By Jonathan Kellerman

FICTION

Gone
Rage
Twisted
Therapy
The Conspiracy Club
A Cold Heart
The Murder Book
Flesh and Blood
Dr. Death
Monster
Billy Straight
Survival of the Fittest

The Clinic
The Web
Self-Defense
Bad Love
Devil's Waltz
Private Eyes
Time Bomb
Silent Partner
The Butcher's Theater
Over the Edge
Blood Test
When the Bough Breaks

NONFICTION

Savage Spawn: Reflections on Violent Children
Helping the Fearful Child
Psychological Aspects of Childhood Cancer

FOR CHILDREN, WRITTEN AND ILLUSTRATED

Jonathan Kellerman's ABC of Weird Creatures
Daddy, Daddy, Can You Touch the Sky?

By Faye Kellerman

The Garden of Eden and
Other Criminal Delights
Straight Into Darkness
The Ritual Bath
Sacred and Profane
The Quality of Mercy
Milk and Honey
Day of Atonement
False Prophet
Grievous Sin

Sanctuary
Justice
Prayers for the Dead
Serpent's Tooth
Moon Music
Jupiter's Bones
Stalker
The Forgotten
Stone Kiss
Street Dreams

By Jonathan & Faye Kellerman

Double Homicide

CAPITAL CRIMES

CAPITAL CRIMES

Jonathan & Faye
KELLERMAN

BALLANTINE BOOKS

NEW YORK

Copyright © 2006 by Jonathan Kellerman and Faye Kellerman

Published in the United States by Ballantine Books, an imprint of The Random House Publishing Group, a division of Random House, Inc., New York.

ISBN-10: 0-345-46798-1
ISBN-13: 978-0-345-46798-0

Printed in the United States of America on acid-free paper

www.ballantinebooks.com

2 4 6 8 9 7 5 3 1

First Edition

Book design by Victoria Wong

CAPITAL CRIMES

MY SISTER'S KEEPER

KEEPER

A NOVELLA

ACKNOWLEDGMENTS FOR
MY SISTER'S KEEPER

Special thanks to Chief Douglas N. Hambleton and Officer Joseph E. Okies, Jr., of the Berkeley Police Department; Detective Jesse Grant of the Oakland Police Department; and Dr. Mordecai and Rena Rosen.

1

The club was from another age. So was Mother.

The Woman's Association of Northern California, Conquistadores Chapter Number XVI, was housed in a sumptuous turn-of-the-century, Beaux-Arts-touched-by-Gothic castle topped by crenellations and turrets, and constructed of massive blocks of mauve-gray Deer Isle granite from a long-dead quarry in Maine. The interior was predictable: somber and dark save for stained-glass windows featuring historical Gold Rush scenes that blew jeweled patches on the walls when the sun shone through. Antique Persian rugs softened well-worn walnut floors, the staircase banister gleamed from decades of polish, thirty-foot ceilings were coffered and rimmed with gold. The ground floor of the building held all the public rooms, the two floors above contained sleeping chambers for the members.

Mother had been a member of the Association for more than fifty years and sometimes slept over in a room far too modest for her. But the fees were nominal, and nostalgia was worth something. Her dinners at the club were frequent. They made her feel special.

They made Davida feel like a freak but she gritted her teeth and indulged Mother's preferences because the woman was a not-too-healthy eighty.

Most dinners meant Mother *and* various selections of *dear friends*, each one of them more than a step out of time. The entire concept of the Association with its genteel Gatsby pretensions would have been anachronistic anywhere. Nowhere was it more absurd than here in Berkeley.

A stroll from the club was the People's Park, originally conceived as a monument to free speech but reduced to a square block of homeless encampments and ad hoc soup kitchens. Good intentions in the abstract, but the brown rectangle reeked of unwashed bodies and decaying food and on hot days anyone not blessed by nasal congestion kept a wide berth.

Not far from the park was the Gourmet Ghetto, the foodie mecca that typified Berkeley's mix of hedonism and idealism. And dominating it all, the UC. It was these contrasts that gave the city a unique character, with everything blanketed by a definite Point of View.

Davida loved the city with all its strengths and its foibles. Leftist and proud, she was now part of the system, duly elected state representative from District 14. She loved her district and she loved her constituents. She loved the energy and the electricity of a town stoked by people who cared about issues. So different from her hometown, Sacramento, where dishing dirt was respectable recreation.

And yet, here she was commuting back to the capital.

All for a good cause.

Tonight the dome-roofed, hush-hush dining room was dense with tables dressed with starched linen and sparkling silver and crystal, but shy on diners. Members were dying off and very few women elected to follow in their mothers' footsteps. Davida had joined the Association a few years back because it was politically smart to do so. She knew most of the members as friends of her mother and they enjoyed the attention she paid them. Their monetary contributions were stingy compared to their assets, but at least they gave—more than Davida could say about a lot of her own allegedly altruistic pals.

Tonight, it was just Davida and Mother. Their server handed them menus and Davida and her mother silently scanned tonight's choices. The entrées, once biased toward steaks and chops, had conceded to present-day realities with more chicken and fish. The food was excellent, Davida had to grant that. In Berkeley, bad food was almost as serious an iniquity as being a Republican.

Mother insisted on flirting with the waiter, an elfin-looking man in his thirties named Tony who was undoubtedly gay. Mother damn well knew he was gay but she batted her lashes like a moony adolescent.

Tony played his part by smiling and batting back. *His* lashes outclassed Mother's—thicker and darker than any man's deserved to be.

Davida knew Mother was worried, trying to mask it with a false cheer. Still dwelling on the *incident*.

Though it had seemed like a big deal last week—and certainly demeaning—Davida now had the perspective to see it for what it had been: a stupid prank executed by stupid people.

Eggs. Sticky, repellent, but not dangerous.

Still, Mother brooded as she forked her shrimp cocktail. Davida's minestrone soup remained untouched because dealing with Mother tightened up her esophagus. If the wall of silence didn't come down, both of them would end up with indigestion and Davida would leave the club in need of . . . something.

Davida loved her mother, but Lucille Grayson was a supreme pain in the ass. Lucille called Mr. Eyelash over, asked for a refill of Chardonnay and drained it quickly. Maybe alcohol would settle her down.

Tony returned and announced the specials. Mother ordered the blackened Chilean sea bass and Davida opted for the linguini with chicken in vodka and sun-dried tomato sauce. Tony gave a dancer's bow and sailed away.

"You look good," said Davida. Not a lie. Lucille maintained clear blue eyes, a sharp nose, prominent chin and strong teeth. Thick, luxuriant hair for an old woman, once auburn, now a gray one shade darker than the club's granite walls. Davida hoped she'd age as well. Decent odds; she bore an uncanny resemblance to Mother and at forty-three, her own auburn waves lacked a single silver strand.

Mother didn't answer.

"Your skin looks great," said Davida.

"It's the facials," Mother responded. "When—*and if*—you go to the spa, ask for Marty."

"I'll go."

"So you say. How long has it been, Davida, since you've taken care of your skin?"

"I've had other things on my mind."

"I bought you a certificate."

"It was a terrific gift, thank you, Mother."

"It's a stupid gift if you don't use it."

"Mother, it doesn't have an expiration date. Don't worry. It'll get used. If not by me, I'm sure Minette will be happy to indulge."

Mother's jaw set. She forced a smile. "No doubt she would be. However, *she* isn't my daughter." She picked up her wineglass and sipped, trying for nonchalance but a trembling lip betrayed her. "You have a little bruise . . . on the apple of your right cheek."

Davida nodded. "The cover-up must have come off. How bad does it look?"

"Well, darling, you wouldn't want to face your public like that."

"True." Davida smiled. "They might think that you were beating up on me."

Mother didn't appreciate the humor. Her eyes misted. "Bastards!"

"I agree." Davida took the old woman's hand, the skin nearly translucent, traced with delicate veins the color of a misty sky. "I'm fine. Please don't worry."

"Any idea yet who did it?"

"Stupid kids."

"That's ambiguous and elusive and I'm not the press, Davida. Have the police made any arrests?"

"Not yet. I'll let you know when it happens."

"When, not if?"

Davida didn't answer. A Latino busboy murmured something polite and removed appetizer dishes. Moments later, he returned with the entrées. Davida wondered why, in fine restaurants, the busboys always served the meal. What were the waiters? Food Transport Consultants?

She thanked him in Spanish and swirled a forkful of pasta. "Delicious. How's your food, Mother?"

"Fine." Again blue eyes clouded. Lucille looked close to tears.

"What is it, Mother?"

"It could have been bullets."

"Luckily, it wasn't. So let's just enjoy this meal and being together." Which was an oxymoron because whenever they were together conflict was inevitable.

Mother harrumphed, and then abruptly plastered a smile across her face as she waved across the room to two women who'd just entered.

Darlene MacIntyre and Eunice Meyerhoff. The duo hobbled over to the table, tongues clucking in unison. Darlene was short and pudgy, Eunice tall and severe with impossibly black hair drawn back in a Dragon Lady bun.

Lucille blew air kisses.

"Darling!" Eunice gushed. "How *are* you?"

"Fabulous, what else? Enjoying a dinner with my busy daughter."
Eunice turned her eyes to Davida. "Are you all right, honey?"

"I'm fine. Thanks for asking."

"That was just *terrible*!"

Lucille said, "Not to mention frightening."

Darlene said, "*Motherfuckers*!"

Davida broke into laughter, but was grateful that the room was empty. "I couldn't have said it better, Mrs. MacIntyre." She took a sip of her wine. "Would you two like to join us?"

"We wouldn't dream of intruding," Eunice said. "Your mother rarely sees you."

"Is that what she tells you?"

"*All* the time, dear."

Davida shot a mock-stern look at Mother then focused her gaze back to the two old women. "Well, then, it's lovely to see you both. Enjoy your evening."

"You, too," Darlene answered. "And don't let those assholes get you down."

When they'd toddled off, Davida said, "I hardly *see* you?"

Mother reddened slightly. "Eunice is a troublemaker . . . I don't complain about you chronically, Davida. That battleaxe is smitten with jealousy because *her* Jane detests her."

"Isn't that a bit of an exaggeration?"

"Hardly, Davida. Eunice sided with Jane's ex during the last divorce. Though I suppose one can understand her frustration, seeing as it was a *third* divorce." Sly smile. "Or perhaps sixth. Or *twenty*-sixth, I've lost count."

"Third," Davida said. "I heard about Eunice taking Parker's side. On top of being tacky and disloyal, it was misguided. Parker Seldey's a jerk and a maniac."

"But good-looking."

"Once upon a time. I hear he has quite the temper."

"So do I, but that doesn't concern Eunice. Because he was courtly to her—remembering her birthday, that kind of nonsense." Lucille sighed. "One's blood is one's blood. Still, by the same token, despite Eunice's quirks, Jane shouldn't despise her."

"She's angry at Eunice, but she doesn't hate her, Mother. Believe me, I know."

Jane Meyerhoff had been Davida's friend since grade school and one of her roomies at the UC. Both had been rebellious teenagers, smoking dope, skipping school, hauled in more than once for petty theft in Sacramento. Stupid self-destructive acts committed because neither girl liked herself.

Jane had carried fifty extra pounds and hated her "summer squash" nose. She starved and vomited the weight off during her freshman year in college, got the nose job as a junior. But old self-images die hard, and Jane had never been comfortable with who she was.

Probably never would be comfortable, Davida decided with some sadness.

She, on the other hand, came to grips with herself well before college. Everything changed a few months before her senior prom when she came out.

Like birthing a child: painful, but you had something to show for it. Coming out meant life was suddenly honest—illuminated by a clean, bright light Davida had never imagined.

She chewed her pasta while glancing across the table. Mother had many faults, but homophobia wasn't one of them. She'd never given a rat's ass that her only surviving child was gay.

Perhaps it was because Mother, though resolutely heterosexual, didn't care for men in general and hated Davida's father, in specific.

The Honorable Stanford R. Grayson, District Court Judge (ret.), now lived in Sarasota, Florida, where he played golf with a second wife twenty years younger than Lucille. Mother had been thrilled when the old man got re-hitched, for now she had something else to complain about. And Father had step-grandchildren with Mixie, so he ignored Davida and left her all to Lucille.

If Mother ever felt pangs about her lack of grandchildren, she never expressed her longings to Davida.

Mother picked at her food and pushed it around on her plate. "How often do you see Janey?"

"A bit more since she moved to Berkeley." Davida smiled tightly. "I try to keep in contact with all my old college roomies."

Mother had wanted her daughter to go to Stanford. Davida insisted on Berkeley. Once there, she'd never really left, working first as an assistant to the mayor, then moving to the capital, where she gofered for Ned Yellin, the most progressive member of the assembly. Ned's shockingly sudden death from a heart attack had propelled her own career.

Now she represented her district with workaholic pride and loved her job.

Although there were days like yesterday that made her wonder why she'd ever shaken the hornet's nest that was state politics. It was challenge enough to deal with the vagaries of constituents basically in harmony with her views. Working with—and around—her less-enlightened colleagues could be as frustrating as . . . there really wasn't anything worse.

Less enlightened; her euphemism of the month. Bigoted and biased would be more accurate. Then again, everyone had his own agenda. She certainly had hers and it had nothing to do with sexual orientation.

When she was ten, her older sister Glynnis had finally succumbed to her protracted battle with rhabdomyosarcoma, a rare muscle tumor. Davida had loved her sister and watching Glynnis spend her last days confined to a hospital bed, hooked up to tubes, clammy gown wrapped around a sallow, stick-thin body, bleeding from her gums and nose . . .

Glynnis' blood cells were in steady retreat and there were no new donors to be found.

Stem cells would have saved Glynnis, Davida was convinced of that. How different would things have been for the Grayson family if the scientific community had been funded righteously?

Two and a half years ago, Davida had been heartened when the people voted in an initiative funding a state stem-cell institute. But years later, she was disillusioned and angry: all the institute had accomplished was creating a board of directors and issuing a namby-pamby mission statement.

"Science works gradually" was the excuse. Davida wasn't buying it. People like Alice had the answer, but Alice hadn't even been consulted by the new board—Davida's repeated requests notwithstanding.

She decided she'd waited long enough. Buttressed by a battalion of scientists, doctors, clergy, humanists and genetic sufferers, she went to war every day in Sacramento, laboring to convince her *less-enlightened* colleagues that a less grandiose but more efficient legislative approach was the answer.

And got precious little for her efforts.

It wasn't that the stodgy pols really cared about aborted fetuses, because she'd learned that few pols cared about anything other than getting reelected. Though they screamed a good case. Six months into her struggle, she was convinced it was *Davida* they were rejecting. Because of who she *was*.

Day after day of wearing out her vocal cords, making deals she really didn't want to make, wasting hours on mind-numbing meetings. Now eggs in her face, on her blouse . . . right there on the capitol steps, the humiliation.

What a mess—there was a metaphor for you.

Mother's voice snapped her back to the here and now. Prattling on about dangers lurking around every corner.

According to Lucille, Davida was a major target of every white-supremacist hate group in California, not to mention Bible Belt pro-lifers, hypermacho antigay farmers from the San Joaquin Valley, and, of course, misogynists of every stripe and gender.

She recalled Mother's first words after the election results were tallied and Davida's supporters broke into raised-fist cheers in the social hall of the old Finnish church.

Be careful, dear. Don't get cocky and think because you can get elected here that you're really popular.

Mother was being her typical negative self, but there was some truth to her admonitions. Davida knew she'd made many enemies, many of whom she had never met.

"Don't worry, Mother, I'm fine."

"On top of that, you work too hard."

"That's what a public servant does, Mother."

"If you're going to keep such long hours, you should at least be compensated for your efforts. Like in the corporate world. With your experience, you could write your own—"

"I don't care about money, Mother."

"That, my dear, is because you've never been without it."

"True, Mother. Fortunate people go into public service to pay back. Stop worrying about me."

Lucille Grayson's look was injured. And frightened. She'd lost one daughter. Survival could be a burden, thought Davida. But she tried to be compassionate. "No one wants to hurt me. I'm too insignificant."

"That's not what I saw on TV."

"They'll have an arrest soon. Whoever did it wasn't clever. Probably imbeciles from the White Tower Radicals."

"They may not be clever, Davida, but that doesn't mean they're not dangerous."

"I'll be especially careful, Mother." Davida took a bite, put down the fork and wiped her mouth. "It's been lovely, but I have piles of paperwork and it's past nine. I have to get back to the office."

Mother sighed. "All right. Go ahead. I have to pack up myself."

"You're not staying overnight?"

"No, I have a meeting tomorrow morning with my accountant back home."

"Who's driving you, Hector?"

"Guillermo."

"He's a good guy." Davida stood up and helped her mother to her feet. "Do you need any help packing?"

"No, not at all." Lucille kissed her daughter on the cheek. "Let me give you a ride to your office."

"It's a beautiful night, Mother. Not too cold and not too foggy. I think I'll walk."

"Walk?"

"It's not late."

"It's dark, Davida."

"I know everyone en route and as far as I know, none of them plans to egg me. You be careful yourself. I don't like you going home so late. I wish you'd sleep here overnight."

Not inviting Mother to her own apartment; there were limits.

Lucille said, "Sacramento is only an hour away."

Davida smiled. "Not the way Guillermo drives."

"A shorter journey means less opportunity for problems, dear. You have your business, I have mine."

"Fair enough." After bidding good-bye to Mother's friends, Davida accompanied the old woman out of the dining room and helped her up the staircase to her room. "I'll talk to you tomorrow, Mother. And I'll tell Minette you said hello."

"But I didn't."

"In domestic matters, honesty isn't always the best policy."

2

Walking through the stillness of Berkeley's business district, a thin fog veiling street signs and darkened storefronts and tickling her nose, Davida jammed her hands into her pockets and enjoyed the solitude. Then the silence got to her and she shifted to Shattuck Avenue, the core of the Gourmet Ghetto. The cafés that lined the street teemed with life. As much a concept as a place, the ghetto featured an architectural mix, like Berkeley itself, that refused to conform to anything resembling a standard. Fussy Victorian morphed to Arts and Crafts California bungalow to Deco to Fifties Dingbat. There were a few nods to the contemporary, but permits were hard to come by and developers often gave up.

Though she'd never admit it to anyone, Davida had long come to realize that Berkeley, like any other small, affluent town, had its own conservative core—change was threatening unless it toed the party line. In this case, the party was hers and she loved the controlled heterogeneity.

Walking with her head down, she trudged up Shattuck, breathing in lungfuls of foggy, saline air. Ducking into her office, she checked the messages on her cell. There were dozens of them but the only one that interested her was from Don. Once upon a time, she had known his number by heart. A lifetime ago.

She hit the green call button. His wife answered.

"Hi Jill, it's Davi—"

"I'll get Don for you."

"Thank you." Their typical conversation. Five words from Jill

Newell was a discourse. The woman just couldn't get past her husband's old high school romance. Davida thought Jill's pettiness astounding after all these years. Especially considering who *Davida* was. But forget logic; Jill simply hated her.

Don came on the line. "Congresswoman Grayson."

"Detective Newell. What's the word?"

"Actually, I do have some news. We got a couple of eyewitnesses on your egg throwers. Couple of moron brothers, Brent and Ray Nutterly. We paid them a visit at their trailer, which conveniently reeked of weed. They're spending the night in the slammer courtesy of SPD. We may be able to send them up for six months to a year for what they did to you, but they aren't going to do any hard time."

"Tell the DA to go for the max." Davida Grayson, brand-new convert to tough sentencing.

"Absolutely," said Don. "Everyone from the chief on down is pissed at them for making us look bad. Toss the capital police into the equation and they're definitely not winning any popularity contests."

He lowered his voice. "Davy, I don't have to tell you this but you know there are others waiting in the wings who are a lot more malicious than those two assholes. Think about hiring a bodyguard."

"Not a chance."

"Just until you get further along on your bill. All that walking around—"

"Exactly. I need mobility and accessibility. Thanks for your concern, Don. Now I have another favor. My mom's due to come home in about an hour, hour and a half. She's been looking a little feeble and refuses to have anyone live with her. Guillermo will drop her off but at this hour, I don't like her being conspicuous. Could you send a squad car past her house just to make sure she's okay?"

"Not a problem. When are you going to be in the neighborhood? I've been thinking about a barbecue."

"Sounds great, Don, but you know how swamped I've been."

"I know."

"Say hello to Jill and the kids for me."

"Didn't Jill answer the phone?"

"She didn't seem too loquacious."

There was a pause before he answered. "That's Jill."

After the phone rang three times, Minette picked up the receiver. She was finishing up the last of her bourbon and the smoky aftertaste lingered on her palate. Just as cigarettes had lingered back in the Good Old Nicotine Days.

She stretched on the sofa and caressed her body. Tonight, she had on a lacy red uplift bra, matching thong, and thigh-high stockings purchased at Good Vibrations. She'd looked forward all day to peeling them off in front of her partner. Slowly. Agonizingly slowly.

The thought of stripping made her horny. She whispered an enticing hello into the receiver.

Davida said, "Hi, honey."

"Hel-lo." Minette hoped she didn't sound as drunk as she felt. "I've been *waiting* for you."

Ooh, that sounds good was the answer over the line. Then the pause Minette hated. "I've got some pressing paperwork tonight, Min. It's going to take some time for me to go through all of it."

"How long is some time? A minute, an hour, a day, a week?"

"More than a minute and less than a week."

Minette did not laugh. Davida tried to keep her patience. She knew Min had been drinking because she was slurring her words, but now was not the right time to get into it. "I've got a committee hearing on the bill in two days, the wording needs to be perfect or some yahoo's going to jump on it."

"Another committee?"

"And two more after that, but things will ease up, soon, I promise."

"No, they won't," said Minette. "You'll find some other cause to rob all your time."

Davida tried to change the subject. "Did you finalize the Tecate reservation?"

"Yes—why? Do I have to cancel it?"

"No, no. The entire week is engraved into my BlackBerry. I can't wait."

"Me, neither." But Minette couldn't muster up much enthusiasm. Davida had aborted their spa vacation at Rancho La Puerta twice before. "When are you coming home?"

"I'll try to make it before one, but don't wait up."

Meaning she wasn't coming home. Minette sighed. Stroked a lace bra cup. Hooked a thumb inside. "Don't work so hard, baby."

"Thanks for being so understanding, honey. I love you."

Minette's *I love you, too,* was cut short by the click.

Pouting, she hung up. Nine thirty-five, and she looked and felt every bit as sexy.

The evening was still very much alive. She pressed a memorized set of numbers into her cell phone, then hit the send button. When the caller answered, Minette tried to steady her voice. "As expected, she's coming home very late tonight if at all. What are your plans?"

"Well, I guess I'm coming over to your place."

"How long will that take?"

"Give me an hour to make excuses."

"I'll see you then. Oh, and pick up a bottle of Knob Creek," Minette said. "We're out of joy juice."

3

The call came in at eight twenty-two AM, just enough time to interrupt Will Barnes's treadmill torture. Every day, he blasted his joints into oblivion with the faint hope that the mindless machine would increase his life expectancy. Will's father and grandfather had died of heart disease in their early sixties. Will's cardiologist said his ticker looked great, but the unspoken message got through: take special care.

He slowed the pace, said, "Barnes."

The Loo said, "Davida Grayson was found dead in her office."

Barnes was so stunned that he almost tripped. Hopping off the machine, he wrapped a towel around his thick, sweaty neck. "What the hell happened?"

"That's what you're supposed to figure out. I'll meet you at the crime scene. Amanda is also on her way. Lucky for you, you've got a pard who knows how to work the media, because this is going to be high profile. Cap has scheduled a press conference at eleven. Town hall meeting will be at seven tonight. We need a quick close, Will, before the community goes haywire."

"Can I put my pants on first?"

"Sure. You can even do it one leg at a time."

William Tecumseh Barnes was a wide-shouldered guy with a football-flattened nose and soft blue eyes. Prone to a beer gut and a double chin, he sometimes reckoned himself over the hill. But women liked those baby blues and he had his own hair, most of it still brown with a dusting of pewter at the temples. He'd gone from high school halfback to the army to law enforcement, spending fifteen years at Sacramento PD, ten as a homicide detective, until family matters brought him to the Bay Area.

Will's only sibling, Jack, was a gay man who made a living out of being a gay man. Jack had moved from Sacramento to San Francisco at sixteen and by twenty had been a "well-known activist," a fanatical in-your-face kind of guy who'd managed to offend everyone.

Will knew the abrasiveness went beyond idealism; he'd spent half his youth cleaning up Jack's messes. But family was family, even if Will hadn't ever really understood his brother.

When Jack was murdered, their parents were long gone and Will faced his grief alone. As the case grew cold, he knew what he had to do. Recently divorced with no kids or baggage keeping him in the capital, he requested a temporary leave of absence. That turned into two years as he searched for his brother's killer. Bit by bit, as he probed into Jack's death, he came to know Jack's life. Jack's friends grew to trust him, confided in him, related snippets that came together like the squares of a patchwork quilt. In the end, Jack's death turned out to be one of those stupid homicides: an argument with the wrong person.

When it was time to return to Sacramento, Will discovered that he loved the beauty of the Bay Area, and had grown to respect—albeit in a begrudging way—the political diversity. He applied to Berkeley PD because a detective position had just opened and because chasing down his brother's killer had left him drained and exhausted and it seemed like a cushy, small-town job.

Not this morning, with Davida Grayson a vic.

Will showered and shaved and locked up his piece of California real estate—a two-bedroom, one-bath, eight-hundred-square-foot bungalow. When Will plunked down a thirty-five-thousand-dollar deposit on it fifteen years ago, it had been a dump. Now his mess was fixed up and prettified and damn if it wasn't the best investment he had ever made.

The area around Grayson's district office on Shattuck was roped off with yellow tape. All the magpies were in place: local TV, radio, the papers. Barnes spied Laura Novacente from the *Berkeley Crier* and gave her a wave. They'd dated a couple of years ago and though it had ended, it had not ended badly. Laura weaved and elbowed herself through the throng and sidled up to him, making sure to give a little hip-to-hip contact.

"What's going on, Willie?"

"You tell me, Laura." Barnes looked around for Amanda Isis. His partner lived in San Francisco, in a twenty-three-room Pacific Heights mansion overlooking everything. It would take her at least another half hour to make it over the bridge. "You got here before I did, lady."

"You don't listen to your own scanners?"

"Not at eight in the morning, I don't."

"I heard she was shot in the head."

"Then you heard more than I did."

"Give me something, Willie."

He sized Laura up with a swift sweep of the baby blues. Ten years younger than him, with long gray hair that flew in the wind like the mane of a galloping horse. Still that trim figure; he wondered why the two of them had gone south. "Captain's arranged some kind of press conference—"

"I thought we were friends."

He loved the urgency in her voice. Had heard it many times before in a different context. "Your number is still lodged in my brain, Laura. If I find out anything, I'll give you a ring, maybe we can meet."

"The usual place?"

"I'm a creature of habit, Laura."

Davida was slumped over her desk, face cradled in the crook of her arms as if she'd been napping away her last moments on earth. Detective Amanda Isis preferred to think that the transition from a temporary sleep to a permanent had been painless. The nape of Davida's neck was blown wide open, pellets hitting with enough force to shred her spinal cord. Just about decapitated.

Amanda was medium-sized, slim, thirty-eight, delicately beautiful with honey-colored hair layered short and enormous brown eyes. She had on a charcoal pantsuit that didn't show the dirt. Armani Couture, but tailored to look run-of-the-mill.

The scene was gruesome and bloody with crimson spray all over the desk and the walls. Not at all the kind of murder that Amanda was used to seeing. When BPD dealt with homicides, they were usually drug killings confined to the dark alleys of the West Berkeley region, brutal but ultimately mundane crimes that often germinated in Oakland.

Amanda studied the body again. Someone had been *serious*. When she looked closely, she could see shotgun pellets embedded in flesh. Brushing honey-colored locks from her eyes, she turned to Will. "This is nauseating."

"Lots of spray . . . a couple of partial shoeprints." Barnes pointed to several spots. "If the past is any predictor of the future, someone somewhere is dumping bloody clothing. But the idiots always think twice about tossing the shoes."

"Who called the murder in?"

"Jerome Melchior—Davida's chief aide. I've got him stowed away in a cruiser, drinking coffee, hoping we can steady his nerves. I'd like to interview him while his memory is fresh, get him away from the magpies before the press conference."

Barnes checked his watch. "We've only got about an hour, Mandy. Ready to hustle?"

"Go interview him, I'll take over here. Then, while I'm working the microphones with the brass, you can have a look around and we'll compare notes."

"You got it." His perfectly organized partner. After a year they synched well, like a nicely tuned clock. Will hadn't been thrilled to work with someone who'd married into a hundred million bucks, had heard the ice-queen dilettante chatter, figured how could it be otherwise. But Amanda worked as hard as anyone. Harder. Maybe those lottery winners who claimed they'd never quit their day jobs were righteous.

She smoothed the jacket of one of those designer pantsuits with gloved hands, took another look at Davida and shook her head. "You ever have any dealings with her, Will?"

"Not professionally." Barnes sighed. "She's a Sacramento girl. I knew her."

"Well?"

Barnes shook his head. "Her older sister, Glynnis, was a couple of years younger than me. She died when Davida was a kid. My brother, Jack, knew Davida in high school. They ran in different circles, but I know when she came out in her senior year, it had a big impact on Jack." He turned to face her. "What about you and Larry? You guys go to parties with pols."

"Good deduction, Detective Barnes. Yeah, I've run into her a few times but no extended conversations. She came across as a reasonable person. Not pro-police but not as antagonistic as some of the others we've had. When she talked, though, she got animated. I guess that was passion about what she believed in."

"If you're passionately *for* something, chances are there's somebody that's passionately *against* the same thing."

"The stem-cell deal, that egging last week," said Amanda. "Wonder if SPD has anything on that."

"I still know people over there. I'll check."

"Maybe we should visit the capital," Amanda suggested. "Scope out her enemies and her friends."

"At the capital, they can be one and the same. Sure, good idea, but I think hobnobbing with those in the know is more up your alley, Mandy."

"What's your forte, compadre?"

"Talking to *her* folk."

Amanda knew he meant the gay and lesbian community. Of all the contacts that a detective might cultivate, she couldn't have thought of a more odd combination than Will and gays. But he got info from them like no one else could. Perhaps they trusted him because he was the last person in the world to be condescending or patronizing. "Sure you don't want to take on the Gray Suits, Willie? It was originally your territory."

"My territory, but never my people."

4

Jerome Melchior sat with his head between his knees in the backseat of the cruiser. He was compact with weight-lifter arms that stretched the sleeves of his black long-sleeved tee. Weeping his eyes out.

Melchior looked up as Barnes approached. Deep-set dark eyes, cinnamon hair highlighted gold and cut close to the skull. He wiped his eyes, dropped his head again. Barnes slid in next to him. "Horrible morning, Mr. Melchior. I'm sorry."

Melchior sucked in air. "I thought she was sleeping. Sometimes she does that."

"Falls asleep at her desk?"

The aide nodded. "When she pulls an all-nighter."

"How often was that?"

"More often lately because of her bill."

"Stem-cell bill?"

"Yes."

Barnes patted Melchior's shoulder. Melchior straightened and threw his head back and stared at the roof of the police car. "My God, I can't believe this!"

Barnes gave him time. "When did you realize she was dead?"

"I don't know why. I just came over and gave her a gentle shake on the shoulder. When I pulled my hand away there was blood on my fingers. It didn't register at first . . . then it . . . did." Melchior reached around and touched the nape of his neck. "The *hole.*"

Barnes took out a notepad. "So nothing immediately clued you in that something was wrong?"

"Nothing looked out of place if that's what you mean." He regarded Barnes. "I touched her again. Blood all over my hands, I'm sure I left bloody fingerprints—oh, God, is that going to mess up your investigation?"

"Not since you've told me. Your call came in to dispatch at around eight in the morning. How long after the discovery did it take you to call emergency?"

"About . . . two minutes, maybe less. But I was so fucked-up I dialed 611 instead of 911, I was shaking so *hard.*"

"That's normal, Mr. Melchior. Let's talk about Ms. Grayson. Politicians have lots of people who don't like their views. Anyone in particular stand out?"

"Not enough to kill her."

"Give me names anyway."

"I'm talking other representatives," said Melchior. "They may be sleazy but they're not . . . okay, okay . . . Mark Decody from Orange County . . . Alisa Lawrence from San Diego couldn't stand Davida, either. They're both Republicans. She was also having some problems with a Democrat. In name only. Artis Handel. He's actually been the most ferocious about the bill."

"Why?"

"Catholic and makes a big point of it. The whole abortion-fetus thing."

"Anyone else?"

"There's a civilian—a nutcase, really. Harry Modell. Executive director of some fringe group called Families Under God. We're talking extremists. I've heard their unspoken motto is kill liberals, not babies. He's a kook and a grandstander, can't say I've ever thought of him as this bad but . . . who knows."

"How'd Davida react to the egg throwers?"

"That." Melchior frowned. "She sloughed it off as crazy kids. I agreed, but now . . . ."

Melchior cried some more. When he was through, Barnes offered him more coffee.

"No, thanks."

"Anything else you'd like to say or add that you think might help?"

"No, I'm sorry."

"How about I call you in a day or so? Sometimes after the shock wears off, you remember things."

"Sure."

"In the meantime . . ." Barnes took out his card. "If you think of anything else that might help me out, give me a call."

Melchior stuck the card in a trouser pocket.

"One more thing, sir. Would you happen to know any of Representative Grayson's passwords for her computer?"

"Why?"

Stupid question but Barnes had heard so many of those in situations like these. "There may be important information in there. The entire machine will be taken to an expert who'll dissect it, but any help you can give us now to speed up the investigation would be appreciated."

"Well," said Melchior, "once in a while, she did ask me to check her e-mail . . . when her laptop wasn't working or . . ." He took Barnes's pad. "Give me a few minutes to think."

"Take your time."

When the aide was finally able to focus, Barnes had a list of five passwords. "That's great, sir. Would you like an officer to take you home?"

"That would be nice." Melchior smiled. "Your brother was a legend."

"Especially in his own mind."

Melchior gave an honest laugh. "He seemed very passionate. I didn't know him well."

"That makes two of us."

The scene had become dense with live bodies skittering around like ants. Two CSU techs, a police photographer, a pair of investigators from the coroner's office—Tandy Halligan, big and tall and female, Derrick Coltrain, small, black, and male.

"How's the hubby?" Coltrain asked Amanda.

"Retirement doesn't wear well on him." Ten years ago, she'd met Lawrence Isis, a half-Irish, half-Egyptian Copt software engineer at a campus concert—Celtic folk music, Amanda had gone on a lark, a friend's urging. The chemistry had been instant, despite the fact that Larry resembled Woody Allen with dark hair and a terrific tan. He'd signed on early at Google, rose through the company, accruing stock. Lots of stock. After living well below their means in Amanda's Oakland condo, they'd made the quantum leap to the mansion two years ago. Seventeen rooms still empty, but Amanda loved the echoes. Larry, though, needed a hobby.

Derrick Coltrain said, "I wouldn't mind early retirement if I had all the toys."

Giving her a curious look. The unspoken message: what the hell are *you* doing here?

On a day like this, good question. She'd gone through Grayson's phone, had progressed to the representative's state-issued BlackBerry. The woman's life had been a series of endless meetings. Over the last two years, she'd scheduled one vacation—a trip to Tecate, Mexico. Probably the spa. Amanda and Larry had been there. She loving the exercise, he bemoaning the lack of wireless.

Coltrain said, "What's he into, the genius?"

"He's thinking of starting up another business."

"Hey, let me know when he's about to go public."

Tandy Halligan said, "By the time it goes public, it'll be too late." She began the process of examining the body. Going slowly, nervous, which wasn't like her. But what if the head detached from the body?

Carefully, she lifted each hand, examined digits closely. "No ligature marks on the wrists. Fingers and nails look clean and undisturbed, doesn't appear there's much, if anything, to scrape."

Steeling herself, she rotated the head to get a side view of the face.

"No scratch marks on the right side . . . none on the left either. But there is a sizeable bruise on her forehead."

"She was sitting at her desk, someone came from behind, shot her and she fell forward," Amanda said. "Or she napped through the whole thing and the impact bounced her forehead into the desk. The floor is old wood planks, it squeaks when you walk on it. Alone, late at night, if she was awake she'd have heard someone behind her."

Tandy said, "Unless she was too focused. Like talking on the phone, or typing."

Amanda wondered if there had been an intruder. No pry marks on the front entrance, the lock was a dead bolt, solid, in working order. The windows also appeared untouched. "Or she wasn't concerned because it was someone she knew. Which doesn't negate the sneak-up-

and-blow scenario if the killer paid her two visits. The first was a ruse, to get the door unlocked. The second was to blast her."

Derrick Coltrain said, "Can I suggest something? Sometimes representatives make a fetish about keeping their doors open. To be accessible, kind of a Berkeley thing."

"At that hour?"

No answer.

Amanda said, "Any idea when she was murdered?"

"Maybe six to eight hours ago but that's just a guess."

Will entered the office and heard that. "Between two and four AM?"

"It's a guess," said Tandy. "Ask Dr. Srinivasan."

Amanda said, "No pries on windows or doors. You know her to leave her door open?"

"She had a rep for hospitality," Barnes said. "Continuous coffee-pot, plate of crullers. For anyone who stopped in, including the homeless. It was chilly last night. Maybe she let one of them crash in the outer office while she worked. Maybe he had a psychotic break."

"A homeless man with a shotgun?"

Barnes shrugged.

Amanda said, "I went through her cell calls last night. Lots came in but she only returned a few. One she returned was to a Donald Newell in Sacramento—"

"Donnie's a homicide detective." Barnes sighed. "I think they were friends in high school."

"Another homeboy. How big was your town?"

"Big, but small. Shit, I wonder if Donnie knows. I'll give him a call."

Simultaneously they looked back at the body. Tandy was in the process of wrapping it up in plastic sheeting when screaming outside the office froze her. Through the window, Amanda saw two policemen trying to restrain a hysterical young woman. She was trim with shoulder-length platinum hair, pink cheeks, and Marilyn Monroe lips. Tight black leotard top over low-rider jeans, high-heeled sandals.

The two detectives rushed outside.

"What's going on?"

"I'm going in!" screamed the blonde. "Bastards!"

The cops looked to the detectives.

Amanda said, "Crime scene, no entrance."

The young woman cursed. Her cheeks were tear-streaked, her eyes were bloodshot, and her breath reeked of alcohol. "Do you know who I *am*?"

"No, ma'am."

"Her lover! Did you hear me—her goddamnfucking *lover*!"

"Sorry for your loss," said Barnes.

"You still can't go in there, but let's talk," said Amanda. She placed her arm around the blonde's shoulders, closing her nostrils to the booze stink. A smell she knew so well, growing up.

The blonde relaxed. Sniffed. "I'm Minette. Her lover."

Amanda motioned the cops to let her go. "Let's go somewhere quiet, Minette."

5

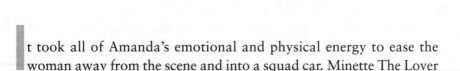

It took all of Amanda's emotional and physical energy to ease the woman away from the scene and into a squad car. Minette The Lover sobbed until she'd cried herself dry. Amanda offered her a tissue.

"Thank you."

"I'm so sorry, Minette. What's your last name, please?"

"Minette Padgett. What ha . . . happened?"

"We're at the beginning of the investigation, Minette. I wish I could give you some details but I can't."

"But she's . . . gone?"

Feeble hope in her voice; this part never got any easier. "I'm sorry, but she is gone." Fresh batch of tears, an explosion of grief. "Minette, right now we're getting information about Davida. Is there anything about her life that might help us out?"

"What do you mean? Like did she have enemies? She had a slew of them. Assholes in the capital hated her because she was gay. Lots of people didn't like her messing with stem cells."

"We got some names from her aide: Harold Modell—"

"Motherfucker."

"Mark Decody and Alisa Lawrence—"

"Motherfuckers*sss*."

"Artis Handel—"

"Turncoat." Minette looked up. "She expected grief from the others, but Artis . . . he's a Democrat, she was especially upset about him."

"Anything more you can tell me about any of them?"

Minette thought a moment, then slowly shook her head. "They were just giving her a hard time. *Politics.*"

"Anybody else I should know about?"

"I don't know . . . I can't think—my head is . . . I can't *think.*"

"What about personal relationships, Minette? Did she have any problems with friends or relatives?"

"Her mother's a profound pain in the ass, but that's just the usual mother–daughter thing. She doesn't have any sibs. Her father lives in Florida in case you want to talk to him."

"Why would I want to talk to him?"

"Because he's an asshole and deserted Davida emotionally after he remarried."

Amanda wrote that down. "Anyone else?"

A pretty brow knitted, then returned to youthful serenity. "Look, I just can't *process* right now." A big sigh. "Has anyone called her mother?"

"We'll take care of that."

"Thanks, 'cause I sure don't want to do it. The old bitch doesn't like me, never did no matter how hard I tried."

"Why do you think that is?"

"I don't know. If I did, I'd work on it. Sometimes it's like that, you know. People take an instant dislike to you. Sometimes *I* take an instant dislike to someone. In Lucille's case, I think we took an instant dislike to each other."

"Tell me about your relationship with Davida."

Minette snapped her head up. "What about it?"

"I know this sounds insensitive but I have to ask it, Ms. Padgett. Were there any problems between you two?"

The young woman shot her a look of disgust. "No, there weren't any *problems* between us two!"

"I've been married for ten years, Ms. Padgett. There are always ups and downs. Please don't take it personally."

Minette didn't answer but it was clear from the look on her face that she wasn't mollified.

"So things were fine—"

"I think I already answered that." Minette faced Amanda. "So you'll call the old lady?"

"Yes."

"Good, because I got a lot of shit to deal with and someone has to start making arrangements. It might as well be her."

"My God! Davida Dead?" Don Newell's voice bellowed through the phone. "That's fucking crazy! What the hell happened, Willie?"

"You know how it works, Don. I wish I had more details but I don't."

"Davida . . . oh, man, that's—at least tell me how she died."

Barnes figured there was no sense being coy. "Twelve-gauge shotgun."

"Oh, man—a typical shotgun *thing*?"

"It was ugly, Donnie."

"That's insane . . . fuckingshit almighty—does her mom know?"

"It's being handled, Donnie."

"If Lucille Grayson hasn't left for Berkeley, I'm taking her personally. Even if she has left, I'm coming down."

Newell's basso was rimmed with a weird, almost hysterical tension. Even allowing for the shock, Barnes wondered what the connection was between a married Sacramento homicide cop and a gay representative. Now wasn't the time to press.

He said, "Donnie, everyone knows she had enemies in the capital. That egging may have been more than a prank. We could use you on home turf. Unless we get a quick solve down here, my partner and I will be coming your way soon, anyway."

There was a long pause. "Will, I'm not dumb and I know what you're thinking because if things were reversed, I'd be thinking the same thing. There was nothing between Davida and me other than a casual friendship. *Nothing*. Get it?"

"Sure do," said Barnes, lying smoothly.

"Why would there be anything, Will? Davida's gay. Sure, once we were close—yeah, yeah I'll stay out of your business but I will talk to Lucille. Two kids and now she's lost both of them."

"Don, do me a favor, assemble everything on Davida that you can. When I see you next, it'll be nice and official."

"It *is* official, Will. I mean it's personal, but it's official too."

"Ain't that the truth," said Barnes. "Now I need to get this out in the open, Don. You talk to her last night?"

"Checked her cell?" said Newell. "Yeah, sure, I called her because we arrested a couple of White Tower boys for the egging. Brent and Ray Nutterly. But I know it wasn't them who killed her because we put their asses in jail."

"What about their buddies in the organization?"

"We were just starting to work that angle, as a matter of fact, because of other things."

"What other things?"

"A couple of months ago, she got an anonymous threatening letter. Low-level stuff—you know, letters cut out of a magazine. We could never could trace it to anyone specific but I wanted to do more. Davida said no, didn't want me making a big deal about it. She said too much of that kind of publicity gave the bastards what they wanted and made her look bad."

"Look bad how?"

"She was big on her public image, gay and progressive but above the fray—her words. She also didn't want anyone to think that she wasn't accessible. Looks like she was too fucking accessible—I should have been more insistent! Damn it, just last night I told her to think about hiring a bodyguard. She blew me off."

"Tell me more about her political enemies."

"Enemies is too strong a word. I'd call them opponents. No one crazy enough to kill her, Will."

"Did she ever talk to you about specific people she was afraid of?"

"First of all, we didn't talk on a regular basis. Second, if she did, don't you think I'da told you? Paranoia wasn't Davida's style. Just the opposite; she minimized danger. When this letter thing came up, she was blasé. To my eye, the woman was never afraid of anything."

While the Loo, the captain, and Amanda Isis fielded questions from the fire-stoking press and strident community activists ready to be outraged about anything, Barnes went through the evidence picked up by CSU. Doorknobs had been wiped clean—a tell, in itself, that supported premeditation—but a partial bloody thumbprint was found on an interior jamb. Bloody shoeprints were of interest, as were multiple red fibers, stray hairs, a used coffee cup, and a cigarette.

Pathology would analyze forensic information taken off the body. Amanda had gone through Davida's cell phone and her BlackBerry. That left Barnes with the onerous and time-consuming task of scouring

Davida's computer, desk calendar, business files and written correspondence.

With Melchior's password list in front of him, he sat down, flexed his fingers and began. Several screen names appeared but none of them looked to be an official representative address with the .gov suffix. An hour of trial and error later, he hit the winning combination. Screen name: DGray, password: LucyG.

Her mom as entry to cyberspace.

Forty-eight e-mails.

He printed them all out. The vast majority were what seemed to be inconsequential communications from friends and community members. A few were personal—mostly from "Mins," two of those graphically sexual.

Lovers hot to trot. There didn't seem to be anything overtly hostile in any of the exchanges with Minette Padgett although in two of the letters, Mins complained about the long hours that Davida was keeping.

So did Lucille.Grayson@easymail.net. Mom was *very* unhappy about Davida's lack of attention to her own well-being. Her latest one implored her daughter to be careful. Something beyond the egging? Mom was a must-interview.

Barnes felt someone looking over his shoulder. Max Flint, the CSU computer guy. "You got into her e-mail. I'm impressed."

"I had a cheat sheet." Barnes gave Flint the list of passwords. "Should I be looking for anything specific?"

Barnes checked his notes. "Dig up whatever you can find regarding the victim and Representatives Alisa Lawrence, Mark Decody, Artis Handel and Eileen Ferunzio . . ." He spelled Eileen's last name. "She was doing political battle with all of them and I heard some of it was intense. Plus, there's a guy, Harry Modell, executive director of Families Under God. See if he wrote anything threatening to her. Finally, give me anything that might've been sent by the White Tower Radicals. Looks like they were behind the egging and possibly a threatening note."

"Lots of enemies," Flint said.

"She was a politician."

6

When the woman stepped outside of the silver Cadillac Fleetwood Brougham, both Barnes and Amanda took note of how dignified she looked. Head held high, shoulders back, thin as paper in a black suit, white silk blouse, seamed stockings and orthopedic pumps straining to be fashionable. Atop her gray coif was a black pillbox hat fronted by a small veil. A uniformed chauffeur held her arm and propelled her forward. Taking her other arm was a rawboned, stoop-shouldered man of medium height and weight. His tightly waved hair was equal parts sand and salt but his handlebar mustache was completely white.

The Donnie Newell that Barnes remembered was a skinny blond kid, skateboarding up and down the basketball courts, getting in everyone's way. Neighborhood boys used to call him "Surfer Joe," a ludicrous moniker because Sacramento was hot and dry and hours from the ocean. In a snapshot of time, Donnie had turned middle-aged.

So what did that say about Barnes?

He glanced at Amanda. The woman was married to a gazillionaire and was pushing forty but she was beautiful, bright, funny and could've passed for a grad student. If you scratched the designer duds.

Born under a lucky star. He harbored a pang of envy then his eyes went back to Lucille Grayson's withdrawn face, staring out at nothing with vacant eyes.

Both kids gone. Hell on earth, what a jerk he was for being petty.

On the other side of the crime-scene tape, the captain was still answering press questions. Good; it kept the focus away from Lucille.

Amanda saw him studying the old woman. "As you remember her?"

"She looks older but not that much older. I think women of that generation dressed dowdier—or maybe I should say age appropriate. Man, I'd like to have a nickel for every fifty-plus woman I see walking around in a miniskirt." Barnes raised his eyebrows. "Not that I'm complaining."

Amanda tolerated the borderline-letch dialogue. Everyone had to deal with sorrow in their own way.

The two detectives began walking toward Lucille, but before they could formally introduce themselves, Ruben Morantz emerged from the crowd and intercepted, offering the frail woman his hand and a round of sympathy.

Maybe some of it was heartfelt, Barnes allowed. The mayor of Berkeley had known Davida Grayson for years and had worked with her on various committees. Though they had had their conflicts, they had also shared victories. Morantz was slight and mild-looking with a narrow torso and sloping shoulders. Innocuous on first impression, but the restless brown eyes, dazzling white smile, and perpetual tan were pure politician.

Hizzoner wore a long black coat over a white shirt, gold tie and tan slacks. Pointy toes of lizard-skin cowboy boots poked under the break of his pants. While he and Lucille chatted, Barnes managed to grab Donnie Newell's attention. Donnie excused himself and walked over.

"Lookin' good, Willie. I think the climate agrees with you."

"You don't look so bad yourself."

"A little thicker in the gut. A little grayer in the head."

"That's how it goes." Barnes made introductions and then looked back at the old woman. "Poor Lucille. I don't know how she's standing on two feet."

"She's tough but how much can even a tough woman take, losing two children?"

The mayor led Lucille away from the crowd, and back to the limo, which the two of them entered.

Amanda regarded Newell. "How well do you know Mrs. Grayson?"

"Davida used to have me look in on her once in a while." Newell smiled at Amanda. "Guess I should bring you up to speed. Davida and I were an item in high school. She came out her senior year, but I suspected something wasn't right long before. She liked to . . . well, experiment is the best way I can say it. I didn't care. I had more fun with that girl. She was a pistol, she and her best friend, Jane Meyerhoff—can't tell you her latest married name. Don't reckon if I ever knew it, she's had so many. I heard the last one ended really messy." Newell turned to Barnes. "Janey lives here now, doesn't she?"

Barnes nodded. He knew all about Janey because he'd picked her up at a bar and they'd dated a few times. Janey wasn't so much a pistol as a machine gun. "Bring the file, Donnie?"

Newell held up a manila envelope. "Been looking into the Nutterly brothers. Far as I can tell, these two boys are a step below Neanderthal, but that doesn't mean they're not dangerous. Stupid and mean is a dangerous combination, right? Still, I don't think they'd act without receiving orders from someone else."

"And who might the order-giver be?" Barnes asked.

"The head of the White Tower Radicals is a guy named Marshall Bledsoe who lives in Idaho."

"I know Bledsoe," Barnes said. "When I was in Sacramento he was rumored to be the main architect of the synagogue bombings. That's twenty years ago. He was a madman then, I don't see him getting sane magically. But from bombs to eggs?"

"Unless that was a ruse," Newell said.

Barnes ran with the idea. "Davida's thinking that whoever's after her is gunning for her in the capital. Then they get her in the safety of her own office."

"Along those lines, the threatening letter was sent to her in Sacramento."

"What threatening letter?" Amanda asked and Barnes realized he'd forgotten to tell her.

Newell opened up the envelope and showed them a copy. Magazine letters of all shapes and colors cut and pasted to form an ominous message.

IMMORALITY LEADS TO DEATH!

It seemed like a silly prank, the kind of thing Amanda might have laughed off as some nutcase gone awry with a scissors and stack of *People* magazines. "Any idea of the authorship?"

"No prints or fibers or saliva. It was dropped off in a taped envelope with no return address. No stamp or cancellation marks, either.

Someone dropped it in her mail slot in Sacramento. That narrows it down to about a million people. I wanted to pursue it, but Davida nixed questioning her colleagues. She was trying to woo a couple of detractors, hoping to sway them to see the light and didn't want the police turning them hostile. So we dropped it." Newell grimaced. "In light of what happened, big mistake."

Barnes asked, "Were you thinking the White Tower was behind it?"

"At that point I didn't because they hadn't bothered her yet."

"Bledsoe's still in Idaho?"

Newell nodded. "It would be nice if he stepped over the border. He's got some outstanding traffic warrants here in California."

Something was tickling Barnes's brain as he watched as Hizzoner and Lucille Grayson emerge from the back of the limo. The old woman remained erect and dry-eyed. Soon the shock would lift and grief would engulf her. He needed to talk to her while she could still talk.

"Where's Mrs. Grayson going, Donnie?"

"To see her lawyer. Final arrangements."

Amanda said, "Would you mind introducing her to us . . . or rather me? You people already know each other."

"It's been awhile," Barnes said. Then he remembered what was nagging at his brain. "Doesn't Marshall Bledsoe's mother live in LA?"

Newell shrugged. "Don't know."

"I think she does. San Fernando Valley as I recall. Now Thanksgiving is, what . . . a week away? I wonder if Marshall will be paying Mom a visit." Barnes smiled. "If he has warrants, we have probable cause."

"I'll have to coordinate with LAPD," Amanda said. "In the meantime, let's talk to Lucille Grayson, then I want to poke around the capital. I know some politically connected people so maybe I won't be as threatening as Don."

"Plus, you're a lot prettier and tons more charming," Newell said.

Amanda's smile started off frosted but thawed in a nanosecond. "People may like me, but no one doesn't *love* my husband's money."

"Willie Barnes." Lucille eyed him head to toe. "You grew up and you got old."

Barnes winked. "That about sums it up, Mrs. Grayson."

The old woman sighed. "I never did get a chance to tell you how sorry I was about your brother, Jack."

"You sent me a lovely sympathy card, ma'am."

"Did I?"

"Yes, you did. I appreciated it and wrote you back."

"Well, then . . . now I'm telling you in person how sorry I was."

"Mrs. Grayson, I am so sorry about Davida. She was a fine woman and a real asset to this community. She was loved, respected and admired. It is a profound loss for everyone, but my heart goes out to you. I'm truly sorry."

Lucille nodded. "Thank you, Will."

"This is my partner, Detective Isis, ma'am." Barnes watched Lucille give Amanda a polite nod.

Amanda said, "Solving this isn't only our top priority, it's Berkeley's top priority."

The old woman nodded and turned back to Barnes. "What do you think about the mayor, Willie?"

Thrown by the question, Barnes formulated his answer as quickly as he could. "He's very concerned, ma'am."

"Concerned for Davida or concerned for the town's image?" When Barnes didn't answer, she said, "I have an appointment with my lawyer in a half hour. If you need to reach me, I'll be at the club for the next couple of days."

"Thank you, Mrs. Grayson, I appreciate your cooperation. Could you spare a few minutes for a couple of questions?"

The old woman didn't agree but she didn't walk away. Amanda went first. "Did Davida express any concerns for her safety after the recent incident in the capital?"

"I was much more concerned than Davida." Lucille raked nails down her cheek, creating temporary stigmata. "My daughter was fearless." She looked at Newell for confirmation. "You remember those Nazis, don't you, Willie?"

"I don't know the Nutterly brothers, but I sure as hell remember Marshall Bledsoe. Donnie tells me he moved to Idaho."

"But he's still got followers in Sacramento. And I see him around from time to time."

Newell said, "Do you, ma'am? When was the last time?"

The old woman's eyes clouded. "I'd say . . . last year . . . maybe it was longer, but I'm sure he goes back and forth."

Amanda said, "Next time you see him, Mrs. Grayson, give us a call right away. He has outstanding traffic warrants in the state of California so we can arrest him."

"That's all you've got on him?" Lucille said. "Traffic warrants?"

"It's enough to bring him in. Especially if you think he had something to do with Davida's death."

"I'd certainly look at him first. Also that Modell man. He used to send her the nastiest mail."

"Harry Modell," Barnes said. Seeing Amanda's inquisitive look, he added, "Families Under God, I'll fill you in."

Newell said, "She never mentioned any hate mail from him."

"Davida thought he was a crackpot," Lucille said. "She thought the letters were funny although I failed to see any humor in them."

"She showed you the letters?" Amanda asked.

"Yes, she did. I kept a few of them. I thought she should send them to the police, but she refused and she forbade me to do it. Said it was a waste of their valuable time."

"You wouldn't still have those letters, would you?" Amanda asked.

"Of course, I have them. In my files at home. I wanted to keep them . . . just in case." Without warning, the old woman's eyes watered. She unfolded a silk handkerchief and dabbed her eyes.

Amanda said, "Who else should we be looking at, Mrs. Grayson?"

"Oh . . . I don't know."

"What about her partner, Minette?"

The old woman's eyes narrowed. "What about her?"

"How'd they get along, for starts?"

"I'll give you my observations, but I'm warning you, they're colored. I don't like the girl."

"Why not?" Barnes said.

"I think she's a mooch, an attention seeker, and a drunk. When Davida first introduced us, it was hate at first sight. But I could tell Davida was smitten. The girl was a gorgeous thing about five years ago. In that showgirl way. Now the bourbon's caught up with her." Lucille lowered her voice. "My daughter never said a word about their relationship—good or bad. But lately, I could tell there were problems."

"How so?" Amanda asked.

"During our lunches and dinners, the girl was constantly calling . . . interrupting. I could tell that Davy was not happy. She'd get this tight look around her eyes and whisper something like, '*Can we talk about this later?'* Not a single meal passed without intrusion." A wistful sigh. "And I saw Davy so seldom."

"But you never heard Davida complain about Minette?"

"Only to say that the girl didn't like her keeping such long hours. Probably the only thing the girl and I ever agreed on." Lucille peered into Amanda's eyes. "Now, I'm *not* saying that the girl had anything to do with Davida's death. But I am saying that there was a reason that Davida spent so much time away."

"Do you think it's possible that Davida was seeing someone else?" Amanda asked.

Lucille shrugged. "Well, let me put it to you this way. Her father never placed a premium on fidelity. If that was the only bad trait that Davy inherited from him, she did quite well."

7

There were numerous cafés in downtown Berkeley, but for some reason Barnes always went to Melanie's—a little hole-in-the-wall that served a mean bran and raisin muffin and a decent cup of no-frills coffee. Of late, Barnes was adding milk to the froufrou level because his stomach rebelled when he drank too much black. Melanie's was about half a storefront wide, and when the place got crowded, he had to walk through the door sideways.

Laura Novacente was sitting at what used to be their favorite corner table, her long gray hair tied up in a knot. When he sat down opposite her, she slid the cappuccino in front of him. "Hey there. How's it going?"

"You're looking good. I like that red dress on you. Brings out your coloring."

"The tape recorder is going, Smooth-guy." Laura pointed to a small lump under a napkin.

Barnes smiled. "It was a compliment. If I get slapped with sexual harassment you're going to be hearing from my attorney for entrapment."

"What entrapment?"

"The red dress. It brings out your coloring."

Laura laughed. "Is your attorney cute?"

"She's very cute."

They drank coffee for several moments. Laura said, "Time for business: do you have something I can print?"

"All business?"

"I don't waste the paper's money on flirting."

"How about this," said Barnes. We are 'still at an initial inquiry stage, exploring all open avenues.' "

Laura got that I'm-hungry-and-grumpy look. "You can do better, Will."

Barnes reached over, uncovered the tape recorder, switched it off, and looked her in the eye. "I've got about five minutes before someone realizes I'm not where I'm supposed to be. In short, we got plenty of suspects, but no good ones."

"What about her partner, Minette?"

"What about her?"

"I heard there was trouble in paradise."

"Like what?"

"Just that. Rumors."

"Thanks, I'll look into it."

"C'mon, Willie. I promise I won't print anything. Just give me an idea of what you're thinking."

"Your promises aren't worth much, Laura."

She showed teeth. "Neither are yours, darling, but let's not hold it against either one of us."

"Okay . . ." He leaned over the table, so close he could smell her perfume. "We're working on Minette's alibi. She claims she was with a friend part of the night, but not the entire night."

"Who's the friend?"

"She's not too forthcoming on that. We're looking into it. Any suggestions?"

"I hear Minette was in and out of a series of relationships before she settled down with Davida. She's pissed off a lot of people. She also drinks."

Willie nodded.

"That doesn't surprise you."

"Davida's mother called Minette a drunk. Think she's cheating on Davida?"

"I wouldn't be surprised." Laura took a sip of her café mocha. "I gave you something, so how about a little reciprocity?"

"Davida had lots of enemies in the capital."

"And the sky's blue, so what? Everyone knows the capital runs on bile but how many politicians are mowed down with a twelve-gauge shotgun?"

"Who told you about the weapon?"

"Word gets around." Laura ran a finger across her lips.

Barnes stared at her.

She said, "Loose lips at the crime scene—your own people."

"Great. Anything else I should know about?"

"Don't be sulky, Will, it's how I make my living. How about giving me something that every other reporter doesn't have?"

With her tentacles, maybe she'd learn something and trade it back to him. "We're investigating some hate mail."

"From . . ."

"You can use the hate-mail part, but not the name. Agreed?"

"Absolutely."

"I mean it, Laura."

"So do I. Who's the hate-mailer?"

"Some whack job named Harry Modell, executive director of Families Under God. Ever hear of them?"

"I have. Modell sent her nasty stuff, huh?"

"According to Lucille Grayson. The old woman still has the letters. Plus—and you can print this—rumor has it that Ray and Brent Nutterly from the White Tower Radicals are going to be charged with the egging incident. Police have eyewitnesses, including several who recorded the whole incident on their phone videos. You want more information, talk to Detective Don Newell, Sac PD."

"That's good, Will, I can run with that. Thanks so much."

Touching his hand.

He said, "Speaking of running, I'd better get back."

"The White Tower boys . . . ," Laura said. "They're into survivalism."

"And a shotgun's a hunting weapon. Unfortunately, the Nutterly brothers were behind bars last night, so it wasn't them." Barnes stood up. "I took a chance meeting you like this, Laura."

"I appreciate it."

"Dinner sometime?"

Her smile was wistful. "I wish you had asked me two weeks ago."

Seeing someone. Barnes working his smile hard. "Good for you."

Her cheeks were flushed. She touched her hair. "It probably won't work out, but what the hell, Willie. Live dangerously."

Since Lucille Grayson was staying in Berkeley for the night, Don Newell and Amanda Isis took the train to Sacramento together, leaving Barnes behind with the nasty job of sorting through thousands of Davida's computer files, decoded easily by Max Flint.

Seated in a comfortable chair, rocked by Amtrak's wheels, the Sacramento detective was fighting the urge to sleep. He glanced at his seatmate. A few calls had filled in her history. A Google gazillionaire. And definitely someone with clout. By the time they stepped onto the train, she had appointments with three different state reps.

Now she was napping, pretty face all peaceful and unlined.

Newell forced his eyes open. Lucille Grayson had chosen to remain in Berkeley until the body was released, and entrusted him with a key to her house and directions where to look for Harry Modell's hate letters. Newell had called up his partner, Banks Henderson, and told him to meet him there at the old lady's place with an SPD video cam and a civilian witness. He didn't want to be accused of planting anything.

He sneaked a sidelong glance at Amanda. Good-looking woman—great-looking really, with that soft skin—kind of a fifties-movie-star glamour.

Maybe she knew she was being watched because she woke up and got back to work on her Starbucks. Without looking at Newell, she began writing furiously in her pad.

"Inspiration?" Newell wasn't so much curious as he was trying to stay awake. Making conversation with a pretty woman was a bonus.

Amanda looked up. "Just writing down any possible questions I can think of for the pols."

"C'mon," he said. "What's the likelihood that it's a politician?"

"Low, I grant you. But so many of these people attract hangers-on and whackos. It'd be stupid not to ask them, right?" She gave Newell a hard look.

He said nothing.

"Is there a problem," she said, "my operating in your territory?"

"Not mine at all. Capital police territory, we just cover the real people." Newell's smile didn't get Amanda's lips curving. "No, no problem. Even if it was my turf. I was just thinking out loud. Truth is, I have seen plenty of those yokels and no matter how they undermine each other on one bill, next day they've got their arms around each other on another one. Take Davida. She's worked on several projects with Eileen Ferunzio and at that time, they were the best of friends."

"You kept in contact with Davida."

"We'd run into each other now and then. Like I said, work brings me to the cap. I used to see Eileen and Davida eating lunch together all the time." Newell shrugged. "Not so much lately."

"Any occasional lunches between you and Davida?"

Newell's smile was easy, but cold. "Oh, I see where this is going. Let me get it on the table: we were just friends . . . not even close friends. My wife didn't like her."

"Why's that?"

"Jill's just that way. She met the woman and took an instant dislike to her. Every time Davida called I knew it was her, by the look on Jill's face."

"Why'd Davida call you?"

"I was her contact in the police department, she was my contact in the halls of government. Mutually beneficial relationship, but nothing more. The woman was gay, Amanda. That means she don't like men."

"Some gays have relationships with the opposite sex."

"Well, if she was doing a guy, I didn't know about it. Why would I? We didn't work like that."

Amanda nodded. "You don't mind my asking you these questions, do you, Don?"

"Not at all," he said glibly. "It's good for me. Gives me empathy for what it's like on the other side of the table."

8

Winding through the Berkeley hills on streets barely wide enough for a compact, Barnes went over the crime scene in his mind. After much prodding and some not-so-subtle threats, Minette Padgett had finally coughed up an alibi name.

Kyle Bosworth hadn't said much over the phone other than to admit being with Minette from ten PM to a little past two. When Barnes wanted to interview him in person, Bosworth balked, but Barnes assured him it wouldn't take more than a half hour of his time. Besides, it was better to have such interviews prearranged than to have the police barge in on him.

Finding the address, Barnes wedged his tiny wheels into a half space and felt lucky to get that. The sidewalks were pushed up and cracked from majestic pines that shadowed postcard lawns. About half of the houses were turn of the century, mostly California bungalows. The others were expensive remodels. Up in the hills, the real estate, like the air, was rarefied.

A tall, emaciated man answered Barnes's knock. His amber hair was messy; his brown eyes, raw and red and drooping. He wore a blue flannel robe over red flannel pajamas, sheepskin slippers on narrow, pale feet. He gave Barnes a quick once-over.

"Mr. Bosworth."

"In person."

"Would you like to see some identification?"

"Not necessary. You look like a cop." Bosworth's smile was feeble. "*Hollywood's* image of a cop."

Barnes went inside. "Those guys are macho and good-looking."

"Yeah, but there's always one guy . . . how should I put it? You know, the older, craggy one who drinks too much, but still shows the rookies how it's done."

"That's me, huh?"

"That's you. Have a seat. Do you want some coffee?"

"I wouldn't mind." Barnes remained standing. "Did I wake you, Mr. Bosworth?"

"Actually Minette woke me. The first time she called, she was hysterical and she made me hysterical. It took a Valium to calm me down."

"What time was that?"

"Right after she heard the news, about eight thirty maybe. The second time was a half hour ago."

"What did you two talk about?"

"She said the cops were probably going to ask me questions."

"Did she tell you anything else?"

"Like what?"

"Did she give you instructions what to say to me?"

"She told me to tell the truth."

"And the truth is?"

Bosworth pointed to an oversized, square-back oak chair with plump red cushions. "Just what I told you. I was with her from ten to about two in the morning."

"What were you doing?"

"I was with her." Bosworth rubbed his eyes and yawned. "That's all you need to know."

Barnes said, "Do you have a live-in partner, Mr. Bosworth?"

Bosworth looked at him. "Interesting that you didn't ask me if I have a wife."

"My brother was gay. If I look like Hollywood's crusty old cop, you look like the good-looking but dissolute, gay interior designer."

"Set designer, please. I worked in Hollywood for ten years. I'll go get some coffee." When Bosworth stepped into the kitchen, Barnes took a peek around the place. The house wasn't large, but it was done up nicely. All the original mahogany woodwork had been refinished,

from the wainscoting to the crown molding. Leaded windows show-
cased a terrific view of the bay. The Craftsman-style furniture looked to
be good-quality reproductions.

"How do you take yours?" Bosworth called from the kitchen.

"A little milk and sugar."

Bosworth returned with a mug on a red lacquer tray. "Here you
go."

"Thanks." Barnes took his coffee and finally sat down.

"You referred to your brother in the past tense. AIDS?"

"Jack was murdered ten years ago. His death is what brought me to
Berkeley."

"Oh jeez, I'm sorry."

Barnes sipped coffee, placed the mug on the tray, took out his pad
and a pencil. "How long have you known Minette?"

"We've traveled in the same circles for at least four years."

"How long have you known her *well*?"

"About a year. We hooked up at the gym. Both our partners keep
long hours. I prefer men, she prefers women but both of us have an
aversion to loneliness. I'm sure Yves suspects something although I
doubt if he suspects it's Minette. When he comes home, there's always
tasty food on the table and a clean house so he doesn't ask too many
questions."

"What does Yves do?"

"He's a patent lawyer for Micron Industries. They're very demand-
ing, but he's paid extremely well."

"Where was he last night?"

Bosworth stared at him.

Barnes smiled.

"Actually, Detective, he was working at home. When I told him I
needed to visit a friend in trouble, he barely looked up from his paperwork."

"Was he up when you came home?"

"Yes. And I suppose you can ask him what time I came home. But
I'd prefer that you don't tell him any more details than necessary."

"Did you know Davida Grayson as well as you knew Minette?"

Bosworth laughed. "Are you asking if I ever slept with Davida? I
must really look like a stud."

Barnes waited.

"I've never slept with Davida. Lately Minette wasn't sleeping with her, either. She was beginning to wonder if there was someone else in Davida's life."

"Did she mention any names?"

The question gave Bosworth pause. "I don't feel good getting someone involved based on Minette's paranoia."

"Minette's paranoid?"

"She can be when she drinks." Bosworth sighed. "Okay. Minette was sure Davida was fooling around with a woman named Alice Kurtag. *Dr.* Alice Kurtag. She's a research scientist at the UC and her specialty is gene splicing. She's a consultant on Davida's bill. It seemed normal to me that they'd spend a little extra time together."

Barnes looked up from his notes. "And what did Minette say to that?"

"She didn't say anything. Maybe she's just justifying her bad behavior by transferring it to Davida."

"Do you know Alice?"

"I've met her a couple of times at Davida's parties."

"Is she gay?"

"I don't know. Both times I met her, she wasn't with a man, but that doesn't mean anything. She was mixing but she wasn't flirting. She just seemed . . . I don't know . . . very businesslike. I don't know anything about science or politics so we didn't talk a lot."

"Mr. Bosworth, would you mind if I tested your hands for gunshot residue?"

"Me?" Bosworth appeared shocked. "I've never held a gun in my life!" He held out his hands. "I just got a manicure yesterday. Will it ruin my nails?"

"It's a simple swab called a DPA test. If you fired a gun, you'll get little blue specks. If you didn't, you won't get any discoloration."

"Did Minette agree to this?"

"She did. The swab turned up negative."

"Do I have to agree to it?"

"No, but why wouldn't you?"

"I don't like being considered a suspect." When Barnes didn't answer, Bosworth said, "Look, if I do it, does that mean that you won't have to talk to Yves about yesterday night?"

"Not necessarily. But if you don't have gunshot residue, I'll put you a little farther down on the list. If Yves verifies your story, you'll be way, way down the list."

"Why would I make the list at all?"

"Don't take it personally, Mr. Bosworth. It's a very long list."

Finishing her meal, Eileen Ferunzio wiped her mouth then reapplied her apricot shimmer lipstick. Amanda noticed that the state representative had barely made it through half of her Caesar salad. The woman looked drawn, her complexion ashen except for two smudges of pink that ran along her cheekbones. Her eyes were an uneasy mixture of green and brown, shifting with the intensity of the light. Eileen was a big woman—five eight or nine—with sturdy, square shoulders, long legs and a strong handshake. At odds with all that were her tiny wrists. Today those wrists were adorned by a gold Lady Rolex and a gem-studded gold cuff bracelet.

Amanda had met her at fund-raisers and she greeted Amanda by first name. Larry's money.

"You're not hungry, Eileen?"

"How can I eat? This whole thing is just terrible! I . . ." Eileen's eyes moistened. "Do you know why it happened?"

"I wish I did." Amanda put down her turkey wrap and wiped her mouth. "That's why I'm here. What can you tell me about Davida?"

"She was a colleague and a friend." Again Eileen's eyes moistened. "I've known her for a while. Even before she got elected to the House, we worked together on various issues."

"Which issues?"

"Davida's a lawyer, you know. She went to Hastings."

"Yes, I heard something about that." Amanda smiled at Eileen. "Which issues did you work with Davida on?"

"She had worked as a lobbyist for The Partnership Against Domestic Violence. She was very effective. I, of course, am an activist in that area."

Amanda said, "Eileen, I heard that you and she had been at odds on this latest bill—HS . . ."

The state representative looked away. "We had our differences, sure." She turned back to Amanda. "What of it?"

"Given your voting record, I would have assumed that the bill was something you would have wholly endorsed."

"Then you would have been wrong."

Tension in Eileen's voice. Amanda said, "What didn't you like about the bill?"

"Just about everything." Eileen shook her head. "In theory, cell lines and cell cloning seems to be the kind of issue that every liberal should get behind. In reality, we are pouring millions of dollars into something that has yet to be proven to be consistently if at all effective. I'm progressive but I am fiscally responsible and the initiative-based institute has accomplished nothing, so far. I happen to believe there are sufficient monies allocated for stem-cell research and related topics. I didn't feel it was prudent to allocate the amount of money Davida was talking about."

"Which was?"

"A half billion dollars over the next three years," Eileen said. "She was dreaming. I told her to pare it down and then we could discuss the matter intelligently and who knows, she might even be able to sway me. She refused, so I refused."

"What did that do to your friendship?"

Eileen's eyes narrowed. "What are you suggesting?"

"I'm just asking a question."

"Oh please!" Eileen's face darkened. "I'm not stupid, and I resent the implication. I had nothing to do with Davida's death and I'll take a lie-detector test if you want to pursue this. But it is beyond insulting!"

"Where were you last night?"

"At home sleeping in bed with my husband."

"Not at the capital."

"Nor anywhere near Berkeley."

Eileen's district was a six-hour car ride from Davida's. Amanda asked, "How did you travel here this morning?"

"I took a seven o'clock from my local airport. Anything else?"

"No offense intended, Eileen. I'm doing my job."

Eileen huffed. "I suppose you are, but surely some independent thinking is called for." Then, as if realizing something, she flashed a sudden, plastic smile. "I'm sorry, Amanda. This is all just so . . . traumatic."

Larry's money.

Amanda smiled back. "Just a few more questions?"

Sigh. "Sure."

"How did your opposition to the bill affect your friendship with Davida?"

"It put a strain on it but we remained on speaking terms. It certainly didn't discourage Davida from calling me frequently. Trying to convince me to change my mind. And I called her after the egging incident. I told her how horrified I was."

"What did she say?"

"She thanked me for my sympathies, but she told me she'd rather thank me for my support. Then she went to work on me again. She was so persistent that I agreed to meet her later this week. She seemed so pleased about that." Eileen swabbed her eyes with her napkin. "That was the last time I spoke to her. If you want to find out who did this, talk to those fascist cretins."

"Which cretins in particular?"

"The Nutterly brothers."

"They were in jail when Davida was shot."

"Amanda, there are a helluva lot more White Tower boys than just the Nutterly brothers, and they all seem to congregate around Sacramento. Why aren't you talking to them?"

"They're on our official list."

"Why are you talking to me *first*?"

"Because you were her friend, and I figured you could tell me who in the legislature was really after her."

Eileen shook her head. "Lord knows the legislature has its share of SOBs but no one there would have *killed* her, for God's sake. Stick around long enough, we're all at odds with one another sometimes. That's just the nature of the beast."

"Did Davida ever talk to you about Harry Modell?"

"That psychotic weirdo? What about him?"

"I heard he sent her threatening letters."

"He sends everyone threatening letters—" Eileen blanched.

"Including you?"

"Oh my God!" she whispered frantically. "Do I have something to worry about?"

"Do you still have the letters, Eileen?"

"In my nut file. I'll get them to you ASAP." She signaled the waiter for the bill. Her face had taken on deep worry lines. "Answer me honestly. Should I be nervous? I mean . . . should I get a bodyguard?"

Amanda thought about that, had no clear answer. She said, "Until we know more, I don't think it would hurt."

Spoken like a true politician.

9

As luck would have it, Barnes found a parking space right on Telegraph, the avenue swimming with the typical time-warp mix of hippies, retro-hippies, one-note fanatics and junk entrepreneurs looking scruffier than any of the others. The uniform was torn jeans, message T-shirts, leather headbands and glassy eyes. Booths were set up on the sidewalks, hawking everything from Maoist theory and anti-Amerikan nihilism to mood rings, organic Viagra, and scented candles. Music blared from speakers attached to competing CD stores. The resulting aural broth was a wall of white noise to Barnes's ears, but what did he know, he'd never progressed much past Buck Owens.

Noise and body odor notwithstanding, Barnes was happy to be there. The day had turned sunny, the skies were clear and his lungs needed to suck in something other than death. On Telegraph, that meant secondary smoke not from tobacco.

Back in the Stone ages, when he'd been an eighteen-year-old high school graduate, advanced education in his circles meant two years at a community college learning animal husbandry. He'd been a decent, but uninspired student and a good varsity football player. Unfortunately there weren't a whole lot of jobs for "good but never, never, ever gonna make it to the pros" running backs. Ergo, the military, and that had been okay for a few years. When he finished up his tour, he had narrowed his future to farming, trucking, or the police academy. Law enforcement was the decision because it seemed like more fun, and Barnes had some book smarts so he advanced within a narrow sphere.

As a detective, he got to use his brain, and, sometimes, he felt like he had a good one.

Still, whenever he had any business at the UC, he felt uncomfortable. He had never attended classes at a genuine university, and the Berkeley campus was as big as a city. It had its own government, its own police force and its own set of rules, explicit and otherwise.

As he walked along leafy lanes, some of the buildings were downright imposing, others looked as inviting as a concrete bunker and he felt like an invader from outer space. Invader past his prime.

Using his little map as a guide, he couldn't help but notice how young the kids were and that made him feel even older.

Dr. Alice Kurtag's lab was housed in a six-story, post-modern, brick and concrete structure that had been retrofitted for earthquakes. Berkeley wasn't perched directly on the San Andreas Fault, but like all the Bay Area, the ground was plenty seismic and no one could predict when The Big One was coming.

And yet, thought Barnes, we pretend. He entered Kurtag's building, drawing stares from a clutch of grad students. Kurtag's lab on the fourth floor was sizeable; her office was not. Her private domain barely held a desk and two chairs. It did have a nice view of the city and the water beyond. The fog had lifted several hours ago and the burn-off had produced a blue sky streaked with white clouds and contrails.

Kurtag looked to be in her fifties, a handsome woman with strong features and a short efficient hairdo. She had blond streaks running through dark hair, and strong brown eyes. She wore little makeup, just a dot of red on her cheeks and something soft and wet on her lips. She had on a long-sleeved green blouse, black slacks and boots. Her ears were adorned with diamond studs. Her nails were short but manicured.

"Do you know anything about a memorial service?" she asked Barnes.

Her voice was soft and surprisingly airy.

"No, Doctor, I don't. But I'm sure there will be one as soon as the coroner releases the body."

"I suppose it's premature at this stage."

Barnes nodded.

"This is just terrible. What happened? Was it a robbery?"

"I hate to sound evasive, but we just don't have all the facts. I know the city council is going to hold a town hall meeting tonight at seven. Maybe we'll know more by then."

"I certainly hope so. This is so upsetting. I work late at night. I'm alone here myself quite often. I'd hate to think of a predator stalking single women. And of course, poor Davida."

"How's the security here?"

"It's a university. It's filled with people who belong and people who don't. Most of the time, I bury my nose in my work and don't look around too much. Now I'm so upset, I can barely concentrate."

"Were you and Davida close?"

"Over the past year, we'd become very close, working on her bill. Now . . . without her as an advocate . . . I really don't know what chance we have for passage."

Barnes said, "When was the last time you saw her?"

"Yesterday afternoon." The doctor's voice cracked. "It seems so far away now."

"What was the occasion?"

"She stopped by to pick up some reports for some lobbyists. She was going to hit the capital full force this week and needed all the scientific information I could muster. I had some of the material ready, but not all of it. She was going to come by this afternoon to pick it up . . ." Again, her voice broke, but this time her eyes filled with tears. "I'm sorry."

"It's a terrible thing," Barnes said. "Did you socialize with Davida outside of work?"

Alice Kurtag wiped her eyes with a tissue. "With Davida, everything was work—from her parties to her meetings. Occasionally, when we were working long hours, we'd treat ourselves to dinner and a movie. Neither of us have children to rush home to." The scientist smiled sadly. "We weren't lovers if that's what you're hinting at."

Barnes gave her a neutral shrug. "Did she ever confide in you?"

"Now and then, I guess. She'd tell me how worried she was about the bill. She only had support in the House if every one of her fellow Democrats chose to back her up. Some had changed their minds, others gave her a hard time from the beginning."

"How so?"

"They objected to the cost of funding the proposition, said give the initiative-funded institute a chance." Kurtag frowned. "Science doesn't come cheap. What worthwhile endeavor is cheap?"

"Did she ever talk to you about personal fears?" When Kurtag seemed puzzled, Barnes clarified his question. "Was she specifically afraid of someone or something?"

"She never said anything to me . . . other than to complain how betrayed she felt."

"Betrayed?"

"By her colleagues."

"Which ones?"

"I don't recall. I organize data, conduct experiments, write reports, Detective. I don't do the actual lobbying." She paused. "There was a woman representative . . . Elaine something."

"Eileen Ferunzio."

"She's the one. Davida was furious with her. Apparently, Davida had recently thrown her support behind one of Eileen's bills, so when she didn't get reciprocity, she felt totally betrayed. But there was never any hint that Eileen was dangerous. That's absurd."

Barnes wondered. "We've heard Davida had received some threatening letters."

"Threatening letters?" Alice thought about that. "Oh, from that crackpot down in Orange County? She seemed more amused by it than scared."

"Do you remember the crackpot's name?"

"Harry something."

"Harry Modell?"

"Yes." The doctor appeared annoyed. "If you know all of this, why are you wasting my time?"

"I know some things but not everything. So she didn't take Modell's threats seriously?"

"Not to my eye. She mentioned something to the effect that she knew things about him, and that all his threats were nothing but bluster."

"What kind of things?"

"She didn't specify."

"Blackmail things?"

"Oh please, why would she waste time blackmailing a loser like him?"

Barnes pressed on. "After Davida mentioned these 'things,' did the threatening letters stop?"

"I really don't know. It wasn't the focus of our meetings."

"How often did she mention Harry Modell?"

Expansive. "Maybe twice, three times."

"When was the last time she mentioned him?"

"I haven't the faintest idea, Detective."

"A week ago? A month ago?"

"Maybe a month, but I couldn't swear to it. Really you're making too big a deal out of him. Is that all? I'm distracted enough as it is. I really need to get back to work."

"Please, Dr. Kurtag, just bear with me. Did Davida ever talk to you about Minette Padgett?"

Alice appeared uncomfortable. She didn't answer right away. "You think Minette murdered her?"

The frankness of Kurtag's question took Barnes aback. "What do you think?"

"I think that unless you think Minette had something to do with her death, I don't want to talk about her."

Barnes ignored her and pressed on. "Minette was having an affair . . . with a man. Did Davida know?"

Kurtag's eyes hardened. "Davida didn't place a premium on her domestic life. She had bigger issues to deal with."

"What does that mean? She knew but didn't care?"

No answer.

Barnes said, "Was she was going to dump Minette? Was she having an affair herself?"

Alice Kurtag's eyes drifted to the ceiling. "It would be helpful if you asked your questions one at a time."

"Okay," said Barnes. "Did Davida know about Minette's affair?"

"She hinted about it—Minette thinks she's subtle, but she's not. But she didn't seem to care, Detective. She was getting a bit tired of Minette's whining."

"Was she going to dump Minette?"

"That never came up."

"Do you know if Davida was involved with someone else?"

"No, I don't. Frankly, I don't see when she would have had the time."

"I'm sorry to have to ask you this, Dr. Kurtag, but where were you last night?"

Alice was silent. Then she said, "Where I am practically every night. Here, at the lab, working."

"Alone?"

"Yes, alone. Who else works at two in the morning?"

Davida had been at her desk at two in the morning. Barnes kept his thoughts to himself. "When did you leave the lab?"

"I didn't. I slept here last night."

"Where?"

"At my desk."

And Barnes thought he had a lonely life. "Do you often sleep at your desk?"

"Not *often*." Alice shot him a cold stare. *"Occasionally."*

"If I offended you," Barnes said, "that wasn't my intention. I have to ask sensitive questions, Doctor. Right now, I'm trying to piece together a time line. So you were here all night?"

Kurtag showed him her profile. Tight lips, squinty eyes. "All night," she said softly.

"Alone."

"I already told you that."

"You're sure no one saw you here?"

Kurtag's smile came nowhere near mirth. "I suppose that means I have no alibi."

"Would you mind if I gave you a gunshot residue test—just a swab of your hands?"

"I would mind because I resent the implication. But go ahead, do it anyway. Then you can leave."

10

The Ronald Tsukamoto Public Safety Building housed both the fire and police departments of the city of Berkeley. The two-story entrance was shaped like a sewing spool with the bottom foot lopped off. It was Deco in style, each of the two semi-circular levels punched with large rectangular windows that sat atop each other with geometric precision. The paint job, however, was pure Victorian—ecru trimmed in robin's eggshell blue and bright white.

Once inside, anyone having business with BPD waited in a rotunda with multi-colored abstract mobiles hanging from the ceiling. A spiral staircase with spaghetti-thin railings wound its way to the second story. The station was pleasant and clean, with checkerboard flooring and soft natural light filtering in from the generous windows.

The actual working interior was plain-wrap cop shop: windowless beige walls, fluorescent lighting, small cubicles with charmless but functional workstations. The equipment was often mismatched, and in the case of some of the computers, sorely outdated. The conference room furniture consisted of white plastic tables and black plastic chairs. Maps of the district, a calendar, a video screen and a chalkboard made up the wall decor. An American flag stood in one corner, the Golden Bear stood sentry in another.

It had been a hellish morning for Berkeley PD, but it was the captain on the hot seat. At six years away from retirement, Ramon Torres now had to explain to the mayor, the governor, and his highly vocal constituency how a beloved state representative had been nearly decapitated in her office and no one knew a damn thing about it.

The captain was short, stocky with leathery brown skin and piercing eyes one shade lighter. Each month expanded his bald spot; what little hair remained was black and that offered him some consolation. He winced as he read through the hate-spewing letters penned by Harry Modell, executive director of Families Under God.

Torres put the missives down and looked across the conference table at Isis and Barnes. Two of his best detectives and they'd learned nada.

"They're obviously written by someone who's bigoted and mean-spirited, but I don't see enough actual threat for us to act. The First Amendment doesn't discriminate between civil and barbaric."

Barnes said, "I'm not recommending that we prosecute him, Cap, but both Amanda and I think it'd be negligent if we didn't at least talk to him."

Amanda said, "He's written other poison-pen letters to female members of our state congress. If something happens to one of those ladies, we'll be in deep waters."

Headlines flashed in Torres's head. Talking heads on the tube, his own name bandied about like a cussword. "How many women are we talking about?"

"At least two."

"What about men?" Torres asked.

Amanda said, "None so far, but Detective Don Newell from Sacramento PD is investigating."

Torres said, "Then maybe you should wait until Newell makes his report before I allocate the funds to send you down south."

"I have another reason for wanting to go to LA this week, sir," Barnes said. "Detective Newell arrested two losers who were behind the assault on Davida Grayson last week."

"The egging."

Barnes nodded. "Coupla morons named Ray and Brent Nutterly from the White Tower boys. Their boss, Marshall Bledsoe, might be visiting LA."

"Bledsoe," said Torres. "Suspected synagogue bomber but he was never charged. Egging seems lightweight for him."

"True, sir, but Newell is pretty sure the Nutterly boys wouldn't have acted without Bledsoe's go-ahead. In light of Grayson's murder, we should question him. That's two obvious reasons for going south."

"Obvious," Torres repeated.

Amanda said, "Bledsoe lives in Idaho but we've got a bench warrant for outstanding traffic violations. His mother lives in the San Fernando Valley and Thanksgiving's coming up."

"Dropping in on Mommy," said the captain. "You do any prep on this?"

"We called LAPD West Valley Division and they called saying there's a pickup with Idaho plates in Mom's driveway. That was an hour ago."

Barnes said, "Four months ago, Modell moved about ten miles north of Bledsoe's mother."

"Convenient," said Torres. "Do the two of them know each other?"

"Good question."

Torres glanced at his wristwatch. "It's too late to put you two on a plane and get you back in time for town hall. If Bledsoe is visiting Mom for the holidays, he isn't going anywhere. The community meeting's been pushed back from seven to eight. Community affairs is making up a list of mock questions. Go over them so you're prepared. I know I don't have to tell you this but I will anyway. No mention of Modell or Bledsoe by name. If someone asks about suspects, tell them we're focusing our attention on a few persons of interest. You do all that, you can book tickets to La La Land."

"Thanks, got it," Barnes said.

"Meanwhile," said Torres, "go down to the morgue in Oakland and see what forensics you can get on Grayson. Coroner's running a full toxicology screen. Given an overkill shotgun thing in the wee hours of the morning, I'm still seeing red flags for a dope deal gone sour. Her blood turns up dirty, we've got a new kind of complication. Afterward, grab some dinner and clean up before town hall. I want you both presentable."

"We're not presentable?" Amanda asked.

"You are," Torres said. "Barnes looks a little wilted."

"I'll unwilt, sir, maybe even shave. When should we leave for LA?"

"Book a seven AM tomorrow. Call up Southwest and JetBlue. Go with whoever's cheaper."

It took ten minutes for Amanda to connect with the deputy coroner in charge of Davida Grayson's autopsy. Dr. Marv Williman was in his late sixties but had the voice of a much younger man. "Detective Isis. Well, this is kismet. I was just about to call you."

"And here I am," Amanda answered. "Will Barnes and I are on our way to see you."

"I finished up the autopsy an hour ago. That means we can meet somewhere other than the crypt."

"That's fine with me. I'm wearing a designer suit."

"Hoo hah," said Williman. "Berkeley's coming up in the world. I'm a little hungry. There's a great Italian place named Costino's about three blocks from my office, more trattoria than osteria."

"Sounds good." Amanda secured the address. "We'll see you in about thirty, forty minutes."

"What sounds good?" Will asked.

"We're meeting Dr. Williman at an Italian restaurant instead of the morgue."

"Pasta in place of pancreases, excellent. It's been awhile since I ate something serious."

"What constitutes awhile?"

"Depends on my mood."

The pasta was excellent but Barnes was so hungry, he barely registered the taste until he polished off the plate. Linguini with fresh tomatoes, basil, garlic, smoked ham and fresh parmesan cheese. Williman seemed equally enamored of his osso buco. Amanda nibbled one slice of her mini white pizza and picked at her salad greens.

"Are you going to eat that?" Will asked, pointing to the pizza.

"Knock yourself out," Amanda answered. "Want a slice, Marv?"

Williman said, "You're not going to eat it?"

"I'm full."

"Big lunch?" Barnes asked.

"Just trying to take off a little weight."

"Where?" both men asked simultaneously.

"I hide it well." She put down her fork. "So what can you illuminate for us, Dr. Williman?"

The doctor took a gulp of Chianti and set down his wineglass. "Actually I have a couple of important things to pass on."

"Wait a minute." Barnes wiped his face with a napkin, appalled at all the sauce it had soaked up, then fished out his notepad and pen. "Okay, go, Doc."

Williman opened his briefcase and handed Amanda and Barnes a two-page stapled summary of the autopsy. "I haven't finished the complete transcription but I wanted to give you this right away."

He let them scan, then continued. "As you can see, the tox screen came up negative for the usual array of street drugs—"

"Is that blood alcohol level right?" Barnes remarked.

"Ah, you noticed. Very good. Yes, we ran it twice. Did this woman hit the bars last night?"

"I was told she went out to dinner with her mother at the ladies' club then headed straight to the office. According to the server, they left around nine. Her mother was the last person to see her alive, other than the killer."

Williman said, "I don't know about you, but I couldn't work very effectively with a BAL of .22. Any idea how much alcohol she consumed over dinner?"

Amanda said, "According to the waiter, it was the old lady who was shooting back the booze. Davida just had a single glass of wine."

"Well, she made up for lost time, later. And her drinking wasn't a one-shot deal. Her liver was in the early to middle stages of fatty cirrhosis."

Amanda said, "I don't recall anyone saying Davida was a heavy drinker. It's Minette who imbibes."

Barnes said, "The people I've talked to say Davida spent most of her time working, a lot of that alone. Maybe she was a secret drinker."

Williman said, "She got booze in her system somehow. Chronically."

Amanda said, "A BAL of .22 could explain why she was napping at her desk and didn't hear anyone enter her office."

"True," said Barnes. "I like that."

"I've got something else to add to the mix," Williman said.

"Don't tell me," said Barnes. "She was pregnant."

"Close—"

"She had had an abortion?"

"No—"

"Willie, you're fixating on her female parts," said Amanda.

"Because everyone's fixated on their respective parts."

"In this case," said Williman, "Detective Barnes is on target. Davida had gonorrhea."

The table went silent. The doctor continued. "Now, I'm not saying it isn't possible to transfer the disease from female to female, but it's considerably more likely to transfer the disease from male to female."

Amanda said, "Did she know?"

"There were no external symptoms," said Williman. "With women especially it can be like that. Makes it worse, by the time you find out, there's damage."

Barnes said, "Did you happen to find semen? Something we can send to the lab for DNA?"

"No semen, just bacteria," said the pathologist. "And it took an eagle eye to spot 'em floating around." He polished his knuckles. "So to show your gratitude, I'll let you pick up the tab."

11

The Berkeley City Council met in the old unified school district building—an imposing two-story white, Neoclassical structure adorned by Corinthian columns and topped by a cupola with a spire that reminded Barnes of an old-fashioned Prussian army hat. It was next to the police station and the juxtaposition of newer Deco and older Beaux Arts was yet more stylistic chockablock.

By seven forty-five, the auditorium was filled to capacity, with spillover distributed to two additional rooms set up with video monitors.

After going over the list of mock questions, Amanda felt well prepared. Barnes, on the other hand, was nervous. Intellectuals scared him and everyone in Berkeley imagined themselves an intellectual. Using big words when simple ones did the job just fine, going on talking jags and rambling from topic to topic and never making a point.

Maybe that was the idea, to be so vague that the debates would go on forever.

Barnes didn't deal much with the locals. Homicides in Berkeley were usually drug-related, the bad guys imported from Oakland— Alameda County's *real* city. Lucky for him Amanda was a great mouthpiece and would be doing most of the talking.

The two of them sat backstage in a room not much bigger than a closet, waiting for their cue to go onstage. The city council was talking about safety issues, trying to calm down a jumpy, muttering audience. Pronouncing profoundly about vigilance, caution and the need for a "supplementary police presence"—which brought on a whole different flavor of muttering.

This part of the meeting had been allotted thirty minutes but had already eaten up an hour. Not necessarily the council's fault—though every one of them could speechify like Castro. Tonight, it was the public who kept interrupting with pointed questions. Gray-haired guys with ponytails and women in blousy dresses wearing the kind of makeup that resembled no makeup at all. Words like "accountability" and "personalized security" and "Guantanamo-type vigilance" kept cropping up. So did "necessary evil," countered by quotes from Che Guevara and Frantz Fanon.

Amanda finished her crossword and put the paper down. She leaned over and whispered, "Eventually, we need to compare notes. Every time I have something to ask you, there's always a third party in the room."

"Anything specific?" Barnes whispered back.

"For starters, who told you Davida kept long, lonely hours?"

"Her mom complained she worked too hard and too long."

"That could be just a mother talking."

"Minette Padgett also mentioned that Davida worked too hard."

"That could be a lonely lover talking."

Barnes grinned. "How about this, Mandy: Alice Kurtag, the scientist helping with the stem-cell bill, said *she'd* worked long hours with Davida. Some nights they'd go to dinner, come back and confer in the lab."

"Hmmm . . ."

"Exactly," said Barnes. "She swears there was nothing between them."

"Was Minette ever with them during these work orgies?"

"If she was, Kurtag didn't mention it. Let's ask Minette."

"Did Kurtag say anything about Davida drinking in excess?"

"No." An idea was scratching Barnes's brain. "It's funny. Minette's been described as the drunk but Davida's liver was in trouble."

"The two of them drank together."

"Maybe together and in excess," Barnes said. "Davida wasn't characterized as a drunk but maybe she was good at maintaining."

"And Minette's younger," said Amanda. "Give her time to develop her own cirrhosis."

Barnes nodded.

Amanda thought a moment. "If someone knew Davida drank herself asleep, be easy to take advantage and shoot her while she was out."

"And who would know more about her drinking habits than Minette?" said Barnes. "Minette's hetero fling, Kyle Bosworth, told me he left the apartment by two in the morning. Kyle's partner verified Kyle was home around two fifteen. Minette had plenty of time to go down to Davida's office, share a bottle with her lover, wait until Davida had nodded off and blow her head off."

"Clear opportunity," said Amanda. "Clear means if we can connect her to a shotgun. Now what's the motive?"

"Davida had the clap and Dr. Williman said it was passed easier from man to woman. Maybe she was having her own hetero fling."

"Still, it's not impossible from female to female," she said, louder. Barnes put his finger to his lips and Amanda dropped her voice. "Any indication that Davida had a man on the side?"

"Not yet. No special guy shows up in any of her e-mails."

Amanda played with her hair. "To my mind, Willie, it makes more sense that Minette got it from Kyle and gave it to Davida. Minette was the one with the free time to carry on an affair and we *know* she slept with a man."

"Dr. Kurtag thought Davida might have suspected Minette's affair. Maybe she learned Minette had given her gonorrhea and blew up bigtime. When Davida tried to break it off, Minette became enraged, an argument ensued and boom."

Amanda said, "Minette passed the gunpowder test."

"All that means is that she washed her hands really well. Man, I'd just love to examine her clothing for blowback blood spray . . . or powder."

"Do we even know if Minette ever came near a shotgun, let alone knows how to use one?"

Barnes shrugged, took out his pad and pen, and scribbled some notes.

An assistant to one of the councilwomen poked her head in. "Berkeley PD, you're on in two."

The detectives stood. Amanda lifted Barnes's bolo tie, let it fall back to his chest and smiled. "This and that big-ass belt buckle, pard. Taking out a billboard that says, 'I'm a shit kicker'?"

"Hey," said Barnes. "This is the land of tolerance. And you're doing most of the talking, Ms. Couture. Ready for your close-up?"

Amanda smoothed her black wool skirt and tucked in her white blouse. "Ready as I'm going to be."

As they neared the stage, she saw Will straighten his tie. Tight jaw; she hadn't meant to rattle the big guy.

She said, "I like your theory about Minette drinking with Davida and blowing her head off. And I'd love to see Minette's clothing, too. Unfortunately, a theory's not enough to get us a warrant to search her apartment."

Barnes'ss brain ran through a series of possibilities. Now his jawline was a track for ball bearings. "How about this: Minette's apartment is also Davida's apartment. We shouldn't have any trouble getting a victim warrant. If we happen to find bloody clothing and brain tissue in the sink's drain traps . . . well, then, that's the way it goes sometimes."

"Viva accidents," said Amanda.

"That and Zapata," said Barnes. "He's one of the good guys around here, right?"

As he stepped into his pajama bottoms, Will thought about the town hall meeting and the press conference. Amanda had summarized the investigation better than he could've, speaking clearly and simply, personable but terse. Captain Torres did a decent job of easing community fears, keeping his cool under a barrage of questions thoughtful and stupid.

Then there was *him*.

Speaking into the microphone with that little nervous stutter in his voice that told the world he was a shit-kicking dufus. The tie and buckle didn't help either; he could almost taste the contempt.

Made him drawl even more, until he ended up sounding like Gomer Pyle on downers.

What a—he stopped. Self-reflection was for chumps.

The phone rang. Good. Maybe Laura, that new relationship biting the du . . . Torres's voice shot over the line. "You know the warrant that you requested to search Davida's apartment?"

"I haven't put it in yet, Cap."

"Don't bother, you won't need it. Minette Padgett called in a 911 emergency about twenty minutes ago. The whole damn place has been ransacked."

"They got me as I walked through the door," Amanda said. "What about you?"

"I was just about to go to bed."

Amanda made a sour face. "I wasn't anywhere near going to bed. This commute is a killer. I really should move."

"You shouldn't even be working," Barnes retorted. "Man, if I had a thousandth of your money, I'd be sailing or playing golf or—"

"Willie, if you quit the force, you'd be cranky twenty-four/seven."

"I'm already cranky twenty-four/seven!" Barnes looked around at the living space in complete disarray. "What a total shit pile."

"That's the bad news," Amanda said. "The good news is now we can look for evidence against Minette without raising any hackles. So stop sneering, pard, and let's get to work."

Barnes took out a camera and began snapping pictures. Had it been tidy, the living room would have felt generous with the wall of picture windows and a high ceiling. But it was hard to look beyond the mess. Craftsman-style seating had been overturned, madras throw pillows were strewn across the floor. Oak bookshelves had been emptied, a couple of cheap glass vases—the kind that come with flower deliveries—were shattered.

The only breakage in plain sight. The open floor plan allowed Barnes a view of the kitchen. Cupboard doors flung open but the crockery within was untouched. The contents of the kitchen drawers, on the other hand, had been emptied and dumped on the floor.

The detectives walked as best as they could, trying not to squash evidence under the soles of their paper-sheathed shoes. The condo had three bedrooms—a master and two smaller guest rooms identical in size. The first of the smaller bedrooms had been converted into a home office; the floor space of the second was taken up with gym equipment.

When you got past the disorder, the master bedroom was a great space—generous and airy with a striking view of the city below and the bay beyond. Davida's sanctuary at the end of a hectic day?

The room's current ambience was chaos, clothing tossed on the floor, drawers dumped, bed linens stripped from the mattress.

The first word that came to Barnes's mind was "staged." Despite countless movie scenes, most thieves didn't randomly ransack because disorder made it difficult to find valuables.

He nodded at Amanda and she got it without his having to say a word. The two of them moved to the home office and surveyed a snowstorm of paper through the doorway. Same drawer-emptying, file-dumping mess, books and videos on the floor, the swivel desk chair overturned in a way that suggested calculation. Barnes's large feet couldn't manage a baby step without crunching something under his feet and he retreated.

"Someone really did a number," Amanda said.

Barnes said, "All this disorder and the plates and dishes are intact? A lot easier to clean up paper and upright couches and chairs, much bigger hassle clearing broken china."

"Why would Minette stage this?"

"Could be her or someone setting her up." Thoughts were rolling around Barnes's brain. "Or maybe even the real deal. When I mentioned Harry Modell to Dr. Kurtag, she told me that Davida wasn't afraid of him because she knew some *things* about him."

"What things?"

"She didn't tell Kurtag. Someone crazy, who knows what they'll do."

Amanda considered that. "Maybe, but it's a reach so unless we know Modell's here in town, he's low on the list."

"Minette's at the top?"

"You bet. Wonder where she is."

"Torres took her complaint and let her go."

"Torres is taking citizen complaints now?"

"Significant other of a high-profile vic," said Barnes. "She's staying with some friends for a couple of days. Which I like. We can sift through the stuff without her poking around in our business."

Amanda surveyed the toss. "How long do you think it will take us to go through all this material?"

"Most of the night," Barnes said. "When's our flight to LA?"

"Seven AM."

"I wonder if we can move it to eleven without getting someone's nose out of joint."

She smiled. "Sneaking in the shut-eye?"

"Both of us. You can bunk down at my place if you want. Save you a trip over the bridge."

"I thought you'd never ask."

12

Barnes's cell chirped just as the garbled PA voice issued a boarding announcement. He fished the phone from his pocket. "Did she just call our flight?"

Amanda looked up from her paperback. "Uh-uh, Phoenix."

"How do you understand anything she said? It just sounds like static." He pressed the green button. "Barnes."

"Sorry to bother you, Detective. It's Alice Kurtag."

Barnes wedged the phone between his shoulder and ear, and found his notepad. "No bother at all, Dr. Kurtag, what can I do for you?"

"I don't know if this is important or not, but you asked me to call you if I thought of anything."

"What's up?"

"As I told you before, my relationship with Davida was almost exclusively business. I barely knew Minette and I didn't know most of their friends."

"Okay," Barnes answered.

"I doubt if this is important, but I recall that about a month ago, Davida dropped by the lab with a friend—an old friend. Someone she had gone to high school and college with. They looked . . ." There was silence for a moment. "I don't know how to put this. They looked comfortable with each other."

The implication was obvious. Barnes said, "More than chummy?"

"Well, they were laughing and touching each other. Of course they *were* old friends."

"Do you remember this person's name?"

"Jane. I honestly can't recall if Davida mentioned her last name. If she did, it's eluding me."

Jane. That threw Barnes. Nothing about Jane ever seemed remotely gay. Just to make sure, he said, "What did this Jane look like?"

"Tall, slim, pretty, Davida's age—long jet-black hair, very striking hair. And maybe a bit . . . shopworn? I don't want to be unkind but it was as if she'd been through a lot."

No doubt who she meant. Jane sure hadn't had good luck with men. "Could it have been Jane Meyerhoff?"

"Yes, it *was*—now I remember, she *did* use her last name! You know her?"

"She's indeed an old friend of Davida's. All right, Dr. Kurtag, thanks for the information." Tacking on the basic detective's parting shot: "Anything else you'd like to add?"

"Actually, yes."

But she added nothing.

Barnes said, "Go on. I'm listening, Doctor."

"Davida told me that she and Jane were going to be away for a couple of days to do some white-water rafting. Davida told me that she had had an intense week and Jane had been going through a very messy divorce. Both of them needed to unwind and both of them loved physical challenges. She told me her cell wouldn't be operative, but she gave me a contact number if something important came up in my research. She said the number was only for me and that I shouldn't give it out to anyone else."

"Who would you give it to?"

"Since we were working together so often, people would sometimes call me looking for Davida."

"Which people?"

"At the capital. Sometimes friends."

"Anyone specific?"

Silence.

"Doctor?"

"Minette called frequently," said Kurtag. "Eight, ten times a day."

"That is pretty frequent."

"In regards to this other woman, it could be totally innocent. Perhaps Davida was taking the trip just to grab a little well-deserved privacy."

The one-hour flight from Oakland to Burbank was on time and bliss-fully free from squalling children. As soon as the plane began its descent, Barnes turned to Amanda. "I've been thinking."

She grinned. "That's always dangerous."

"That's why I don't do it often. In terms of staging, what about that crank letter Donnie Newell showed us? Someone cutting block letters from a magazine and pasting them on a piece of paper. How Hollywood is that? We should really talk to Newell again."

"Minette's been harassing Davida for a while?"

"The woman does seem to like her fair share of attention. Maybe she was upset when Davida didn't take the letter seriously."

Amanda nodded. "Good point. Now how does it connect with Minette as the murderer?"

Barnes conceded that he had no answer. "There are other reasons to talk to Donnie. He was Davida's ex-boyfriend in high school before she came out. Remember he said something about Davida being a pistol? How'd you take that?"

"That she was hot in bed." Amanda shrugged. "So they probably fucked. What's the big deal? It was a long time ago."

"It struck me that Donnie remembered the relationship so clearly and chose to mention that aspect of it with Davida lying dead with her head nearly blown off."

"Men are always thinking about sex."

"True, but that thing he told you—his wife hating Davida. Obviously, the two of them were still in contact."

"Minimal contact according to Newell."

"What's minimal to him may have seemed like maximal to Minette. Also, from dating her in high school, do you think Donnie knew about Davida's drinking?"

Amanda laughed. "What are you suggesting?"

"I'm not suggesting anything,"

"Yes, you are and it seems a big jump."

"What?"

"You're seeing Newell as a suspect. First of all, we know he was in Sacramento the day of the murder because she called him."

"Exactly. And we don't know the nature of the call . . . only what Newell told us. Maybe she says c'mon down to the office for a late-night fling and they spent a little time together. Minette told us Davida had planned to pull an all-nighter. Who said it was to work? She and Donnie are alone . . . drinking and . . ."

"And what?"

"Dunno, something went awry. You know people can get crazy when they're under the influence."

"Do you not like this guy or something? Some kind of high school thing?"

"I barely knew Donnie. I remember him as a skinny blond kid, that's all."

Amanda wagged a finger at him. "Your imagination is doing over-time, Detective Barnes. Maybe it's sleep deprivation."

"Or lack of useful evidence in the apartment," Barnes said. "At the very least, I want to talk to Newell about Davida Grayson and Jane Meyerhoff. He inferred they'd both been party girls. Pair that with Kurtag telling me Davida and Jane were going away together, and not to tell Minette, and I'm wondering: is their relationship new or were Davida and Jane picking up where they left off in high school and col-lege? I'm also wondering if Jane was the reason that Davida came out."

"How does that tie in with Newell?"

"Maybe Donnie did a threesome with the girls and Davida discov-ered she liked Jane better than him."

"And . . . ?"

"And, maybe Newell felt threatened."

"So he decided to pop her after what . . . twenty-five years?"

Barnes smiled. "Yeah, it's thin—but think of this. Williman told us male-to-female's an easy way to transmit the clap. And Donnie's male."

"You know what I think?"

"What?"

"You want to interview Newell in hopes he'll give you lurid details about a threesome."

"Maybe." Barnes laughed. Then he turned serious. "No way to bring up gonorrhea with him in a cop-to-cop chat . . . okay, let's shift gears: if there was a sexual relationship between Davida and Jane, it could be a motive for *Minette* being jealous. Jane just moved back to Berkeley about a year ago. After three failed marriages, maybe she wanted something from her youth."

Amanda regarded her partner. "Didn't you date Jane?"

"Uh, yeah, but not for long."

"Why not?"

"She was a piece of work. No such thing as a casual conversation, everything was a debate."

"Did it end badly?"

"No, it just ended. I stopped calling and she didn't care."

"Seeing as there's no hard feelings, why don't you ask her about her relationship with Davida instead of asking Newell?"

"Because Davida was murdered and I don't know how truthful Jane will be with me. I can approach Donnie differently."

"Cop to cop," she said. "But you can't bring up venereal disease."

Barnes grew silent. "Okay, the whole thing sucks."

"Hey," she said, "I like the way your mind works, I'm just trying to keep things organized. Are you really suspicious of Newell?"

"Maybe intrigued is more the right word."

The plane's wheels hit the tarmac and a flight attendant launched into the usual spiel, pretending they had a choice who to fly with. When the announcements were over, Amanda said, "I like the Davida/Jane thing. I don't know if it's relevant but it's always good to look at close friends first."

Barnes said, "I reckon we should also think a little bit about what we're gonna do in LA, especially since the department paid for luxurious transportation. Who's our contact at LAPD?"

Amanda checked her notes. "Detective Sergeant Marge Dunn. She told me her lieutenant—his name is Decker—is very curious about Marshall Bledsoe."

"What mischief did that dirtbag pull off there?"

"A local synagogue was ransacked about five years ago and Decker always felt that there was someone behind the scenes."

13

Amanda couldn't help it; she was a Bay Area snob.

San Francisco was a city; LA was a monster. The freeways stretched for miles without a break in the urban ugliness and the traffic never seemed to let up.

At least this time of year, the sky was clear and blue, a welcome change from the fog. Dirty air, but warm enough for the Berkeley detectives to roll down the windows of their compact rental. The tin can wheezed at the slightest hint of an incline. Barnes drove while Amanda navigated. Allowing for ten minutes of getting-lost time, it took them an hour and a quarter to reach the West Valley stationhouse—a square, windowless brick thing. Larger than Berkeley PD, but minus the style.

There she was, Ms. I'm-So-Sophisticated. No matter how hard she fought clichés, Northern Cal—and her own social status—wouldn't be denied.

She tried to focus on their case, but no new ideas had surfaced since she and Will had deplaned. They walked to the station entrance in silence, and were met in the lobby by Detective Sergeant Marge Dunn.

She looked around forty—tall, big and blond with soft brown eyes and a bright smile. Escorting them up to the detectives' room, she knocked on the wall to the lieutenant's cubicle even though the door was open.

The man who waved them in was in his fifties—a fit fifties. A moustachioed redhead with flecks of white in his hair. He wore a blue buttondown shirt, coral silk tie, gray slacks, shiny black wingtips. Amanda thought he could've easily been a lawyer. When he stood up, the top of his head wasn't that far away from the ceiling.

Another big one. She put him at six four, minimum. He extended a huge, freckled hand to her, then to Will.

"Pete Decker," he said. "Welcome. Have a seat." He offered them two plastic chairs. "You two want anything to drink?"

"Coffee would be nice," Barnes said.

"Times two," Amanda said.

"Pot's low, I'll make a fresh one," Marge Dunn said. "You want some, Loo?"

"Absolutely, thanks," Decker answered. "And while you're out there, ask dispatch to send another cruiser by Bledsoe's house to see if the truck's back in the driveway."

Barnes said, "Bledsoe's gone?"

"Probably out with Mom. I don't see him leaving town before Thanksgiving." Decker looked Barnes and Amanda over without making too much of a show of the scrutiny. Crossing long legs, he leaned back in his chair. "I wanted to keep a low profile so we don't spook him. All the bozo has to do is take out a checkbook, pay his fines and he's out. We're hoping he isn't savvy enough to know that, although if he murdered a state representative, he's not naïve. What evidence do you have on him?"

"Nothing," Barnes answered.

Decker smiled. "Well, that's not good. We need some excuse beyond unpaid parking tickets to bring him in for questioning."

"Bledsoe's head of the White Tower Radicals," Amanda said. "Two days before Davida Grayson's murder, two White boys egged her on the steps of the state capitol. We think Bledsoe gave that order and maybe more."

"Yeah, I heard about that," said Decker. "Those two are locked up, right? Have they implicated Bledsoe?"

"No, but Bledsoe doesn't need to know that," Barnes said. "Maybe if we scare him enough, we can pry something out of him."

Marge Dunn came back in with the coffees. "No truck in the driveway."

Decker said, "Anything else besides Bledsoe on your agenda?"

"One other interview," Barnes said. "Some bigot named Harry Modell, heads a group called Families Under God. We found three very nasty letters that he wrote to Grayson."

Amanda said, "If you want us to wait for Bledsoe first before we interview Modell, we can do that. We'll work around you."

Decker said, "Someone from West Valley should make the arrest, and if I'm going to give up a detective, you might as well interview Modell and make good use of your time." He turned to Marge. "How's your schedule looking?"

"Holiday light," Marge answered. "I can wait around until he shows. Just need my thermos and my iPod."

Harry Modell's address was a trailer park nestled in the oaks of the foothills among miles of unspoiled landscape. Not a hint of a dug-in structure could be seen anywhere. "Happy Wandering Mobile Community" consisted of fifty slots, all occupied, with generators going full blast.

Modell's slice of LA real estate was Space 34. His TravelRancher was sided in yellow vinyl with white trim. Perched on a flat roof, a dish aimed south. As Barnes and Amanda climbed a makeshift plywood ramp to the front door, they saw TV images blinking through a stingy front window. Barnes knocked on the door, waited an appropriate amount of time, got no answer and knocked again.

A voice from inside told him to go away.

"Police," Barnes yelled. "We need to speak with you, Mr. Modell."

The voice, louder, creaky, told him to fuck himself.

Barnes blew out air and looked at his partner. "We can't force our way inside."

"The guy sounds old," Amanda said. "We're worried for his safety."

"That's not going to—" Abruptly the door swung open. The man in the wheelchair was ancient with a cue-ball head, sunken, jaundiced eyes and ill-fitting dentures that clacked as he rotated his mandible. Small-jawed face once round, now sagging in the middle like a bell pepper. Grainy complexion, more wrinkles than smooth flesh. Stick legs, but his arms were surprisingly muscled. Probably from wheeling around.

"Mr. Modell?"

"What the fuck do you want?"

"To talk to you."

"What the fuck about?"

"May we come inside?" Amanda asked.

Modell eyed Amanda. "You can, he can't."

"We're a team, sir."

"Then go play a fucking game." But Modell didn't wheel back into the trailer and Amanda saw something in his eyes other than hostility.

A faint longing.

She smiled.

Modell said, "Ahh, why the fuck not, I'm bored." He propelled the chair to the side so they could enter.

They walked into a hothouse. The temperature must have been hovering in the nineties. Three humidifiers filled the cramped, dim space with mist. The upside of the oppressive micro-climate was tables of flora—bromeliads, African violets, wild beautiful blooms Amanda didn't recognize.

She began to sweat and glanced at Will. He took off his jacket. His shirt was sodden.

Modell ignored them and wheeled to the only surface devoid of plant life—a rickety card table that hosted bottles of pills, an ancient-looking burrito and the TV remote. Modell muted the sound but left the picture on. Some old movie in black and white.

Amanda said, "We have a few questions for you if you don't mind."

"I do mind," Modell said, clacking his teeth. "But can I stop the minions of HAG?"

"HAG?"

"Heathen Atheistic Government."

Modell reached over to pinch off a papery old African violet bloom.

Barnes got right down to business. "Could you tell me where you were two nights ago?"

Modell squinted at the detective. "I'm always here. Does it look like I can go anywhere?"

"You moved to this trailer park recently," Amanda said.

"You got that right, lady. I sold my house in Orange County, pocketed an absurd profit and decided to spend my days doing what I do best—communicating with atheists, reprobates and perverts. God knows there are enough of them to fill my time."

"Communicating with letters," said Barnes.

"Lost art," said Modell. "All that e-mail buggery. When I was at my peak, I sent out thirty, forty a day. Now I'm down to five. The hands." Waving gnarled digits. "Damn shame, the perverts seem to be multiplying faster than ever."

"Which perverts have you written to lately?"

Again, Modell squinted. "What the fuck do the police care about an old man writing letters?"

Amanda said, "An old man who heads Families Under God."

"Not anymore. I gave that up two years ago. Don't you police people keep abreast of the times?"

"Why'd you resign?" Amanda asked.

"I started the ministry thirty years ago all by my lonesome. Built it up big." He shook his head. "Too big. The members decided they needed a board. To do what, I don't know, but the assholes started telling me how to run my organization. So I told them to fuck off and I quit. Damn shame, at our heyday we were a powerful force against the perverts. What they're doing now, don't know, don't care. I write five letters to perverts, God's happy. Now if you don't tell me what you want, you can just leave. At least, *you* can leave. I don't mind if the lady stays . . . unless you're one of those lesbos. Then you can be the first out the door."

"You don't like lesbians?" Amanda asked.

"What's to like? They're homos and they're perverted."

"Did you ever write a letter to State Representative Davida Grayson?" Amanda asked.

"Aha!" Modell jabbed a finger upward. "*Now* I see what this is about. The lesbo representative." Big smile. "But that happened up north."

"We're from up north," Amanda told him. "Berkeley PD."

"You came all the way down just to see little ol' *me*? Lady, I'm *flattered*!"

"You did write to her," Barnes said.

"Fuck yeah I wrote to her. I wrote to her many times. The pervert was not only a lesbo, she was trying to cut up unborn babies for her own selfish purposes."

Amanda said, "Stem-cell research."

Modell seemed to levitate out of his chair. "Stem-cell research *bull*! Nothing good will ever come from butchering human babies, young lady, and I certainly don't want to pay for such shit with my tax dollar." He sank back down. "Yeah, I wrote to that sodomite, told her what I thought of her bull and of her being a lesbo. Told her everything she needed to hear."

"Which was?"

"Women got no business being in politics, it turns them into perverts like Grayson. I'm certainly not mourning Grayson's demise, but if you think I had anything to do with her murder, you are seriously misguided and as stupid as she was."

Barnes loosened his tie and undid the top button of his shirt. Amanda gave him a tissue from her purse and both of them mopped their brows. She said, "Politicians receive negative mail all the time, sir, but your letters were especially nasty."

"Lady, I'm a nasty, God-driven man. I don't deny it. But last I heard you can't arrest someone for that."

"You can arrest someone for threatening harm."

"I didn't threaten harm, mister. I just told her the truth . . . that she was going to burn in hell for eternity, two seconds flat her flesh would look like pig cracklings and her insides would boil like soup. I told her she was so far gone even Jesus wouldn't know what the hell to do for her. You want to arrest me for truth-telling, go ahead and give me the entertainment and the publicity and maybe I'll start another church. Do one of those *websites*."

Amanda said, "Is there anyone who can verify your whereabouts for the last couple of days?"

"Lady, I'm damn flattered that you think I have enough energy to fly up to that pinko city and pop the lesbo. Fact is, I'm eighty-four, for the last ten of those wheelchair bound and a good day for me is when I wake up and move my bowels without straining."

"You could've hired someone," Barnes said.

"I could go to the novelty shop, buy a big nose and say I was a Jew—listen, you two, just because I decided to use my First Amendment privileges and tell the perverts what I think of them doesn't mean I have to sit hear and listen to your bull. Your bosses will be hearing from me. Get the fuck out of here before I run you over with my chair."

Barnes started the engine and let it idle while he pulled out his cell phone. "Other than providing entertainment for the old bastard, that was a colossal waste of time."

"Had to be done," Amanda said.

He fooled with the phone, scowled. "Can't get my messages. No reception in this dump."

"Thought you liked rural living."

"Rather have twenty rooms with a view. Let's go back to the West Valley and see if anything's up with Bledsoe. Unless you want to grab something first? We can eat in the car."

"Nutrition sounds good as long as it's not hamburgers."

"What's wrong with burgers?"

"Larry got a new barbecue. Turbo-powered and he's collecting marinades."

"Boy needs a hobby, huh?"

She shrugged. "He'll find something."

"I'll find a Subway or something. It ain't Chez Panisse but what is?"

14

Delicately, Marge Dunn unwrapped the wax paper that held together a turkey and cheese sub. "Wow, thanks for thinking of me. I'm hungry." She steadied the sandwich then took a big bite. "Mmmmm . . . that's good."

"Amanda's idea, she's the considerate one," Barnes said. He was sitting shotgun in an LAPD unmarked; Amanda was in the backseat and Marge was at the wheel.

Marge spoke over her shoulder. "Thank you, Considerate One."

"No prob."

The car fell silent until Barnes grumbled, "You think this joker is going to show?"

Marge wiped her mouth. "I don't see why he'd leave if he came down to be with Mom for the holidays. And if he does leave, that tells us something." She regarded Barnes. "I really like the silverwork on your belt buckle. What kind of stone is that? Green turquoise?"

"Exactly."

"Nice."

"Got it in Santa Fe. Ever been there?"

"Sure," she said. "I go there a lot. Sometimes during opera season, if my daughter's schedule permits."

"Never been to the opera."

Amanda said, "Will's into Buck Owens."

"Me, too. I'm eclectic. Big loss, Buck."

"Dwight Yoakam's carrying it on," said Will.

"He rocks but still, it's not the same." Marge finished her sandwich and stowed the trash in a plastic bag. "The opera house is really special. It's outdoors with this beautiful view of the mountains. Sometimes crickets sing along." Big smile. "Sometimes, they're on key. They've got great chamber music, too. And country at some of the casinos. Great little town, culture-wise."

Barnes sneaked a quick look at Marge's left hand. No ring. "Whole Southwest area is a pretty part of the country."

"Magnificent . . . a real break from LA." Marge turned around again. "Have you ever been there, Amanda?"

"Once and it was gorgeous."

Barnes said, "I remember the food being good."

"That, too," Marge said. "If either of you go again, give me a call, I'll tell you some good restaurants."

Barnes said, "I just might do that."

The two of them swapped brief smiles. Further interchange was cut short a black pickup truck tooling down the road. Instinctively, all three detectives slouched down in their seats.

Marge said, "Let's wait until they're out of the car."

The truck pulled into the driveway. A man got out on the driver's side carrying several bags of what looked to be groceries. Seconds later, an older woman opened the front passenger door. She was pear-shaped, gray-haired and slow-moving. He had wild unkempt hair and several days of dark beard growth. He wore a white T-shirt, a denim jacket and jeans, white sneakers. She had on a long gray sweater, a blue turtleneck, and black polyester pants. Her sneakers were black.

With Bledsoe's hands occupied, the situation for arrest was ideal.

"Let's do it," Marge said.

The three detectives jumped and swarmed the unsuspecting duo.

"Police, Mr. Bledsoe, don't move," Marge barked. As soon as Barnes relieved Bledsoe of his bags, the women brought his arms around his back and Marge slapped on the cuffs. "Good afternoon, Mr. Bledsoe, we have a bench warrant out for your arrest for outstanding traffic warrants—"

"You've got to be shittin' me." Bledsoe's voice was lazy.

"No sir, I am not." Out of the corner of her eye, Marge saw something blurry coming at her nose. She ducked, but a hard object made contact with the left side of her forehead. Flailing fingernails. The contact stung.

Amanda caught the old lady's arm midair. Laverne Bledsoe's breath was ripe with liquor and garlic.

"That was really stupid." Amanda spun Mom around. "Now you're under arrest for assault on a police officer."

Laverne responded by trying to stomp on Amanda's shoe. Amanda stepped back, but the old woman caught her on the tip of her toe. She wrestled Granny down to the ground and snapped Laverne's hands behind her back maybe a little more forcefully than necessary. The cuffs clicked.

Bledsoe remained completely passive, watching from the sidelines. Almost amused. "Are you going to arrest my mom, too?"

"Looks that way," Amanda said, bringing the squalling woman to her feet.

"She's sixty-eight."

Barnes said, "She assaulted two police officers."

"That's bogus. This whole arrest thing is bogus."

The old lady began cursing but Bledsoe stayed quiet. Marge patched in a call for transport.

Laverne looked at her son with panicked eyes.

Bledsoe spoke in a monotone. "Calm down, Ma, it's not good for your heart."

"Shitheads!" Laverne screamed. "Manhandling an old woman!"

Barnes saw blood on Marge's temple. "Got a Band-Aid? She got you."

Marge touched her head. "Bad?"

Barnes gave a slight shake of his head. As a black-and-white pulled up, Amanda tightened her grip on the granny. Carefully, she escorted the irate woman to the confines of the backseat. The uniforms wrote down basic facts and drove off.

Barnes said, "That was something!"

Marge got a Band-Aid and Neosporin from the first-aid kit in the unmarked's trunk and Amanda tended to the wound.

"I actually took the time to do my makeup this morning. What a waste!"

"You look fine," Barnes said.

Marge smiled. "How's your foot, Amanda?"

"She's no lightweight but I'll survive."

Marshall Bledsoe said, "You calling my mom fat?"

When no one answered, he said, "I need to be with her. To calm her down. Her heart's not so good."

Marge said, "Why's she so riled up anyway?"

"One, she's sick of you guys badgering me. Two, that's just her. She riles easily especially when she's had a few beers."

"How many is a few?"

Bledsoe thought a moment. "I think she drained a six-pack, but that's just getting started. In her prime, Ma could keg with the best of them."

A second cop car picked up Bledsoe and delivered him to the station. The detectives got there first and worked out the interview.

Smoking and sipping coffee, Bledsoe slumped, loose-limbed, in a hard chair that he seemed to find comfortable. So relaxed he could have been zoned out in his living room watching the game. Marge was willing to let Laverne go, but the old lady refused to leave without her son, so she was in a room next door.

None of the detectives had any idea what they'd get out of Bledsoe, but they had him in custody for a few hours until his traffic arraignment. The court had to add up all the fines and penalties. With skipping out on a warrant and some luck, there'd be jail time.

Since it was LAPD territory, Barnes and Isis deferred to Lieutenant Decker. The big man announced he and Barnes would go in first and the women would do round two if there was anything worth pursuing. Decker opened the door, lumbered in and sat opposite Bledsoe. Barnes sat on Bledsoe's right.

"How are you doing, Marshall?"

"How's my mom?"

"Waiting for you."

"She needs to eat. She has yo-yo blood sugar."

"She had lunch on the taxpayers' money."

"Any way we can rip off this illegitimate government is great." Bledsoe shook his head. "Would you like to tell me what's really going on?"

"You're a lousy driver," said Decker. "You owe the city, the county, and the state a lot of money."

"You know that's horseshit," said Bledsoe, still without passion. "For the police to make a house call, you must think I know something important."

Decker leaned back in his chair. "And what important thing would you know?"

Bledsoe stubbed out his cigarette. "I don't have to talk to you clowns. All I have to do is lawyer up and that ends that."

"No curiosity?" said Decker.

"What am I supposed to know?"

"Exactly."

"Huh?"

"It's complicated," said Decker. Now Bledsoe was confused and trying hard not to show it. Decker shot Barnes a nod.

Barnes leaned in close to Bledsoe. "You're known as a leader, Marshall. You give the orders, you don't take them."

Bledsoe shrugged.

Decker's turn to lean forward. "We had a synagogue desecrated a few years ago. The guy who took the fall was some mope named Ernesto Golding. Definitely an order-*taker*."

"Who were his people?"

"White Tower Radicals," Decker lied. "An organization near and dear to you."

Bledsoe smiled and fluffed his beard. "If you're asking me if I'm a member, I plead proud and guilty. But whatever you're talking about, that Jew place or any other place, it wasn't me."

"I didn't say it was you," Decker said. "Did I say it was you?"

Bledsoe was quiet.

"Marshall, I believe you. You know why? Something that important—trashing a Jew place—Ernesto had to be taking orders from a guy higher up than you."

Marshall blinked. "And who would that be?"

"Ricky Moke—"

"Ricky?" Bledsoe laughed. "Right."

"He's the man, Marshall."

Bledsoe laughed again. "Don't you turkeys know anything? Moke's dead. He was eaten by a bear."

"A mountain lion."

"Either way he's still animal shit. Before that, he was a peon."

"That's not what I hear."

"Then you hear shit."

"Either way," said Decker, "Ricky's gone. You're saying that makes you the big guy?"

Bledsoe started to smile, cut it short, stayed silent.

Decker said, "How did it feel having someone like Moke muscle in on your authority?"

"Right." Bledsoe huffed. "Ricky was a *peon*."

"So correct me, Marshall. Tell me what you know about the ransacking of the synagogue—straighten me out."

"I don't know shit about it, never followed any of that. And since Moke is dead and Golding was popped, I guess you'll never know what really happened."

"If you didn't know anything about the case, how do you know Golding's dead, let alone popped?"

Bledsoe smacked his lips together and said nothing.

"We can dance like this for a while but bottom line, you're in trouble, Marshall. At this point, you could use someone on your side."

Bledsoe let out a lone chuckle. "Let me set you straight, man. I didn't ransack any kikehouse down here, and that's the truth. Theoretically, if I had been involved, it wouldn't have been a ransacking. Something would have exploded and you can bet your ass, there would have been kikes inside—the younger the bet—" His chair flew out from under his butt and unceremoniously, he toppled to the floor. "What *the fuck*!"

"Sorry, I tripped and knocked your chair." Decker exchanged glances with Barnes. Barnes didn't emote.

Then the lieutenant turned to Bledsoe, gave him a tight smile and righted the seat. "Here, sit back down, Marshall. What were you saying?"

Bledsoe got up from the floor, wiped off his pants, stayed in the corner.

Decker was still smiling. "Have a seat."

"I'd rather stand."

"Have a seat." Decker's tone took on menace. Reluctantly, Bledsoe sat down. Decker continued, "Well, you might not have witnesses against you for the synagogue but Detective Barnes here has very good news for us. His witnesses against you are still alive."

"Witnesses against . . ." Bledsoe's brow creased. "What the hell are you talking about?"

"Two boys in the White Tower Radicals, Bledsoe," Barnes said. "They nailed you on Davida Grayson."

"*Who?*" Bledsoe asked.

"C'mon, we know you ordered the hit," Barnes lied. "And those two boys are in custody and tripping over their feet to testify against you—"

"Who the *fuck* is Davida Gray?"

"She's a state representative from Berkeley," Barnes said. "She was found the night before last in her office with her head blown off."

Bledsoe's expression made Barnes's mood sink. Genuine puzzlement. It took the scruffy bastard a few moments to find his voice. "Uh . . . didn't that happen up in Northern California?"

"Yes, it did," Barnes said. "I'm from Berkeley PD."

"You don't have jurisdiction down here," Bledsoe said.

"But I do," Decker said. "Ransacking a synagogue is one thing, Marshall. Gunning down an elected official is taking your shit to a whole different level."

Barnes said, "We can't help you unless you start helping yourself. And you can start helping yourself by telling us what happened."

Bledsoe leaned back in his chair. "I honestly don't know what the *fuck* you're talking about." He crossed his arms. "You guys are throwing me shit and trying to make me think it's perfume."

"Why would we do that?" Barnes said.

"Because that's what you clowns do. Let me tell you something. You and your Jew masters are all on borrowed time."

Barnes said, "Marshall, why would we waste our time coming down here unless we had you cold?"

"'Cause you're afraid of me and what I represent," Bledsoe answered. "I don't know anything about the dyke."

"How'd you know she was a lesbian?"

"Because I read, Jack. Who are these imaginary fairies testifying against me?"

"Your peeps, Marshall."

"Who?"

"Ray and Brent Nutterly?"

"Oh Christ!" Bledsoe made a pained face. "Those two idiots! They're saying I had something to do with blowing a diesel dyke's brains out?"

Neither Barnes nor Decker answered.

"I've been with my *mom* for the last week! The pop was just a couple of days ago, right? I'm a superhero for the people, but even I can't be in two places at the same time." Sly smile. "Maybe next year. I'm working on my superpower mojo."

Decker said, "Where were you the night before last?"

"I told you, I was with my mom."

"That tells us bullshit cause she'll lie for you," Barnes said. "Let's try again. Where were you the night before last and what were you doing?"

Bledsoe tapped his toe. "Let me think, let me think. Uh, last night . . ." He snapped his fingers. "We watched a DVD—*Boldface Liars* . . ." A laugh. "You two should know about that."

"The night *before* last night," Barnes said.

"Okay, okay . . . uh . . . let me think."

"Make it a good one, Marshall," Decker said.

Another snap of the fingers. "Mom and I went out to dinner. Cody's Family Restaurant, I paid with a credit card. That should be even easy enough for you clowns to check out."

Barnes said, "What time did you eat?"

"Nine . . . maybe a little earlier. The place was pretty empty. The waitress's name was Kris. Big tits, ugly face. Anything else?"

"What'd you eat?" Barnes asked.

Bledsoe laughed. "Chili cheeseburger, onion rings and a Coors. Mom had the same except she ordered curly fries. She loves her curly fries."

"What did you do after dinner?"

"Went back to Ma's, drank a couple of brews . . . watched a little TV. I guess I knocked off around twelve."

"What were you watching?" Barnes asked.

"Uh . . . some old movie. Robert Mitchum and some nice-looking piece of old-fashioned ass. Piece of shit. I turned it off before the end. Can I go now?"

Barnes remained stoic but Bledsoe's alibi was too damn specific and he wasn't happy. If someone verified him in LA at nine, it would have been difficult—though not impossible—for him to travel four hundred miles, do the murder in the early-morning hours and drive back down. There were also planes, but Barnes figured a guy like Bledsoe would be memorable, easy enough to check out. Bledsoe could have ordered the hit, so he wasn't off the hook. But bottom line: no evidence to pursue an investigation.

Decker asked, "How did you know Ernesto Golding was popped?"

"Good news travels fast."

Again, Decker kicked the chair out from under Bledsoe's ass. Marshall cursed and stood up, again, wiping off his pants. "Shit! You can keep persecuting me, man, but it won't help your fucking cause! I had nothing to do with his death or the lesbo."

"So how do you know about Ernesto Golding being popped?" Decker said.

"I knew the cunt that set him up."

"Name." Decker flexed a leg.

"Ruby Ranger. She's doing a long stretch of time, which is probably okay for her. I think she also likes girls. Guess they're everywhere." Big grin. "Minus one."

A knock; the door opened. Marge Dunn handed Decker a piece of paper. Decker read it and nodded. "Your arraignment is scheduled in two hours, Marshall. You'll be put in a holding cell and when the time comes, cuffed again and driven to court. After you pay your fines, you'll be lucky to have cab money. Then again, you can always hock your truck. You won't need it since your license will be revoked—"

Bledsoe gave a sick smile. "You've got to be shittin' me."

"You got three speeding tickets, two going excess of eighty-five."

"This is so bogus."

"Then there are all the parking violations. What's the problem, Marshall? Have trouble reading signs?"

Something in Bledsoe's eyes told Barnes that Decker had hit a nerve.

Decker said, "The grand total for your ass to stay out of jail is five thousand, six hundred and twenty bucks."

Bledsoe glared at Decker, muttering to himself. "Fucking asshole kike!"

Decker's leg shot out again and Bledsoe buckled under his own weight and went down. He looked up from the floor, spittle running down a corner of his mouth. "I'll have your badge for this."

Decker laughed. "Great. I could use a vacation."

15

After Bledsoe was duly escorted out of the interview room, Barnes shut the door and lowered his voice. "Little rough, don't you think?"

Decker faced Barnes, eye to eye. "Let him sue. I meant what I said."

Barnes dropped the issue. Why piss off someone who was helping him out? Besides, he'd been in similar situations.

Decker said, "If Bledsoe gets jail time and his alibis don't check out, I'll give you a call and you and your partner can take a shot at him again." Tight smile. He brushed back the ginger mustache. Bristly hairs spread and fell back into place. "It'd probably be better if I wasn't around. Marshall wasn't my most sterling interview."

"Seemed fine to me, Lieutenant. Thanks for the help."

Decker stretched. His hands reached the ceiling. "Look, I caused him some grief and I'm not sorry about that. I know he's caused mischief down here. But I'm thinking that alibi had too much detail for you guys and if he's right about the time frame, it's going to be tough tying him in directly."

"I was thinking the same thing," Barnes concurred.

"Cody's restaurant is about twenty minutes from here," Decker said. "Marge will give you directions."

"Thanks. We'll track down Kris the waitress and see what she says. Even if she alibis him, we'll check the airports to make sure he didn't take a quick hop north."

As they left the room, Decker said, "I would've liked to see it work out better for you. Murder trumps everything and that guy should be put away."

Barnes said, "He was a long shot, Lieutenant. Egging's a far cry from blowing someone's head off." He took out his card and handed it to Decker. "If we can ever reciprocate, just let me know."

"Will do. And have Marge Dunn give you her card . . . just in case you need anything else."

"I'll do that," said Barnes. "Just in case."

Kris, the thirty-year-old blond waitress with a large chest and a face Barnes thought more okay than ugly, remembered both Bledsoes. How could she forget them? He was a surly jerk and Mom was foulmouthed.

"They left like a dollar tip on a twenty-dollar tab and acted like I was lucky to get that."

"Do you remember what time they left?" Amanda asked her.

Kris twirled a strand of too-yellow hair. "Late, like ten. Like I remember thinking that if I could, you know, finish off with these assho . . . these people, like I'd be done for the evening. I was more gone than there, you know?"

"Thanks for helping us out," Barnes said.

"Sure. Is he, like, in trouble?"

Barnes shrugged.

"He must be in trouble. Like why else would the police be asking about him? Doesn't surprise me. He had a strange look."

"Strange, how?"

Kris bobbed her head up and down. "You know . . . looking over his shoulder a lot."

"Really?" Barnes asked.

"Sort of." Again, she bobbed her head up and down. "Kind of. Or maybe he was just hungry and wanted his food faster than we could give it to him."

Amanda said, "You should be a detective yourself."

"Thanks." Kris smiled a mouth of white, straight teeth. "I watch a lot of *Law & Order,* especially *SVU.* Christopher Meloni is hot."

As soon as the plane took off, Amanda closed her eyes and fell asleep. The state of bliss lasted approximately fifteen minutes, until turbulence woke her up with a start. A flight attendant was urging everybody to return to their seats and buckle up. Amanda looked to her left, at Barnes gripping the armrests with white knuckles. The plane rocked in a sea of wind, and Barnes turned green around the gills.

She said, "Turbulence isn't dangerous."

"So they say."

"It's true. You should feel it in a small jet. Cork in a bathtub effect. You get used to it."

Barnes stared at her. "Well, thank God, I don't ever foresee me having that problem."

"Hey, how many times have I offered to give you a ride somewhere gratis?"

"I hate flying."

"You get all the catering you want."

Will's big hand clamped on his gut.

Uh-oh, wrong thing to say.

She kept her mouth shut and the turbulence faded.

"Really," she said. "Hitch a ride with us one of these days."

"Too rich for my blood," said Barnes.

Amanda didn't answer.

He said, "Don't be sore, pard."

"The hell I won't. Being pissed is a God-given right even for rich folk." She wagged a finger at him. "And it's rather poor judgment of you to alienate me, especially after making a date with that tall drink of water. You might need a lift to LA."

Barnes reddened. "We didn't make a date—"

"You exchanged numbers, William. What do you call that?"

"Just being polite—"

Amanda laughed. Will's blush was hilarious. From green to pink; today her partner was a Christmas tree.

She said, "She seemed nice if my opinion means anything. And she certainly understands the biz."

"It's nothing, Amanda. Just being courteous."

"You're not going to call her?"

"I didn't say that. Should the timing be right—"

"Uh-huh."

"Can we drop this?" The seat belt sign turned off. Barnes felt more relaxed. He didn't mind her ribbing but now he wanted to focus on work. "How about we talk about the case since that's what we're getting paid for?"

"Mr. Workaholic," she said. "Yeah, you're right. Now that Bledsoe and Modell have sunk to the bottom of our short list of suspects, I'm not feeling too perky. But I guess it puts us back in standard territory: someone close to Davida."

Barnes nodded. "Someone close enough to her to know she was a closet drinker. The question is, who among her friends did she piss off that bad?"

"The gonorrhea can't be ignored. Who she got it from and did she give it to someone. Tomorrow, we should talk to Minette and find out if she knew Davida was sick. If she doesn't, she's got to get tested. And if she doesn't test positive, we have to find the partner who gave it to Davida if for no other reason than the public health issue."

"And if Minette is infected," said Barnes, "we have to find out if Minette gave it to Davida or was it the other way around."

"You talked to Minette's boyfriend . . . what's his name?"

"Kyle Bosworth."

"What about him as the bad guy?"

"What's his motive?"

Amanda said, "Maybe he gave the clap to Minette, who gave it to Davida. Maybe Davida was going to tell Kyle's partner about his infidelity and Kyle killed Davida to shut her up. People lead that kind of complicated life, anything can happen."

"From what people have been telling us about Davida and Minette, I don't see Davida caring all that much about Minette's indiscretions."

Amanda thought for a while. "Then what about this, Will: Alice Kurtag told you she thought Davida might have been having an affair with Jane Meyerhoff. Didn't you say that Jane was married a bunch of times?"

"Three times. Donnie Newell said it."

"The point is, Jane has sex with men."

Barnes felt his cheeks go hot and looked away, but Amanda didn't appear to notice. "Maybe *Jane* got the clap and gave it to Davida, who gave it to Minette, who gave it to Kyle. That would be a reason for Minette to be furious. In addition to it being evidence of Davida's infidelity—"

"Alleged infidelity. And Minette definitely cheats."

"So she rationalizes it—Davida works all day, leaves her high and dry, but Davida has no excuse. The fact that Minette chose a man could be her way of pretending it didn't count."

"Kind of nutty. And narcissistic."

"She has that theatrical quality about her, Will. Phoning ten times a day, maybe staging that break-in. The point is, Minette had plenty of reason to be angry at Davida. And she'd likely know about Davida's drinking. Who better to sneak up and blow Davida's head off? Plus the fact that it was probably done when Davida was sleeping could indicate a woman."

"Why?"

"We're a sneaky bunch."

"Hey," said Barnes, "I'm bringing you up on sexism charges at the next Berkeley Truth Council."

"Don't go there, pard."

Both detectives laughed.

Barnes said, "Do you think that little Minette is big enough to handle a shotgun?"

"Talk about sexism—yeah, I do. All she had to do was handle it for one blast."

"Her hands were clean," Barnes said. Answering his own question: "So she washed them good."

"Minette as the shooter would also explain staging the ransacking. What better way to turn suspicion away from yourself than to be a victim of a crime?"

Barnes turned silent.

After a few minutes, Amanda asked him what was on his mind.

"You're making sense, Mandy."

"Let's ask around about Minette before we talk to her. You must know some people in common."

"Why?"

"You seem to know everyone else attached to this case."

"Sacramento," said Will. "It can be a small town. Everyone went to public school back then. Even rich kids like Davida and Jane ended up at the same high school as us regular folk. Their fathers owned the ranches and our fathers worked the ranches . . . you really see this as a female thing?"

"Why not?"

"To me, it feels like a man's murder—cold, calculating, precise."

"Davida didn't have many men in her life," Amanda said.

"She had a few . . . starting with Donnie Newell."

"Back to him?"

"I'm not saying he did it. But they were close enough at one time for Donnie to say she was a pistol . . ." A pause. "Both her and Jane . . ." Again, Barnes fell silent. "I am not sex-obsessed. At this moment. I'm just saying there could be something that goes way back. And speaking of men, Jane's last divorce was extremely messy."

"How do you know?"

"I asked around," he said. "Other high school buds. Her last husband was a financial type who lost his job. Jane didn't take well to that and she didn't want him getting any of her first two husbands' cash."

"Asking around," said Amanda, so quietly Barnes had to read her lips over the plane's roar.

Annoyed. He'd hotdogged it without telling her.

"Like I said, it's a small town, Mandy."

"So you did."

The place was dark and smoky with the band playing Texas swing. There was sawdust on the floor and beer was flowing in a continuous stream from tap to glass. Just a half hour from Berkeley, Mama's was a different world. Barnes was on his second Heineken but his third plate of Buffalo wings, wondering if she'd bother to show. She hadn't sounded all that enthusiastic over the phone, but who could blame her? They'd never progressed beyond a few months of dating and a couple of meaningless bounces between the sheets.

Besides, as he'd explained, the call was business, not personal.

A shapely blonde approached his table. Tall. Like Marge Dunn. Narrower, with coltish legs—a body that could definitely handle the miniskirt. But unlike Dunn, this face was worn, desperation tugging down the eyes. Barnes wasn't in the mood to play therapist to another wounded soul.

"Looking for some company?"

Barnes smiled and shook his head. "Unfortunately, I'm meeting someone here."

"Some other time?" she suggested.

"Life is long."

The blond woman didn't exactly know how to interpret that. She walked away with an exaggerated sway in her hips and for a moment, Barnes wondered if he'd done the right thing by shutting her down.

His ruminations were interrupted when he spotted Jane at the door. He stood and waved her over. She'd dressed way over the Mama's level: tailored black pantsuit, sapphire-blue silk scarf worn like a choker around her neck, filmy edges shimmering in the turbulence created by dancing bodies.

She walked gingerly across the sawdust in pointy, high-heeled black boots, carrying an oversized black bag that could have been crocodile. She had a long face and long teeth but elegant carriage and demeanor and a lush body saved her from horsy. Her jet-black hair was poker straight and thick, and flowed over her shoulders like an oil spill. She came over and gave him a quick peck on the cheek. Her eyes were soft blue, red around the edges.

"Thanks for meeting me on such short notice," Barnes said.

She looked at the chair, brushed off the seat with a paper napkin and sat down. "You couldn't do better than this dive?"

"It's on the way to Sacramento."

"Thank you and I appreciate that, but so are a few fine restaurants, Will."

"I like the music. How about some wings and a beer?"

"How about no wings and a Scotch?"

"That can be done." Barnes signaled the waitress and ordered a Dewar's on the rocks. Jane reached in her bag and pulled out a pack of cigarettes. "You always were kind of a cowboy." She lit up and blew out a plume of smoke. "So, what was so urgent that it couldn't wait?"

"I'm talking to just about everyone who knew Davida, and you knew her very well."

Jane shrugged. "And?"

"What can you tell me about her?"

Her eyes got wet. "She was a remarkable person. Committed to what she believed in, very comfortable in her own skin. I admired her so much, I still can't believe . . ."

She started to cry. Barnes was right there with a napkin, but she elected to pull out a tissue from her exotic skin bag. She blew her nose and dabbed her eyes just as the waitress plunked down the glass. Barnes paid the bill and the tip and edged the glass closer to Jane. She sipped, took a second swallow. Half the whiskey was gone before she decided to resume the conversation.

"I talked to Lucille this afternoon. She and my mom are good friends."

"Like you and Davida."

Jane smiled. "Second generation . . . anyway, the poor old woman is having a rough time. I'm spending the night with her . . . I don't want her alone."

"That's really nice of you, Jane."

"Actually, I was thinking of moving in with her for a while . . . just until . . ."

Barnes waited for more.

"I don't know what just until means," Jane said. "She's not even my mother and I feel the need to look after her. Make sure she doesn't sink into a bad depression, although who could blame her if she did?"

Barnes nodded.

Jane said, "My mother never needs anyone. So strong. She comes across DAR but back when we had the ranch, she'd be sinking posts with the guys."

"I know," said Will.

"You were one of them?"

She didn't even remember.

He said, "Summer job, I worked at a whole bunch of ranches. Your mom was tough." Speeding up in that big, pink Lincoln, not a glance at the hired help as the car kicked up dust.

"Do you think it's weird that I want to stay with Lucille? I haven't asked her yet. I suspect she'll say no."

"She probably will refuse your hospitality, at first. Later on . . ." Barnes shrugged.

She frowned.

He said, "You feel close to her, it's no sin."

"I've known her forever. We've all known each other so long." She finished her Scotch and Barnes called for a refill.

He said, "It's nice to stay in contact with old friends. And Davida and you were very old friends."

Jane nodded. "We hadn't been in much contact for about fifteen years. But when I moved back to Berkeley, we picked up where we left off."

Whatever that meant. "Did that cause any problems with Minette . . . your being so close to Davida?"

Jane stared at him.

He said, "Being such an old friend. Minette impresses me as the emotional type, with or without a good reason."

"You've got that right, Will. Minette has a lot of problems and jealousy was one of them. She resented Davida nursing me through my divorce. Once Parker lost his money, his entire personality deteriorated. He'd waver between being a vicious bear and a passive lamb, you can't even imagine. One moment, I was afraid he'd assault me, the next he'd be sobbing on the phone, begging me to come back to him. I'm sure you remember."

Their big stab at dating had come just as Jane had split from Parker. One of those accidents, Barnes running into Jane on Shattuck, he coming off shift, exhausted, in a down mood. She leaving Chez Panisse. Alone. Needing to talk to someone.

They went for drinks. One thing led to another. She had a gorgeous body but her enthusiasm waned midway through.

He said, "I remember you being nervous about him. I don't remember you saying he wanted you back."

"I didn't want to burden you with sordid details, Will. It was totally my fault that Parker and I got married. When I met him, I admired his machismo and his take-charge attitude. It took about four months to realize how controlling he was. That's always been my mistake. I hook up with the ultramacho men and get surprised when they turn brutal. Call it growing up with a dominant mother and a father who wasn't. I suppose I got used to people pushing me around and long for the daddy I never had . . . that's what I really liked about Davida. She always let me be me."

"You two travel together at all?"

Jane lifted her head from her Scotch, looked him square in the eye and didn't answer him.

Barnes said, "Alice Kurtag said you two went away together for a few days to unwind."

"Yes, we did." Jane was still trying to stare him down. "What better way to get your mind off of your troubles? I was involved in a horrible divorce and Davida was stressed about the stem-cell bill. We went hiking and white-water rafting."

"Sounds like fun."

"It was the best weekend I'd had in a long time."

"Jane, I'm sorry to have to ask you this, but were you involved with

Davida? I'm bringing it up because Davida was infected with gonor-rhea and if you were—"

"Are you serious?"

Barnes nodded.

"Hah." Jane shrugged. "She never said a word to me about that. Then again, why would she? I would imagine she'd be embarrassed about it." She glanced at her watch, finished off her Scotch and started to open her wallet.

Barnes stopped her. "My treat. So you're okay healthwise."

"I'm fine. Perfect. And in answer to your question, Davida and I were just friends. Period. I'm sure Minette gave it to her." She stood up. "It's getting late."

"What's the rush? It's not that late and you've only got about thirty miles to go."

"All true, Will, but still I'm done here."

16

"I can't believe you talked to her last night!"

Amanda was clearly pissed. Barnes said, "It was an impulsive thing."

"First you call around old high school buds, then you meet with one of them who's a serious witness all by your lonesome. What's gotten into you, Will?"

He gave the honest answer: "Don't know."

Amanda shook her head, rummaged in her purse. Fishing out a Ghirardelli chocolate square, she unwrapped and ate. Not offering him one from her stash, as she usually did.

"Sorry," said Barnes. He'd parked the car in front of Davida Grayson's complex. "I know. It was stupid and I apologize. But it's done. So can we move on?"

Amanda wasn't about to let go so easily. "Did you at least learn anything other than that Jane's back in Sacramento? And why?"

No answer.

She said, "Thought she moved back to Berkeley."

"Guess she moved back."

"You didn't ask her?"

"It didn't seem relevant."

"Only her sex life was."

"She claims there was none with Davida."

"You believe her?" said Amanda.

"Don't know. Don't know if it matters, Mandy."

"Well, as soon as she gets back, I want a crack at her. Just because she denies having the clap doesn't make it true. And seeing as how you were both drinking none of it can be entered into the case file."

"No reason for her to lie—"

"Well, we won't know until we *officially* talk to her, will we? *Partner.*"

He gave her a few minutes to cool down. She ate another chocolate. Made a show of chewing it slowly.

"Mandy, maybe I'm off but I'm thinking right now, our minds should be on Minette and not on Jane. Per our previous discussion. And unless you can stop glaring at me, we can't go in and interview her."

Silence.

"Man—"

"Forget it, just don't do it again, okay, Will? For your own sake. It looks bad."

"You're right. I was wrong. Shall we move on?"

"Absolutely."

"Was that a female or a male absolutely?"

"What's the difference?"

"A male absolutely is absolutely. A female absolutely is I'll drop it for now but I'll bludgeon you with it later on."

"A female absolutely."

"That's what I thought."

The disarray had been cleared, but the condo was far from clean. The kitchen was piled with dirty dishes and the dining room table held cartons of take-out Chinese. At nine in the morning, Minette was still in a terry bathrobe and mules. Her eyes and nose were puffy and red and her hair could have used a good scrubbing. The faint odor of alcohol lingered on her breath and in the unit.

"Thanks for seeing us so early," Amanda said.

"Sure . . ." Minette was still dazed. "Have a seat. Anywhere's fine."

The two detectives looked around and found space on a Craftsman-style sofa. It was as flat as a bench and merciless on the ass. "Thank you," Barnes told her.

"You want some coffee? I sure as hell need a cup for myself."

"I'd love some," Amanda said. "But let me make it, Minette. Why don't you sit down and relax?"

"That would be nice."

Amanda went into the kitchen and began to open the cupboards and refrigerator, looking for coffee. Minette made no effort to direct her. The open space gave Amanda an earful of conversation.

"Rough night?" Will asked.

"Probably one of many." Minette's eyes watered. "It's so surreal. I just can't believe . . ." The tears came down. "I'm still in shock."

"I can't tell you how sorry we are for your personal loss, Ms. Padgett."

"The hardest part is that bitch mother. She won't let me plan anything." More tears. "She's taking the body back *to Sacramento*. Davida *hated* Sacramento! She had nothing but bad memories."

"Can I ask what those bad memories are? It might be relevant to the case."

Minette clamped her lips together. Then she said, "You know . . . her parents' divorce . . . her coming out . . . it was painful."

"I'm sure it was tough," Barnes said, "but she traveled there often for work."

"She worked there, but she lived here!" Minette folded her arms across her chest.

Barnes backed it up. "It's must be very painful to be excluded from the funeral plans. I'm very sorry, Minette."

The woman lowered her voice but her tone remained harsh. "It's goddamn painful." A sigh. "I'm so damn angry. It's not your fault you're here to listen to me bitch but I make no excuses for my behavior."

Barnes glanced at his watch. They'd been in her place over ten minutes and she had yet to ask about progress on her lover's murder or the ransacking of the condo. He wished Amanda would hurry up with the coffee. He didn't want to approach touchy subjects without her.

Minette said, "I need to sleep for about six months and wake up after this entire nightmare is over. I had to take the phone off the hook and turn off my cell. I'm sick of people calling. They don't really care about me. All they want to know is the gory details."

"Gory details?"

"You know, like was there a struggle, did she put up a fight?" She looked at Barnes. "*Did* she put up a fight?"

Barnes said, "From what we could tell, she appeared to be sleeping at her desk. Did she do that often . . . fall asleep while working?"

"All the time . . . especially when she pulled all-nighters."

"Did you often visit her office and find her asleep?"

"Not *often*." Minette's eyes narrowed. "Sometimes I'd bring her dinner and we'd eat together."

Amanda came back with a tray of mugs, milk, sugar, and Splenda. "Here we go. I poked around in your cabinets. I hope these cups are okay."

"They're fine." Minette doused her coffee with milk and artificial sweetener. "I don't want you to think that I made a habit out of going to her office. I never liked to bug her when she was working."

Barnes nodded, thinking about ten calls a day to Dr. Kurtag's office.

"I mean, occasionally, I'd surprise her," Minette said. "Couple of times I did find her asleep at her desk. And here, too. At her home office. She'd fall asleep. She was very tired. You can imagine."

Barnes nodded, and glanced at Amanda who was ignoring his pleading eyes. "If you wouldn't mind, Ms. Padgett, we do have a couple of questions for you."

"Call me Minette." She sipped coffee and nodded. "Go ahead. I'm more awake now."

Barnes decided to forestall the bombshell. "Would you like to know about our progress on the ransacking of your apartment?"

Minette looked momentarily confused. "Oh . . . yes, of course. Did you find the bastard?"

"No, but we're getting close," Barnes lied.

"What do you mean?" Minette asked. "What have you found out?"

"We're not at liberty to discuss everything, but we found some interesting forensic evidence." Barnes was pleased with his glib tone of voice.

"Like what kind of forensic evidence?"

"For starters," Amanda said, "it doesn't appear that the vandals were out for anything specific. We think they just wanted to make a mess."

"Were? There were two of them?"

"Or maybe just one," Barnes said. "The point we're trying to make is that the mess appeared to be superficial—"

"Not when you're the one cleaning it up," Minette said.

"I'm sure that's true, but we think someone is trying to throw the police off track."

"How do you know that?"

"We can tell these things, Minette. There's just something about it that looks funny. As soon as we know more, we'll pass on that information to you. In the meantime, can you think of anyone who has access to your condo?"

"My housekeeper and the condo manager."

"We'd like to talk to them," Amanda said. "Could you get me their numbers?"

"Sure." She got up and came back a few minutes later with the information. "Emilia has worked for us for two years. I don't see her doing anything like that, but the manager is kinda creepy."

"Creepy in what way?"

"You know . . ." She lowered her eyes. "Lewd looks."

"We'll check him out."

Minette's eyes drifted to the wall clock. She stood and wandered around the room. "Anything else?"

Amanda said nothing, deferring to Barnes. He was senior anyway. Let him handle it.

He said, "Could you sit back down for just a moment, Minette?"

"Why?"

"Please . . ." After Minette sat, Barnes said, "There's no easy way to say this, so I'm going to be blunt. Did you know that Davida Grayson was infected with gonorrhea?"

"Gonorrhea?" Minette appeared truly stunned. "Like in *STD gonorrhea*?"

Amanda nodded. "The coroner found evidence at the autopsy."

"Holy moly *shit*!" In a few ticks of time, the woman's features had turned from baffled to enraged. She flung her coffee cup across the room. "That motherfucker *bastard*!" She got up and started to pace. "I'll kill him. I swear to God I'll kill the fucking bast—" She stopped talking and turned to the police. "I don't mean that literally. I'm just so fucking furious! How could he *do* this to me?"

"Who is he?" Amanda asked.

"Kyle of course! Kyle Bosworth." She spat out the name. "Son of a bitch!"

"Are you sure you got it from him?" Barnes asked.

She turned her wrath on him. "Look, Detective, I don't know what you think about me and frankly right now, I don't give a shit. I only began seeing Kyle because I was so goddamn lonely. I loved Davida but it gets real old drinking by yourself. If she would have been a tiny bit more available, I wouldn't have had to look elsewhere!"

Amanda said, "I don't think he meant it that way, Minette—"

"It sure as hell sounded accusatory."

"I think he meant to ask if it were possible that someone gave the disease to Davida other than you."

That suggestion did little to mollify Minette's fury. Her face turned bright red. "If Davida didn't have time for me, she certainly didn't have time for another woman!"

"Or man?" said Barnes.

"You two have a lot of nerve! And for your information, Davida wasn't into men!" She burst into tears. "I'd like you both to go now."

Amanda said, "We don't mean to be intrusive, Minette—"

"But you're going to be anyway. I really need you both to leave."

Barnes said, "You need to get tested."

"What do you think? Of *course* I'll get tested!"

"When you get the results, could you give us a call, please?"

"No, I won't give you a call *please*. I don't give a shit about you or her or anything else!" A new batch of tears. "Why is everyone always fucking me *up*?"

"I'm sorry," Amanda said.

"No, you're not!" Minette wiped her eyes. "I'm going to call up that bastard and give him a piece of my mind!"

Barnes said, "I don't blame you for being angry, but maybe you should wait until you're tested. If you come back negative, you may be angry at the wrong person."

Minette shook her head. "It's impossible for me to be angry at the wrong person because I'm so fucking angry at *everyone*!"

Barnes kept his eyes on the picture window, the one that framed a magnificent view of the bay. A lot more interesting than watching Kyle Bosworth pace back and forth. The man was raking his hair with long, slender fingers. The parallel rows cut into the shafts reminded Barnes of a field during planting season. Summers working the ranches.

Notepad in hand, Amanda kept refocusing in on the moving target. "I'm sorry that you had to find out from us. You should know that Minette accused you of giving it to her."

"The bitch!" Bosworth exclaimed. "The absolute bitch!"

"I take it you don't agree?"

"No I don't agree! I don't know *what* that wicked witch was talking about! I was clean when I met her and if anybody gave anything to anyone, it was she who gave it to me!" He muttered as he paced. "This is great! This is just fucking great!"

"So you had no idea you might be infected," Amanda stated.

"None whatsoever!" He glared at her. "I had no symptoms—have no symptoms. Why would I be infected? I don't routinely go around cheating on my spouse. Minette was a distraction and only because Yves works too hard."

Same thing Minette said about Davida, Barnes thought.

"Minette wasn't even a serious distraction," Bosworth continued. "I like women but I prefer men. Why in the world would I suspect I was infected with anything?"

Amanda said, "Not to get too clinical, but symptoms of the disease appear much earlier in men than in women."

That stopped Bosworth's running a rut in the rug. "The symptoms. Burning, pus, hard to pee—no, I've never had it but in this day and age one educates oneself." He brightened. "The obvious conclusion from no symptoms is no clap. I know it can be latent, but pu-leeze."

Suddenly standing straight.

Amanda said, "Mr. Bosworth, you need to talk to a doctor. Men do get more obvious symptoms and they get them earlier than women do but there are no hard-and-fast rules."

Barnes said, "Also it's easier for a man to give the disease to women than for men to get the disease from women."

Kyle stared at him. "Are you saying that *Yves* gave me a dose?" Anger tightened his face. He started pacing again. "I'll kill that bastard! I should have known all those late nights were more than work!"

"Whoa, whoa, whoa," Barnes said. "Before you consider homicide, maybe you want to get yourself tested. It could be that Yves has been working late at night and you're not infected at all."

Kyle stopped moving and stared into space. "Yes, that probably should be the first step . . . maybe I'm not even infected . . . first things first, eh? Maybe I'm clean. That would certainly be nice. Heh heh—if you two will excuse me now, I have to make a rather embarrassing appointment."

Amanda stood up from the couch. "Will you let us know the results as soon as you find out?"

"What's it your business?"

"It might have some relevance to Davida Grayson's murder."

"Ruling me out!" Kyle proclaimed. "And here I was enjoying being a suspect—so delicious, when you know you're innocent."

"You will let us know, sir?"

"Yes, of course, but please don't call me, let me call you. If I get a reprieve on this, I don't want Yves to know I was tested. I think he'd tolerate my indiscretion, but the man has an absolute *phobia* of germs."

17

The two interviews turned out to be the highlights of the detectives' day. The remainder of their time was spent chasing down leads that dead-ended. At five in the afternoon, Barnes put in calls to Minette Padgett and Kyle Bosworth, reminding them to phone as soon as they got their test results. They didn't expect to hear from Minette but held out hope that Bosworth would cooperate.

Bosworth figured a negative would rule him out—if only life were so simple. No disease meant only that Kyle was out of the infection loop. Though if there was a good reason to seriously suspect him, neither Barnes nor Amanda could come up with it.

Flagging blood sugar made it hard to work and before returning to their cubicles, they made a pit stop at Melanie's, snagging Barnes's favorite corner table. Will stoked his engine on black caffeine and Amanda ordered a decaf, no-sugar-added vanilla latte with nonfat milk.

Barnes said, "Are you sure there's even coffee in that concoction?"

"I don't know how you drink it black. Rots your stomach lining."

"It's already rotted from dealing with all these deceptive jokers. Lord, give me a dishonest drug dealer any day of the year. At least I know what I'm dealing with."

"Notice how Minette didn't make eye contact when she was talking about her 'creepy' condo manager." Amanda made quotes with her fingers. "While we were in LA a couple of the uniforms canvassed the complex. The residents had nothing but nice things to say about Davida." She sipped foamy milk. "Minette was a different story."

"How so?"

"She wasn't friendly, for one thing. Her downstairs neighbor had a run-in with her about making too much noise late at night. Davida smoothed it over by assuring they would take off their shoes after ten."

"Minette being difficult is a given, Mandy. Now we've got to get from there to murder."

"Sure be nice if we had the shotgun."

Barnes said. "We don't even know if Minette has ever fired a gun. We should see if she has any permits on file."

"I can do that." Amanda regarded her partner. "You're still skeptical about her."

"She was with Kyle until early morning and both of them were more than a little looped. Davida was murdered with a dead-on, single shot. Even with a shotgun that requires coordination."

"Hard to get it wrong when you're a foot away from the person who's sleeping."

"I still say the murder looks male—more violent than it needed to be. It was done up close and personal by someone who knew how to use a gun. This was not the work of a hysterical drunken woman."

"Another sexist no-no." Amanda grinned. "Does male mean you're back to Don Newell?"

"He called Davida and she called him back. We're taking Donnie's word what the conversation was about. I think I can justify speaking to him again."

"Let's say it's Newell. Why would he kill Davida?"

"First thought is he was having an affair with her and she threatened to tell his wife."

"The wife who hates Davida, quote unquote," said Amanda. "Meaning there's another suspect. But if Davida knew about the resentment, why would she threaten to tell Newell's wife? Also, from everything I've ever heard about her, she had a vested interest in being gay."

"So maybe Donnie threatened to expose her."

"Why would he do that? He's got a wife and kids, he's got a good position with Sacramento PD. Even if they screwed once in a while, he wasn't in love with her and had to know there was no future in the relationship. Also, you yourself said he seemed shocked by the murder. Give me a reason why he'd drive down to Berkeley and blow her head off with a shotgun."

"I don't have a good reason, Amanda. And I'm not saying he did it. I'm just saying it looks like a man did it." Barnes's cell rang and he glanced at the number. "It's Bosworth." He depressed the green button. "Barnes."

"Kyle Bosworth, Detective." There was lightness in the man's voice.

"Thanks for calling back," said Barnes.

"So far so good," said Bosworth, as if talking to himself "A couple of the blood tests will take a little time, but my doctor's nearly certain I'm clean." His voice turned hard. "No thanks to that bitch!"

"Good to hear, Mr. Bosworth. For all we know, Minette may be clean, too."

"Then how did Davida—oh, sure. Our late state rep wasn't a saint. Sure, why not, we're all human. Ta ta, Detective, I'm going to go out and have a wonderfully cholesterol-laden dinner—"

"Did Minette ever talk to you about problems between Davida and her?"

No response on the other end. "Hello?"

"Yes, Detective, I'm still here. Anything Minette says needs to be taken with an entire quarry of salt."

"What did she tell you, Mr. Bosworth?"

"I should preface what I'm about to tell you. Our fling—Minette and me—what we said and what we did was often the product of overindulgence."

"You drank together."

"Minette was a *huge* drinker and not a pleasant drunk. When she got pickled, she'd go into a litany of complaints about everyone and everything. She told me—while drunk—that she was sure that Davida was fooling around on her."

"Did she suspect anyone specific?"

"I'm sure she suspected a lot of people. With enough bourbon in her, she could be downright paranoid."

"Did she mention any names?"

"Nothing I recall."

"Can you remember if Minette specified Davida's paramour as being male or female?"

Again, Bosworth went silent, causing Barnes to ask if he was still on the line. "Yes, yes . . . Davida with a man? Well, *that* would be interesting. I've never heard anything about her swinging both ways but I'm not terribly surprised. We all have a bit of both yin and yang in us whether we admit it or not."

The best place to reinterview Minette was the station. They flipped a coin. Amanda lost the toss and made the call.

To get Minette in, Amanda decided to appeal to the woman's vanity. Minette picked the phone up on the third ring, whispered a boozy hello.

"Ms. Padgett, I'm so sorry to bother you again, but this is Detective Isis. If I could just a have a moment of your time, I'd be very grateful."

"Wha-at?"

"My partner and I . . . we were discussing things and we both decided that we really needed your help. Would it be possible for you to come to our office to chat with us for a bit?"

"What about?"

"We're making some headway, but you knew Davida better than anyone else and we could use your insight."

"I did know Davida better'n anyone, so you tell me why tha' bitch won't let me do anythin' at the memorial."

There was no way the woman was fit to interview tonight, but maybe Amanda could set something up for tomorrow. "How about this, Minette: come in and help us out and I'll call Lucille Grayson and make a personal appeal for you to be part of the service. How does that sound?"

"You'll never change the hag's mind. She's a real *bitch*."

"Let me try, Minette." Amanda took in a silent breath and let it out. "When can you come in?"

"Not tonight. Too late."

It was quarter to six. Lord only knew how long she'd been hitting the bottle. "You're right. How about tomorrow, say ten AM?"

"Mebbe eleven."

"Eleven would be perfect. I'll call you at ten thirty to see if you're on schedule?"

"Sure. Bye."

"Oh, by the way, did you get tested yet?"

A long pause. "Good news. The doctor thinks I'm clean."

"That's very good news."

"I suppose. Bye."

Amanda placed the phone back in the cradle.

Being clean meant Minette realized that her worst fear had been true. Davida had been cheating on her. The big question was with whom? Minette must be wondering the same thing. That could explain her drinking this early.

She looked around the squad room for Barnes—tucked into a corner, facing the wall, talking on the phone. She went over and tapped him on the shoulder. Barnes whispered a *gotta go* into the receiver and disconnected his cell.

"Who were you talking to?" Amanda asked casually.

"No one."

"On the phone, talking to no one. They've put people away for far less, Will."

"It wasn't business-related."

Amanda's smile widened to a grin. "You were talking to that cop in LA—"

"Amanda—"

"What was her name?" Amanda snapped her fingers. "Marge. Tall drink of water, but nice-looking, I'll grant you that."

"She adopted an orphan in her teens. The kid goes to Caltech. We were just talking about kids."

"You've never had any."

"I was doing the listening."

"Willie and Margie sitting in a tree—are you going down south or is she coming up north?"

"She's got a couple of days off. Can we move on to business?"

"Sure, because I took care of some. Minette's coming down to the stationhouse tomorrow at eleven."

"You got her to come in?" Barnes nodded with approval.

Amanda punched his shoulder lightly. "Call it the old charm. I'm going home now to work my magic on my husband. Unless you want my advice on something."

"Like what?"

"Like where to take Margie. They're predicting high sixties with sunshine. You should rent a convertible and take her to wine country. Spring for some bucks and stay at the Sonoma Mission Inn."

That actually wasn't a bad idea, but damn if Barnes would give her any satisfaction. "You can go now, Mandy. I'll be in around nine tomorrow."

"Me too, God and traffic willing. I'll call Minette at around ten thirty tomorrow to remind her about the appointment. She's already a bit inebriated, so I'll probably have to remind her of our conversation. No doubt she'll be hung over and in a foul mood."

Barnes said, "I'll pick up some juice, donuts, whatever. Every little bit helps."

"If only it were that simple," Amanda said. "Get aspirin, too."

18

At ten thirty in the morning, Minette was still in bed, having forgotten about the appointment. Amanda decided the most efficient thing to do was just pick her up and bring her in. It took a full hour for the woman to dress and another half hour of plying her with designer coffee until she seemed coherent enough to interview. Even with the star treatment, Minette was surly. Her makeup couldn't hide the bags under her eyes, making them look more muddy than exotic. Her hair was in need of a good brushing as well as a root job. She was dressed in crumpled khakis, a white tee and sneakers. The woman was lanky and thin and from the back she could have passed for an adolescent boy.

Amanda escorted her into the interview room and helped her to a chair. "Can I get you anything to eat?"

"It makes me nervous when you're too nice," Minette groused.

"That's just the way we are. Here to help." And we need *your* help. "A munch?"

Minette considered her response as if world peace depended on it. "I suppose I wouldn't mind a muffin. Anything reduced-fat."

"Not a problem. Be right back."

While Amanda got someone to pick up the muffins, Barnes watched Minette through a one-way mirror. She seemed more tired than nervous and to underscore the point, she lay her head down in the cradle of her arms and closed her eyes. Five minutes later, she was snoring.

Amanda came into the observation room. Barnes said, "If the woman has anxiety, she's hiding it well."

"Maybe she has nothing to feel guilty about."

"We all feel guilty about something, it's a matter of degree." A policewoman entered and handed Amanda the goody bag. She passed it to Barnes, who pulled out a bran muffin and chomped half of it in one bite. By way of explanation, he said, "No time to eat this morning."

"What were you doing while I was babysitting Ms. Padgett?"

"The official memorial service for Davida is tomorrow afternoon at two in Sacramento. I want to set up an interview with Lucille Grayson afterward."

"Thanks for telling me."

"I'm telling you now," Barnes said. "I got us tickets for the noon train." He finished his muffin and stood. "Ready?"

"Sure, let's see what Sleeping Beauty has to say for herself."

Gently, Amanda rocked Minette's shoulder. Minette woke up with a start and it took her a few moments to remember where she was. A thin line of drool had slipped out of the corner of her mouth. She sucked it up and wiped her lips with the back of her hand. "Wow." Minette sipped her coffee. "I'm more tired than I thought. Do we really have to do this now?"

"The sooner we finish, the better our chances of catching a murderer," Barnes told her.

"Have a muffin." Amanda offered her the bag. "You can keep all of them if you want."

Minette extracted the blueberry. "One's fine. Thanks."

"Here's some napkins . . . need a refill on the coffee?"

"Sure."

"Be right back."

As soon as Amanda left, Barnes said, "Again, I'm sorry for your loss."

"Thanks. Can we get on with this?" She looked at her watch. "I really got things I need to do."

Barnes smiled and Amanda came back in with the coffee.

"Here we go. Anything else?"

"Ms. Padgett is a busy woman," Barnes said without a trace of irony. "We should get started. Before we get into Davida, I have a couple of questions for you concerning the break-in at your condo."

Minette peered over the rim of the coffee cup. "Yeah?"

"You reported that you didn't think anything was missing. Is that still correct?"

"I didn't say that. I said I'm not sure."

"But your valuables . . . cash, jewelry, expensive items . . . were all accounted for?"

"I think I'm missing cash."

"You think?" Amanda asked.

"Yeah, Davida always kept cash on hand. Couple of hundred. Maybe more. I only found fifty so maybe the burglars took the rest."

"And your jewelry?"

Minette shrugged. "I guess it's all there. I didn't check every piece. What does this have to do with Davida's murder?"

"Maybe nothing." Barnes moved in closer. "We have a little bit of a dilemma, Minette, and we need your help. At first, we thought that the break-in was done by Davida's murderer, that he or she was looking for something specific. Makes sense, right?"

Minette nodded.

Barnes went on. "But then we realized Davida's office wasn't ransacked. So we're figuring why would your condo be ransacked and not the office?"

Amanda said, "So now we're thinking that the two incidents might be unrelated."

"What do *you* think?" Barnes asked.

"How the hell would I know?" Minette was irritated. "That's your job."

"Fair enough," Barnes answered. "So my first question is, who would want to ransack your condominium and not take anything valuable?"

"Am I supposed to answer that?" Minette frowned. "If I could answer that, we wouldn't be talking."

"Well, here's the thing: we didn't find any pry marks or forced entrance. We're figuring whoever messed up your place had a key."

Minette took a few moments to collect her thoughts. She looked from detective to detective, then down at her watch. "I *told* you we had a creepy manager. Did you check *him* out?"

"We did," Amanda said. "He was working on the plumbing at one of your neighbors' homes that night."

"Till midnight?"

"Beyond. Seriously clogged line."

"So he couldn't have done it," said Barnes.

Minette didn't reply.

He pressed her: "Who else had a key to your condo?"

"Lucille Grayson," Minette said. "You know, I wouldn't be surprised if she did it."

Amanda acted as if she took that seriously. "Why would she do that?"

"To piss me off. I told you the woman hates me."

Barnes said, "Sorry, that night she was at the club with some friends. We know for a fact."

"Well . . . that's what her friends would say."

"She was identified by dozens of people, and her nurse stayed with her the entire time. She wasn't anywhere near the condo." Barnes tried to get the woman to make eye contact. "Minette, one way or the other, we're going to get to the bottom of the ransacking—"

"Shouldn't you be concentrating on the murder?"

"We're doing both," Barnes said. "And right now, we'd like to rule out a connection between the murder and the ransacking. To do that, we've really got to find out what happened at your place. Whoever did it, Minette, I just want you to rest assured that we're going to nail him—or her—and throw his—or her—sorry ass in jail."

Amanda said, "So if you know *anything* about it, now's the time to say something because Detective Barnes and I really don't want to be spinning our wheels."

"See that's what gets us really pissed off . . . when people lie to us."

"Yeah, that really is a nuisance," Amanda concurred.

Barnes said, "Even though we realize that sometimes people don't lie to us on purpose, know what I'm saying?"

Minette shook her head slowly. Bloodshot eyes focused on something in the distance.

Amanda said, "People sometimes lie to protect someone or something. Would you know anything about that, Minette?"

"No." Her voice was strong, but she started gnawing on her thumbnail. "You said you needed my help. What do you want from me?"

"For one thing, we'd like to know who might have ransacked your condo," Barnes said. "Because it's definitely an inside job."

"How can you be so sure?"

"No valuables are missing."

"I told you, some cash might be missing."

"That's just for show," Amanda said. "Know how we know that?" No answer. "The ransacking was messy, but all of your dishes remained in the kitchen cabinets. None of that stuff was touched. A lot of disorder but almost no breakage."

Barnes said, "Easier on whoever had to clean it up."

Amanda said, "You know, Minette, if you have something to tell us, tell us now before it gets too far."

Barnes said, "We know you've been under terrible stress."

Amanda said, "We know you haven't been yourself at all. We understand that it's been an emotional time for you."

Barnes smiled.

Amanda smiled.

Minette's left cheek quivered. She hugged herself. Yanked at an errant strand of hair. "You have no idea."

"How could we understand such loss?" Amanda said. "We can't and we're not even going to try. But we do have to get to the bottom of what happened in your condo. We do have to know what really happened."

"What do you mean?" Minette sniffed. "If I knew what happened, I'd tell you."

Barnes's smile turned reptilian. "We think you know *way* more than you're telling us."

"So now's the time to get it off your chest," Amanda broke in. "While we can still help you."

"I don't understand," Minette whispered.

"If you tell us what happened, Minette, we can do something for you. You know, being so stressed out and all, we'll understand."

"But," said Barnes, "if we waste valuable time trying to solve the ransacking and things begin to point in your direction . . ." He shook his head. "That's going to look very bad, Minette. Very, very bad."

Amanda leaned forward. "We think you know who did it, honey, and now's the time to tell us. Because if you don't tell us now, we can't help you."

"And we really want to help you."

"Yes, we do want to help you. But first we've got to know what really happened."

Minette cried silent tears. Amanda reached over and took her hand. "It's all right, honey. You can tell us. It must be so hard for you. It must have always been so hard for you with Davida being away all the time."

"I thought she was *working*." Minette's voice was clogged with emotion. "Now I realize she had someone *else*!" She burst into tears. "How could she do that to me! That bitch! A bitch that *came* from a bitch!"

"I'm so sorry," Amanda said. "You must be terribly disillusioned with her."

"Totally." She sniffed back tears. "I thought she was working so *hard*."

"You must be so angry."

"I'm furious!"

"I bet," Barnes said. "But you suspected the affair, didn't you?"

Quickly, she made eye contact with Barnes, then broke it off. "I suppose I did."

"You came home after the press conference, didn't you?" Barnes said.

Minette hesitated. Gave a guilty-kid nod.

"You came home . . . alone, disillusioned, confused, upset . . . all those things, right?"

Nod, nod.

"Alone in the place that you once shared with Davida," Amanda said. "You must have been beside yourself with confusion and anger."

Barnes said, "So to get rid of those horrible feelings, maybe you threw something at the wall."

"Just because you were so upset," Amanda added.

"I was *very* upset."

Barnes said, "And then it went from there."

No answer.

"We need your help, Minette. We need the information straight-arrow truthful. You need to tell us what happened after you got home from the press conference."

"I was upset," Minette said softly. "I threw a pillow at the wall." The two detectives waited for more. "And . . . then I threw another pillow . . . and another. And then I turned over one of the couches. I was

surprised that it wasn't all that heavy. So I turned over the other one."
She was breathing harder now. "And then I saw Davida's office, looking all neat . . . like it hadn't been used in ages because it hadn't been
used in ages. And I just knew in my heart of hearts that if she wanted
to really work, she could have worked at home. So I began to take
things out of her file cabinets . . . and tear them up . . . and toss them
because it's not like she needed them anymore . . ." Tears were stream-
ing down her cheeks. "And then I went on to the closets. And I threw
clothing all over the place . . . and then the dressers. And then . . ."

She was sobbing hard.

"I realized I had made a gigantic mess and that I'd have to clean it
all up. And I was so alone and lonely and . . ."

More sobbing. Amanda offered her a tissue. "So then what did you
do?"

"I turned the sofa back and put back a pillow, but that only made
me angrier. And I felt so stupid. And scared . . . I don't know who
killed Davida, honestly, I swear I don't know!"

"Okay, we believe you." And Barnes did . . . sort of. She seemed
too hysterical to pull it off. But he kept an open mind because he had
been fooled before. "You were scared being alone. Then what?"

"I totally freaked myself out," Minette said. "I started thinking—
you know, like your mind gets hold of something and just keeps going?
That's what happened to me, the thoughts took over. Like whoever
hurt Davida . . . maybe he's coming to get me. And here I was alone in
the place, which was now a total mess. I was so scared! I wanted to call
the police. But I felt stupid telling them that I was freaked out and
scared . . . you know?"

"That's what we're here for," Barnes said.

"Yeah, right!" Minette dried her eyes with a tissue. "You guys are
quick with traffic tickets, but if I told anyone I was scared, I bet not one
cop would have come out to see me."

She had a point, Barnes thought.

Amanda said, "You must have really felt alone."

"I did."

"So then what did you do?" Barnes prompted.

"I called the cops and told them that our place had been tossed. I
needed people to stop already with Davida and focus on *me*. She was
dead, but I *wasn't*."

Minette's egotism took neither detective by surprise, but her admission did.

"In the future," Barnes said, "if you feel scared again, there are people who can help you and you don't have to fib to get them to talk to you."

"That's all it was meant to be," she sobbed. "A stupid fib because I was desperate! Am I in trouble?"

"You filed a false police report," Barnes said, "so that could be trouble, yes. But I think the judge will take into consideration your circumstances."

Minette nodded. "I should probably contact my lawyer."

"Probably," Amanda said. "If you can't afford one, the county will give you one free of charge."

"I'm okay with money." She stood up on wobbly feet. "Can I call my lawyer now?"

"First, we need to read you your rights."

Minette sat through the beginning of the routine, numb, inert. When Barnes got to the part about an attorney being provided, she said, "You just said that. I know all of it anyway from TV. I watch a lot of TV because she left me all the time."

"She's vain and egotistical and self-centered," Barnes said once they returned to the other side of the one-way mirror. "But the real question is, did she murder Davida? We went through her house and her clothes. No blood-spattered clothing, nothing with gunpowder residue, no shoes with trace evidence of blood or carpet fiber. No gun registration and there's no evidence that she's owned an illegal firearm."

"She could have hired someone."

"Why would she want Davida dead?"

"Because she was cheating on her. Because Davida left her alone once too often."

"Minette dealt with that," said Barnes. "Doing her own cheating."

"Minette is a selfish little bitch who probably flew into a narcissistic rage when she found out that Davida had someone on the sly."

"Okay, so you like her."

Amanda's smile was weary.

Barnes said, "You really like her for it?"

"No, but I don't want to rule her out. She's unstable and she knew Davida's habits better than anyone."

No sense belaboring the subject. "Are you coming to Sacramento with me tomorrow?"

"Of course. Why are you even asking?"

"The memorial's scheduled the day after the funeral. I set up the interview with Lucille Grayson for when it's over." Barnes smiled like a cat with feathers in his teeth. "Is that okay?"

"What's on your mind, Willie?"

"After the funeral, I'm going to Don Newell's place for dinner at five thirty."

She stared at him. "And I'm not invited."

"I can get you invited."

"But . . ."

"It's up to you."

"But you didn't mention me the first time around."

"It was more of a social thing—old-boy barbecue."

Amanda whistled. "Oh, man. First high school buds, then Jane Meyerhoff, then this. Maybe you'd like to take over the entire case by yourself?"

"C'mon, Amanda, don't be—"

"You think I'm losing my touch? I was the one who just got Minette to confess to the break-in."

Barnes had seen that as teamwork. He said, "That was great, but with Donnie Newell, there might be things I can—he might be uncomfortable talking in front of you."

"Good-old-boy sex talk?"

"Woman talk," said Barnes. "Specifically his relationship to Davida."

"While you're with him, I could talk to the wife who hated Davida. Or is she too hysterical and weak to pull it off?"

"I thought about that, Mandy, I really did. But then instead of the dinner being a friendly invitation, and the boys retiring for a cigar, it's too much like a cop interview. You know, you take one, I take the other."

He was making sense, although Amanda hated to admit it. "If you exclude me from anything one more time, I'm walking. This is a partnership, remember?"

"Mandy, you know how much respect I have for you—"

"Don't go there, Will. I'm too pissed off for condescension."

"Look, I really do respect your opinion. As a matter of fact, I took your advice."

She regarded him with narrowed eyes. "What advice?"

"You know . . . me and Marge Dunn. I rented a convertible. We're going to drive through Napa and Sonoma, do a couple of tastings."

Actually, Barnes hadn't prepared a damn thing but Amanda's idea had been a good one, and it seemed like a dandy time to tell her. "Any idea if there's a cheese shop en route? I think a cheese, fruit and wine picnic would be great. You agree?"

Amanda sighed. "Actually, I do have an address. Also, try The Olive Press near Sonoma. And if she's still tolerating you by the end of the day, I've got some dinner recommendations."

"That would be super—"

"Now cut the crap and rent that car and stop bullshitting me. I'm still pissed, Will."

"I know you are. How about coffee at Melanie's? I'll pay."

She cracked up. "You think you can get me to come around with a measly mocha latte?"

"Lunch?"

"You're getting warmer."

"Chez Panisse? I know one of the waitresses, maybe if it's slow—"

"Thanks, love to." Amanda smiled. "I'll pull out the car while you check your wallet."

19

Though she had no children, Davida Grayson had left behind a legacy. Her lust for life, her obsession with justice for the underclass, her dogged pursuit of righteousness were iterated and reiterated by each speaker. Those who eulogized her knew her well enough to make it sound real. Everyone pledged not to let Davida's dream of creating a new stem-cell line perish with her.

In the end, Lucille Grayson had acted with class and had allowed Minette Padgett to speak. Surprisingly, Minette was clear of thought and steady of balance. She spoke briefly—always a sign of discretion—and from the heart. If Barnes hadn't known what a nutcase she was, he might've choked up.

When the hour was up, the casket was loaded into the hearse, and a community that had loved Davida offered its final good-byes. The graveside service was to be a small and private affair.

Amanda checked her watch as she and Barnes filed out of the auditorium. They joined the massive black wave undulating toward the exits. It was shortly after three. "Your man-to-man dinner still on for five thirty?"

"Far as I know."

"Did you see Newell here?"

"I looked for him, couldn't find him anywhere," Barnes answered. "We've got time to kill. Want to grab a cup of coffee?"

"Why not?"

She walked slightly ahead of him, made her way through the throng. Civil but still pissed off.

Outside the auditorium, Barnes caught up with her. "I called Newell this morning. You're invited for dinner."

"Why the change of heart?"

"Because you should be there. After dinner, I'll take Donnie, and you occupy Jill Newell, just like you said."

Neither detective spoke for several footsteps.

Barnes said, "You know I'm a loner, Amanda. I work well with partners but only up to a point. I feel a little bad about that, but not too bad. I am what I am. But that doesn't mean that when someone calls me on my bullshit I can't set it right."

They walked a couple more steps in silence.

"Did you tell Newell I was definitely coming?"

"I said you might. Didn't know if you had other plans."

"I don't now."

"So I'll call Donnie and tell him it's a go."

"How about if I call Jill and ask her if it's okay for me to come to dinner? Then when she says yes, I'll thank her personally and ask her if I can bring anything."

"Woman to woman," said Barnes.

"Person to person."

As a state capital, Sacramento played a fine host to its politicians. It had classy restaurants, several art museums courtesy of Crocker Bank, concert halls, a few theaters and the ARCO arena with its NBA team, the almost-champ Kings. But like most cities, it had multiple identities.

In Sacramento's case, that meant a mining history and agricultural presence. When the Kings made the play-offs, the fans came armed with cowbells.

Barnes had grown up in a semi-rural, farming community twenty quiet miles from the capitol dome, where, like most of his schoolmates, he learned how to shoot a rifle and use his fists. The music of choice was country for the masses and bluegrass for those serious about guitar and fiddle. Having a gay brother and living in Berkeley had altered Barnes's perspective but had never totally erased it. As Amanda had pointed out, sometimes he reverted to the cowboy thing. Sometimes to his detriment.

But this wasn't one of those times. Sitting at the Newells' big pine dinner table, wearing his bolo tie, a soft pair of Wranglers and well-broken boots, he felt right at home.

The ranch-style house sat on ten acres of oak and eucalyptus in a semi-agi neighborhood with barns and paddocks. The furniture was a chain-store leather ensemble complete with two La-Z-Boy lounge chairs fitted with cup holders that faced a sixty-inch flat-screen TV. Whatever art in sight was made by the Newell kids. Most of the table conversation centered on the kids asking the adults to pass around the food. Everyone praised Jill on her fine cooking, which was no lie. Jill seemed to take little joy in the attention. Shy woman, she always had been.

During the meal, Barnes snuck several sidelong glances at Amanda who ate sparingly and complimented the behavior of the Newells' three kids.

As far as Barnes could tell, no thanks to Don who was loose and jocular and made no attempt to act parental.

It was Jill who ran a tight ship.

She was statuesque, about five ten, with a weathered oval face, high cheekbones, and piercing brown almond eyes that suggested Indian blood. Her lips were full but she rarely smiled. Her hands had been roughened by use, her fingers long but her fingernails short. She wore tight jeans and a loose-fitting sweatshirt. Her chestnut-colored hair was tied up in a high ponytail.

Like that artist . . . Georgia O'Keeffe.

"I don't remember the last time I ate so well." Barnes patted his stomach. "Man, that was terrific, Jill. Those ribs, unbelievable."

Jill acknowledged the comment with a slight smile and a soft thank you. When she got up to clear the plates, so did Amanda.

"Sit, Amanda," Jill told her. "The kids will do it."

"I really don't mind," Amanda said. "Besides, I know it's a week-day and they must have homework. I sure don't mind helping if you want them to get a jump on it."

"Well, okay—if you're sure?"

"Positive."

Jill nodded. "All right, you three, you caught a break. Go to your lessons and no computer privileges until all three of you are through."

She turned to her oldest—a fifteen-year-old boy named Ryan. "If I catch you sneaking online before you're done, there will be hell to pay. Understood?"

Her son gave her a look somewhere between a smile and smirk. "I hear you. Thanks for dinner." Then he grinned at his father, who gave him a wink behind Jill's back.

Amanda, the millionaire, fit in seamlessly. She said, "I can wash or dry."

Barnes knew she'd grown up hard. Could still relate to anyone.

"We have a dishwasher," Jill said.

"Even better, I'll load."

"You need help, hon?" Don asked, not even pretending to mean it.

"We're fine," Amanda answered.

Don said, "Jill, would you mind if I show Will your new shotgun?"

"Go ahead," Jill said.

"*Your* new shotgun?" Amanda said.

"Jill's a crack shot," Don said. "We could use people like her for SWAT but I'd rather have her cooking."

Jill frowned. "Shooting people don't interest me."

"See, there's where we're different." Newell managed to kiss his wife before she could turn away. "See you in a bit, ladies."

After they were gone, Amanda took in a pile of dishes and began to push the leftover food into the garbage. "Where'd you learn how to shoot?"

"My daddy. He took me hunting when I was ten. At the time, I hated it, but I loved my daddy, so I went along. I never like to kill any animals, so I took up skeet. I discovered I had a good eye and good co-ordination. When I was fifteen, I started entering competitive shooting. I have enough blue ribbons to paper my powder room. But to me, competition is silly . . . a guy's thing, you know? But it made my daddy real proud. The shotgun's for turkey hunting. Donnie bought it for me—one of those gifts men get you 'cause they want to use it themselves."

"Donnie's the hunter in the family?"

Jill nodded. "I used to just tag along, you know, but lately I decided if I was going to cook the holiday turkey, I should be honest about where our meat comes from. So now I pull the trigger. I gotta say, there is nothing like fresh game. It is positively delicious."

"I'm sure that's true."

"You hunt?"

"No . . . but neither did my dad . . . not that it mattered." Amanda smiled. "I didn't have such a great relationship with my father, but I don't dare complain. My husband more than makes up for that deficit."

Jill was silent. Then she said, "We all have our crosses to bear. Donnie's got good intentions." She shrugged. "You know what they say about good intentions."

"I do."

"He just gets caught up in stuff," Jill said. "He don't always think things through. It's cost him some promotions."

"How's that?"

"Instead of studying for the Sergeant's tests, he's helping this old friend or that old friend or just shooting the bull down at Brady's." She faced Amanda. "Sometimes people take advantage of him."

"That's not good."

"Not good at all." Jill exhaled. "But like I said, he's a good man."

Actually, she said he had good intentions, but Amanda didn't correct her. "How long have you two been married?"

"Twenty-one years. We met in high school."

"Oh." Amanda feigned ignorance. "Did you know Davida Grayson? She was also a local."

"Yes, I knew Davida."

"Were you at the memorial service today?"

"Donnie was, but I couldn't make it. Conflict with the school . . . parent-teacher thing." Jill shrugged. "It must have been sad."

"Very."

"To be honest, I didn't want to go . . . too freaky, you know? To know someone who was murdered."

"Were you and Davida friends?"

"Oh heavens no. I didn't like her at all back then, but that was probably ignorance. She'd already come out when I was a sophomore and I thought it was gross—you know, women with women."

"Sure."

"Anyway, that was a lifetime ago. It didn't help my feelings that Donnie had dated her also. Did you know that?"

Amanda shook her head. Keep those bald lies coming.

"Anyway, after she came out, Donnie was sorely traumatized. He got lots of ribbing from his friends."

"I can imagine. Did you start dating him right after?"

"Pretty much, yeah. The rest, like they say, is history." Jill smiled tightly. "How many children do you have?"

Changing the subject. Amanda said, "None, yet."

"They bear watching. Kids. My oldest one really bears watching. He's sneaky . . . like some other people I know."

The implication was obvious, but Amanda didn't press her for more. When people opened up too quickly, there was often a backlash of anger. "You ever practice shooting on your own property? What do you have here, like twenty acres?"

"Ten and a half but it looks bigger 'cause a lot of it's clearing. Sometimes when I'm in the mood, I do target practice on a bull's-eye that I got hanging on the trees. If I used my shotgun on the oaks, I'd blow them to a stump."

"Well, maybe one day we can go shooting together. I'm not a bad shot but there's certainly room for improvement."

Jill hid a smile. "Be happy to show you whatever I know."

"That would be great." Amanda was very satisfied with the turn of events. Both Donnie and now Jill could be suspects. If she went shooting with Jill, it would be a good way to pocket some shotgun casings.

Barnes looked at the twelve-gauge Browning Gold Lite pump gun. "Nice piece of equipment. Didn't know you were a hunter."

Newell gave him a chance to hold it, then took it back and placed it on the gun rack, locking the bar into place. "Oh, yeah, for some years now. Life can get tedious, Willie. A man needs a hobby." He turned to Barnes. "You've been itching to get me alone all evening. What do you want to talk about?"

"What do you think?"

"Don't turn that question with a question shit on me," Newell said. "I've been a cop long enough for you to respect me. Now either spit it out or go home."

Barnes said, "Fair enough. You need to tell me about your relationship with Davida Grayson and you need to be honest."

Newell smiled and shook his head. "I knew this was coming."

"So you've had time to think about it."

"Nothing to think about, Willie. Davida was an old friend and a controversial politician. If she needed police help, I was happy to give it to her. Buddy, that's it."

"What about your past with the woman?"

"That's what it is, Will. It's a past."

"I need to know about it, Donnie, because this case seems to re-volve around it."

"How so?"

Barnes was caught in his lie. "Wish I could tell you, but you know the drill."

"Am I considered a suspect?"

"You were one of the last people to talk to her. I only have your word what the conversation was about."

The men were silent. Newell shrugged. "Like I said, there's been nothing between us for the last twenty-five years. Not that I would have minded, because at one time, I was crazy about that girl. She fucked like a bunny, you have no idea. When you're seventeen, that's all a girl's got to do to make you crazy about her."

"I know all about that," Barnes said. "So you had no idea she was gay."

"I don't think *she* had any idea she was gay."

Barnes was silent.

"All right, maybe she did know," Newell told him. "She was the one that suggested doing a threesome with Jane Meyerhoff. I was a normal, red-blooded American teenage stud and that meant I was horny all the time. When she suggested a threesome, man, I thought I died and went to heaven. I guess looking back at it, she used me to get to Janey."

"How'd it happen?"

"It was one of those pivotal moments, Willie. We were double dat-ing and went back to Jane's house because her parents were never home . . . always off to some fancy destination. There were four of us—Jane's date, some loser, Derek Hewitt."

"I remember Hewitt," said Barnes. "Tall, skinny, dumb."

"And rich—rich was a big thing to Janey's parents. Anyway, we were downing shooters and smoking weed and getting high. Hewitt got sick to his stomach and fell asleep on Janey's bed. The rest of us were feeling no pain. When Davida threw out the suggestion, Janey and I thought she was joking."

Newell turned grave. His voice lowered. "But she wasn't. It hap-pened slowly . . . you know, just kissing and copping feels. Then . . . bam . . ." Newell was sweating. "Afterward was the scary part. Jane freaked out. It took the both of us and a lot more weed to calm her down, convince her that it was no big deal, only normal experimentation. A couple of months later, Davida came out. She and Jane remained friends, but I became an outsider real quick."

"So Davida and Jane hooked up that long ago?"

"I rightly don't know if they did or didn't. Eventually, I started dating Jill, 'cause she was hot, too, wanted it all the time. Though looking back it seems like she was . . . you know, maybe acting? Like she really didn't like it as much as she pretended?"

"How'd Davida react to your hanging with Jill?"

"Don't know that she reacted at all. Davida and I were pretty much avoiding each other. Mostly I was avoiding her. I was embarrassed— stuff guys said."

"I can understand that."

"Like I couldn't compete with a carpet muncher, crap like that." Newell frowned. "Jane and I went our separate ways and she went back to Hewitt, until we graduated high school. Then Jane and Davida went off to the UC and Hewitt went to Stanford and I went to community college. We're talking ancient history, pal."

Barnes nodded.

"Willie, the last time I had really anything personal to do with Davida is when I brought her to the senior prom and that's the truth."

"You took Davida to the prom?"

"What a dumb-ass thing to do. Jill has never let me forget it."

"Why'd you do it?"

"Because Davida begged me and I guess I thought I owed her something for the great sex. I'd only been dating Jill for a few months and the girl was a sophomore. I figured she'd have two more chances in her junior and senior year. Also since Davida was a lesbian, I thought Jill wouldn't care." He laughed. "Boy, was I one stupid shit."

"And you haven't done anything sexually with her since she came out?"

"I believe I already answered that."

"Don't get testy, Donnie, I have my reasons for asking. Davida had gonorrhea and it didn't come from her girlfriend, Minette."

There was a long silence.

Newell looked up at the black sky. "Did it come from a guy?"

"I have no idea, Don, but we do know that the bug is passed more easily from boy to girl than from girl to girl."

"Son of a bitch," he whispered. "So she was carrying on with a man."

"Maybe."

"If she would have asked me for a tumble, I don't know what I would have done. She was still a fine-looking woman." His blue eyes focused in on Barnes's face. "Lucky for me, she didn't put me in that bind."

"Where were you the night Davida was murdered? Every minute of the night."

"Home in bed."

"Mind if I test any of these shotguns for ballistic comparison?"

Newell thought long and hard. "What, that rifling stuff? Hell, I couldn't care less but if I agree Jill's gonna wonder why. I don't want to give my wife any reason to suspect me of anything, Willie. Even though I didn't do nothing. You know how it is, sometimes that just don't matter to the missus."

More silence.

"Why don't you see how far your investigation takes you without my guns? If you're still curious, then I'll comply. But I sure as hell won't be happy about it. Who in their right mind would be happy being viewed as a murder suspect?"

20

Lucille Grayson lived in a three-story Victorian, shingle-sided and stately. The curving front porch was set up with wicker furniture, including an old-fashioned swinging love seat. The house had been painted a soft cream and trimmed in a green that blended with the surrounding acreage. Specimen oak, eucalyptus, sycamore and pine dotted the velvet lawn. Flower gardens shouted color, orchards of citrus and peach and plum pumped out fruit well beyond the growing season.

Inland California was flat, hot and dry, but this neighborhood had been bulldozed into hillocks and irrigated nearly a century ago. With Gold Rush optimism and enough trucked-in water, anything could happen.

Barnes and Amanda were almost a half hour early and they secreted themselves under an oak whose boughs hung so low they nearly touched the ground. Sipping the Peet's coffee they'd picked up along the way, they watched visitors arrive and leave.

During the entire drive, Barnes had slept. Now he yawned and blinked himself awake.

Amanda had stayed up just as late, then made the drive back to San Francisco. She'd ended up talking to Larry, then cuddling, then more, and hadn't slept much at all. What a doll her husband was, but she knew eventually fatigue would beat her to the ground. Right now, though she felt amped. "Good morning. So what do you think?"

Barnes said, "About what?"

"About Barry Bonds taking steroids. About your old homeboy Donnie Newell. Still suspicious of him?"

"Haven't ruled him out, but he said we could test his guns and he didn't give off any obvious tells. Honestly, I don't know, Mandy."

"Well, I'm liking Jill Newell. She's always resented Davida, she doesn't trust her husband and she knows how to shoot. If Don and Davida rekindled their passion and Jill found out, she'd be *major* pissed."

"I don't think they were doing the nasty."

She took in her partner's eyes. "Why not?"

"When he told me they weren't, he seemed straight."

"And you believe him, just like that."

"He was upfront about everything, Mandy, not a trace of edge. When I told him about the gonorrhea his reaction was resentful, almost outraged, but not nervous. It was more like: if Davida was going to fuck a guy, it should have been him."

"Ah, vanity, vanity, the male species is thy name."

"I don't think that's the quote, pard. Anyway, he started reminiscing and it sounds like he and Davida had quite a thing going before she came out."

He filled Amanda in.

She said, "All the more reason for wanting to start up again."

"I guess . . . yeah, he was bragging, but it had more of a . . . wistful quality. Like life was better back then. We're talking over twenty years ago. I'm not saying Don's been an angel but if he cheated, I don't see it with Davida. Because I think he would've told me."

"Stud talk, guy to guy."

"It's what we do."

"On the other hand, maybe that was a ploy, big fella," Amanda said. "He confesses to what you already know so he doesn't have to tell you anything new."

"You could be right."

Amanda smiled. "So we've basically reversed positions. I'm liking Jill and possibly Don, and you're not."

"That's what we do, right? The old open-minded waltz."

Moments later, when he'd finished his coffee: "I'd feel a whole lot better if we had some kind of forensics."

"Let's see what happens when we test the Newells' guns. Any reason we didn't take them last night?"

"I told Donnie I'd hold off. He didn't want to give Jill the idea that he might be even a remote suspect."

"When's the right time, Will, after he's dumped the guns?"

"I took down the serial numbers. He's not gonna dump anything."

"One minute you've got a hard-on for him, the next minute you let him off the hook? I don't understand you."

Barnes turned to her. "Right now, even if the Newells are involved, we got shit on the case. If we rule their guns out, we'll have less than shit."

"So we engage in major denial to forestall disappointment? You are not making sense. We need to go back today and get the guns."

"Suit yourself, but my gut says it isn't either of them."

"So who does your gut say it is?"

"So far my gut's only good at eliminating suspects, not catching them."

Amanda regarded her partner—paler than usual and his hands had a slight tremor. "Maybe you should ease off on the all-black, Will."

"It's not the coffee, Mandy, it's being back here. I used to clear brush over there." Pointing. "Couldn't have been more than fourteen, no one ever offered me a drink . . . yeah, I'm a bundle of raw nerve endings. Tom Clancy was right: you can't go home. Furthermore, you shouldn't even if you could."

"That was Thomas Wolfe."

"Thomas Wolfe? The writer in the white suit?"

"That's Tom Wolfe."

Barnes was irritated. "What I'm trying to say is I'll be happy to get the hell out of here."

The interior of the mansion was hot and close and noisy. A horde of well-wishers drank Chardonnay, munched on tea sandwiches and made small talk. Lucille Grayson held court from a camel-back, ruby brocade chair in a simple black dress, black stockings and black ortho-pedic shoes. Her makeup was discreet, her eyes dry as a San Joaquin summer.

When she saw Barnes, she cocked a beckoning finger. He quickly made his way through the crowd. "Again, I'm so sorry, Mrs. Grayson."

Lucille couldn't hear him. She shouted, "Go into the parlor. I'll meet you there in twenty minutes."

Barnes had no idea where the parlor was. He'd never gotten past the front room.

Davida had always met him outdoors. Stealing away was part of the thrill.

The two of them, under the stars, smelling the menthol of eucalyptus, faint overtones of horseshit.

Her hair, the quick uptake of her breath . . .

He sidled through the crowd and searched for the parlor.

This day and age, who had a parlor? Amanda, as stylish as any of Lucille's friends, saw him and made her way over.

"She wants to meet us in the parlor, wherever that is."

"House like this it would be off the side with a porch view."

She pointed and he followed, once again groping through the mob until he felt a hard tap on his shoulder.

He looked back, faced Jane Meyerhoff's steely eyes.

She yelled, "Something I can help you with?"

"Where's the parlor?"

"Why?"

"Meeting Lucille there."

Jane pointed exactly where Amanda had. Grabbing Barnes's hand, she accompanied the two detectives to a carved door, then stepped forward and flung it open.

The room was musty, high-ceilinged, draped in heavy red velvet fringed with gold. Nail-head chairs and tufted ottomans were arranged in formal seatings. A mirror-backed walnut bar was stocked with bottles and crystal stemware.

To Barnes's eye, it resembled a Spaghetti Western whorehouse. He wondered if Davida had brought any boys here.

Jane closed the door behind her and looked Amanda over. Both of them in black suits, svelte, groomed like champs. Like a photo from a charity luncheon.

"Jane Meyerhoff." She proffered a hand. "I don't believe we've met."

"Amanda Isis."

"Would you like a drink?"

"Water."

Jane's eyes drifted to Barnes.

"I drink whatever you're pouring."

"Well," said Jane, inspecting the bottles, "Lucille has Glenlivet, Glenfiddich, Glenmorangie . . . aren't you a bourbon man?"

"At times."

"The second row is Wild Turkey, Knob Creek—"

"Jane, anything's fine. And just a finger's worth. We're paying our respects but we're also working."

"Working with Lucille?"

"Wherever it takes. Thanks for directing us."

"Not a problem." Jane poured the drinks, allowed herself two fingers of vodka. "Lucille asked me to handle things today. You know, help marshal the great unwashed." Tilting her head toward the door. Waves of chatter leaked through the wood. "I didn't speak. It might've provoked Minette."

"Not the time or the place," Amanda said.

"Precisely."

Barnes said, "You and Minette don't get along?"

Jane took a long swallow of vodka. "No one gets along with Minette. If you'll excuse me, I should see how Lucille's doing." She hurried out.

Amanda said, "Sensitive topic, Minette."

Before Barnes could answer, the door opened and Lucille entered, holding a cane and clutching Jane's arm.

Barnes pulled out a chair and Jane eased the old woman into it.

"Something to drink, Lucille?"

"Johnny Walker, rocks. Red or black, at this point I'm not tasting anything."

As Jane poured: "Make it a double, dear."

"Thanks so much for agreeing to see us, Mrs. Grayson," Amanda said.

Lucille gripped the handle of her walking stick. Carved ivory—a woman's bust. "Perhaps I should thank you. It's a good excuse to get the hell out of there."

Jane handed her the drink and Lucille polished it off with astonishing speed. "Ah, that's good. Take over for me, Janey. Someone has to hold down the fort."

Jane said, "You're sure you don't need me here?"

Lucille waved a dismissive hand. "Go on out there and make sure no one steals the silver."

Jane sighed heavily and left.

Lucille looked at Barnes. "I'm assuming, Willie, that you and your pretty partner wish to talk to me without her hanging around."

"You read my mind, Mrs. Grayson."

"Your mind is not that tough to decipher."

Barnes smiled. "You cut me to the quick, Mrs. Grayson."

"I'm good at that." Lucille's eyes misted. "Davida was good at it also, though she was patient with me. I'm sure I was a giant pain in the posterior."

"I'm sure you weren't—"

Lucille patted his hand. "You didn't know her very well, did you, Willie?"

Barnes kept a straight face. "She was younger than me. In Jack's class."

"Jack knew everyone . . . and everyone's business."

"True enough."

"How long has it been since he passed away?"

"Ten years."

"Really? I can scarcely believe how quickly the time passes."

"It does indeed, Mrs. Grayson."

"You can only imagine how rushed life has become for an old lady like myself. I recall all of them as youngsters. Glynnis, Jack . . . and now Davida. Life has dealt me bins of shit, but I refuse to die." She waved her glass. "Thank God for alcohol. Get me another, Willie."

Barnes complied. Lucille faced Amanda. "I'm not being very polite, am I? Going on about old times with which you're not familiar." She looked around absently, as if studying the overstuffed room for the first time. "I'll need to get back to the barbarians shortly. What is it that you want to ask me?"

Barnes rubbed his hands together. "This might get a little prickly . . ."

Lucille sat and drank and waited, impassive.

"Do you know if Davida was having an affair?"

Lucille's eyes whipped away from Barnes's face and settled on the fireplace. She took another sip of whiskey. "I don't like Minette, never did, and Davida was well aware of that fact. If my daughter had someone else, she wouldn't have told me because I would have nagged her to dump Minette once and for all."

"Let me rephrase the question," Amanda said. "If Davida had someone else, who might it have been?"

The old lady shrugged.

Amanda said, "Is it possible that it could have been a man?"

Lucille didn't answer right away. "No, I don't think so. Davida got a lot of mileage out of being a lesbian."

"All the more reason to keep an affair with a man hidden."

"A man . . ." As if considering an exotic species. "No . . ." Lucille shook her head. "I knew my daughter better than one might think. She wasn't interested in men." Another sip of whiskey. She stared at Amanda. A smile spread slowly. "As the saying goes, it takes one to know one."

Barnes almost choked on his drink although Lucille's admission shouldn't have come as a shock. It was well-known around town that she'd treated her husband coldly, had had no use for men since the divorce. He thought that resulted from a bad marriage, but maybe he'd mixed up cause and effect.

"One of the reasons I didn't like Minette," Lucille said, "is that she wasn't *real*. Just a shallow, stupid girl using my daughter as a meal ticket. Now it's out in the open . . . what that little bitch was doing all those nights my daughter was working."

Barnes rubbed his chin. "I think Davida was doing more than working, Mrs. Grayson. Davida had gonorrhea but Minette is clean. There was someone else in your daughter's life."

Lucille took a deep breath and let it out. "I see."

"That's why I asked if there was a man in her life," said Amanda. "The disease is passed easier from male to female than from female to female."

"Aha . . ." Lucille nodded. "I see your logic, but I still know my daughter. If she got the disease, it was from a woman, most probably a woman who sleeps around with men."

"Any candidates?" Barnes asked her.

Lucille smiled. "You're wondering about Jane."

"Jane moved back to Berkeley. She and Davida reignited their friendship."

"That silly boat ride. Why anyone would subject themselves to bumping and . . ." Lucille checked herself. Finished her second drink. "Could Davida and Jane have had a *thing*? Oh, yes, definitely."

Sitting back and enjoying the look on the detectives' faces.

Amanda said, "Definitely."

"I know it for a fact, dear. Not that either one would tell me. But I'm able to recognize love when I see it. Davida always loved Jane. It just took Jane twenty years and all those ridiculous marriages to decide she loved Davida."

21

Excusing herself, Lucille left them alone in the parlor. Barnes steadied his hand with more bourbon.

Amanda drank water and said, "Well that was earth-shattering."

"Jane and Davida. Just like the old days. I told Jane about the gonorrhea when we met up a couple of nights ago. She was pretty casual about it, suggested Davida had gotten it from Minette. Now I'm thinking she was out to make a point: this has nothing to do with me."

"Maybe a diversion, but maybe also the truth, Will. No matter what Mother says, Davida could've been flinging with a Y chromosome."

"We've gone over all of her e-mails for the last three months—personal and business—haven't found anything hinting at a secret male lover."

"Nor have we found anything linking Jane to Davida."

Barnes conceded the point. "Maybe Jane's still in denial about her own sexuality."

"Or Lucille has it all wrong."

"It's not just Lucille, it was Alice Kurtag, too."

Amanda's turn to concede. "Jane wanted the relationship but wasn't ready to come out."

"Mandy, what if Jane was all thrilled about hooking up with Davida and Davida wanted to go public? Jane wasn't ready for that. She goes to Davida's office to beg her to hold off on any announcements, but Davida refuses."

"She visits with a shotgun in hand?"

"So they drank together and had an argument. Jane left and re-turned to do the deed. Donnie Newell told me that Jane freaked out big-time after they did a threesome. If Davida threatened to out her, she could've freaked out again."

"Maybe Newell was taking the heat off himself and directing you elsewhere. And we know he owns shotguns."

Barnes gathered his thoughts. "Okay. You win. I'll go back and round up Newell's guns."

Amanda applauded silently.

Barnes said, "That doesn't mean that Jane is off the hook."

"All this time, you've been saying the crime had a masculine qual-ity to it. Then we get a decent male suspect and/or his eagle-eye shootin' wife and you switch to Jane Meyerhoff. Does Jane even know how to shoot?"

"Never saw her actually do it but she grew up on a ranch—okay, enough of this, I've been blabbing so much I might as well run for city council. We'll get the guns and we'll talk to Jane, see if we can't get her to admit to the affair."

"How do we crack her?"

"Lucille figured it out, it's useless denying it."

"Lucille's a lesbian with a lesbian daughter. She could be accused of overactive gaydar. Jane denies it, it's her word against Mother's."

"Then we lie, tell Jane that *Davida* told Lucille about their affair in no uncertain terms, and Lucille told us. Then we sit back, no judging, and watch how she reacts."

"Ah, the suspense," said Amanda. "I love my job."

Lucille's visitors had thinned, but the mansion still buzzed with late-comers. After mingling for a few minutes, Amanda and Barnes found Jane in the kitchen, placing cucumber, cress and egg salad finger sand-wiches on a silver tray. She looked up and resumed her work.

Barnes said, "We need to talk some more."

"About what?" Forced lightness in her voice.

Barnes placed a hand on her arm. Immediately, Jane's eyes watered. Barnes whispered, "Lucille told us."

Tears etched a meandering trail through Jane's foundation. "Told you what." No question mark in her inflection.

"About you and Davida."

Jane stared at the refrigerator.

Barnes said, "She told us."

"What does an old woman know?"

"Davida told her everything."

"I don't believe that."

"Lucille wants to make it public."

Jane's face infused with color. More than a blush—the deep hue that comes from a hard slap. "But why would she want . . ." She shook her head. "Can't we discuss this later?"

"I'm afraid not," Amanda said.

Barnes said, "The only way we're going to get your side of it is if you tell us."

Jane wiped her hands on a napkin and picked up the tray. Amanda took it from her and placed it out of reach. The gesture—being deprived of her task—made Jane sag.

"My side of it." Sick smile.

Barnes said, "How long have you been involved with Davida?"

"Please, Will." Jane's eyes were pleading. "Can't you just let things be? My *mother* is here. She *doesn't* know and I really don't see the point of her finding out now that Davida's gone."

"I'm not talking to your mother, Janey, I'm talking to you. How long have you been involved with Davida?"

Jane's eyes skittered between Amanda and Barnes, then trailed back to the fridge. Amanda followed her gaze. Nothing to see on the old Sub-Zero. No cutesy, kitschy magnets, no personal touches. The kitchen was as sterile as an operating room.

Jane said, "Since I filed for my divorce." Her shoulders lowered another inch. "Parker went crazy, started doping more heavily, became an absolute psychotic *shit*! I called Davida for support because . . . I don't know why . . . she'd always been there when I was down . . . before all those men, and she did it again, became my main source of support. Because *Mother* had zero tolerance for my complaints against Parker, sometimes I think she preferred Parker to me—never arguing with her, dressing right. Then he goes and turns into such a *shit*! But it's my fault, spoiled Janey whining about another man gone bad. Parker played it. Horrible to me but courtly to her. Mother is not only a gossip, she is also the most superficial person I know. Makes Minette look like Gandhi—if Davida hadn't been there for me, I would have had a total breakdown!"

She stopped talking abruptly, gasped for breath. Cried and didn't bother to wipe her face.

Amanda got a napkin and did it.

Jane didn't seem to notice the kindness.

Amanda said, "Were you two planning a future together?"

"We weren't planning anything! Nothing was planned, it just happened! Even after we continued to see each other I told Davida I wasn't sure. Davida certainly didn't push me. She was a busy woman. She had things other than sex on her mind."

"You know about the gonorrhea. I assume you've been tested."

Jane looked down at her feet. "I am currently on medication. Apparently, I was asymptomatic."

"Do you know who gave it to you?"

She laughed bitterly. "That could be a bit of a list . . . including my ex. Among his many other transgressions, the man got around. Of course, Mother doesn't know anything about that. She thinks the divorce was another one of my quote unquote impulsive follies!"

Barnes said, "Janey, did Parker know that you and Davida were intimate?"

"I don't see how he could've. I haven't spoken to the asshole in over seven months."

Amanda said, "How do you think he'd react if he found out that you not only left him, but you took up with a woman?"

"How would he find out?"

"Lucille knew," Barnes said. "Alice Kurtag also suspected there was something between you two. Even Minette wondered about the two of you being more than friends."

"Word gets around, Jane," Amanda said. "So please answer the question. How would Parker react if he thought that you left him for Davida?"

Jane licked her lips. "When he's threatened, Parker can be an extremely violent man. Over the past seven months, I've heard his drug use has gotten out of hand."

"What does he take?"

"Weed, coke, pills." Bitter smile. "An eclectic man."

"Does he know how to shoot a shotgun?" Barnes asked.

Jane blanched. "Parker loved to hunt. Loved guns—I never let him keep any of them in the house. He was too unpredictable."

"Where'd he keep them?"

"In storage. I couldn't tell you where."

Amanda said, "Where can we find Parker?"

Jane licked her lips again. "We owned a cabin near the river, about an hour from here. As part of the divorce settlement, I agreed to let him buy me out at a bargain price. Even with that, he hasn't paid me. Lord only knows where he'll get the money. Among Parker's other wonderful traits is a congenital inability to keep a job."

"The deed's still in your name?"

"It is until he comes up with the cash."

"So the cabin is yours but he lives there?"

"He might," said Jane. "For all I know he's in Timbuktu. I always hated the place. Dirty, lousy plumbing—roughing it was his idea." Her eyes softened. "When Davida and I were on the river, roughing it seemed fine—"

Amanda broke in: "Do we have your permission to enter the property, including the interior of the cabin?"

"Sure, why not—" She gasped. "You really think he—oh, God, oh, God." Rising to her feet, hands fisted. "Go. If it was him, go and *kill* him. I'll draw you a *map*."

Barnes floored his Honda. The car balked, tried to tackle the grade, kicked back, finally slipped into gear and chugged along.

Blackness all around. Amanda rechecked her gun and wondered if the backup they'd called would get there. Rural sheriff, claiming to be understaffed. He hadn't sounded too impressed to begin with and "Berkeley" had caused him to grow silent.

That's unincorporated land, not really our jurisdiction.

Whose is it?

Good question. I'll see what I can do.

The tiny car continued to labor up the mountain road. Why did a big man like Will drive such dinky wheels?

Up here in the boonies, small things like insufficient acceleration mattered. Jane's scrawled map was helpful to a point, then everything started to look the same and landmarks vanished in the darkness. The GPS Amanda had attached to her handheld computer had been rendered useless ten miles back, reception blocked by massive oaks and giant redwoods.

"What's wrong?" said Will.

"With what?"

"You're fidgeting. Like you do when you have serious doubts."

"If we really suspect this joker of blowing off Davida's head, we could be making a big mistake by going in alone."

"Davida was sleeping. We're wide awake."

"Mr. Macho."

"Hey," he said, "it's a social call. We'll ring the guy's doorbell and act nice and polite."

"It's almost ten PM and we didn't clear it with Torres."

"We tried. Is it our fault he's at a fund-raiser?" Shaking his head. "Community gardens, there's a law-enforcement issue for you."

Amanda went silent.

Five miles later, Barnes said, "You know, maybe it's a good idea for you to wait in the car, especially if Parker doesn't cotton to women."

"I should just sit by and watch as Parker plugs you in the gut?"

"If you hear rat-a-tat put the pedal to the metal and get the hell out of here. You've got someone to go home to."

"Not funny, Will."

Barnes smiled. Wondering if he'd really been aiming for humor.

He slowed to five per, had Amanda shine a flashlight on Jane's map, drove another ten miles and forked left. "Nothing is going to happen to me or to you. We're just paying the guy a visit, that's all."

Amanda shook her head. "Just make sure your gun is drawn."

They came to a dirt lane marked by a small wooden sign, nearly overtaken by vines and suckers.

RISING GLEN NO TRESPASSING.

A chain-link gate sagged on its hinges. Barnes got out. No lock, the clasp wasn't even set in place. Swinging the gate inward, he got back in the car and coasted down on a rutted dirt lane.

Amanda said, "It's so dark I can barely see my hands."

Barnes stopped, had another look at the map, clicked off the flashlight. "When we come to a pond, it's fifty yards to the right."

Moments later, Amanda spotted a pinpoint of light.

A sliver of moon breaking on water. She pointed. "Over there."

Off in the distance, another dot of illumination. Amber, like the lit end of a cigarette.

They watched for a while. The dot never moved.

Barnes said, "Probably a porch light." He aimed the Honda at it, driving carefully along the curving surfaces of the pond bank.

A small structure came into view. More of a lean-to than a cabin, fashioned of rough planks and topped with tar paper. Low-wattage porchlight, no illumination through any of the windows.

Parked to the side was a Chevy Blazer, long unwashed, tires so underinflated they were perilously close to flat.

Barnes said, "Guy treats his wheels like that, he's not taking care of himself."

Amanda said, "I'm sure he'll love getting woken up."

Barnes killed the headlights, switched off the engine. The two of them got out of the car, just stood there. Something small and frightened scurried into the brush. An owl hooted. A burble sounded from the pond.

The air smelled pure, herbally sweet.

Amanda said, "Is that the theme from *Deliverance* I hear wafting through the piney woods?"

Both detectives checked their weapons and headed for the cabin.

Barnes whispered, "You hear anything, save yourself and the young'uns and take the wagon back to Laramie."

Amanda said, "Let's get this damn thing over with."

"You bet," said Barnes, figuring he sounded pretty mellow. The gun in his hand was so cold that he wondered about frostbite.

Halfway to the cabin's front door, the detectives agreed that Barnes would do the talking and Amanda would be on the watch for any weird behavior on Parker Seldey's part.

A second after they'd reached that accord, two booms exploded into the night and the sweet air turned sulfurous.

Barnes hit the ground and reached out to push Amanda out of the firing line. She did the same for him and their fingers touched momentarily.

Then both of them stretched on their bellies and two-handed their guns.

A hoarse voice screamed, "Get the hell off my property!"

Barnes screamed back: "Police. We just want to talk to you, Mr. Seldey."

"I don't want to talk to you!"

A flash from the doorway was followed by another concussive burst. Something whizzed by Barnes's right ear. Sighting a stand of small oaks, he crept and slithered for cover, while motioning for Amanda to do the same.

Not knowing if she could see him.

Hearing her I-told-you-so. Minus the usual good-natured inflection.

She did have someone to go home to . . . he made it to the trees.

Amanda had gotten there first.

Both of them holding their breath as Parker Seldey stepped into the porch light. Rifle in one hand, flashlight in the other.

Seldey swept the earth with the electric torch.

Amanda whispered, "Don't move, pard." Without warning, she crouched, straightened a bit, kept her body low, and ran toward the car.

Seldey shouted something incoherent and aimed the rifle at her back. Barnes fired first. Seldey pivoted toward the source, shot three times, missed Barnes by inches.

Barnes scooted back, struggling for silence. Seldey advanced on him, sweeping with the flashlight, muttering, breathing hard.

When he was twenty feet away, Barnes began to make out details, limned by sparse moonlight. Baggy T-shirt, shorts, bony knees. A thatch of hair, the woolly outlines of an untrimmed beard.

Seldey got closer. Barnes smelled him—the hormonal reek of fury and fear.

Seldey swept the ground. The beam must've caught a glimpse of something because Seldey hoisted the rifle and aimed—

Noise to his back made him pivot. A car engine racing.

Seldey aimed at that—was knocked backward by white light.

Amanda flashing the high beams, blinding Seldey.

The startled man fired into the sky.

Barnes was on him, wresting the gun away, pounding Seldey's face.

No resistance from Seldey and Barnes rolled him over, put his knee on Seldey's back. Was ready to cuff him but Amanda did it first.

Everyone panting.

They rolled Seldey over and had a look at him. Mountain-man hair almost obscured patrician features. Sharp brown eyes. Maybe not sharp. Inflamed.

Seldey said, "Why're you here? There's no full moon, they only come with the full moon."

"Who's they?" said Amanda. Squeezing the words out between gasps.

"My friends. The forest people." Seldey laughed. "Just kidding. Do you guys have any weed?" Rattling the cuffs. "And maybe you should take this shit off. If you do, I can put you out of your misery."

22

Within an hour, dozens of enforcement officials had collected outside the cabin. Parker Seldey was taken away and the structure was taped off.

By the early-morning hours, an arsenal had been removed, including three shotguns. Seldey was living like a savage in the insect-infested cabin, with no outdoor plumbing and food rotting in tins. No phone or computer but Seldey had brought a ham radio and a battery-op VCR. A CS unit from Sacramento scoured his meager belongings. Don Newell showed up at three AM but didn't do much other than stand around.

Barnes and Amanda borrowed a sheriff's phone that worked and told the story to Captain Torres. Being woken up didn't endear them to the boss and Torres wasn't mollified by Amanda's assurance that they'd had consent from the legal owner to enter the property.

Blood spatter on Parker Seldey's jeans and shirt calmed him down a bit.

"But I'm reserving judgment until you get real evidence."

That happened two days later—a rush DNA matched the blood to Davida and word had it Seldey's attorney would be going for a plea, some sort of mental health explanation.

Barnes gave Laura Novacente the exclusive. In return, she invited him to her place for an "intimate dinner." Being a gentleman, Barnes let her down easy.

Laura showed class. *Call if it doesn't work out, Will.*

Of course, I will.

The citizens of Berkeley were pleased with the arrest of Parker Seldey for the murder of Davida Grayson. Seldey being a registered Republican turned satisfaction to glee and someone talked about silk-screening a T-shirt capitalizing on that fact. Final message yet to be decided.

Everyone settling down.

Except Amanda Isis.

Early Friday morning found Barnes and Amanda at their favorite corner table at Melanie's. He was on his second double espresso and his third muffin. She sipped foam off of her cappuccino and picked at her croissant.

Barnes was in a great mood, looking forward to a second weekend with Marge Dunn. He'd volunteered to fly to LA but Marge asked if she could come back up north.

Smart woman; nothing was as beautiful as the Bay Area on a crisp, cool day. Barnes figured to ask Amanda for more social advice, because the weekend in Napa had turned out perfect. He'd arrived with several ideas to run by her, but she was quiet—almost sullen.

"What's wrong?" Barnes asked.

"Nothing."

"Don't give me that. You didn't like the wine I sent you or something?"

"You didn't have to send me wine, Will. I was just doing my job."

"Your job was saving my life. The guy at the liquor store told me it was good stuff."

"It was and I thank you."

"So what's bugging you, Mandy? And be honest. I'm not good at this shrink stuff."

"Speaking of shrinks, I just talked to the psychiatrist who's taking care of Seldey," she said. "She says the guy's clearly psychotic."

"I don't need a shrink to tell me that."

"He's actively paranoid, Will, as in unable to form a coherent plan of action. Yesterday he had to be straitjacketed because he scratched himself raw. He claimed that voices were telling him to repent by skinning himself like they did to Jesus in that Mel Gibson movie."

"So he's faking it, trying for reduced culpability."

"He's not trying to get out of anything. Just the opposite, he keeps ranting about shooting Davida, saying he's proud of it."

"All that's the DA's problem."

"Maybe it's our problem, Will. As in getting the entire picture. You see a guy that disordered planning a careful murder all by his lonesome? He says *voices* told him to kill Davida. What I'm wondering is, was one of them real?"

"Someone coached him?"

"Davida may have welcomed the homeless but given all Jane told Davida about Parker, you see Davida letting him in at two AM? His having a key would change the equation. What if someone pointed him in the right direction and said 'Go boom'? Someone who knew him, realized he was crazy. Someone who had power over him. And might have a key. And knew she was drinking because she drank with her."

"Jane?"

"Who else?" Amanda said.

"Why would Parker obey her? They hated each other."

"That's according to Jane. What do you remember about him?"

"Not much, he wasn't a local. I think he grew up in Hillsborough or some other high-priced spread. Maybe went to Stanford."

"Will, I've been asking around discreetly. No one from the good old days knows him, and he didn't grow up in NoCal, he's from Massachusetts."

"So?"

"My point is that everything we know about him has been filtered through Jane. Jane told us she expected Parker to pay off the cabin. But if he was that compromised mentally, how could that happen? Maybe she let him stay because he was useful to her. She kept him on the side because she knew she was going to use him to murder Davida."

"If Parker was crazy, why would Jane rely upon him? Hell, why would she marry him in the first place?"

"Maybe his pathology was under control—medicated officially or otherwise. Maybe being married to Jane helped him maintain. When she petitioned for divorce—and the paperwork says she initiated—he broke down. As to how she'd rely on him, she knew him well enough—understood which buttons to push."

"Sounds like a movie," said Barnes. "You're stretching. Why?"

"It just doesn't sit right with me. The guy's too crazy to do it all by his lonesome."

"What's Jane's motive?"

"Davida was going to dump her and it pissed her off. Or Davida was about to *out* her and she couldn't handle it. You saw how squeamish she was when we talked to her at Lucille's. What better way to get rid of Davida than to sic poor psychotic Parker on her, telling Parker that it was all Davida's fault that they broke up in the first place? Davida dies, Parker's locked up. Talk about killing two birds."

"Inventive," said Barnes. "You thinking of quitting and writing screenplays?"

"Granted, I can't prove any of it, and maybe it'll turn out to be fantasy. You want me to check it out alone, or with you?"

"That's my choice?"

"You bet, pard."

Barnes pinged a spoon against his demitasse. "If Parker's *that* disturbed, maybe he's got some prior hospitalizations that will tell us more about how his head works. Why don't you check that out?"

"And you'll talk to Jane."

"I was thinking I'd look into Jane and Parker's financials, see if she was supporting him and for how long. You want us to do everything together, fine, no more cowboy."

Amanda laughed. "No, I was just asking. Let's divide it up. You can even wear that string tie."

23

It took the detectives several days to get a reluctant go-ahead from Captain Torres. With the evidence presented and corroborated, the boss had no choice but he told them to be "tactful." Whatever that meant.

Giving the order to both of them but looking straight at Barnes. Amanda had covered him, claiming the hotdog to Seldey's cabin was a joint decision, but Torres was no fool.

He kept his mouth shut and said, "Yes, sir." Saluted behind Torres's back as the captain hurried off to a meeting.

The Woman's Association was doing a brisk lu   , tables of genteel ladies exercising their jaw muscles on gossip   he tri-tip special. Barnes felt stiff in a jacket and tie, but Amanda glided through the dining room in a navy suit with matching pumps.

The table they were looking for was in the corner. Six septuagenarian females chattering and wielding silverware with finishing-school precision. Five of them focusing their attention on a black-haired dowager in a black knit suit and pearl earrings. A thin old woman, bordering on emaciation, with shoe-polish hair drawn back in a bun. Her blue eyes flashed with excitement as she spoke.

Eunice Meyerhoff enjoyed holding court.

When Barnes and Amanda reached her table, she looked up. Blinked. Smiled.

"Good afternoon, Detectives, what are you doing here?"

Barnes said, "Hi, ladies, how's everything?"

The women clucked pleasantries in unison. Eunice said, "We're just about done with our meal. Would you like to join us for dessert?"

Amanda said, "Actually, Mrs. Meyerhoff, we need to speak to you in private. Just for a second."

Eunice's companions stared at her. She bristled. Beamed. "Why, of course."

Barnes took her by the elbow. As they crossed the dining room, Eunice waved to other diners. When they got past the tables, her jaw tightened around her smile. "What is this about, Detective Barnes?"

"We need your help," said Amanda.

"And how long will it take? Today is Boston cream pie, which I adore. The kitchen generally runs out if one hesitates too long."

"Maybe the ladies should order dessert without you," Barnes told her.

Eunice stiffened in his grasp. Skinny but tough, like an old wild turkey, annealed by challenge.

Out in the lobby, Eunice said, "Where shall we chat?"

Amanda said, "Let's use your room. Nice and private."

"I don't—well, if you insist." A frail smile. "I suppose . . ." She patted Barnes's arm. "So muscular, William. You were always a good worker."

The elevator ride was silent. Eunice fished out her key and opened the door to a surprisingly shabby little room papered in a lilac print. The carpet was worn, the drapery was gray and dusty and the place emitted a nursing-home smell. Leaded-glass windows let in some natural light but the day was overcast. Nearly all the space was taken up by a queen bed, a simple wood chair, a chipped nightstand that held a clock radio and an old Bakelite dial phone, and a folding suitcase rack.

Ancient Vuitton valise on the rack.

Eunice sat down on the chair. Slumping, as if making the most of her advanced age. But there was something sharp and distrusting in those eyes.

Barnes said, "I have a few questions for you, Mrs. Meyerhoff. It has to do with some of your bank transactions."

Those sharp eyes narrowed. "Well, I don't think my finances are any of your business."

"I'm sorry for the intrusion, but we had to obtain certain facts."

"What facts?" Her tone had hardened.

"Generally, your spending is quite light," Amanda said. "That's why we were surprised by two recent withdrawals that were substantial."

"Two cashier's checks," Barnes added. "Ten thousand dollars each, over the last forty-five days."

"So?" said Eunice. "Last time I checked the federal government was still allowing me to spend my own money."

"We know who cashed them," said Amanda.

The old woman grew silent. One red-nailed hand scratched the other.

"Parker Seldey," Barnes said. "That's quite a lot of money to give an ex-son-in-law."

"We don't like him much," Amanda said. "He tried to shoot us. We're curious why you like him."

"You were trespassing!" Eunice blurted.

"No, ma'am," Barnes said, "Jane gave us permission to enter the premises and Jane owns the premises."

"Parker didn't know that."

A pause.

Barnes said, "That's our point. You seem quite fond of Parker."

Eunice's mouth screwed up. "Whatever issues Jane has with him, he's always been a gentleman with me. What's wrong with that?"

"Nothing's wrong with it," Barnes said, "though I'm sure it's hurtful to your daughter."

Eunice grunted. "As if she cares what's hurtful and what's not."

"She's been hurtful to you?" Amanda asked.

"I can't remember a time she *hasn't* been hurtful! Always taking up with bums or drug addicts—using drugs herself, the stories I could tell you. Do you think that's a daughter who cares about her mother's feelings?"

"I'd say no," Amanda said.

"Darn right, no!"

"Still," said Barnes, "your being so close to Parker isn't exactly sitting right with Lucille Grayson."

"Am I supposed to care about that witch?" Eunice's eyes spat fury. "Always bragging, bragging, bragging about her perverted daughter. I think I've had quite *enough* of Lucille Grayson, yes I have. I don't give a hoot about her or her lesbian daughter and I don't give *two* hoots what she thinks about me."

"Is that why you're paying for Parker Seldey's defense?" Barnes said, risking a guess.

When Eunice didn't answer, he thought: Yes! Sherlock lives!

Amanda read his mind, ran with it. "Your hiring Parker's lawyer really puzzles Lucille Grayson."

The old woman folded her arms across her chest. "I told you I don't care about that biddy."

"Your personal relationship with Lucille is none of our business," Amanda said.

"Darn right!" Eunice said.

"However," said Barnes, "Davida Grayson's murder is our business. Parker confessed to killing her, so we know who actually pulled the trigger. We also know someone paid him to do it."

"Those cashier's checks of yours, Mrs. Meyerhoff. We know exactly what they were for because Parker told us. And it looks pretty incriminating. The first one was issued awhile before Davida was murdered, but the second was issued and cashed the day after her death."

"Payment for a job well done?" said Barnes.

Eunice chewed her lip. Scarlet lipstick smudged the meager flesh.

Amanda said, "What did you tell him, Mrs. Meyerhoff? That Davida was responsible for Jane leaving him?"

"She *was* responsible!" Eunice snapped. "If it hadn't been for that pervert, Janey wouldn't be doing sick things."

"What kind of sick things?" Barnes asked.

"I'm a lady!" Eunice retorted. "I don't talk about things like that!"

"So you do blame Davida for Jane's behavior."

"You bet your backside I blame Davida. She's always been responsible for Janey straying—back to grade school."

"It wasn't Davida who's been married three times," Barnes pointed out.

"Of course not. Why would she marry? She was a pervert! And Lucille defending her all the time. Enjoying it—if you ask me she's that way, too." Eunice punched a palm with her fist. Not much sound. Small bones.

She said, "After that biddy told me what Janey and her daughter were doing, I had to do something! No decent mother would do any less."

"So you talked to Parker about it," Amanda said.

"He was just as frustrated with Janey as I was."

"I see," Barnes said. "You know, Mrs. Meyerhoff, I think at this point, we need to inform you of your rights."

"My rights?" She stared at him. "Is it your intention to arrest me?"

"Oh, yes." Barnes stated the Miranda rights and asked her if she understood them.

"Of course I understand them! I'm old but I'm not senile."

"You don't have to talk to us," Barnes said, "but if you want to tell us your side of the story, now's the time."

"We might be able to help you if we knew your side," Amanda said. "But like Detective Barnes said, you don't have to talk to us."

"I know that!" Eunice squeaked. "I have nothing to hide. I'm proud of what I did. I defended my daughter. I prevented her from further debasing herself with that pervert!"

"Why don't you start at the beginning?" Amanda said.

Barnes said, "The more we know, the more we can help you."

"There's nothing to tell," Eunice said. "I told Parker what needed to be done and he agreed. I told him I'd give him money to pay off Janey for his cabin, but I don't think he even cared about that. He was as furious at Davida as I was. I knew that Davida was a horrid alcoholic—God only knows how much she and Janey used to pack away in high school. I also knew that Janey had a key to her office. I took it one day and I made a copy. I told Parker to wait until the time was right."

"Meaning?"

"When that pervert got herself so damn drunk, she'd fall asleep."

"How would you know that?" Amanda asked.

"Because I had Parker install a hidden video camera."

Barnes felt himself go hot. CSI had torn through the office. A lunatic plants a bug and no one finds it. "Where'd he install it?"

"Exactly where I instructed him to, in the light fixture above her desk," Eunice said. "You know you can get tiny, tiny cameras no bigger than a nail head? I learned that from a movie and found the equipment online. She giggled. "Of my friends, I'm the only one online. One must change with the times."

Amanda said, "So you knew when Davida was asleep because of the secret video camera. Where was the monitor?"

"I used to carry it with me, teeny little thing, sometimes the reception was fuzzy but as long as I was here in the city it worked fine. I don't have it anymore. I have no use for it now that the pervert is gone."

"So what happened when you found Davida asleep?"

"I think that's obvious," Eunice said.

"Tell us anyway. Better in your words than someone else's."

A sigh. "I happened to be in town, as Davida supped with Lucille. I knew Davida drank alone, at night, figured dinner with that biddy mother of hers would drive her to drink *that* night. I contacted Parker through his shortwave radio. It took about two hours for him to get down here and by that time, Davida had passed out."

"Who had the key?"

"I did. I sneaked out of the club . . . those old guards . . . not worth a plugged nickel. I met him outside and we drove to the office." Eunice smiled. "I kept guard while he did what he needed to do."

A liver-spotted hand flew to one ear. "I heard the blast, it sounded pretty darn loud to me but no one seemed to notice. Parker emerged. He wore a long coat that concealed the gun and looked just like one of those homeless bums you people coddle. He escorted me back to the club. The guard was sleeping." She chuckled. "Not that it mattered. Who'd want to break in and harm a few old ladies?"

Eunice stood and offered fragile wrists. "If you get pleasure arresting an old lady, indulge yourselves. I have heart problems and recurrent breast cancer. I am proud that I helped rid the world of that witch. That is my legacy to my daughter. Go ahead, Detective, cuff me."

Barnes complied. More symbolic than precautionary. The bracelets were too big for her.

As they left the room, he took her elbow again.

"Ah, a gentleman! I've always appreciated a courtly man." She smiled at Barnes, but he didn't smile back. She let go with a big sigh. "Well, if you're going to be *that* way about it, I suppose I *should* call my lawyer!" She turned to Amanda. "My cell phone's in my purse. His name is Leo Matteras and he's in the directory. Could you dial it for me, honey? Even if my hands weren't tied up, I'd have some problems. Old alluring eyes just aren't what they used to be."

24

Barnes and Amanda found Jane sitting in a teak chair on the rear deck of her rented house on Oxford Street.

The place was a smallish English cottage, beautifully designed and festooned with iceberg roses. High spot on the street; the Berkeley hills were verdant, the view across the bay picture-perfect.

Jane hadn't bothered to notify the DA she'd moved. Nor had she told them she was planning to travel to Europe. That nugget had come to Barnes by way of an old Sacramento classmate, a woman named Lydia Mantucci, who'd never liked Jane and had forwarded the gossip with glee.

No one answered his knock on the stout, hand-carved door but a walkway on the far side of the house led to a flight of wooden steps that they climbed.

It was late afternoon and cold wind blew across the water. Jane had dressed for a warm-weather fantasy: black, short-sleeved polo shirt, khaki shorts, oversized sunglasses. Her skin was prickled by goose bumps and she hugged herself.

Intentional suffering? Amanda wondered. Jane had lost weight and with no makeup and her hair drawn into a high ponytail, she looked plain and worn.

She wasn't surprised to see them.

"You detected me," she said. "Drink?" Indicating a half-empty bottle of Sapphire gin and an ice bucket.

"No, thanks," said Will. "Nice view."

"When I pay attention it is. I got the place cheap because the previous tenant was denied tenure and left in a snit without giving notice or paying two months' rent."

"Angry professor."

Jane smiled. "Angry assistant professor of ethics."

Amanda said, "When are you leaving for Italy?"

Jane removed her sunglasses. The sclera of her eyes were pink, smudgy pouches had formed under the lower lids, and her eyebrows drooped. "You're worried *I'll* leave in a snit?"

"The DA's office sent us," said Will. "They may need you to testify that you gave us permission to be on the property."

"I already put that in writing for the DA."

Amanda said, "If the defense makes a big deal out of our right to search, in-person testimony will be required."

Jane turned away and stared at gray water and milk-colored sky. "Plus, they're hoping I'll testify against Mother."

"Have they asked you to do that?"

"No, but that was the clear subtext. I even received a little lecture about there being no filial privilege under the law."

Amanda said, "So when are you planning to leave and where exactly are you going?"

Jane said, "That's the linchpin of the defense? You people trespassed?"

Barnes said, "Probably not but we've got to be ready for anything."

"*Probably* not?"

"There's talk Parker will be pleading diminished capacity. And that your mother's lawyer will be delaying to the max."

Jane faced them again. "Matteras? He's probably hoping she'll die first, so he can avoid having to earn his retainer. Fat chance."

"She's healthy?"

"Only the good die prematurely." Jane's hands clenched. "Like Davida. God, I miss her."

She sniffled and poured gin and drank way too much and suppressed a belch. "Don't worry, I'll be there if I'm needed. In the meantime, I have to try something new."

"What's that?" said Barnes.

"Being alone."

"You're sure that'll be good—"

"As sure as I've ever been about anything. Look at me, Will. Pathetic." She touched her chest, let her hand trail down to her abdomen. Her legs were prickled and white. Long, sleek legs, legendary in high school, maybe still her best feature. But for the first time, Barnes noticed encroaching signs of age: spider veins, hints of varicosity, patches of pucker and slack.

He said, "You look great, Jane."

"I look like shit, but thanks for lying. Even though you were never really good at it . . . think about it, Will: have you ever seen me alone for any significant stretch of time?"

Barnes considered that. Jane laughed. Not a pleasant sound. "Exactly. It's an addiction as much as any other."

"What is?"

"Needing people. To hell with Streisand. Fools like me are anything but lucky. I don't know how I ended up this way but I'm sure as hell going to try to find out."

"In Europe," said Amanda.

"Florence, to be specific," said Jane. "I've been there with each of my glorious spouses. Mother took me when I was twelve, fourteen and sixteen. I figured it would be a good place to start. If I don't fall apart, I can work my way up to some meaner places." She laughed. "Maybe I'll tour Beirut."

Amanda said, "Testing yourself."

"It's about time," said Jane. "I'll probably flunk. Lord knows I've failed every other life lesson."

Barnes said, "Jane—"

Jane wagged a finger. "Hush, bad liar. Right now, nothing is sure to churn my stomach more than reassurance."

Amanda said, "Good, because this is a business call, not psychotherapy." Using a voice so cold Barnes had to fight not to stare.

Jane's face went white.

Amanda stepped closer, took the glass from her hand and set it down hard on the table. "If you're serious about growing up, losing the self-pity is a good place to start. Bottom line: you need to cooperate fully. If you don't, you'll be subpoenaed as a material witness and we'll confiscate your passport. We need all your flight information as well as your addresses overseas, so start dictating."

She whipped out her pad.

Jane said, "All I know so far is my flight number and my hotel in Florence."

"Then we'll start with that. You need to know that if the DA's not satisfied with what we bring back, you won't be getting on any planes."

Jane tried to lock eyes with her but Amanda's stone face made her turn away. "My, but you're a tough one."

"More like a busy one," said Amanda. "Let's stop screwing around and get some facts down on paper."

Twenty minutes later, walking back to their car, Barnes said, "Aren't we the stern, unrelenting authority figure."

Amanda got behind the wheel.

As she fooled with her hair and started the engine, he said, "I'm sure there was a reason."

Amanda pulled away from the curb, driving faster than usual. She covered half a block and stopped, keeping her eyes on the street.

"No big riddle," she said. "I felt sorry for her. So I gave her what she needed."

MUSIC CITY BREAKDOWN

A NOVELLA

ACKNOWLEDGMENTS FOR
MUSIC CITY BREAKDOWN

Special thanks to Chief Ronal Serpas, Commander
Andy Garrett, and Sergeant Pat Postiglione of the Metro
Nashville Police Department, and to the
inimitable George Gruhn.

1

A beautifully carved mandolin in a velvet-lined case was stashed in the bedroom closet of Baker Southerby's house.

The instrument, a 1924 Gibson F-5 with just a little pick wear below the treble f-hole, was worth more than Baker's house, a little frame bungalow on Indiana Avenue in the west Nashville neighborhood known as The Nations. The area was solid blue-collar with some rough edges, lots of residents living paycheck to paycheck. The house was the only one Baker Southerby had ever known, but that didn't make it more than it was. The Gibson, rare because it had been a commercial failure, was now a serious six-figure collector's item, a fact Baker's partner liked to obsess on.

"One just sold at Christie's for a hundred and seventy, Lost Boy."

"You follow auctions?"

"I was curious."

When Lamar Van Gundy got like that—usually when the two of them were grabbing a quick meal—Baker kept chewing his burger and pretended that he'd gone deaf. Mostly that worked, but if Lamar was in a mood and persisted, Baker's next retort was as automatic as voice mail: "And your point is?"

"I'm just saying it's a gold mine."

"Pass the ketchup, Stretch. Stop hoarding it in the first place."

Lamar's huge hands stretched across the table. "Here. Drown your grub in the stuff, El Bee. One *seventy,* what does it take to impress you?"

"I'm impressed."

"When's the last time you played the damn thing?"

"Something that pricey no sense risking damage."

"What, you got epilepsy, gonna drop it?"

"You never know, Stretch."

Lamar said, "*You* know and *I* know and *everyone* knows that they sound better when you play 'em. You open up the soundboard a bit, who knows, you could push it to one eighty."

"And your point is?"

Lamar tugged a moustache end. "Someone didn't take his Midol. Why do you hate the damn thing when it's like the most important thing you own?"

Baker shrugged and smiled and tried not to think about a little boy's voice cracking, honky-tonk smoke, loose laughter. Curled on the backseat as the old van bumped over country roads. The greasy way headlights could wash over rural asphalt.

Lamar saw Baker's smile as consistent with his partner's quiet manner and sometimes that would be End of Topic. Three years they'd been working together, but the big man had no clue Baker's show of teeth was forced. For the most part, Lamar could read people real well, but he had his blind spots.

Times when Lamar wouldn't let go, his next comment was so predictable it could be from a script. "You own a treasure and your alarm system sucks."

"I'm well-armed, Stretch."

"Like someone couldn't break in when you're on the job." Deep sigh. "One seventy, oh Lord, that's *serious* money."

"Who knows I own it other than you, Stretch?"

"Don't give me ideas. Hell, George Gruhn could probably unload it for you in like five seconds."

"Is it dropping in value as we speak?"

This time, it was Lamar who was hard of hearing. "I consigned my '62 Precision with George last year. Got twenty times what I paid for it, bought a three-year-old Hamer that sounds just as cool and I can take it to gigs without worrying about a scratch being tragic. George has the contacts. I had enough left over to buy Sue flowers plus a necklace for our anniversary. The rest we used to pay off a little of the condo."

"Look at you," said Baker, "a regular Warren Buffett." Having enough, he rose to his feet before Lamar had time to reply, went to the men's room and washed his hands and face and checked the lie of his buttondown collar. He ran a sandpaper tongue over the surface of his teeth. Returning to find all the food gone and Lamar tapping a rhythm on the table, he crooked a thumb at the door. "Unless you're planning on eating the plate, Stretch, let's go look at some blood."

The two of them were a Mutt-and-Jeff Murder Squad detective team operating out of the spiffy brick Metro Police Headquarters on James Robertson Parkway. Lamar was six-five, thirty-two, skinny as a shoe-string potato with wispy brown hair and a walrus moustache like an old-time gunslinger. Born in New Haven, but he learned southern ways quickly.

Baker Southerby was two years older, compact and ruddy with skin that always looked razor-burned, bulky muscles with a tendency to go soft, thin lips and a shaved head. Despite Lamar's tendency to digress, he'd never had a better partner.

Nashville homicides had dropped to sixty-three last year, most of them open-and-shuts worked by district detectives. The routine killings tended to be gang shootings, random domestics, and dope dealers cruising into town on the I-40 and getting into trouble.

The three, two-man Murder Squad teams were called out on who-dunits and the occasional high-profile case.

The last new murder Southerby and Van Gundy had worked was a month ago, the shooting of a foulmouthed, substance-abusing Music Row promoter named Darren Chenoweth. Chenoweth had been found slumped in his Mercedes behind the crappy-looking warehouse that served as his Sixteenth Avenue office. An unindicted co-conspirator in the Cashbox payola scandal, his death was a head-scratcher with serious financial overtones, possibly a revenge hit. But it closed four days later as just another domestic gone bad, Mrs. Chenoweth coming in with her lawyer and confessing. A quick plea down to involuntary manslaughter, because fifteen witnesses were willing to testify Darren had been beating the crap out of her regularly. Since then Baker and Lamar had been working cold cases and closing a nice number of the green folders.

Lamar was happily married to a Vanderbilt Med Center pediatric nurse with whom he'd just bought a fifth-floor two-plus-two condo in the Veridian Tower on Church Street. Stretch and Sue used overtime to pay off the mortgage and they treasured their meager free time, so Baker, living alone, volunteered to take all the late-night and early-morning calls. Do wake-up duty in a nice, quiet voice.

He'd been up watching old NFL reruns on ESPN Classic when the phone rang at three twenty AM on a cool April night. Not Dispatch, Brian Fondebernardi calling direct. The squad sergeant's voice was low and even, the way it got when things were serious. Baker heard voices in the background and immediately thought, *Complications.*

"What's up?"

"I disturb your beauty sleep, Baker?"

"Nope. Where's the body?"

"East Bay," said Fondebernardi. "First, below Taylor, in a vacant lot full of trash and other nasty stuff. Almost a river view. But you asked the wrong question, Baker."

"Who's the body?"

"There you go. Jack Jeffries."

Baker didn't answer.

Fondebernardi said, "As in Jeffries, Bolt, and Ziff—"

"I got it."

"Mr. Even Keel," said the sergeant. A Brooklyn native, he worked at a whole different pace, had taken awhile to understand Baker's slo-go style. "Central Detectives buttoned down the scene, M.E. investigator's down there now, but that won't take long. We got a single stab wound in the neck, looks to be right in the carotid. Lots of blood all around so it happened here. Lieutenant's on her way, you don't want to miss the party. Call the midget and get the heck down here."

"Hi, Baker," Sue Van Gundy answered in her throaty, Alabama voice. Too fatigued to be sexy at this hour, but that was the exception and though Baker thought of her as a sister, he wondered if maybe he should've agreed to date her cousin the teacher who'd visited last summer from Chicago. Lamar had shown him her picture, a pretty brunette, just like Sue. Baker thinking *Cute,* then *Who am I to be picky?* Then figuring it would never work, why start.

Now, he said, "Sorry to wake you, Sue. Jack Jeffries got himself stabbed."

"You're kidding."

"Nope."

"Jack Jeffries," she said. "Wow, Baker. Lamar *loves* his music."

Baker restrained himself from saying what he knew: *Lamar loves everyone's music. Maybe that's the problem.*

He said, "Millions of people agree with Lamar."

"Jack Jeffries, unbelievable," said Sue. "Lamar's out like a light but I'll nudge him—oh, look, he's waking up by himself, got that cute look—honey, it's Baker. You've got to work—he's comin' round, I'll make some coffee. For you, too, Baker?"

"No, thanks, had some," Baker lied. "I'll be by in a jif."

Sue said, "He's so tired—up doing our taxes. I'll make sure his socks match."

Baker drove his department Caprice to Lamar's high-rise and waited on the dark street until Lamar's whooping-crane form lurched out the front door, a paper bag dangling from one gangly arm. Lamar's walrus moustache flared to the periphery of his bony face. His hair was flying and his eyes were half-shut.

Baker wore the unofficial Murder Squad uniform: crisp button-down shirt, pressed chinos, shiny shoes, and a holstered semi-auto. The shirt was Oxford blue, the shoes and the gun-sack, black. His sore feet craved running shoes but he settled for crepe-soled brown Payless loafers to look professional. His Kmart preppy special shirt was broadcloth laundered spotless, the collar starched up high the way his mother had done it when he was little and they all went to church.

Lamar got in the car, groaned, pulled two bagels out of the bag, handed one to Baker, got to work on the other, filling his stash with crumbs.

Baker sped to the scene and munched, his mouth still fuzzy, not tasting much. Maybe Lamar was thinking about that when he swallowed hard and dropped the mostly uneaten bagel into the bag.

"Jack Jeffries. He's pure LA, right? Think he came here to record?"

"Who knows?" *Or cares.* Baker filled his partner in on the little he knew.

Lamar said, "Guy's not married, right?"

"I don't follow the celebrity world, Stretch."

"My point," said Lamar, "is that if there's no wife involved, maybe it won't dud out to a stupid domestic like Chenoweth."

"A four-day close bothers you."

"We didn't close squat, we took dictation."

"You were happy at the time," said Baker.

"It was my anniversary. I owed Sue a nice dinner. But looking back . . ." He shook his head. "Total dud. Like a solo that dies."

"You prefer a sleep-destroying WhoDun," said Baker. Thinking: *I sound like a shrink.*

Lamar took a long time to answer. "I don't know what I like."

2

John Wallace "Jack" Jeffries, a natural Irish tenor prone to baby fat and tantrums, grew up in Beverly Hills, the only child of two doctors. Alternately doted upon and ignored, Jackie, as he was known back then, attended a slew of prep schools, each of whose rules he violated at every turn. Dropping out of high school one month short of graduation, he bought a cheap guitar, taught himself a few chords and began thumbing his way eastward. Living on handouts, petty theft, and whatever chump change landed in his guitar case as he offered renditions of classic folk songs in that high, clear voice.

In 1963, at the age of twenty-three, usually drunk or high and twice treated for syphilis, he settled in Greenwich Village and attempted to insinuate himself into the folk music scene. Sitting at the feet of Pete Seeger and Phil Ochs, Zimmerman, Baez, the Farinas was educational. He had a better shot actually jamming with some of the younger lights—Crosby, Sebastian, the heavy girl with the great pipes who'd begun calling herself Cass Elliot, John Phillips who'd do a favor for anyone.

Everyone liked California Boy's voice but his temperament was edgy, pugilistic, his lifestyle an all-you-can-smoke-snort-swallow buffet.

In 1966, having failed to snag a record deal and watching everyone else do so, Jeffries contemplated suicide, decided instead to return to California, where at least the weather was mellow. Settling in Marin, he hooked up with two struggling folkies named Denny Ziff and Mark

Bolt whom he'd seen playing for not much better than chump change in an Oakland Shakey's Pizza.

In what subsequent armies of publicists termed a "magical moment" Jeffries claimed to be munching on a double-cheese extra-large and admiring the duo, while realizing something was missing. Rising to his feet, he hopped on stage during a spirited a capella delivery of "Sloop John B" and added high harmony. The resulting melding of voices created a whole much greater than the sum of the parts and brought down the house. Word of mouth seared through the Bay Area like wildfire and the rest was music history.

The real story was that a speed-shooting promoter named Lanny Sokolow had been trying to get Ziff and Bolt past the pizza circuit for two years when he happened across a chubby, longhaired, bearded dude crooning to a giggly bevy of porn actresses at a Wesson Oil party sponsored by the O'Leary Brothers, San Francisco's favorite adult theater tycoons. Even if Sokolow hadn't been racing on amphetamine, that high, clear voice would've tweaked his ear. The fat guy sounded like an entire angels' chorus. Hell if this wasn't exactly what his two borderline-intelligence baritones could use.

Jack Jeffries's response to Sokolow's greeting and attempted power shake was, "Fuck you, man, I'm busy."

Lanny Sokolow smiled and bided his time, stalking the fat kid, finally getting him to sit down and listen to some demos of Ziff and Bolt. Caught at a weak moment, Jeffries agreed to take in the Shakey's show.

Now, Sokolow figured, if *three* edgy temperaments could coexist . . .

One thing about the official version *was* true: word of mouth was instantaneous and super-charged, nudged along by a new electric thing called folk-rock. Lanny Sokolow got his trio amplified backup and a series of freelance drummers, and booked them as opening acts at Parrish Hall and the other free venues on the Haight. Soon, The Three, as they called themselves, were opening for midsized acts, then major headliners, actually bringing in serious money.

An Oedipus Records scout listened to them lead in for Janis on a particularly good night and phoned LA. A week later, Lanny Sokolow was out of the picture, replaced by Saul Wineman who, as head man at Oedipus, rechristened the group Jeffries, Ziff and Bolt, the sequence of names determined by a coin toss (four tosses, really; each of the three demanded a turn but none was happy until Wineman stepped in).

The trio's first three singles made Top Ten. The fourth, "My Lady Lies Sweetly," hit Number One With A Bullet and so did the LP, *Crystal Morning*. Every song on the album credited the trio as writers but the real work had been done by Brill Building hacks who sold out for a flat fee and a strict nondisclosure pact.

That exposé was among the almanac of allegations listed in Lanny Sokolow's breach-of-contract lawsuit, a marathon feast for attorneys that dragged on for six years and ultimately settled out of court, three weeks prior to Sokolow's death from kidney disease.

Six subsequent albums were penned with some help from Saul Wineman. Four of the five went platinum, *My Dark Shadows* dipped to gold, and *We're Still Alive* tanked. In 1982, the group broke up due to "creative differences." Saul Wineman had moved on to movies and each of the trio had earned more than enough to live as a rich man. Residuals, though tapering each year, added cream to the coffee.

Denny Ziff burned through his fortune by backing a series of unfortunately written and directed independent films. By 1985, he was living in Taos and painting muddy landscapes. In '87, he was diagnosed with small-cell carcinoma of the lung that killed him in three months.

Mark Bolt moved to France, bought vineyard land and turned out some decent Bordeaux. Marrying and divorcing four times, he sired twelve children, converted to Buddhism, sold his vineyards and settled in Belize.

Jack Jeffries chased women, nearly lost his life in a helicopter flight over the Alaskan tundra, vowed never to fly again and bunked down in Malibu, overindulging in any corporeal pleasure at hand. In 1995, he donated sperm to a pair of lesbian actresses who wanted a "creative" kid. The match took and one of the actresses gave birth to a son. Jeffries was curious and asked to see the boy, but after the first few visits where Jeffries showed up toasted, the mothers termed him unfit and filed a cease-and-desist. Jack never fought for contact with his son, now a high-achieving high school senior living in Rye, New York. Rug-rats had never been his thing and there was all that music yet to be made.

He slept till three, kept a small staff that pilfered from him regularly, drank and doped and stuffed his face with no eye toward moderation. The residuals had trickled to a hundred G a year but passive income afforded him the house on the beach, cars and motorcycles, a boat docked in Newport Beach that he never used.

From time to time, he sang on other people's records, gratis. When he performed, it was as a solo act at local benefits and venues that got smaller and smaller. Each year he put on more weight, refused to cut his hair, now white and frizzy, even though every other m.f. had sold out to Corporate Amerika.

He hadn't been to Nashville since That Time but remembered it as a cool place, but too far to drive. So when the owner of the Songbird Café sent out a mass e-mail requesting participants in a First Amendment concert inveighing against federal snooping in public libraries, he tossed it. Then he retrieved it, read the list of those who'd agreed to attend, and felt crappy about having to say no.

Hemmed in, like maybe the cure was worse than the disease.

Then he happened to bring his guitar for repair into The Chick With the Magic Hands and started talking to her and she made a suggestion and . . . why not, even though he didn't have much hope.

Give it a try, maybe it was time to show some *cojones*.

Two months later, would you believe it, it *worked*.

Ready to fly.

Good name for a song.

Jack Jeffries, lying dead in a weed-choked, garbage-flecked lot a short walk from the Cumberland River, would be a no-show at the Songbird concert.

Cleared by the M.E., Lamar Van Gundy and Baker Southerby gloved up and went to take a look at the body. The okay didn't come from an investigator; an actual pathologist had shown up, meaning high priority.

Ditto for the appearance of Lieutenant Shirley Jones, Sergeant Brian Fondebernardi, and a host of media types kept at bay by a small army of uniformed cops. The two local homicide detectives had signed off to the Murder Squad, more than happy to be free of what was looking like the worst combo: publicity and a mystery.

Lieutenant Jones handled the press with her usual charm, promising facts as soon as they were in, and urging the newshounds to clear the scene. After some grumbling, they complied. Jones offered words of encouragement to her detectives, then left. As the morgue drivers hovered in the background, Sergeant Fondebernardi, trim, dark-haired, economical of movement, led the way to the corpse.

The kill-spot was a shadowed wicked place reeking of trash and dogshit. Not really a vacant lot, just a sliver of clumped earth shaded by the remnants of an old cement wall that probably dated to the days when riverboats unloaded their wares.

Jack Jeffries lay on the ground, just feet from the wall, vacant eyes staring up at a charcoal sky. Dawn was an hour away. Cool night, mid-fifties; Nashville weather could be anything, anytime, but in this range, nothing would weirdly accelerate or slow down decomposition.

Both detectives circled the scene before nearing the body. Each thinking: *Dark as sin: a body could walk right by it at night and never know.*

Fondebernardi sensed what was on their minds. "Anonymous tip, some guy slurring his words, sounds like a homeless."

"The bad guy?" said Lamar.

"Anything's possible, Stretch, but on the tape he sounded pretty shook up—surprised. You'll listen when you're finished here."

Lamar got closer to the body. *The man was obese.* He kept that to himself.

His partner said, "Looks like he let himself go."

Sergeant Fondebernardi said, "We're being judgmental, tonight, Baker? Yeah, aerobics would've made him prettier but it wasn't a coronary that got him." Flashing that sad, Brooklyn smile, the sergeant leaned in with a flashlight, highlighted the gash on the left side of the victim's neck.

Lamar studied the wound. *All that music. That voice.*

Baker kneeled and got right next to the corpse, his partner following suit.

Jack Jeffries wore a blousy, long-sleeved black silk shirt with a mandarin collar. His pants were lightweight black sweats with a red satin stripe running the length of the leg. Black running shoes with red dragons embroidered on the toe. Gucci insignia on the soles. Size 11, EEE.

Jeffries's belly swelled alarmingly, a pseudo-pregnancy. His left arm was bent upward, palm out, as if caught in the act of waving good-bye. The right hung close to a spreading hip. Jeffries's long white hair was a droopy corona, some of it floating above a high, surprisingly smooth brow, the rest tickling puffy cheeks. Muttonchops trailed three inches below fleshy ears. A fuzzy moustache as luxuriant as Lamar's obscured the upper lip. Would have hidden both lips but for the fact that the mouth gaped in death.

Missing teeth, Baker noted. Guy *really* let himself go. He pulled out his own penlight and got eye to eye with the wound. Two or so inches wide, the edges parting and revealing meat and gristle and tubing. An upwardly sloping cut, ragged at the top, as if the knife had been yanked out hard and caught on something.

He pointed it out to Lamar. "Yeah I saw that. Maybe he struggled, the blade jiggled."

Baker said, "The way it climbs is making me think the thrust was upward. Could be the stabber was shorter than the vic." He eyeballed the corpse. "I'd put him at six even, so that doesn't clear much."

Fondebernardi said, "His driver's license says six one."

"Close enough," said Baker.

"People lie," said Lamar.

Baker said, "Lamar's license says he's five nine and likes sushi."

Flat laughter cut through the night. When it subsided, Fondebernardi said, "You're right about lying. Jeffries claimed his weight to be one ninety."

"Add sixty, seventy to that," said Baker. "All that heft, even if he wasn't in shape, he'd be able to put up some resistance."

"No defense wounds," said Fondebernardi. "Check for yourself."

Neither detective bothered: the sergeant was as thorough as they came.

"At least," said Lamar, "we don't have to waste time on an I.D."

Baker said, "What else was in his pocket besides the license?"

Fondebernardi said, "Just a wallet, morgue guys have it in their van but it's yours to go through before they book. We're talking basics: credit cards, all platinum, nine hundred in cash, a Marquis Jet Card, so maybe he flew in privately. That's the case, we might get a whole bunch of data. Those jet companies can book hotels, drivers, the whole itinerary."

"No hotel key?" said Lamar.

The sergeant shook his head.

"Maybe he's got friends in town," said Baker.

"Or he didn't bother with the key," said Lamar. "Celebrity like that, people carry stuff for you."

"If he is in a hotel, where else is it gonna be but the Hermitage?"

"You got it," said Lamar. "Ten to one, he's got the Alexander Jackson suite or whatever they call their hotshot penthouse."

Sounding like he yearned for all that, thought Baker. Dreams died hard. Better not to have any.

Fondebernardi said, "Anything else?"

Baker said, "The big question is, what was he doing in this particular spot? It's industrial during the day, empty at night, pretty much away from the club scene, restaurants, dope dealers. Even the Adult Entertainment Overlay doesn't reach here anymore."

"One exception," said the sergeant. "There's a dinky little club called The T House two blocks south on First. Looks like some kind of a hippie joint—hand-painted signs, organic teas. They advertise entertainment no one's ever heard of. Place opens at seven and closes at midnight."

"Why would Jeffries be interested in that?" said Lamar.

"He probably wouldn't, but it's the only place anywhere near here. You can check it out tomorrow."

Baker said, "I'd be wondering if he found himself a hooker, she brings him down here for a shakedown. But nine hundred in the wallet . . ." He checked the body again. "No wristwatch or jewelry."

"But no tan lines on either wrist," said Fondebernardi. "Maybe he didn't wear a timepiece."

"Maybe time wasn't a big deal for him," said Lamar. "Guys like that can have people telling time for them."

"An entourage," said Baker. "Wonder if he private-jetted in with some people."

"It might be a good place to start. Those service places are open twenty-four/seven. Anytime, anywhere for the rich folk."

The sergeant left and the two of them walked around the site several times, noting lots of blood on the weeds, maybe some indentations that were foot-impressions but nothing that could be cast. At four fifty AM, they okayed the morgue drivers to transport, and drove dark, deserted downtown streets to the Hermitage Hotel on Sixth and Union.

On the way over, Baker had called the toll-free number on the Jet Card, dealt with resistance from the Marquis staff about relinquishing flier information, but managed to ascertain that Jack Jeffries had flown into Signature Flight Support at Nashville International at eleven AM. They were not forthcoming about any of his fellow passengers.

The rich and famous demanded privacy except when they wanted publicity. Baker saw it all the time in Nashville, hotshot country stars hiding behind big glasses and oversized hats. Then when no one was noticing them, they talked louder than anyone else in the restaurant.

Lamar parked illegally at the curb, right in front of the Hermitage night door. Nashville's only "AAA Five Diamond Award Recipient" was a gorgeous heap of Italian marble, stained-glass skylights, insets of Russian walnut carved exuberantly, restored to 1910 opulence. Locked up after eleven, the way any sensible downtown hostelry should be.

Baker rang the night bell. No one responded and he tried again. It took three more tries for someone to come to the door and peek around the side windows. Young black guy in hotel livery. When the detectives flashed I.D., the young guy blinked, took awhile to process before unlocking the door. His badge said WILLIAM.

"Yes?"

Lamar said, "Is Mr. Jack Jeffries the rock star staying here?"

William said, "We're not allowed to give out guest—"

Baker said, "William, if Mr. Jeffries is staying here, it's time to switch to 'was.' "

No comprehension in the young man's eyes.

Baker said, "William, Mr. Jeffries was found dead a couple of hours ago and we're the guys in charge."

The eyes brightened. A hand flew to William's mouth. "My God."

"I'll take that as a yes, he's registered here."

"Yes . . . sir. Oh, my God. How did it—what happened?"

"That's what we're here to find out," said Lamar. "We'll need to see his room."

"Sure. Of course. Come in."

They followed as William sped across the monumental lobby with its forty-foot coffered ceiling inlaid with stained glass, arched columns, brocade furniture, and potted palms. At this hour, dead-silent and sad, the way any hotel gets when stripped of humanity.

Baker remembered more motels than he could count. He thought to himself: *Doesn't matter what the tariff is, if it ain't home, it's a big fat nowhere.*

William nearly flew behind the walnut reception desk and set about playing with his computer. "Mr. Jeffries is—was—in an eighth-floor suite. I'll make you a key."

"Was he staying alone?" said Baker.

"In the suite? Yes, he was." The kid wrung his hands. "This is horrible—"

"Alone in the suite," said Lamar, "but . . ."

"He arrived with someone. That person's staying on the fourth floor."

"A lady?"

"No, no, a gentleman. A doctor—I guess his doctor."

"Mr. Jeffries was sick?" said Baker.

William said, "I didn't see any symptoms or anything like that. The other guest is a doctor—I really couldn't tell you what it's all about."

"Anyone else arrive besides this doctor?"

"No, sir."

"A doctor," said Lamar. "Did he and Mr. Jeffries seem to be hanging out?"

"I recall them leaving together. At the end of my first shift—I do doubles when I can. Paying for college."

"Vanderbilt?"

William stared at him. The absurdity of the suggestion. "Tennessee State but I need to pay room and board."

"Good for you, education's important," said Lamar. "What time we talking about, Mr. Jeffries and his doctor leaving?"

"I want to say eight thirty, maybe nine."

"How was Mr. Jeffries dressed?"

"All in black," said William. "A Chinese-type shirt—you know, one of those collarless things."

Same outfit they'd just seen.

Baker said, "So he and this doctor went out at eight thirty or thereabouts. Did either of them return?"

"I couldn't say. We were pretty busy, and mostly I was checking a large party of guests in."

"Anything else you can tell us about this doctor?"

"He did the checking in for Mr. Jeffries. Mr. Jeffries just kind of stood back. Over there." Pointing to a towering palm. "He smoked a cigarette and turned his back on the lobby like he didn't want to be noticed."

"And let the doctor check him in."

"Yes, sir."

"When the two of them left, what was their demeanor?"

"You mean were they in a good mood?"

"Or any other kind of mood."

"Hmm," said William, "I really couldn't say. Nothing stands out in my mind one way or the other. Like I said, it was busy."

Baker said, "But you noticed them leaving."

"Because he's a celebrity," said William. "Was. I don't know much about his music, but one of our bookkeepers is in her fifties and was really excited he was staying here."

"Any idea why Mr. Jeffries was in Nashville?"

"Actually, I do," said William. "I believe there's a benefit concert at the Songbird, and he was going to sing. The performance list, according to the same bookkeeper, is quite impressive." Deep sigh. "I know he brought his guitar with him. Bellboys were competing to carry it."

William's eyes rose to the glass coffers. "The doctor brought one, too. Or maybe he was just carrying Mr. Jeffries's spare."

"A doctor roadie," said Baker. "What's this person's name?"

More fooling with the computer. "Alexander Delaware."

"Another state of the union heard from," said Lamar, cuffing Baker's shoulder lightly. "Maybe he's from The Nations."

"Oh, I don't think so." William was humorless. "He lists his address in Los Angeles. I can give you the zip code and his credit card information if you like."

"Maybe later," said Baker. "Right now, give us his room number."

3

oom 413 was a short walk from the elevators, down a silent, plush hallway. The corridor was empty save for a few room-service trays left outside doors.

Nothing outside Dr. Alexander Delaware's door.

Baker knocked lightly. Both detectives were surprised when a voice answered right away. "One second."

Lamar checked his watch. It was close to six in the morning. "Guy's up at this hour."

Baker said, "Maybe he's waiting for us so he can confess, Stretch. Wouldn't that be nice and easy?"

Muffled footsteps sounded behind the door, then a blur washed across the peephole.

"Yes?" said the voice.

Baker said, "Police," and placed his badge a few inches from the hole.

"Hold on." A chain dropped. The doorknob rotated. Both detectives touched their weapons and stood clear of the door.

The man who opened was forty or so, good-looking, medium height, solidly built, with neatly cut dark curly hair and a pair of the lightest gray-blue eyes Lamar had ever seen. Wide eyes, so pale the irises were nearly invisible when they engaged you straight on. In the right light, that Orphan Annie thing. They were slightly red-rimmed. Boozing? Crying? Allergies brought on by Nashville's high pollen count? No sleep? Pick a reason.

"Dr. Delaware?"

"Yes."

Lamar and Baker stated their names and Delaware offered his hand. Warm, firm shake. Each detective checked for fresh cuts, any evidence of a struggle. Nothing.

Delaware said, "What's going on?" Soft voice, low-key, kind of boyish. "Is Jack okay?" He had a square jaw, a cleft chin, a Roman nose. Dressed for lounging around, in a black T-shirt, gray sweats, bare feet.

As Lamar peered past the guy, into the room, Baker had a second look at the hands: smooth, slightly oversized, with a faint spray of dark hair across the top. The nails of the left hand had been clipped short but those on the right grew just past the fingertips and were tapered to the right. Possibly a classical guitarist or some other type of fingerpicker. So maybe the second guitar was his.

No one had answered Delaware's question. The guy just stood there and waited.

Baker said, "Any reason Mr. Jeffries wouldn't be okay?"

"It's six in the morning and you're here."

"You're up," said Baker.

"Trouble sleeping," said Delaware. "Jet lag."

"When'd you get in, sir?"

"Jack and I got in at eleven yesterday morning and I made the mistake of taking a three-hour nap."

"May we come in, sir?"

Delaware stepped aside. Frowning as he ushered them in.

Smallish, standard room, nothing fancy about it. A neat-freak, Lamar decided. No clothes in sight, every drawer and closet door shut. The only way you'd know the room was occupied was the guitar case near the bed, pillows propped up against the headboard and the comforter slightly mussed—indented where a body had reclined.

On the nightstand was an old-fashioned glass in which two ice cubes melted, a minibar-sized bottle of Chivas in the wastebasket. There was also a large-format magazine—*American Lutherie.*

Another music wannabe? Lamar waited for Baker's reaction. Baker was impassive.

Lamar had a closer look at the mini-bottle. Empty. Doctor mellowing out from insomnia with a drink and a read? Or calming himself down?

He and Baker pulled up chairs and Dr. Alexander Delaware perched on the bed. They gave him the bad news straight out and he placed a palm to his cheek. "My God! That's horrible. I'm . . ." His voice trailed off.

Baker said, "How about filling us in?"

"About what?"

"For starters, how about why Mr. Jeffries travels with a doctor."

A deep sigh. "This is . . . you've got to give me a few minutes."

Delaware went to the minibar and took out a can of orange juice. He drank it quickly. "I'm a psychologist, not a medical doctor. After a helicopter mishap several years ago, Jack developed a phobia of flying. I was treating him for it. Nashville was his first actual flight after the near crash and he asked me to accompany him."

"Leave all your other patients and go with him," said Baker.

"I'm semi-retired," said Delaware.

"Semi-retired?" Baker said. "That would mean you work some-times?"

"Mostly police work for LAPD. I've been consulting on and off for several years."

"Profiling?" said Lamar.

"And other things." Delaware smiled enigmatically. "Once in a while, I'm useful. How did Jack die?"

"That's your whole practice?" said Baker. "Consulting for LAPD?"

"I also do court consults."

Baker said, "You don't see patients but you were treating Jack Jeffries."

"I don't see many long-term patients. Jack came to me through my girlfriend. She's a luthier, has worked on Jack's instruments for years. Awhile back, he mentioned to her that he'd been invited to sing at the Songbird Café for the First Amendment gathering, and was frustrated that his anxiety prevented him from going. He was open to treatment and my girlfriend asked me if I would see him. I was between projects, so I agreed."

Lamar uncrossed and crossed his legs. "What do you do for that kinda thing?"

"There are lots of approaches. I used a combination of hypnosis, deep muscle relaxation and imagery—teaching Jack to retrain his thoughts and emotional responses to flying."

"That include drugs?" said Baker.

Delaware shook his head. "Jack had engaged in decades of self-medication. My approach was to see how far we could get without medication, get him a backup prescription for Valium, if he needed it during the flight. He didn't. He was really doing well." He ran a hand through his curls. Tugged and let go. "I can't believe—this is . . . grotesque!"

A solemn headshake, then he strode to the minibar and retrieved another can of orange juice. This time he spiked it with a bottle of Tanqueray. "Time for me to self-medicate. I know enough not to offer you any booze, but how about soft drinks?"

Both detectives declined.

Baker said, "So you were his hypnotist."

"I used hypnosis along with other techniques. Jack invested serious money in a Jet Card as a way of encouraging himself to keep practicing. If the flights to and from Nashville went smoothly, the plan was for him to try another trip alone. The success he'd achieved so far—mastering his fear—was good for him. He told me he hadn't accomplished much for years, so it felt especially good."

"Sounds like he was depressed," said Lamar.

"Not clinically," said Delaware. "But yes, he'd reached an age, was looking inward." He drank. "What else can I help you with?"

"How about an accounting of his—and your—movements from the time you arrived in Nashville?" said Baker.

Again, the pretty boy raked his curls and threw them a look with those pale, pale eyes. "Let's see . . . we got in around eleven in the morning. We flew privately, which was a first for me. A limo was waiting for us—I believe the company was CSL—we got to the hotel around noon. I checked in for Jack because he wanted to smoke a cigarette and was concerned about being conspicuous."

"Conspicuous, how?"

"The whole celebrity thing," said Delaware. "Being mobbed in the lobby."

"Did that happen?"

"A few people seemed to recognize him but it never got beyond looks and whispers."

"Anyone scary-looking?" said Lamar.

"Not to my eye, but I wasn't looking for suspicious characters. I was his doctor, not his bodyguard. All I remember were tourists."

"How about the few people who recognized him?"

"Middle-aged tourists." Delaware shrugged. "It's been a long time since he was a household name."

"That bother him?"

"Who knows? When he told me he didn't want to be noticed, my first thought was he really did and wanted to reassure himself he was still famous. I think attending the concert was all part of that . . . the desire to get out there and be someone. But not because of anything he said. This was just my perception."

"You checked in, what next?" said Baker.

"I walked Jack up to his suite and he said he'd call me if he needed anything. I went down to my room, intending to take a twenty-minute catnap. Usually I wake up, right on the dot. This time I didn't, and when I did get up, I felt logy. I went to the hotel gym, worked out for an hour, took a swim." A strong exhalation. "Let's see. I showered, I made a couple of calls, did a little reading, played a little." Indicating the guitar case and the magazine.

"Who'd you call?" Baker asked.

"My service, my girlfriend."

"The luthier," Baker said. "What's her name?"

"Robin Castagna."

Lamar furrowed his eyebrows. "She got a write-up in *Acoustic Guitar* last year, right?" When Delaware looked surprised, he said, "You're in Nashville, Doctor. It's the town's business." He pointed to the guitar case. "That one of hers?"

"It is." The psychologist unlatched the guitar case and took out a pretty little abalone-trimmed flattop. Like a 000-size Martin, but no decal on the headstock and the fretboard inlays were different. Delaware fingerpicked a few arpeggios, then ran some diminished chords down the board before frowning and returning the instrument to the case.

"Nothing sounds too good this morning," he said.

Nimble, Baker thought, the guy could play.

Lamar said, "You planning on doing some performance while you're here?"

"Hardly." Delaware's smile was wan. "Jack had his psychologist, the guitar is my therapy."

Baker said, "So you picked a little, read a little . . . then what?"

"Let's see . . . must've been six thirty, seven, by then I was hungry. The concierge recommended the Capitol Grille, right here in the hotel.

But after I looked at it, I decided I didn't want to dine alone in a place that fancy. Then Jack called and said he wanted to go out and 'score some grub,' could use company."

"How'd he sound mood-wise?"

"Rested, relaxed," said Delaware. "He told me the songs had been going well, no trouble remembering lyrics—which had been one of his main concerns. He made a lot of jokes about old age and hard living causing brain damage. He also told that he was thinking of writing a new song for the benefit. Something called 'The Censorship Rag.' "

"But now he was hungry."

"For ribs, specifically. We ended up at a place on Broadway—Jack's. He picked it out of the restaurant guide, thought it was funny—the name, some kind of karma."

"How'd you get there?"

"We took a cab over."

"It's walking distance," said Baker.

"We didn't know that at the time."

"When did you get there?" said Baker.

"Maybe a little before nine."

"Anyone recognize him at Jack's?"

Delaware shook his head. "We had a nice quiet meal. Jack ate lots of pork shoulder."

"Was he bothered by not being recognized more?"

"He laughed about it, said one day he'd just be a footnote in a book. If he was lucky to live that long." Delaware winced.

Baker said, "So what, he had a premonition?"

"Not about being murdered. Lifestyle issues. Jack knew he was obese, had high blood pressure, bad cholesterol. On top of all the hard living."

"Bad cholesterol but he ate pork shoulder."

Delaware's smile was sad.

Lamar said, "Who paid for dinner?"

"Jack did."

"Credit card?"

"Yes.

Baker said, "What time did you leave the restaurant?"

"I'd say ten thirty, at the latest. At that point we split up. Jack said he wanted to explore the city and it was clear he wanted to be alone."

Baker said, "Why?"

"His words were, 'I need some quiet time, Doc.' Maybe he was on a creative jag and needed solitude."

"Any idea where he went?"

"None. He waited until I caught my cab on Fifth, then started walking on Broadway . . . let me get my bearings—he headed east."

Baker said, "East on Broadway is the center of downtown, and it's anything but quiet."

"Maybe he went to a club," said Delaware. "Or a bar. Or maybe he was meeting up with some friends. He came here to perform with people in the business. Maybe he wanted to meet up with them without having his therapist around."

"Any idea who those friends might be?"

"No, I'm just postulating, same as you."

"East on Broadway," said Baker. "Did you hear from him after that, Doctor?"

Delaware shook his head. "What time was he killed?"

"We don't know yet. Any idea who'd want to do him harm?"

"None whatsoever," said Delaware. "Jack was moody, I can tell you that much, but even though I'd treated him, it wasn't in-depth psychotherapy, so I don't have any window into his psyche. But throughout the dinner, I felt he was keeping a lot to himself."

"What makes you say that?"

"Intuition. The only thing I can tell you that might be useful is that his mood changed toward the end of dinner. He'd been talkative for most of the meal, mostly reminiscing about the good old days, then suddenly he got quiet—really buttoned up. Stopped making eye contact. I asked if he felt okay. He said he was fine, and waved off any more questions. But something was on his mind."

"But you have no idea what," said Baker.

"With someone like Jack, could've been anything."

"Someone like Jack?"

"My experience has been that creative and moody go together. Jack had a reputation for being difficult—impatient, sharp-tongued, unable to maintain relationships. I don't doubt any of that's true, but with me he was pretty pleasant. Though at times I felt he was working really hard to be amiable."

"He needed you to get on and off that plane," said Baker.

"That was probably it," said Delaware.

"Ribs at Jack's," said Lamar. "Any liquid refreshment?"

"Jack had a beer, I had a Coke."

"Only one beer?"

"Only one."

"Pretty good self-control."

"Since I've known him, he's been temperate."

Lamar said, "This was a guy who skydived on acid and raced motorcycles while driving blind."

"I'll amend the statement. Around me, he's been temperate. He once told me he was slowing down like an old freight train. He rarely divulged his private life to me, even after we built up a rapport."

"How long did that take—rapport?"

"Couple of weeks. No treatment's effective unless there's trust. I'm sure you guys know that."

"What do you mean, Doctor?"

"Interrogating witnesses is more about developing a relationship than strong-arming."

Baker rubbed his shaved head. "You counsel the LA po-lice on technique?"

"My friend over there, Lieutenant Sturgis, does pretty well by himself."

"Sturgis with an *i-s* or an *e-s*?"

"With an *i:* like the motorcycle meet."

"You're also a biker?"

"I rode a bit when I was younger," said Delaware. "Nothing big-bore."

"Slowed down yourself?"

Delaware smiled. "Don't we all?"

4

They stayed with the shrink for another twenty minutes, going over the same ground, asking the same questions in different ways in order to tease out discrepancies.

Delaware answered consistently, with no sense of evasiveness. That wasn't enough for Baker to give him a pass, seeing as he was the last person, so far, to see Jack Jeffries alive and most murders boiled down to someone the vic knew. The guy being a doctor didn't mean much, either. Then there was the hypnotist deal, which, no matter what Delaware claimed, was a form of mind-bending.

On the other side, there were no visible cuts on the guy, his demeanor was appropriate, his movements could be traced easily until ten thirty, he had no obvious motive, and hadn't bothered to set up an alibi for the time of the murder.

"Do you know if Jack was married?" Baker asked him.

"He wasn't."

"Any special person in his life?"

"No one he told me about."

"Anyone we should contact in LA about his death?"

"I suppose you could start by calling up his agent . . . or maybe it's his ex-agent. I seem to recall something about Jack firing him several years ago. I'm sorry but if he told me a name, I don't remember it."

Baker wrote down *agent* on his notepad. "So no one keeping the home fires burning?"

"No one that I know about."

Lamar said, "What are your plans now, Doctor?"

"I guess there's no reason for me to stick around."

"We'd appreciate it if you did."

"You were planning to be here till after the concert," Baker said, "so how about at least for a day or so?"

Those pale eyes aimed at them. Small nod. "Sure, but let me know when it's okay to leave."

They thanked him, and went up to the eighth floor. After roping the door with yellow crime scene tape, they gloved, turned on the light and proceeded to paw through Jack Jeffries's magnificent-view suite. During the ten hours Jeffries had lived there, he'd managed to turn it into a sty.

Clothes were strewn everywhere. Empty soda cans, wrinkled bags of chips, nuts, and pork rind whose contents littered the floor. No booze empties, doobies or pills, so maybe Jeffries had told the shrink the truth about slowing down.

In a corner next to a couch, Jeffries's guitar, a shiny jumbo Gibson with a rhinestone-studded cowboy pick-guard leaned against the wall in a precarious position.

Lamar was about to move it, but checked himself. Finish up and take Polaroids first.

On Jeffries's nightstand was the room key they hadn't found in his pocket—so much for that lead. Also, a snapshot, curling at the edges.

The subject was a kid: a big beefy young man, eighteen or so with cropped fair hair. He wore some kind of athletic uniform. Not football, no pads. A wine-colored shirt with a white collar, across the chest WESTCHESTER in gold letters.

Smiling like a hero.

Lamar said, "Looks just like Jack. At least what Jack used to look like, right? This is maybe the kid he had with Melinda Raven and that other actress, whatshername?"

Baker lifted the picture with a gloved hand. On the back, genteel handwriting, feminine, in deep red ink.

Dear J: This is Owen after his last big game. Thanks for the anonymous donation to the school. And for giving him space. Love, M.

"M for Melinda," said Lamar.

Baker said, "What kind of uniform is this?"

"Rugby, El Bee."

"Isn't that British?"

"They play it at the prep schools."

Baker regarded his partner. "You sure know a lot about it."

"One of my many schools played it, but not all that well," said Lamar. "Flint Hill. I lasted six whole months there. If it hadn't been for varsity basketball, I would have been booted in two. Once I discovered guitars and stopped playing sports for the well-heeled alumni, no one had a lick of use for me."

Baker opened a drawer. "Looky here." Holding up a sheet of lined paper with crenellated edges that said it had been torn from a spiral notebook.

Verses in black pen filled the sheet. Block-printed lettering but with flourishes on the capitals.

> Thought my songs would carry me far
> Thought I'd float on my guitar
> But The Man says you're no good for us
> Might as well catch that Greyhound Bus

> Refrain: Music City Breakdown,
> It's a Music City Breakdown
> Just a Music City Shakedown,
> A real Music City Takedown

> Thought they cared about Mournful Hank
> Thought I'd come and break the bank
> Then they made me walk the plank
> Now I'm here all dark and dank
> (Refrain)

"So much for creative output," Baker said. "This is pretty juvenile."

The tall man took the sheet, scanned. "Maybe it's a first draft."

Baker didn't answer.

Lamar said, "Guess the guy didn't figure on getting his throat cut and us archaeologizing all over his shit." Slapping the paper down on the nightstand.

"We should take it," said Baker.

"So take it."

"Someone's cranky."

"Hey," said Lamar, "I'm just feeling for the guy. He beats his fear, manages to fly over here on his own dime just to do some good, and ends up like we just saw him. That's a rotten deal any way you shake it, El Bee."

"I'm not denying that." Baker placed the sheet in an evidence bag. The two of them continued to toss the suite. Going over every square inch and finding nothing interesting except a note on a message pad that seemed to bear out Delaware's story: *BBQ Jacks B'Way bet 4 &5 Call AD or solo?*

The note was in a completely different handwriting from the song lyrics.

"The directions have to be Jack's handwriting," Baker said. "So where'd the lyrics come from?"

"Maybe he had a visitor," Lamar said. "You know, some wannabe using a ruse like room service, then dropping his bad poetry on him."

"So why didn't Jack throw it away?"

Lamar said, "Maybe the guy was dry and he was searching for inspiration."

Baker stared at him. "He musta been desperate to steal from the likes of this."

"Well, he hadn't had a hit in a long time."

"That's thin, Stretch."

"Agreed, El Bee, but it's all I can think of. Let's see if we can't get prints off it anyway, run an AFIS."

Baker jiggled the bag. "What we need to do is bring in the CSers and have 'em print the whole damn pigsty. I'll take the pictures and then we can book."

Lamar stood back as Baker walked around snapping Polaroids. Both of them careful not to disturb easily printable surfaces.

Baker said, "You wanna call Melinda Raven tomorrow morning? Find out if Owen is her kid and ask what his relationship was with his daddy."

"I can do that. Alternatively, we can go to the library and read old *People* magazines. Why play our ace card?"

Baker nodded and continued to snap Polaroids. When he was done, he stowed his camera and headed for the door. Lamar, still gloved, hesitated, then placed Jeffries's guitar on the bed before he closed the door.

5

aker dropped Lamar off at his condo at nine AM. They'd made a short stopover at the lab to run an AFIS fingerprint check on the note. The system was down, try again later.

"I'm going to catch a couple hours of shut-eye," said Lamar. "Okay with you?"

"Better than okay." Baker drove off.

Sue Van Gundy was up, at the dinette table, eating her Special K with sliced banana, decaf on the side. Planning, as was her habit, to leave in twenty for the beginning of her eleven-to-seven shift.

She lit up when she saw her husband, got up, wrapped her arms around his waist, rested her cheek on his flat, hard chest.

"That," he said, "feels nice."

"How'd it go on Jeffries, honey?"

Lamar kissed her hair, they both sat down and he pilfered her decaf. "It went nowhere, babe. We're starting from nothing. And Baker's in one of those snits."

"Because it's music-related." Statement, not a question.

"Three years we've been working together and he still won't tell me why he hates anything to do with tone and rhythm."

"Lamar," said Sue, "I'm sure it's something to do with his folks. Just like that nickname you gave him. He really was a lost little boy, growing up on the road, it couldn't have been anything like a normal childhood. Then they up and *die* on him, Lamar? And he's all *alone?*"

"I know," he said. Thinking: *But there's got to be more.* One time, right after he and Baker had started as a team and he'd learned of his partner's quirk, he'd done some sniffing around, found out Baker's parents had been a pair of singers.

Danny and Dixie, traveling the back roads doing honky-tonk, county fairs, roadhouse one-nighters. Danny on guitar, Dixie on the mandolin.

The mandolin.

A long way from stars, nothing on Google. Lamar dug some more, found the obit in an old newspaper file.

Sue was insightful, but still, there had to be more to it than long-time grief.

She said, "Let me make you some eggs."

"No, thanks, baby. I just need to sleep."

"Then I'll tuck you in."

Baker went home, stripped naked, fell into bed, was asleep before his face hit the sheet.

Much of the afternoon was spent with the two of them sitting at the center table in the pale purple Murder Squad detectives' room, working the phone and sifting through the slew of tips that had poured in after Jack Jeffries's murder hit the news.

TV, broadcast, radio, the final edition of *The Tennessean.* By evening, it would be the national entertainment shows.

Fondebernardi and Lieutenant Jones stopped in to see how everything was going. Both of them too experienced and smart to push because that would accomplish nothing other than make their detectives nervous. But they were edgy, all that media attention.

Baker and Lamar had a data flood on their hands from the blitz of phone tips. Sometimes too much information was worse than none at all. Like a room with fifty different fingerprint patterns. Every call they fielded was from a nut, a psychic or just a well-meaning citizen imagining or exaggerating. Two dozen people claiming to have seen Jeffries in two dozen unfeasible places at impossible times.

A few informants were certain he'd been accompanied by a dangerous-looking person. Half of those described a woman, the other half a man. Details as to height, weight, clothing and demeanor were cloudy to the point of uselessness, but everyone agreed on one thing: a dangerous-looking *black person*. And that included black informants.

The detectives had seen that before, called it The Color Kneejerk, but given a 911 caller who sounded African-American, it couldn't be dismissed.

Then the 911 caller showed up at headquarters, a former merchant marine, now homeless, named Horace Watson, who lived in an east-side shelter and liked to take long walks by the river. The man was seventy-three, wizened and toothless. He was also as white as Al Gore; his southern Louisiana accent misconstrued as black patois.

Lamar and Baker took him into a room and started in on developing a relationship by giving him a Danish and coffee. Watson was already tipsy but outgoing, a nice drunk and eager to help. Volunteering about how he always walked by that area—that particular piece of land because sometimes you could find aluminum cans for the Redemption Center and one time he'd found a watch. Too bad it didn't work.

This time, he'd found more than he was looking for. Freaking out when he saw the dead man, he'd hurried back to the shelter to tell someone. Found a pay phone along the way and made the call.

Now he was wondering . . . ahem . . . about maybe a *ree*-ward?

"Sorry, sir," said Lamar, "no rewards for finding bodies, only murderers."

"Oh," said Watson. Flashing a sunken grin. "Cain't blame a guy for trahn."

They questioned him awhile longer, ran him through the system and got a hit with a few misdemeanors. When Baker suggested a polygraph, Watson loved the idea. "Long as it don't hoit."

"Painless, Mr. Watson."

"Let's do it, den. Always wanna try new t'ings."

Lamar and Baker traded looks.

Stretch cleared his throat. "Uh, sorry, sir, no polygraphers on the premises. We'll call you."

"Oka-ay," said Watson. "I got nuttin a do."

Calls to Jack Jeffries's credit card company, follow-up chats with a supervisor at Marquis Jet and the limo driver who'd taken Jeffries and Delaware to the hotel, and a brief sit-down with the staff at Jack's Bar-B-Que confirmed every detail of Dr. Delaware's story.

No one at the restaurant had noticed where Jeffries had gone.

Baker and Lamar spent the next two hours canvassing neighboring merchants east of the barbecue joint, talking to passersby, anyone who hung out regularly on the numbered streets between Fifth and First.

Nothing.

With little else to go on, the two detectives started making phone calls, splitting the list of the performers for the upcoming "Evening at the Songbird Café for the Benefit and Protection of the First Amendment."

Among the names were some of Lamar's idols: Stretch did his police duty with gusto. Baker made the calls with reticence bordering on hostility. The sum total of twenty-two phone calls yielded the same results, which were no results. Everyone was stunned by the news, but no one had seen hide nor hair of Jack Jeffries. Some didn't even know he had been scheduled to perform. Checking Jeffries's outgoing cell calls verified the stories. If Jack had attempted to reach former buddies, he'd done so on a landline that the detectives were unaware of.

A seven PM call to Lieutenant Milo Sturgis in LA verified Dr. Alexander Delaware's longtime association with the department. Sturgis termed Delaware as brilliant.

"If you can use him," the lieutenant said, "do it."

Baker asked him if he knew Delaware had been treating Jack Jeffries.

Sturgis said, "No, he never talks about his cases. Guy's ethical."

"Sounds like you like him."

"He's a friend," said Sturgis. "That's an effect of his being a good guy, not a cause."

The AFIS report on the scrap of song lyrics from Jack Jeffries's room came back negative for any match with an individual in the system. The crime scene people were still working at the scene and the results would start to trickle in tomorrow.

Baker called the coroner's office and spoke to Dr. Inda Srinivasan. She said, "Obviously tox won't be back for a few days but this was one unhealthy guy. His heart was enlarged, his coronary arteries were seriously occluded, his liver was cirrhotic and one of his kidneys was atrophied, with a cyst on the other not that long from bursting. Top of that, he's got noticeable cerebral atrophy, more like what you'd see in an eighty-year-old than a sixty-five-year-old."

"He was also fat and had dandruff," said Baker. "Now tell me what killed him."

"Severed carotid laceration, exsanguination and subsequent shock," said the pathologist. "My point is, Baker, he probably didn't have long, either way."

6

At seven thirty, they returned to the kill-spot. In diminishing daylight, stripped of hubbub and artificial illumination, the site was even more depressing. Last night's foot-indentations were almost gone, plumped by dew. But streaks of rusty brown remained on the weeds. Fresh dog dropping deposited inches from where the body had lain, the pooch disregarding the boundaries of the yellow crime scene tape.

Why should life stop?

At eight thirty they were starving and went back to Jack's Bar-B-Que, not just for the food, but also hoping someone might remember something.

Baker ordered smoked chicken.

Lamar asked for Tennessee pork shoulder and when the food arrived, said, "It's like some primitive rite."

Baker wiped his mouth with a Wash'n Dri. "What is?"

"I'm eating what Jack ate, like that could transfer his karma to us."

"I don't want his karma. You gonna eat all those onions?"

They wiped their chins and drove to The T House. The front door was open but from the street, the club looked empty.

The interior was a single dim, plywood-paneled room with a warped pine floor, mismatched chairs pulled up to small round, oilcloth-covered tables, a few pictures of bands and singers hanging askew.

Not quite empty; three patrons, all young, emaciated, sullen, drinking tea and eating some kind of anorexic biscuits.

Big and Rich on the too-loud soundtrack, asking women to ride them.

Behind a makeshift bar, a black-shirted, spiky-haired guy dried mismatched glasses. As the detectives stood in the doorway, he glanced their way briefly, then returned to his chore.

Not curious about their presence. Meaning Jeffries probably hadn't been here.

They entered anyway, looked around. No hard liquor permit, just beer and wine and a skimpy selection of that. To the left of the bottles, a blackboard listed two dozen types of tea.

"Talk about selection," said Lamar. "Oolong is one thing, Unfermented White sounds illegal."

Baker said, "Look at this." Cocking his head at the rear of the room where a stage should be. No platform, no drum kit, or any other evidence of live entertainment.

Another dude in all-black fiddled with a karaoke setup.

"They can't hire someone live?" said Lamar. "The Large Pizza Blues just got sadder."

Referencing the old strummer's joke: *What's the difference between a Nashville musician and a large pizza? A large pizza can feed a family of four.*

This town, getting someone to play for cheap was as easy as blinking, but whoever owned this place opted for a computer. Someone turned the volume down on Big and Rich. A young woman wearing a waitress apron over a red tank top and jeans stepped out of a door in the back, checked with all three tea-drinkers, refilled a pot, then went over to the karaoke guy. He offered her a cordless microphone. She wiped her hands on her apron, untied it and placed it on the bar. Untying a blond ponytail, she fluffed her hair, flashed teeth at the nearly empty room, finally took the mike.

The room grew silent. The blond girl wiggled, more nerves than sexiness. She said, "Here we go," and tapped the mike. Thump thump thump. "Testing . . . okay, folks, how're y'all tonight?"

Nods from two of the tea-drinkers.

"Awesome, me, too." Mile-wide smile. Pretty girl, twenty, twenty-one. Small and curvy—five-two or -three, square jaw, big eyes.

She cleared her throat again. "Well . . . yeah, it is an awesome night for some music. I'm Gret. That's short for Greta. Then again, *I'm* kinda short."

Pausing for laughter that never arrived.

The karaoke guy muttered something.

Gret laughed and said, "Bart says we'd best be moving along. Okay, here's one of my favorites. 'Cause I'm from San Antone . . . though I love love love *Nashville*."

Silence.

A third throat clear. Gret threw back her shoulders, tried to stand taller, planted her feet as if ready to fight someone. A musical intro issued from the karaoke box and soon Gret was putting heart and soul into "God Made Texas."

Lamar thought she started out pretty good, belting out the song in a smooth, throaty voice, just above an alto. But she was a long ways from great.

Meaning another rider on the Dead Dream Express. Nashville chewed them up and spit them out the way Hollywood did with starlets. According to what he'd heard about Hollywood; the farthest west he'd been was Vegas, five days at a homicide investigation seminar. Sue had won twenty bucks playing dime slots and he'd lost all that and forty more at the blackjack tables.

He stood there as Gret wailed on, glanced at his partner. Baker had turned his back on the stage, was staring at a blank wall and Lamar caught a glimpse of his profile as Baker winced suddenly. As if seized by a cramp.

Lamar was wondering what was wrong when a nano-second later Gret from San Antone skidded off pitch, maybe an eighth note flat. A few measures later, she did it again and by the end of the verse she was *way* off.

Off the beat, too, hopping in too early on several verses.

Baker looked ready to spit.

How the heck had he heard the bad note *before* she sang it? Lamar wondered. Maybe he was so fine-tuned that the sound waves got there sooner. Maybe that was why, even though he could pick and grin up there with Adam Steffey and Ricky Skaggs—at least according to what people said—he let that F-5 just sit in the—

He stopped himself. Jack Jeffries's throat had been cut and he was here to work.

The song ended. Finally. Gret from San Antone bowed as a pair of hands clapped lazily.

She said, "Thanks, y'all, now we're going to do a little traveling, down to that awesome town so devastated by that evil woman known as Katrina. This is a real oldie, I wouldn't know it but my mama's a big doo-wop fan and back when she was littler than me, I'm talking a real bobby-soxer—y'all know what that is?"

No answer.

Gret made the wise choice of not continuing the digression. "Anyway, back then my mama just loved a boy from New Yawk named Freddy Cannon. Palisades Park?"

Silence.

"Anyway," she repeated, "Freddy also recorded this one back in the dinosaur age." Gret blinked and straightened up. "Okay, here we go, folks. 'Way Down Yonder in New Awleans.' "

Baker walked out of the café and stood out on the sidewalk.

Lamar listened to a few sour beats, then joined him.

"Don't you think we should at least ask if he was in here, El Bee?"

"Yup," said Baker. "I'm just waiting for the static to die down."

"Yeah," said Lamar, "she stinks, poor thing."

"Maybe she's the lucky one."

"Why's that?"

"No one'll give her any false hope and she'll go find a real job."

They watched from the doorway as Gret put the microphone down and resumed her waitress duties. None of the patrons needed her and she headed over to the bar. Sipping a beer, she peered over the foam, locked eyes with the detectives and smiled.

When they approached, she said, "Po-lice, right?"

Lamar smiled back. "Today we are."

"I figured you'd be here," she said. "'Cause Mr. Jeffries was here. I was gonna call you but I really didn't know who to call and I figured you'd be here, soon enough."

"Why's that?"

That threw her. "I dunno . . . I guess I figured someone would know Mr. Jeffries was here and you'd be following up."

Baker said, "Who would know?"

"His entourage maybe?" said Gret, as if answering a question on an oral exam. "I figured someone must have drove him from wherever fancy place he was staying, a celebrity like him doesn't just show up by himself."

"Was he with anyone?"

Gret chewed her lip. "Nope . . . he wasn't. I guess I *shoulda* called. Sorry. If you didn't come by tomorrow, I was *gonna* call. Not that I can tell you anything else except he was here last night."

Baker turned to the bartender who'd ignored them when they entered. Pimply-faced kid, the spiked hair was dyed black. He had a long, gaunt, chin-dominated face, didn't look old enough to drink. Shifty eyes—real shifty eyes. "Anything you want to say, son?"

"Like what?"

"Like were you on last night?"

"Nope."

"Did you know Jack Jeffries was here last night?"

"Gret told me."

"Man gets murdered and he was here last night. We show up and you don't think to mention it?"

"Gret just told me. She said she'd be talking to you."

Gret said, "I really did, Officers. Byron doesn't know anything."

Lamar said, "What's your last name, Byron?"

"Banks," said the barkeep.

"Sounds like you don't enjoy talking to the police, son."

No answer.

"You have experience talking to the police, son?"

Byron Banks gazed at the ceiling. "Not really."

"Not really, but what?"

"I did nine months."

"When?"

"Last year."

"For what?"

"Grand theft auto."

"You're a car booster."

"Just once, I was wasted. Never gonna happen again."

"Uh-huh," Baker said. "Do you have a substance-abuse problem?"

"I'm okay, now."

"Tending bar?" Lamar stood up and stretched to his full height. He did that whenever he wanted to intimidate. "Don't you think it's a little risky for a guy like you?"

"It's tea," said Banks. "I don't do nothing and I don't know nothing. She's the one who was here."

Greta said, "That's really true."

Baker said, "Where were you last night, Byron?"

"Over on Second."

"Doing what?"

"Walking around."

"By yourself?"

"With friends. We went into a club."

"Which one?"

"Fuse."

"That's Techno," said Lamar. "How about the names of your friends?"

"Shawn Dailey, Kevin DiMasio, Paulette Gothain."

"What time were you cruising Second?"

"Until about one or two. Then I went home."

"Which is where?"

"My mother's."

"Where's that?"

"New York Avenue," said Banks.

"The Nations," said Lamar with a quick glance to Baker. Later, if he was in a mood, he'd have some fun. *Neighbors like that and your alarm sucks . . .*

"Yeah. I'm feeling antsy. Can I go have a smoke?"

They took his stats and let him go. The kid walked past the karaoke gear, disappeared through the rear door.

"He's really a nice person," said Gret. "I never knew he was in jail. How could you tell?"

Lamar turned his eyes on the waitress. "We got ways. What's back there, through that door?"

"Just the bathroom and a little room where we put our stuff. I keep my guitar there."

"You play?" said Lamar. "How come you used the machine?"

"House rules," said Gret. "Some kind of union thing."

"Who else was here last night?"

Gret said, "Our other bartender—Bobby Champlain—and me and Jose. Jose sweeps up after we close so he came in maybe ten to midnight."

"Either of them have a criminal record?"

"I wouldn't know for certain, sir, but I wouldn't *think* so. Bobby's around seventy, deaf in one ear, mostly deaf in the other, and a little . . . slow, you know? Jose's real religious—Pentecostal. Bobby told me he's got five kids and works two jobs. Neither of them would have recognized Mr. Jeffries, especially looking . . . well, different. I was the only person who did."

"Mr. Jeffries looked older than you expected."

Nod. "And a lot . . . you know, fatter. We might as well be honest."

"But you recognized him."

"My mama *loved* the trio . . . but her favorite was Jack. He was the star, you know. She has all the old LPs." Sad smile. "We still got a record player."

Baker said, "Who makes the house rules?"

"The owner. Dr. McAfee. He's a cosmetic dentist, loves music. He worked on Byron's mom's teeth. That's how Byron got the job."

"Dr. McAfee around much?"

"Almost never," said Greta. "Bobby Champlain told me he's too busy doing teeth; Bobby started off working here when it opened, around a year ago. Dr. McAfee worked on his teeth, too. He lives in Brentwood. Dr. McAfee, I mean, not Bobby. Nowadays, he hardly ever makes it over. Last couple of weeks, I been opening and closing, and he's been paying me a little extra for that."

"What time did Mr. Jeffries show up?"

"I'd have to say around eleven fifteen, thirty. We close at midnight but the music stops at fifteen to. I was just about to start my second set."

"Singing old favorites," said Lamar.

The girl smiled. Those big eyes were brown and soft. "Singing's in my blood. It's my goal."

"To get a record deal?"

"Well, sure, that would be great. But I just love singin'—sharing what I've got with other people. My goal is to one day be able to do that as my real job." Her lips turned down. "Here I am talking about me and it's so horrible about Jack Jeffries. When I found out, I was so shocked, I can't tell you. He's more from my mama's time but she plays his records all the time and he had a *beautiful* voice. Just gorgeous. She always said it was a gift from God." Small fists clenched. "How could anyone *do* that to him? When I found out this morning, I was *horrified*. And then I said ohmigod, I need to talk to them—meaning you—the police. I thought of 911 but they say if it's not a real emergency, don't use it 'cause it ties up the lines."

"Why exactly," said Baker, "did you think you needed to talk to us?"

Confusion clouded the brown eyes.

Lamar added, "Is there something specific you want to tell us?"

"No, but he was *here*," said Gret. "Sat right in that chair and drank two pots of chamomile and ate yellow-raisin scones with oodles of butter and listened to me sing. I couldn't believe it, Jack Jeffries sitting there *listening* to me! I was so nervous I thought I'd fall down. Usually when I sing I make eye contact—connect with the audience, you know? Last night, I just stared at the floor like a stupid little kid. When I realized it, I looked up and wouldn't you know, he was looking back at me and paying attention. Afterward, he applauded. I nearly ran off to the bathroom, but finally I built up my courage and went back out and got him more tea and told him how much I admired his music and that singing was my goal. He told me to follow my dreams . . . that's what he did when he was my age. For a long time everyone discouraged him but he stuck it out and stuck with it."

Tears welled in her eyes.

"To hear those words from a superstar like that. I can't tell you what it meant. Then he shook my hand and wished me luck. Left a nice tip, too. I ran out to thank him, but he was already talking to that lady and I didn't want to disturb his privacy."

She reached for a bar napkin, and wiped her eyes.

Lamar said, "What lady, Gret?"

"Some older lady. They were talking a little ways up, but not too far from the T. Then he walked her to her car . . . which was parked even farther up."

"How long did they talk?"

"Don't know, sir. I didn't want to stare—didn't want to be rude—so I went back inside."

"But you definitely saw Jeffries talking to this lady."

"Yeah, she just walked up to him out of nowhere. Like she'd been waiting for him."

"Did Jeffries appear startled?"

She thought. "No—no, he didn't look surprised."

"Like he knew her."

"I guess."

"Would you say it was a long conversation or a short one?"

"I really couldn't say, sir."

"Did either of them look upset?"

"No one was laughing but it was too far away to see."

Baker said, "Why don't you show us exactly where they were standing."

Lamar watched from where Gret said she'd been standing and Baker accompanied the girl as she paced off five yards, stopped and said, "Right around here. I think."

East of the café. Direct route to the kill-site.

Baker had her point out where the woman's car had been parked. Another three, four feet east. He brought her back to the café and the three of them stood out on the sidewalk.

"So you can't say how long were they talking," said Lamar.

"I really wasn't staring the whole time." She blushed. "I mean it's natural, I'm not going to run away. Big-time superstar just walks in—just walks *in* by *himself* and sits down and *listens*? We *never* get anyone important, never ever. Not like on Second or Fifth or over at the Songbird. Those places, you hear all kinds of stories about celebrities dropping in at the popular clubs. But we're away from all that."

"Yeah, it is kind of a different location," said Lamar.

"Dr. McAfee bought the building cheap. He's a big real estate investor. I think he's planning to tear it down eventually and build something else. Meanwhile, we're doing music and I'm grateful for the opportunity."

Big brown eyes. Lamar wondered what they'd look like, chilled by failure.

Baker said, "Talk to us about this lady, Gret. What did she look like?"

"That's a tricky one."

The detectives exchanged glances. *That's a tricky one* is often code for "I'm lying through my teeth." Baker said, "Do the best you can."

"Well, she was older but not as old as Mr. Jeffries. Maybe forty or fifty. Shoulder-length dark hair . . . not so tall. Maybe . . . I dunno. Five four or five five." She shrugged.

"What about clothing?"

"A dark pantsuit . . . maybe dark blue? But it could've been gray. Or black. That's about all I could tell you. It was dark and like I said, I didn't want to stare. Now ask me about the car."

"What about the car?"

"Real nice Mercedes-Benz sports car and bright red like a fire truck."

"You didn't happen to catch the license plate?"

"No, sir, sorry."

"Convertible?"

"No, a coupe. No canvas top."

"Red."

"*Bright* red, even at night you could see that. Looked like it had custom shiny wheels. Real shiny. You think she had something to do with it?"

"It's too early to think anything, Gret. Anything else you can remember that might help us would sure be appreciated."

"Hmm." She took hold of her hair, bunched it back in a ponytail, let it drop. "That's really about it."

They asked for her full name, address and phone number.

She said "Greta Lynne Barline." The brown eyes shot to the sidewalk. "I'm in between phones—looking for a better carrier, you know? I'm staying temporarily at the Happy Night Motel. Just a ways down on Gay Street, so I can walk."

The detectives knew the place. One-star joint, not far from their office. It had once been a hotbed of naughtiness before the big vice crackdown. Now the place was trying to grab the tourist trade and an AAA rating. Mostly, it drew truckers and transients.

Greta added. "I had an apartment with a roommate but she left and the rent was too much. I was thinking the eastside, but it's still pretty black. Maybe I'll get a car and live near Opryland." A big smile. "That way I can visit all the time, watch those tropical fish in that restaurant they have."

"Doesn't sound so bad," Baker said. "One last question, Greta, and then I think we're done for now."

"Sure . . . shoot." Another wide smile. She was enjoying the attention.

"Mr. Jeffries was here for about a half hour, maybe an hour?"

"More like a half hour. He left after I stopped singing."

"What was Mr. Jeffries's state of mind when he was here?"

"You mean his mood?" She brightened. "He was happy, really enjoying the music."

7

The red Mercedes was a good lead. How many of those could there be?

The major dealer was Mercedes-Benz of Nashville, out in Franklin, but it was way too late to reach anyone.

"What now, El Bee?" Lamar asked. "Time to pack it in?"

"Actually, I was thinking of heading out to the Songbird. I hear they're doing a tribute to Jeffries that's gonna last pretty late. As long as I'm out, I thought I'd pay my respects."

"And check out the crowd while you're there?"

"Reckon so. You know I'm a big one for multi-tasking. Why don't you come with me, Stretch?" A hint of a genuine smile. "Or do I have to twist your arm?"

Big grin from Lamar. "Buddy, I am so there."

The café and dinner club was located in a strip mall, sharing a common wall with Taylor's Insurance. It had expanded recently, taking over McNulty's Travel, which had gone south courtesy of Internet booking. Bad luck for Aaron McNulty, but a bit of good fortune for Jill and Scott Denunzio, the owners. The club was bursting at the seams and even with the extra room, on specialty nights there wasn't a chair to be had.

The place was dimly lit with a beer and wine bar opposite the front stage. Large fir planks made up the floor and a half dozen ceiling fans were going full blast. About twenty tables were crammed with teary-eyed fans paying tribute to Jack Jeffries. The crowd looked to be well beyond the club's 140 capacity, but neither detective was counting. When they walked in, the stage overflowed with some of music's finest, all of them lifting their voices in unison for a soul-wrenching edition of one of Jeffries, Ziff and Bolt's signature tunes, "Just Another Heartbreak."

Once inside, the detectives leaned against the wall and listened, catching most of the song. Lamar had to remember to blink. Totally entranced by the music. Then thinking yet again about the differences between good, great, and a shot at the gold.

Each individual up there had righteous pipes worthy of several platinum records, but there was something to that saying about the whole being greater than the sum of its parts. Maybe it was the time and the place, maybe it was the emotion, but even Baker seemed under the spell. When they were done, the room remained silent for a few beats, then erupted into heartfelt applause that lasted a good five minutes. The stage cleared and Jeremy Train took the mike.

Mega-popular in the seventies, a chick magnet with his laid-back manner and boyish good looks, Jeremy had preserved amazingly well. He was around five ten, trim and muscled, with the famous stick-straight, shoulder-length hair. The locks were still dark, with a few sparkles of gray that twinkled every time Train moved his head. A couple of wrinkles were carved into his face but they made him look manly. He wore jeans, a black tee, boating shoes without socks. Like Greta Barline had done yesterday evening, he tapped the mike several times. Unnecessary, a singer's tic; he'd just used it for the group number.

"Yeah, I guess it's still hot . . ." A few titters of laughter. "Uh, I want to thank everyone for showing up at this . . . uh, impromptu gathering that was supposed to be for the First Amendment . . ." Applause. "Yeah, right on. Instead, we gather for a much sadder reason and . . . well . . . You know, Jack's music really speaks for what he was . . . more than uh, I can say, you know?"

Applause from the audience.

"But someone should say a few words about Jack and I guess I was elected since I knew him well in our . . . uh, craaazy days." A smile. "Oh man, Jack was . . . well, let's not bullshit around. Jack was one crazy *motherfucker.*"

Applause and laughter.

"Yeah, one crazy motherfucker . . . but a very sensitive human being underneath all that craziness. He could be a mean son-of-a-bitch and then he could turn around and be the nicest guy in the universe. You know, throwing beer bottles out of the car at a hundred miles an hour, sticking his head out, cussing at the top of his lungs. Streaking naked down Sunset . . . man, he loved to get attention and that sure got attention."

Jeremy Train laughed nervously.

"Then Jack would turn around and, shit . . . like once I was admiring a painting he had on his wall and he just took it off the wall and fucking *gave* it to me. I tried to *hey, man,* but Jack's mind was made up and y'all know how stubborn that crazy motherfucker could be."

Nods among the performers.

"Yeah, he was just . . . no one could outdrink him. Certainly no one could out*eat* him."

Subdued laughter.

"Yeah, it didn't end well for Jack and that's really . . ." Jeremy's eyes got moist. "And you know, that's really a shame because lately he was really getting his act together. A new CD was in the works . . . he'd got his bad habits under control . . . except maybe his eating and you know, c'mon, give the guy a break. Things were going better for him personally . . . so maybe Jack ended on a high note after all."

A hard swallow.

"So thank y'all for comin' out here for Jack . . . and let's not forget Denny and Mark. So this is for the trio . . . we love you guys. Keep the faith. And I think we're gonna end on a piece that, hey, Jack, we love you, bro. We're really gonna miss you."

The performers shuffled back on stage, took up their positions and ended with "My Lady Lies Sweetly." When they had finished, the standing ovation was thunderous and long. Lamar had to shout over the *bravos* and *encores.* "Talk to Train?"

"Reckon he'd be the one."

They wound their way through the crowd until they found Jeremy talking earnestly to a bevy of nubile teenage girls, each one looking profoundly sad as Jeremy dispensed his words of wisdom.

"Yeah, that was Jack. Just a crazy guy."

Baker stepped toward him, badge in hand. "Mr. Train, I'm Detective Southerby and this is Detective Van Gundy. Could we have a word with you in private?"

Jeremy's eyes darted from side to side. The dilated pupils could have been from the dark, or from something that would make him nervous to be around the police. Baker interjected, "It's about Jack Jeffries."

Looking a little relieved, Jeremy Train nodded. "Sure . . . uh, wanna step outside so I can take a smoke?"

"That would work," Baker said.

Once outside, Jeremy lit up and offered the detectives a Marlboro. Both declined with a shake of the head. "Bad habit," he said.

"Just think of it as helping the southern economy," Baker said. "I liked what you had to say about Jack."

"It sucked, man . . ." He shook his head in disgust. "I can't talk in public. It's weird, I can write good songs—"

"Great songs," Lamar interrupted.

"Yeah?" A smile. "Thanks. I can sing . . . I dunno, I'm kinda shy in public."

"Not like Jack from what I hear," Lamar said.

"No, Jack wasn't shy about anything. He was just . . . you know, out there. Damn shame." He looked up from his smoke. "You're the detectives who're investigating his murder?"

"We are," Baker said. "Anything about him you can tell us would be helpful."

"The truth is that Jack and I hadn't been in touch like for . . . sheez . . . ten years. You could call him one day and he'd be like real cheerful, then ten minutes later, he'd be cussing you out and hanging up on you . . . the guy was as unpredictable as the weather."

"Yeah, that was his rep," Lamar said. "In your talk on stage, you mentioned that there was a new CD and some personal relationships. What can you tell me about that?"

"The CD was going real well. Actually, he e-mailed me and asked me if I wanted to participate."

"What'd you tell him?" Baker asked.

"I said hell yeah, if the timing works out. He e-mailed me back telling me we'd talk about it at the benefit in Nashville. I was pretty surprised he was comin' out. We all knew he had a fear of flying."

"I'm interested in the personal relationships," Lamar said. "What about those?"

"I think I meant more like his personal life. From what I understand, he was getting his addictions under control . . . alcohol in particular. He was a mean drunk, so that was good."

Baker said, "What about that kid he fathered with that lesbian couple?"

"Melinda Raven . . . yeah, I met her, I think . . . yeah, gay . . . been a lot of women in my life." Jeremy said that without braggadocio, just a statement of fact. "We all thought Jack was a little weird for volunteering, but in retrospect, who knows? For as much as I see my oldest daughter, she could have been put up for adoption. Her old lady likes me to keep my distance except when it comes to child support. If the checks aren't there by the first of the month, she sure doesn't mind calling me up. So maybe Jack had the right idea. Have fun and let someone else take care of the kid." Talking about his ex had hardened his face. "I really don't know if Jack had contact with the kid or not. Like I told you, we've basically been out of contact for ten years. I was surprised by his e-mail, his contacting me after all these years."

Lamar said, "And you told him you'd work with him on his CD?"

"Not work *with* him . . . just participate, like cut a background track, I coulda used Pro Tools, e-mailed it to him. I was happy he called me, but there was this part of me that was a little . . . uh, hesitant. I mean the guy was a real asshole even though he was blessed with the voice of an angel." A chuckle. "We're in the Bible Belt so I guess I can say that God really does work in funny ways."

8

The next morning, Lamar was on the phone with the Mercedes dealer's sales manager, a voluble guy named Ralph Siemens. Siemens gave up a name instantaneously.

"That's got to be Mrs. Poulson. She bought a fire-engine SLK350 two months ago. I only sold two red ones in a long while, everyone wants white or black. The other was to Butch Smiley but he got an SUV."

Defensive tackle for the Titans. Three-hundred-pound black man.

"Is Mrs. Poulson around forty-five with shoulder-length dark hair?" said Lamar.

"That would be her," said Siemens. "You know who I'm talking about, right?"

"Who?"

"*Poulson.* As in Lloyd Poulson? Banking, electronics, shopping centers, whatever else makes money. Real nice gentleman, bought a new sedan every two years. He died last year, cancer. Mrs. Poulson stayed in the house but she also breeds horses in Kentucky. There was talk she was going to move there full-time."

"Where does she live?"

"Where else?" said Siemens. "Belle Meade. Do me a favor and don't tell her I'm the one who told you, but I might as well give you the address 'cause you're going to find out anyway."

Belle Meade is seven miles southwest of downtown Nashville and a whole different planet. Quiet meandering streets wind past Greek Revival, Colonial and Italianate mansions perched on multi-acre lots. Sweeping lawns are shaded by monumental oaks, pines, maples and dogwoods. The town's an old-money bastion with plenty of new-money infiltration, but who-lived-here-before still affects real estate values. Driving through the wide lanes of asphalt, it wasn't unusual to spot trim young women riding beautiful horses around private corrals. The street signs said it all: a racing horse with a colt behind a low-slung fence. Equestrian sports ranked right up there with golf and family football games as Sunday pastimes.

The town's two thousand residents had been absorbed into the Metro Nashville utility grid years ago while managing to keep their high-priced real estate officially independent, with its own police force. Autonomy, and some believed psychological segregation from Nashville as a status symbol, was so important to the landowners of Belle Meade that they agreed to pay taxes to both cities.

No big strain; average family income nudged two hundred thousand, highest in the state. The locals were ninety-nine percent white, one percent everything else. Kids who wanted to go to Vanderbilt could, for the most part. Not much reason, in the past, for Lamar and Baker to drive through. Over the last three years, Belle Meade had registered no homicides, one rape, no robberies, four assaults, most of them minor, and a quartet of stolen cars, two of them joyrides by local teens.

That kind of peace and quiet left the twenty-officer Belle Meade police force time to do what had made it famous: mercilessly enforce the traffic rules. Including no special treatment for cops; Lamar drove down Belle Meade Boulevard slowly and carefully.

Making a quick turn, passing Al and Tipper's place, he found the address easily enough. Pinkish cream, flat-topped thing about ten times the size of a normal house, set behind iron fencing but with a nice clear view of a three-acre swath of bluegrass. In the center of a circular driveway, a one-story fountain burbled. The red Benz was parked right in front, along with a Volvo station wagon. Pines so dark they almost looked black had been barbered to cones and were positioned at the front of the mansion, like sentries. Toward the front of the property, hanging over the fence, were some of the biggest oaks the detectives had ever seen.

As they parked and walked to the gate, Lamar saw how theatrical the landscaping was. The trees and foliage had been manipulated for uneven sun exposure so that the three-story expanse got maximum dappling. There was no lock on the gate. They walked through, made the hike to the front door, rang the bell.

Expecting a maid in full uniform, or maybe even a butler to answer their call: instead, a nice-looking, middle-aged woman in a pink cashmere cowl-neck sweater, tailored white slacks and pink sandals came to the door. Polish on her toenails, but not pink, just natural. Same for her nails, which were clipped surprisingly short. No jewelry except for a platinum wedding band.

She had dark hair, shoulder-length and flipped at the ends, soft-looking skin and blue eyes—true blue, not like the shrink's. Her face was the perfect oval, a bit too tight around the edges but still pretty.

"Mrs. Poulson?"

"I'm Cathy." Soft, thin voice.

The detectives introduced themselves.

"Nashville detectives? Is this for fund-raising? Chief Fortune didn't mention anything."

Letting them know she was connected, that she saw them as beggars.

Baker said, "We're here about an incident that took place in the city, ma'am."

Lamar said, "A murder, I'm afraid. Jack Jeffries."

No shock on Cathy Poulson's smooth face. She nodded. Slumped.

"Oh, Jack," she said. "Please come in."

She led them across an entry hall bigger than their residences, into a sunlit room that looked out to manicured acres of hillocks, streams, stone waterfalls, and tree girdle at the rear. A royal blue Olympic-sized pool was edged with golden tiles and dressed at the corners with more statuary—naked nymphs. A patch of color sparkled off to the left where a rose garden thrived. Green tarpaulin fencings in the distance shouted *Tennis, Anyone?*

A maid in full uniform—young, black, slim—dusted antique furniture.

A rich lady who answered her own door, thought Lamar. Nervous about something?

Cathy Poulson went up to the woman and rested her hand on a shoulder. "Amelia, I need to talk to these gentlemen a bit. Would you please bring us some of that amazing lemonade, then see if the kitchen needs freshening?"

"Yes, ma'am."

When Amelia left, Cathy said, "Please sit. I hope you like lemonade."

Sinking into enormous silk-upholstered chairs, Baker and Lamar drank the best lemonade they'd ever tasted and took in the room. Fifty feet long by half as much wide, with high coved ceilings not much simpler than those in the Hermitage lobby. Stiff arrangements of gleaming, curvy-legged wood tables, delicate chairs and high-back French provincial couches shared space with realistic, soft seating. The walls were pale green silk hung with gilt-framed paintings of still lifes and country scenes. The stone fireplace at the far end was big enough to walk into. A few color photos rested on the carved mantel.

Lamar said he loved the lemonade.

Cathy Poulson said, "It's amazing, isn't it? The key is to use Meyer lemons along with the regular kind. Gives it a bit more sweetness. My husband taught me that. He was originally from California. Fallbrook, that's down near San Diego. His family grew citrus and avocado. A drought and some bad investments wiped them out completely. Lloyd had to start all over by himself and he was successful beyond belief. He died six months ago. He was a wonderful man."

She got up, walked to the mantel, fetched one of the photos and brought it back.

It looked like some sort of charity ball shot, where rich folk pose for photographers as they enter a fancy room. Cathy Poulson stood next to a short, thick, balding man with curly white hair fringing his ears. Red designer gown for her—same color as her car—tux for him. Lloyd Poulson's eyes crinkled when he smiled. His pudgy fingertips were visible around his wife's wasp waist.

He wore thick-lensed, black-framed glasses and had a gut that swelled his cummerbund, appeared to be at least seventy. Cathy Poulson looked like a movie star in the photo. Plenty of jewelry that night— diamonds at every strategic location. The bodice of her red gown was low-cut enough to expose a big, soft expanse of swelling breast. Perfect cleavage, thought Lamar. You'd never know to look at her in the sweater.

"Such a vital man," she said with a sigh. "Prostate cancer. There was pain but he never complained."

"Sorry for your loss, ma'am."

Cathy Poulson picked invisible lint from her sweater, reached for the photo, placed it faceup on her lap. "Sorry to bore you with my personal problems. You've got important work to do and you want to know why I was talking to Jack the night before last."

"Yes, ma'am."

"First off," she said, "it's pretty obvious that I wasn't trying to hide anything. You don't go into that neighborhood with a car like mine, park right out in front, if you're worried about being seen." She tapped the photo. "Who saw me, that girl?"

"Which girl?"

"A little blond girl, I assumed she was a waitress or something like that. She and a Mexican were the only ones left in the place. I saw her watching Jack and me from the doorway."

"Spying?" said Baker.

"Probably, but trying hard not to show it," said Cathy Poulson. "Unable to resist, I suppose. Which is understandable, given how famous Jack is. Was."

She bit her lip.

"I found out about it this morning. Like everyone else. Drinking my morning coffee and reading the paper and there it was." Her eyelids quivered. "I went into the bathroom and was completely sick."

"You knew about the murder but you acted surprised when we showed up," said Baker.

Cathy Poulson blinked. "Pardon?"

"That remark about fund-raising?"

The woman blushed. "That was stupid and snobbish, Detective. Please forgive me. I guess I—I don't know why I said that. I certainly wasn't surprised that you showed up. I knew that girl had seen me and if she told you, you'd probably trace me through my car. And of *course* you'd want to talk to me. I might have been the last person to see Jack before he—*was* I?"

"So far, that's the case, ma'am."

"Well, that's horrible. Repugnant and horrible."

Neither detective spoke.

Cathy Poulson said, "Did the girl tell you that Jack and I didn't leave together? That I drove off and that he stayed behind?"

"No, ma'am," Lamar answered.

"Well, that's what happened. So it's obvious I'm not your culprit." Smiling and aiming for levity, but one hand clawed a white-trousered knee.

Baker said, "Why'd you go down to The T House to talk to Mr. Jeffries?"

"He chose it, said it was off the beaten path . . . how right he was. I knew it was a dump, but Jack could get insistent." She shook her head. "The original plan was for me to be there earlier. I got held up and didn't make it until closing. Jack understood. He could be quite . . . pleasant. When he wanted to be."

"Sounds like you two go back a ways."

Cathy Poulson smiled and sat back and swept dark hair from her face. Light from the rear of the room caught on her platinum ring.

"I suppose you could say that."

"Would you be so kind as to fill us in?" said Lamar.

"About my relationship with Jack?"

"Yes, ma'am."

"Is that really necessary? Seeing as I'm not your culprit."

"The more information we have, the easier our job is, ma'am."

"Believe me," said Cathy Poulson, "I'm not going to be able to make your job any easier because all I can tell you is Jack and I spoke briefly and then I left." A manicured hand graced her left breast. "Please, guys, given all I've gone through this past year, I really can't handle any more stress."

Shifting from "gentlemen" to "guys." This one parceled out the charm. Lamar wondered how much she'd rehearsed, and knew Baker was thinking the same thing.

Baker put on his nice voice and leaned forward. "We have no intention of causing you stress, ma'am. But we do need to compile data."

She stared at him, as if seeing him for the first time. Shifted back to Lamar. "College basketball?"

"No, ma'am."

"Sorry, that was inappropriate. It's just that my son's into sports—basketball, football, baseball, you name it. He just started at college. I'm here all alone. *Feeling* really alone."

"Vanderbilt?"

"Oh, no," she said, with some fervor. "Vanderbilt would've been great, he could've stayed in a dorm room, he knows I'd never meddle, but he'd still have the opportunity to come home on weekends to dump laundry, maybe grant me a few 'Hi, Moms.' No, Tristan's at Brown in Rhode Island. Smallest state in the union and there's where he picks."

"Supposed to be a good school," said Lamar. "Ivy League, right?"

"Right, but so what? My husband went to Chico State College and he was the most successful man I've ever met. Granted, Tristan's an excellent student, his SATs were terrific, and all his varsity letters were impressive. His guidance counselor said he was Ivy League material from the git-go. But Vanderbilt's just as good. Now he's never here. *Never.*"

Raising her volume so by the last word it was like hearing someone else's voice—shrill, angry. A deeper flush took hold of her face and wrinkles started to show around the edges of her makeup, like fault lines.

One of those mood-disorder things? Lamar wondered. *Or is she trying to tell us something? Because this one sets things up like a stage director. From the way she plants her trees and arranges her expensive furniture to bringing us lemonade we don't ask for.*

Staying in control.

But if there was a message beyond the fact that she missed her kid, he wasn't picking it up. And for a new widow, he supposed that was a normal reaction.

Still, there was something about her . . . He said, "Must be tough, alone in a big house."

"Alone," said Cathy Poulson, "is tough, anywhere."

Baker smiled. "Could I use your restroom, please, ma'am?"

He glanced at the mantel as he left, and was gone for a while. Lamar digressed by commenting on Cathy Poulson's paintings. She jumped at the opportunity to walk him around the room, announcing titles and artists and describing how and where and when her deceased husband had acquired each picture. When they got to the mantel, he saw mostly pictures of her with a token nod to a few snapshots with the husband. Nothing of the kid.

Baker came back, looking sharp-eyed and ready to say something.

Cathy Poulson got there first, saying, "Okay, I'll be open and tell you everything. If you pledge that you'll do your best not to violate my privacy."

Baker said, "We'll do our utmost best, ma'am." Looking relaxed—too loose, Lamar could tell there was something on his partner's mind.

The three of them sat back down.

Cathy Poulson said, "Jack and I had a relationship—ancient history, before I met Lloyd. I'm from California, too. LA. That's where I met Jack."

Another West Coast connection, like the shrink. Lamar wondered if Delaware knew her, then told himself he was being stupid. Ginormous city like LA, what were the chances . . .

Cathy Poulson said, "That's it."

Baker said, "A relationship."

"Yes."

"Why'd you decide to meet last night?"

"Jack called me to let me know he was in town. Out of the blue, you could've knocked me over with a feather. He said he'd heard about Lloyd's passing and was real sweet about it—Jack could be like that. He said he'd had some rough patches himself but of course nothing comparable to what I was going through . . . which I thought was extremely empathic. I'd heard a bit about what Jack had gone through—from the media, not personally. The lifestyle issues, the career ups and downs. For him to put all that aside and consider my pain, I thought that was . . . kind."

Baker said, "So he called to say hi."

"We talked a bit. He said he'd had a terrible fear of flying after that helicopter thing—I read about that, too. He said he'd lived with his fear for years, finally decided to conquer it and get some therapy. The flight to Nashville was a big accomplishment. He sounded so incredibly *proud*. As if he'd just had a number one hit. I told him that was wonderful. Then we talked some more about Lloyd. Then he asked if I wanted to get together. I suppose I shouldn't have been surprised, but it caught me off guard. I didn't know how I felt about that."

"Not sure you wanted to see him."

"To tell the truth," she said, "we didn't part on great terms. Back in the old days, Jack could be tough."

"How so?" said Baker.

"Mercurial—moody. Drugs made it worse. Then there were all those women. Groupies—do they still call them that?"

"Yes, ma'am," said Lamar. Thinking: *All those gigs I played, never saw a single one.*

"All those groupies," said Cathy Poulson, "you can't really expect a man to be faithful . . . anyway, it was jarring, hearing from him so many years later. Maybe my grief was what led me to say okay, I'm still not sure. He told me there was a club he was going to, over on First, could we meet there. I agreed. But right after I hung up, I regretted it. What in the world was it going to accomplish? I considered calling him back and canceling, but didn't want to hurt his feelings. Especially with his conquering his fear—I didn't want to set him back. Can you understand that?"

"Sure," said Baker.

"I mean that would make me feel guilty, stressing him to the point where he backslid." She glanced to the side. "Back in the good old days, I had plenty of experience with backsliding."

"Drugs," said Baker.

"The whole crazy scene," she said. "Funny thing was, no one really saw it as crazy except me. I never indulged. Not *once, never.* I respect myself way too much for that. Jack, of course, was another story. I spent many a night walking him around. When a doctor needed to be called, I was usually the one who did it."

"You had a close relationship," said Lamar.

"Such as it was. But ancient, ancient history, gentlemen. That's why I wasn't sure I wanted to play the reminiscence game with him. Still, I didn't want to upset Jack, so I didn't cancel. Instead, I showed up late." A glassy smile, almost intoxicated. "I thought that was the perfect solution."

"Showing up late?"

"Of course. That way, we'd have minimal contact but I'd have fulfilled my obligation."

Once again Lamar thought of Cathy as a master director. Baker said, "You'd say hi, nice to see you, then you'd go your separate ways."

"Exactly," said Cathy Poulson. "Frankly, when I saw Jack I was shocked and that made it easier. My image of him was stuck back in the time when we were together. He had been a handsome man. Now . . ."

She shrugged.

"Not too well preserved," said Lamar.

"That makes him sound like a lab specimen but I'm afraid you're right." She sighed. "Poor Jack. Time hadn't been kind to him. I drove there expecting a good-looking man—which was foolish after all those years had passed. What I saw was a heavy old bald man."

Not unlike her late husband, thought Lamar.

She picked up her glass of lemonade. "We had a little hug, chatted briefly, then parted ways. I will tell you this: Jack wasn't upset, the entire encounter was friendly. I got a clear sense that he felt the same way I did."

"Which was?"

"Don't fix it if it ain't broken," said Cathy Poulson. "Whoever wrote that famous book was right. You really can't go home. Psychologically, I mean."

Lamar still had a feeling about the woman and would've stuck around to see if he could tease anything more out of her. But he could tell Baker was antsy. A few more of Lamar's questions made his partner downright restless, perched on the edge of the sofa, ready to spring up like a frog at a fly.

Lamar said, "Thank you, ma'am. If you think of anything else, here's our number." He handed her a card and Cathy Poulson placed it on a table in an absent way that let him know he'd never hear from her again.

She said, "Of course. Would you like me to put some lemonade in a little bottle?"

9

Back in the car, Lamar said, "Okay, what?"

"Okay, what *what*?"

"The way you were itching to book, El Bee. Sportin' a rash?"

Baker grinned huge—an unusual sight. "Drive."

Lamar made his way back to Belle Meade Boulevard, passed more mansions. Engine roar sounded at their rear end. A couple of rich kids in a BMW convertible testing the speed limit. They got inches from his rear bumper. He let them pass, heard laughter.

Baker said, "Did you notice that there's no pictures of her kid in the living room?"

"Sure did. Not too many of her late great husband Lloyd, either. I figure her for one of those narcissists, it's all about me."

"Or maybe something else," said Baker. "When I go to use the facilities, I notice an alcove up a ways. She's got alcoves, niches, whatever, all over the place. Has these little prissy figurines, glass globes, that kind of stuff. But the one near the john has a picture. In a nice frame, just like the ones on the mantel, and it shows her kid. Big old blond bubba, could be a twin of the one in the picture we found in Jeffries's hotel room."

"Owen the rugby player," said Lamar. "By the way, that one is definitely Melinda's kid. I found a picture in an old copy of *People* magazine."

"Good for you," said Baker. "Now just let me stay on track here for a second, Stretch. This other kid—Poulson's kid—is wearing a uniform, too—real football, with the pads and the black stuff under the eyes. And I'm telling you, he could've had the same papa as Owen. Same coloring, beefy, big jaw. To my eye, an even stronger resemblance to Mr. Jack Jeffries. That makes me curious so I turn over the photo and on the back there's an inscription. 'Happy Em's Day, Mom, You Rock, Love Tristan.' The really *interesting* part is the handwriting. Block letters with little flourishes on the caps. I'm no graphologist but to my eye, a dead match in handwriting for those silly lyrics we found in the hotel room."

" 'Music City Breakdown.' "

"What it's looking like," said Baker, "is a whole bunch of stuff broke down."

They drove back to the city, grabbed fast-food burgers and Cokes, took them to the purple room where Brian Fondebernardi joined them around the center table. The sergeant's shirt matched the walls. His charcoal slacks were razor-pressed, his black hair was clipped, his eyes sharp and searching. Dealing with the press all morning hadn't dented him but he wanted a progress report.

Lamar said, "Matter of fact, we have something to report."

When they finished filling him in, Fondebernardi said, "He was a rock star, had beaucoup girlfriends, she was one of them and got knocked up. So?"

"So," said Baker, "the kid's a college freshman, meaning eighteen, nineteen tops. Let's even say twenty if he's dumb, which he ain't because he got into Brown. She was married to her husband for twenty-six years."

"Oops," said Fondebernardi.

"Oops, indeed," said Lamar. "There's a secret worth keeping in Belle Meade."

"Plus," said Baker, "we know the kid—Tristan's his name—had contact with Jeffries."

"Via the handwriting of the song," said Fondebernardi. "Kid could've mailed that in."

"Maybe, Sarge, but Jeffries held on to it. Meaning maybe there was some kind of relationship."

"Or he thought the lyrics were good."

Baker rocked an open palm with splayed fingers back and forth. "Not unless he lost his ear completely."

"Lyrics needed something, that's for sure," said Lamar, "but they were full of frustration—like Nashville screwed him over. Doesn't sound like a pampered rich kid, so maybe there's a side of ol' Tristan we don't know about."

"Someone that age," said Fondebernardi. "He hasn't had time to get frustrated."

"Rich kids," said Baker. "They're used to having their way, get their panties in a sling real easily. Maybe this one wanted approval from Jeffries, didn't get it, and freaked out."

"He's in Rhode Island, Baker."

"We haven't verified that yet."

"Why not?" said Fondebernardi, then he checked himself. "You want my okay before you call."

Baker said, "It's Belle Meade, Sarge."

End of discussion.

The registrar clerk at Brown University was squirrelly about giving out student information.

Lamar said, "You got Facebook, right?"

"Yes."

"Then nothing's secret, so why don't you make my life easy?"

"I don't know . . ."

"I don't want his grade point average, only to know if he's on campus."

"And this is because . . ."

"Police investigation," said Lamar. "You don't cooperate and something bad happens, it's not going to reflect well on Brown. And I know what a great school Brown is. My sister went there."

"Who's that?"

"Ellen Grant," he said, picking a nice Waspy name out of thin air. "She loved it."

"Well," said the clerk.

"On campus or not, we'll do the rest."

"Hold on, Captain." Another little fib.

Less than a minute later: "No, Captain, Tristan Poulson took a leave of absence for the second semester."

"He did the fall semester, then he left."

"Yes," said the clerk. "The freshman year can be stressful."

They called Fondebernardi back to the purple room and told him.

He said, "Rich kid who thinks he's a songwriter, drops out to follow his dream?"

"That, plus maybe Lloyd Poulson's dying got him delusional," said Lamar. "It's possible somehow Tristan figured out Jack was his bio dad. And maybe he found out more than that. The M.E. said Jack's internal organs were a mess, he didn't have long. Maybe Tristan read about Jack's health issues in some fan magazine, worried about that and it tipped him over—get in touch with my bio dad before he kicks, too. Use music to bond. And where else would he go to do that but back home, because here's where the music is. Not to mention Mommy's money and connections."

"Or," said Baker, "Tristan didn't figure out who his real daddy was but he wanted to meet Jack, anyway. Mommy's old boyfriend, who just happens to be a onetime superstar and Tristan's into writing songs. Jeffries might not be able to motivate hits anymore but to a needy kid he could've seemed larger than life."

"Especially," said Lamar, "if Mommy told him detailed stories about the good old days. She's a genteel rich lady now, but likes attention. I can see her basking in old glory."

Fondebernardi didn't answer.

"Fame," said Lamar. "It's the hardest drug of all, right, Sarge? Tristan gets in touch with his songwriting self, writes a plaintive ditty that he sends to Jack."

"Who just happens to be his real daddy," said Baker.

Lamar said, "I haven't seen the kid's picture yet, but Baker says the resemblance is real strong."

Baker nodded. "Strong enough for Mommy to take Junior's pictures off the mantel in case we showed up. Unfortunately for her, she forgot about the alcove."

"Thank God for Baker's bladder," said Lamar.

Fondebernardi said, "Find out everything you can about the kid."

They started where everyone does: Google. Came up with twenty hits, all scores from football games and field hockey matches Tristan Poulson had played in.

Varsity star at Madison Prep, a fancy-pants place out in Brentwood they'd both heard of because Lieutenant Shirley Jones's son had been accepted there on a basketball scholarship. One of two black kids admitted three years ago.

They asked her if they could talk to Tim and told her why.

She said, "You bet. And he knows how to keep his mouth shut."

Tim Jones came to the station after school, all six six of him, carelessly good-looking, still wearing his blazer and khakis, white shirt and rep tie. He hugged and kissed his mother, followed her into the purple room, sat down and attacked the Quiznos Black Angus on rosemary parmesan bread smothered with mozzarella, mushrooms and sautéed onions she'd bought for him.

Baker and Lamar watched in admiration as the kid polished off the full-sized sub in what seemed like a few bites, washed it down with a jumbo root beer, not a crumb or stain on his preppy duds.

"Excellent," he told the lieutenant. "Usually you get me the Italian."

"Special occasion," said Shirley Jones, touching the top of her son's head briefly, then heading for the door. "Talk to my ace detectives. Tell them everything you know and then forget it ever happened. When will you be home?"

"Right after, I guess," said Tim. "Massive homework."

"You guess?"

"Right after."

"I'll pick up some Dreyer's on the way."

"Excellent. Rocky road."

"Ahem."

"Please."

"I knew him," said Tim, "but we didn't hang out. He seemed okay."

"You play on a team together?" said Baker.

"Nope. He did some hoops but just jayvee. Football's his thing. He's built for it."

"Big guy."

"Like a refrigerator."

"An okay guy, huh?" said Lamar.

Tim nodded. "Seemed mellow. He'd play aggressive on the field but he wasn't like that the rest of the time. I went to a few parties with him—jock stuff, after games—but we didn't hang out."

"Who'd he hang with?"

"Other football dudes, I guess. He had a girlfriend. From Briar Lane."

"Remember her name?"

"Sheralyn," said Tim. "Don't know her last name."

"Cheerleader?"

"No, she was more of a brainiac."

"Good student."

"Don't know about her grades," said Tim. "Brainiac's more than good grades, it's a category, you know? Concentrating on books, art, music, all that good stuff."

"Music," said Baker.

"She played piano. I saw her at a party. Tristan was standing with her, singing along with her."

"Good voice?"

"He sounded okay."

"What kind of music?"

Tim frowned. "Something like old jazz, maybe Sinatra, which was kind of weird; everyone thought it was funny they were playing old-people music but they were serious. My mom plays Sinatra. Sammy Davis Junior, Tony Bennett. Has those vinyls, you know?"

"Antiques," said Baker.

Tim said, "She has a typewriter, too. Likes me to know how things used to be."

"What do you know about Tristan's music?"

"His what?"

"We've heard that he wrote songs."

"That's a new one for me," said Tim. "I never heard rumors he and Sheralyn broke up, but maybe he was looking to get another girl."

"Why do you say that?"

"That's mostly why guys write songs."

10

Googling *Briar Lane Academy Sheralyn* pulled up a review in the girl school's campus paper, *The Siren Call*. Last October, the Thespian Club had presented a "post-modern version of *As You Like It*." The reviewer had loved the show, singling out Sheralyn Carlson's portrayal of Rosalind as "mercilessly relevant and psychologically deep."

They traced the girl to an address in Brentwood—Nashville's other high-priced spread. Five miles south of Belle Meade, Brentwood had a higher concentration of new money than its cousin, with rolling hills and open land a magnet for music types who'd cashed in. Faith and Tim and Dolly had Brentwood spreads. So did Alan Jackson and George Jones. Homes ranged from horse estates to sleek ranch houses. Ninety-four percent white, six percent everything else.

Sheralyn Carlson might've posed a problem for the census taker, with a Chinese radiologist mother and a hulking, blond radiologist father who would've looked fine in Viking duds. The girl was gorgeous, tall and lithe with long, shiny, honey-colored hair, almond-shaped amber eyes, and a soft-spoken disposition of the type that tended to reassure adults.

Drs. Elaine and Andrew Carlson seemed like quiet, inoffensive types, themselves. They briefed the detectives on the fact that their only child had never earned a grade lower than A, had never given them a *lick* of problem, had been offered a spot in the Johns Hopkins gifted writer program but had turned it down because, as Dr. Elaine phrased it, "Sheralyn eschews divisive stratification."

"Our view as well," added Dr. Andrew.

"We try to maintain family cohesiveness," said Dr. Elaine. "Without sacrificing free expression." Stroking her daughter's shoulder. Sheralyn took her mother's hand. Dr. Elaine squeezed her daughter's fingers.

"My daughter—our daughter," said Dr. Andrew, "is a fabulous young woman."

"That's obvious," said Baker. "We'd like to talk to her alone."

"I don't know," said Dr. Andrew.

"I don't know, either," said Dr. Elaine.

"*Know,*" said Sheralyn. "Please." Flashing a brief, tight smile at her parents.

The Drs. Carlson looked at each other. "Very well," said Dr. Andrew. He and his wife left the stark, white contempo living room of their stark, white contempo house as if embarking on a trek across Siberia. Glancing back and catching Sheralyn's merry wave.

When they were gone, the girl turned grave. "Finally! A chance to express what's been on my mind for some time. I'm extremely concerned about Tristan."

"Why?" said Baker.

"He's depressed. Not clinically, at this point, but dangerously close."

"Depressed about his father?"

"His father," she said. Blinking. "Yes, that, of course."

"What else?"

"The usual post-adolescent issues." Sheralyn turned her fingers like darning needles. "Life."

Lamar said, "Sounds like you're interested in psychology."

Sheralyn nodded. "The ultimate questions always revolve around human behavior."

"And Tristan's behavior concerns you."

"More like lack of behavior," she said. "He's depressed."

"Going through rough times."

"Tristan's not what he seems," she said, as if she hadn't heard. She had the refined good looks of a beauty queen, but aimed for edgy. Floral minidress, combat boots, henna patterns banding the tops of her hands, four pierces in one ear, three in the other. There was a tiny little dot above her right nostril where a stud had once rested.

"What do you mean?"

"At first glance," she said, "Tristan comes across as Mega Jock From Planet Testosterone. But he's preternaturally sensitive."

"Preternaturally," said Baker.

"We all have our masks," the teen remarked. "A less honest person might have no trouble donning his. Tristan's soul is honest. He suffers."

Neither detective was really sure what she meant. Lamar said, "Is he going through an identity crisis of some kind?"

She looked at him as if he needed tutoring. "Sure, why not."

"Changing his ways," said Baker.

Silence.

Lamar said, "We know he took a leave from Brown. Where is he?"

"At home."

"Living with his mother?"

"Only in a physical sense."

"They don't get along?"

"Tristan's home is not a nurturing place."

"Conflict with his mother?"

"No-o," said Sheralyn Carlson. "For conflict, there needs to be involvement."

"Mrs. Poulson's not involved."

"Oh, she is." The girl frowned. "With herself. Such a cozy relationship."

"You don't like her," said Baker.

"I don't think about her enough to dislike her." A second later: "She represents much that repels me."

"How so?"

"Have you met her?"

"Sure have."

"Yet you ask," said Sheralyn Carlson, working at looking amused.

Baker said, "What's her problem, besides being a distant mom?"

The girl took several moments to answer. Twisting those fingers. Playing with her hair and the hem of her dress. "I love Tristan. Not as a sexual lover, there's no longer that spark between us." She crossed her legs. "Words don't do it justice but if I had to encapsulate, I'd say brotherly love. But don't take that as a Freudian hint. Tristan and I are quite proud that we've managed to transition our relationship from the realm of the physical to idealistic companionship." Another long pause. "Tristan and I have both taken on the mantle of celibacy."

Silence.

Sheralyn Carlson smiled. "So-called adults shudder at the notion of so-called adolescent sexuality but when the s.c. adolescent eschews sexuality, the s.c. adults think it's bizarre."

"I reckon that's not too foreign a concept in these parts," Baker said. "Churchgoing people every Wednesday and Sunday like clockwork."

She frowned. "The point is that Tristan and I have opted for a more internal life. Since his senior year."

"Art and music," said Lamar.

"The internal life," the girl repeated.

"Well, that's fine, Sheralyn. And now he's living at home. You see each other much?"

"At home and about."

"About where?"

"He tends to gravitate toward Sixteenth Street."

"Looking for a record deal on Music Row?"

"Tristan is close to tone deaf, but he loves to write. The obvious choice is lyrics. For the last month, he's been attempting to sell his lyrics to the philistines on Music Row. I warned him he'd encounter nothing but crass commercialism, but Tristan can be quite determined."

"From jock to songwriter," said Baker. "How'd his mom take that?"

"She would have to care to take."

"Apathetic."

"She would have to believe that others exist in order to fit into any sort of category such as 'apathetic.' "

Lamar said, "Mrs. Poulson lives in her own little world."

"Little," said Sheralyn Carlson, "being the operative word. She did break out of it long enough to tell Tristan that he was too good for me." Crooked smile. "Because of this." Touching the side of one eye. "The epicanthic fold trumps all."

"She's a racist," said Baker.

"Well," said the girl, "that has been known to exist in various civilizations over a host of millennia."

Aiming for breezy, but recalling the slight had tightened her voice.

One of those high-IQ types who hid behind words, thought Lamar. That rarely worked for any length of time.

He said, "Tristan couldn't have been happy with that."

"Tristan laughed," said Sheralyn Carlson. "I laughed. We shared the mirth."

The detectives didn't answer.

"She," said the girl. Letting the word hang there for a few seconds. "She—okay, let me fill in the picture with an anecdote. When Tristan started at Brown, he was the epitome of Mega Jock with his shaved head and fresh-faced optimism. By the end of his first semester, his hair had reached his shoulders and his beard was full and woolly; he grew a lovely, masculine beard. That's when he began suspecting, but *she* denied everything."

"Suspected what?" said Baker.

"His true paternity."

"He doubted that Mr. Poulson was his—"

"Detective Southerby," said the girl, "why not be honest? You're here because of Jack Jeffries's murder."

Baker had mentioned his own surname once, when first meeting the family. Most people never bothered to register it. This kid missed nothing.

He said, "Go on."

"Throughout Tristan's childhood, *she* had always talked about Jack. Rather incessantly, at times. Tristan knew that her relationship with Lloyd was sexless and he noted the sparkle in her eye when Jack's name came up. He wondered as anyone with a brain would wonder. Then, when the inner world began exerting its pull and he began to write, wonder turned to fantasy."

"About Jack Jeffries being his real dad," said Baker.

"Every adolescent has them," said Sheralyn Carlson. "Escape fantasies, the certainty that one has to have been adopted because these *aliens* one finds oneself living with *can't* be linked to one, biologically. In Jack's case, a rather dramatic physical resemblance kept the fantasy alive." Another crooked smile. "And wouldn't you know."

She crossed the other leg, exposed some thigh, tucked down her dress and ran a finger under the top of a boot.

Lamar said, "Tristan felt he looked like Jack Jeffries."

"He did, I did. Anyone who saw pictures of Jack Jeffries when he was young did. Two things happened that further fed his fantasy before it became reality. Before Tristan left for Brown, I came across a picture of a boy in a magazine. In *People* magazine, an article about sperm donors."

"Melinda Raven's son by Jack Jeffries."

"Owen," said Sheralyn, as if recalling an old friend. "He could've been Tristan's twin. The similarity in age made the resemblance undeniable. That's why the first thing Tristan did when he got to Brown was grow his hair and beard. To compare himself to pictures of Jack taken back in the Hairy Days. The result was beyond debate. Tristan experienced a crisis of sorts. We spent long hours on the phone and decided he needed a paradigm shift. He took a leave of absence, came home, moved into the guest house of Mommy's manse and prepared to confront her. We had strategy meetings beforehand, devising how to approach her, finally settled on simplicity: tell her you know and request verification. Tristan took some time to build up his courage, finally did it, when she was on her way to her country club. We expected initial denial, then confession, then some sort of emotion. *She* didn't bat an eyelash. Told him he was crazy and that he'd better clean up if he intended to ever have lunch with her at the club."

"What did Tristan do?" said Lamar.

"Nothing."

"Nothing at all?"

"Ergo, depression."

"Did he try to contact Jack Jeffries?"

"He did more than try. He succeeded."

"They met?"

"In cyberspace."

"E-mail," said Baker.

"Tristan contacted Jack Jeffries's website, introduced himself, sent a j-peg of his senior photo, as well as a later, hirsute version, and some lyrics. He expected nothing, but Jack answered, said he was happy to hear from Tristan. Said Tristan's lyrics were 'awesome.' "

"How'd Tristan react to that?"

The girl turned away. Placed her hand on a small, white abstract carving resting on a glass and chrome table.

This place is like an igloo, thought Baker. "How did Tristan take that?"

The girl gnawed her lip.

"Sheralyn?" said Baker.

"He cried," she said. "Tears of joy. I held him."

Ten minutes later, Drs. Andrew and Elaine peeked in.

Sheralyn said, "I'm fine," and waved them away and they disappeared.

During that time, she'd verified that the lyrics Tristan had sent were "Music City Breakdown." But she denied knowing about any face-to-face meeting between Tristan Poulson and Jeffries. Nor was she willing to pinpoint Tristan's whereabouts beyond the guest house on his mother's property.

"He's still there," said Baker.

"I believe so."

"You believe?"

"Tristan and I haven't been in contact for several days. That's why I'm concerned. That's why I'm talking to you."

"What did you think when you heard Jack Jeffries had been murdered?"

"What did I think?" she said. "I thought nothing. I *felt* sad."

"Did you consider that maybe Tristan had done it?"

"Never."

"Does Tristan carry a weapon?"

"Never."

"Has he ever shown a violent side?"

"Never. Never never never to any incriminating questions you're going to ask about him. If I thought he was guilty, I'd never have talked to you."

"Why not?"

"Because I'd never do anything to incriminate Tristan."

"Even if he murdered someone?"

Sheralyn rubbed the space to the side of one eye. Same spot she'd touched when discussing Cathy Poulson's racist comment. Then she sat up straight and stared Baker down—something few people tried.

"I," she pronounced, "am neither judge nor jury."

"Just for the record," said Baker, "where were you the night before last, say between twelve and two AM?"

"That's not night, it's morning."

"Correction duly noted, young lady. Where were you?"

"Here. In my bedroom. Sleeping. I make an effort to sleep soundly."

"Good habits," said Lamar.

"I have obligations—school, SATs, theater club, Model UN. Et cetera."

Sounding bitter.

"Headed for Brown?"

"Not hardly. I'm going to Yale."

"Sleeping," said Baker. "First time you heard about Jack Jeffries was . . ."

"When my father brought it up. He's our own personal town crier. He reads the morning paper, and comments extensively on every article."

"You didn't think anything of it, just sad."

"Over the loss of life," said the girl. "Any life."

"Just that," said Baker. "Even though you knew this was Tristan's real dad and Tristan had recently contacted him."

"I was saddest for Tristan. Am. I've called his cell twenty-eight times, but he doesn't answer. You should find him. He needs comfort."

"Why do you think he's not answering?"

"I've already explained that. He's depressed. Tristan gets like that. Turns off the phone, goes inward. That's when he writes."

"No chance he's run away?"

"From what?"

"Guilt."

"That's absurd," she said. "Tristan didn't kill him."

"Because . . ."

"He loved him."

As if that explained it, thought Lamar. Smart kid, but utterly clueless. "Tristan loved Jack even though he'd never met him."

"Irrelevant," said Sheralyn Carlson. "One never falls in love with a person. One falls in love with an *idea*."

11

rs. Andrew and Elaine Carlson verified that Sheralyn had been home the night/morning of the murder from five PM until eight thirty AM, at which time Dr. Andrew drove her to Briar Lane Academy in his Porsche Cayenne.

"Not that they'd say anything else," muttered Baker, as they got back in the car. "She's got them wrapped around her little intellectual finger, could've climbed through a window and met up with Tristan and they'd never know."

"Think she was involved?" said Lamar.

"I think she'd do and say anything to cover for Tristan."

"Her celibate lover. You believe that?"

"Kids, nowadays? I believe anything. So let's find this tortured soul and shake him up."

"Back to Mommy's mansion."

"It's a short drive."

When they got to the Poulson estate, a lowering sun had grayed the house and a padlock had been fixed to the main gate. The red Benz was in the same place. The Volvo was gone.

No call box, just a bell. Baker jabbed it. The front door opened and someone looked at them.

Black uniform with white trim, dark face. The maid who'd fetched the lemonade—Amelia.

Baker waved.

Amelia didn't budge.

He shouted her name. Loud.

The sound was a slap across the genteel, silent face of Belle Meade.

She approached them.

"Not here," she said, through iron gate slats. "Please."

Her eyes were wide with fear. Sweat trickled from her hairline to an eyebrow but she made no attempt to dry her face.

"Where did the missus go?" said Baker.

Silence.

"Tell us, right *now*."

"Kentucky, sir."

"Her horse farm."

"Yes, sir."

"When did she leave?"

"Two hours ago."

"She take Tristan with her?"

"No, sir."

"You're sure about that?"

"Yes, sir."

"We could sit here and watch the house for days," said Lamar. "We could come back with a warrant and go through every room of this place and make a godawful mess."

No answer.

Baker said, "So you're sticking with that story. She didn't take Tristan."

"No, sir."

"No, you're not sticking with it, or no she didn't take him?" Baker's ears were red.

"She didn't take him, sir."

"He in the house, right now?"

"No, sir."

"Where, then?"

"I don't know, sir."

"When's the last time you saw him?"

"When you were here, sir."

"When we were talking to Mrs. Poulson, Tristan was here?"

"In the guest house."

"When did he leave?"

"After you did."

"Why?"

"I don't know, sir."

"Did he take a car?"

"His car," said Amelia.

"Make and model," said Lamar, whipping out his pad.

"A Beetle. Green."

"Did he take anything with him?"

"I didn't see, sir."

"You cleaned his room, right?"

"Yes, sir."

"Any clothes missing?"

"I haven't been in there today, sir."

"What we're getting at," said Baker, "is did he just take a drive into town or do you think he *left* town?"

"I don't know, sir. It's a big house. I start at one end, takes me two days to get to the other."

"And your point is?"

"There are many things I don't hear."

"Or choose not to hear."

Amelia's face remained impassive.

Lamar said, "Tristan left right after we did. Did he and his mother have a discussion?"

"I don't know, sir."

"Why'd Mrs. Poulson decide all of a sudden to fly to Kentucky?"

"It wasn't all of a sudden," said the maid. "She flies there all the time. To see her horses."

"Loves her horses, does she?"

"Apparently, sir."

"You're saying the trip was planned."

"Yes, sir. I heard her calling the charter service five days ago."

"So you do hear some things."

"Depends which room I'm working, sir. I was freshening outside the study and she was using the study phone."

"Remember the name of the charter service?"

"Don't have to," said Amelia. "She uses the same one all the time. New Flight."

"Thank you," said Lamar. "Now where can we find Tristan?"

"Don't know, sir."

"Sure about that?"

"More than sure, sir."

Back in the car, they got the registration stats on Tristan Poulson's VW and put an alert out on the car. They called New Flight Charter, were told in no uncertain terms that the company maintained strict client confidentiality and that nothing short of a warrant would change that.

"That so . . . well, good for you," said Baker, hanging up with a scowl.

"What?" said Lamar.

"They fly big shots like President Clinton and Tom Brokaw, everything hush-hush."

"Hush-hush but they tell you they fly Clinton."

"Guess he's beyond mere mortality. Drive, Stretch."

On the way back to town, they got a call from Trish, the receptionist at headquarters. A Dr. Alex Delaware had phoned this morning, and then again at two. No message.

Baker said, "Guy's probably itching to get back home."

"Guy works with the police," said Lamar, "you'd think he'd know he's free to go, we can't keep him here legally."

"You'd think."

"Hmm . . . maybe you should call him back. Or better yet, let's drop in on him at the hotel. See if he knew Cathy Poulson in her LA days. While we're there, we can also show Tristan's picture around to the staff."

"Two bad we don't have two pictures," said Baker. "Another with all that hair."

"Like father, like son," said Lamar. "It always comes down to family, doesn't it?"

Delaware wasn't in his room. The concierge was sure of that, the doctor had stopped by around noon to ask directions to Opryland and hadn't returned.

No one at the Hermitage remembered ever seeing Tristan Poulson, the clean-cut, high school senior photo version. Asking people to imagine long hair and a beard produced nothing but quizzical looks.

Just as they were about to leave for a drive-through of Music Row, Delaware walked in. Spruced up, LA style: blue blazer, white polo shirt, blue jeans, brown loafers. Taking shades off his eyes, he nodded at the concierge.

"Doctor," said Baker.

"Good, you got my message. C'mon up, I've got something to show you."

As the elevator rose, Lamar said, "How was Opryland?"

Delaware said, "Tracing me, huh? It was more Disneyland than down-home but with a name like Opryland I shouldn't have been surprised. I had lunch in that restaurant with the giant aquariums, which wasn't bad."

"Have a hearty seafood dinner?"

The psychologist laughed. "Steak. Any luck on Jack's murder?"

"We're working on it."

Delaware worked at hiding his sympathy.

His room was the same pin-neat setup. The guitar case rested on the bed.

He opened a closet drawer, drew out some papers. Hotel fax cover sheet, over a couple of others.

"After you left, I started thinking about my sessions with Jack. Something he told me as the trip approached. Dead people don't get confidentiality. I had my girlfriend, Robin, go through the chart and fax the relevant pages. Here you go."

Two lined pages filled with dense, sharply slanted handwriting. Not the clearest fax. Hard to make out.

Delaware saw them squinting. "Sorry, my penmanship stinks. Would you like a summary?"

Lamar said, "That would be great, Doctor."

"As the date got closer, Jack's anxiety rose. That was understandable and expected. We redoubled our efforts to work on deep muscle relaxation, pinpointed the stimuli that really set off his anxiety—basically we gave it the full-court press. I thought we were doing fine but about a week ago, Jack called me in the middle of the night, unable to sleep, agitated. I told him to come over but he said he'd wait until morning. I asked if he was sure, he said he was and promised to show up at nine AM. He arrived at eleven, looking haggard. I assumed it was pre-flight jitters but he said there were other things on his mind. I encouraged him to talk about anything that bothered him. He made a joke about it—something along the lines of 'That's allowed? Good old-fashioned head-shrinking instead of cognitive hoochy-coo mojo mind-bending?' "

He sat down on the bed, touched the guitar case. "That had been an issue right from the beginning. Jack did *not* want psychotherapy. Said he'd had plenty of that during his various rehab stints and that the sound of his own voice bitching made him want to puke."

"Afraid of something?" said Baker.

"Aren't we all?" Delaware slipped off his jacket, folded it neatly, placed it on the bed. Changed his mind, got up and hung it in the closet.

He sat back down. "There's always that possibility. What people in my business call baloney afraid of the slicer. But I take people at their word until proven otherwise and I went along with Jack not wanting to get into topics other than flying. We had a deadline approaching and I knew if Jack didn't get on that plane, I'd never see him again. But now, he'd changed his mind and wanted to talk. I'm not saying what he told me about is profoundly relevant to your case, but I thought you should know."

"Appreciate it," said Baker, holding out an expectant palm.

"What Jack wanted to talk about was family," said Delaware. "That surprised even me because Jack had always been an extremely focused and goal-oriented patient. I'm sure the stress of the upcoming flight released a barrage of unpleasant memories. He started with a brutal upbringing. Abusive father, negligent mother, both of them doctors—respectable on the outside but severe alcoholics who turned his childhood into a nightmare. He was the only child, bore the brunt of it. His memories were so traumatic that he'd seriously considered sterilization when he was in his twenties, but never followed through because he was too damn lazy and stoned and didn't want anyone 'cutting down there before I had enough fun.' But I'm not sure that was it. I think a part of him did yearn for that parent–child connection. Because when he talked about not having his own family, he got extremely morose. Then he brought up something he'd done that made him smile: fathering a child with an actress who was gay and sought him out because she admired his music."

"Melinda Raven," said Lamar.

"So you know."

"That's all we know. Her name."

"The story she put out for the media was sperm donation," said Delaware. "The truth was, Jack and she made love. Several times until she conceived. She had a boy. Jack was not involved in his life."

"Why not?"

"He claimed it was fear," said Delaware. "That he'd mess the boy up. I know Jack's image was that of a rock 'n' roll bad boy, afraid of nothing. And he had taken some outrageous risks during the early days, but those had been fueled by drugs. At the core, he was a highly fearful man. *Ruled* by fear. When he brought up Owen, he looked proud. But then when he got into Owen not being a part of his life, he broke down. Then he started on a long jag about all the other children he might've sired. All those groupies, one-night stands, decades of random promiscuity. He made a joke about it. 'I'm a bachelor, meaning no kids. To speak of.' Then he broke down again. Wondering what might have been. Visualizing himself old and alone at the end of his life."

"With his money," said Lamar, "if he sired kids, you'd think at least some of the women would've filed paternity suits."

"I told him exactly that. He said a few had tried but they'd all turned out to be liars. What concerned him were the honest women too kind to exploit him. Or women who simply didn't know. His phrasing was 'I rained sperm on the world, it had to sprout somewhere.' "

"Why wouldn't women know?"

Delaware ran his fingers through his curls. "At the height of Jack's career, he spent a lot of time in a haze that included group sex, orgies, just about anything you can imagine."

"He partied hearty and now he's worrying about unknown kids?" said Baker.

"He was an old man," said the psychologist. "Getting closer to mortality can turn you inward."

Same phrase Sheralyn had used about Tristan.

Father and son . . .

Delaware said, "What I'm saying is that the issue of family—not having a family—was on Jack's mind as the trip approached. And something else he told me—something I really didn't appreciate at the time—makes me wonder if the trip was really *about* family."

Lamar hid his enthusiasm. "The story was he was coming out here for the Songbird benefit."

"Yes, it was, but you know guys like me." Small smile. "Always looking for hidden meaning."

"What's the thing he told you?"

"The day after he poured out his heart, he came in looking great. Standing straighter, walking taller, clear-eyed. I said he seemed like a man with a mission. He laughed and said I was right on. He was ready to fly, ready for anything God or Odin or Allah or whoever was in charge was going to toss his way. 'Gonna sing my guts out, Doc. Gonna reclaim my biology.' That's the part I overlooked when I first talked to you. 'Biology.' I thought he was relating it to 'guts.' Joking around, that was Jack's style. He made light of things that frightened him until they got to a level where they overwhelmed him."

"Reclaiming his biology," said Baker. "A paternity thing?"

"The day before, all he could talk about was paternity. I should've made the connection."

"And you're thinking that's relevant because . . ."

"I'm no homicide expert," said Delaware. "But I've seen a few crime scenes. The paper said Jack was stabbed and a knife can be an intimate weapon. You need to get up close and personal when you use one. If you tell me Jack was robbed, I'll change my mind. If he wasn't, I'll continue to wonder if he was cut by someone he knew. Given his remark about biology, how resolute he looked before we left, I'll also wonder if he chose Nashville for his maiden voyage—chose that particular benefit, when there are so many others—because he wanted to be here for a personal reason. And ended up dying because of it."

Neither detective spoke.

Delaware said, "If I've wasted your time, sorry. I wouldn't have felt right if I didn't tell you."

Baker said, "We appreciate it, Doctor." Leaning over and taking the fax. "Do you know a woman named Cathy Poulson?"

"Sorry, no."

"No curiosity about why I asked?"

"I've learned to modulate my curiosity. But sure, who is she?"

"Old girlfriend of Jack's. Hung out with him in LA, maybe thirty years ago."

"Thirty years ago, I was a kid in Missouri."

"The thing is," said Lamar, "she also hooked up with him nineteen and a half years ago."

Delaware studied them. "That's a precise time frame. You know because it was punctuated by a specific event."

Baker looked at Lamar. Lamar nodded.

"Blessed event," said Baker.

"Another kid," said the psychologist. "One of the women Jack wondered about. She lives here?"

"Yes, sir. But for now, we're asking you to respect confidentiality. Even though dead people don't get any."

"Of course. Boy or girl?"

"Boy." They showed him Tristan's picture.

He said, "Oh, man, he looks just like a young Jack."

"He writes songs," said Lamar. "Or thinks he does."

Delaware said, "Meaning a reunion could have involved an audition?"

"Maybe not a happy one." Baker removed a folded photocopy of the song from his pad.

Delaware read the lyrics. "I see what you mean. You found this on Jack's person?"

"In his room. How would Jack react to something like this?"

Delaware thought. "Hard to say. I guess it would depend on his state of mind."

"What do you mean?"

"Like I told you, Jack could be moody."

"You're not the only person to tell us that," Baker answered.

"He might even have had a borderline mood disorder. He could shift from amiable to downright vicious pretty quickly. I only saw his angry side a couple of times in therapy, and it wasn't severe. Flashes of irritation, mostly at the beginning when he was ambivalent when I probed too deeply. As I told you the first time, he was mostly amiable."

"When he decided he really needed you to get on that plane with him, he behaved himself."

"Could be," said Delaware.

"So he never got violent with you?"

"No, nothing like that. My hope was that if Jack stuck around long enough to see concrete results—once he was able to imagine himself nearing an airport without getting sick to his stomach—he'd level out emotionally. And that's exactly what happened. Except for that night he called me, what I mostly saw was the charming side."

"But that other side didn't disappear," said Lamar. "He just held himself in check."

"It's possible."

"So someone catches him in the wrong mood, shows him crappy music, he could've turned nasty."

Delaware nodded.

Baker said, "Do that with a kid—a kid you never acknowledged and just met—and things could turn downright ugly."

Delaware looked at Tristan's photo. "He's your primary suspect?"

"He's looking good for it but we've got no evidence." Lamar smiled. "Just psychology."

Baker said, "First we have to find him, so we'd better be doing our job. Thanks for doing yours, Doc. You can head home, now. We need you, we'll phone you."

Delaware handed the photo back. "Hope it's not him."

"Why?"

"It's tough when they're young."

12

ack in the car, Lamar said, "Smart guy."

Baker said, "That's what the LA Loo said."

"What'd you think about his theory?"

"I'm getting that warm, fuzzy feeling, like when everything starts fitting together. Let's find the kid."

"That's the plan."

They cruised up and down Sixteenth, then tried the neighboring streets, searching for the green Beetle, or a big hulking hippie-type with long hair and beard. Or maybe Tristan Poulson had switched back to the clean-cut version.

A couple of prospects turned out to be garden-variety homeless dudes. One of them panhandled and Lamar handed him a buck.

"Father Teresa," said Baker.

"Got to give to get back. Where, now?"

"Drive."

A canvass of the city core turned up nothing.

Baker said, "These are rich people, they lie with more style."

"Meaning he could be in Kentucky, no matter what the maid said."

"Or in that guest house, the Bug stashed in the garage. Did you notice they've got five of 'em? Garages."

"Didn't," said Lamar. "One thing for sure, his mama lied. That big speech about how far away he was in Brown, how much she missed him. That was just one big misdirect . . . same thing as taking his pictures off the mantel before we showed up."

"The mantel," said Baker, "could've been something else. Maybe there never were any pictures of him up there."

"Why not?"

"There were only two with the husband, and both were him *and* her and she's in front. The rest were all her by herself. Lots of those."

"Freakishly self-centered," said Lamar. "Just like Sheralyn said."

"Think about it, Stretch. Her kid drops out of school, changes his appearance, gets depressed. Now he's in big-time trouble as a murder suspect. What does she do? Packs out for Horsey Land."

"Unless she took him with her."

"Either way, we've got no grounds for warrants and are wading through a swamp of lies."

"Okeechobee Okefenokee *Everglade* of lies, El Bee. What do you think the real reason was for her meeting with Jack?"

"Maybe warning him away from the kid?"

"Like, 'Don't be a bad influence,' " said Lamar. "Or it was just what she said. Jack got in touch with his inner parent, wanted to see his kid and the kid's mommy, too. Some sort of family reunion but she wasn't going for it. Either way, if Jack didn't cooperate, she'd have reason to be upset."

"True, but Greta Barline didn't see any animosity."

"And Cathy wants us to think she's clean because she drove off. Even if that's true, what stopped her from circling around, following Jack as he strolled in the dark?"

"Cutting his throat?" said Baker. "You think a nice, well-bred rich lady would stoop to that?" Smiling bitterly.

"More likely it was the kid, El Bee. Big enough to get the job done."

"We were figuring someone shorter than Jack."

Lamar didn't answer.

Baker rubbed his head. "Swamp of lies."

"Don't let your feelings get all hurt. Occupational hazard, you heard the man, even shrinks have 'em."

Baker looked at his watch. Close to one AM and they were nowhere, nothing, no-how. He phoned headquarters, and made sure the alert on Tristan and his car was still in place. Clicking off, he said, "What's the chance Belle Meade's going to help us with surveillance on the house?"

"Heck," said Lamar, "what's the chance, we do it ourselves, they're not going to ticket us for trespassing?"

Waking up Lieutenant Jones at one forty-two AM wasn't a snap decision. Neither was calling her direct without going through Fondebernardi. They took a two-man vote.

"I say do it," said Lamar. "Why have two people pissed off at us?"

Baker said, "Unanimous," and made the call. A brief one.

"She was cool, Stretch, didn't even sound like she'd been sleeping. She's gonna call the Belle Meade chief. Maybe he's a night owl, too."

Moments later, Jones phoned back. "The chief, Bobby Joe Fortune, promised to send a uniform by the Poulson house at regular intervals. First thing in the morning, he'll also notify his department's single criminal investigator, guy named Wes Sims, once worked as a Nashville detective. I know Wes, a good, smart man."

Lamar and Baker were to avoid surveillance, themselves.

"Oh, man," said Lamar.

"Bobby Joe made a good point," said Shirley Jones. "Quiet street like that, you're going to stick out."

"An officer passing at regular intervals won't?" said Baker.

The lieutenant said, "It's something they do anyway."

"Meaning they're not doing anything extra for us."

"Baker," said Jones, "we live on earth, not Mars. Now, why don't you tell me why you're so hot on this rich boy?"

He complied. When he finished, the lieutenant said, "I'm with you, good work. I'll make sure the uniforms really chase *our* streets for him. Now let's all get some sleep, be fresh as daisies for another day of public service."

13

leep was brief. At four AM, a call from headquarters informed Baker that Tristan Poulson had been spotted by a local squad car and taken to headquarters for questioning.

"Nashville PD?"

"We got lucky, sir."

Tristan had been walking along the river, unarmed, no resistance. The VW was parked behind a warehouse, no real intent to conceal. Baker roused Lamar and the two of them drove to work, waited in an interview room for their suspect to arrive.

Tristan was led in, uncuffed, by a female officer. No reason to restrain him, he hadn't been arrested, and had shown no signs of violence.

Lamar thought, *Lucky break his mama being out of town. No lawyer called in and, with the kid nineteen, no legal obligation to call her. The Belle Meade connection will probably end up complicating matters, but let's just see what shakes out.*

Tristan was neither clean-cut or shaggy hippie. His fair hair was long, but washed and combed, his beard trimmed to a neat goatee. He wore a black Nike T-shirt, baggy blue jeans, white running shoes. There was a small gold knob in one ear. His nails were clean. Nice-looking kid, glowing tan, all that beef looked to be solid muscle. More buff than any pictures Lamar had seen of Jack Jeffries, but the resemblance to Jack was striking.

The boy refused to make eye contact. Despite the hard body and the good grooming, the detectives could see the depression Sheralyn Carlson had talked about. Stoop in the walk, shuffle in his gait, staring at the floor, arms swinging limply as if their being attached to his body didn't matter.

He sat down and slumped, studying the floor tiles. Clean tiles; they smelled of Lysol; one thing you could say about the Murder Squad, the maintenance crew was first-rate.

Lamar said, "Hi, Tristan. I'm Detective Van Gundy and this is Detective Southerby."

Tristan slid down lower.

Baker said, "We know it's rough, son."

Something plinked onto the tiles. A tear. Then another. The kid made no effort to stop, or even wipe his face. They let him cry for a while. Tristan never made a move or a sound, just sat there like a leaky robot.

Lamar tried again. "Real tough times, Tristan."

The boy sat up a bit. Breathed in deeply and let out the air and made abrupt eye contact with Lamar. "Is your father alive, sir?"

That threw Lamar. "Thank God, he is, Tristan." Wondering for a split second what Baker would have said if he'd been the one asked. Then, getting back in detective mode and hoping his answer and a subsequent smile would spur some resentment, jealousy, whatever, make the boy blurt it all out and they'd be finished.

When Tristan's attention returned to the floor, Lamar said, "My dad's a great guy, real healthy for his age."

Tristan looked up again. Smiled faintly, as if he'd just received good news. "I'm happy for you, sir. My dad's dead and I'm still trying to figure that out. He loved my music. We were going to collaborate."

"We're talking about Jack Jeffries." Asking one of those obvious questions you had to ask, in order to keep a clear chain of information.

"Jack was my true father," said Tristan. "Biologically and spiritually. I loved Lloyd, too. Until a few years ago, I thought *he* was my true father. Even when I learned that wasn't true, I never said anything to Lloyd because Lloyd was a good man and he'd always been good to me."

"How'd you find out?"

Tristan patted his chest. "I guess I always knew in my heart. The way Mom always talked about Jack. More than it just being the good old days. And how she never did it around Dad. Lloyd. Then, when I got bigger, seeing Jack's pictures, friends would show them to me. Everyone kept saying it."

"Saying what?"

"We were clones. Not that popular opinion means anything. Sometimes, just the opposite. I didn't really want to believe it. Lloyd was good to me. But . . ."

"The evidence was too strong," said Lamar.

Tristan nodded. "Also, it . . . verified stuff I'd always felt." Another pat. "Deep inside. Lloyd was a good man, but—no buts, he was a good, good man. He died, too."

"You've had a lot of loss, son," said Baker.

"It's like everything exploded inward," said Tristan. "I guess that's *im*ploded. Implosion."

Enunciating the word, as if performing at a spelling bee.

"Implosion," said Baker.

"It was like—everything!" Tristan looked up again. Looked at both detectives. "That's why I considered it."

"Considered what, son?"

"Jumping in."

"Into the Cumberland?"

Another weak smile. "Like that old folk song."

"Which one?"

" 'Goodnight Irene.' "

"Great song. Leadbelly," said Baker, and Lamar almost got a stiff neck from not swiveling toward his partner.

The boy didn't answer.

Baker said, "Yeah, that's a great old song. The way that lyric just hits you, like it's not really part of the rest of the song, then boom."

Silence.

Baker said, " 'Sometimes I have a great notion to jump in the river and drown.' Ol' Leadbelly killed a man, spent time in prison, that's where he wrote it and—"

" 'Midnight Special.' "

"You like the old ones, son."

"I like everything good."

"Makes sense," said Baker. "So there you were, imploding. I got to tell you, things go a certain way, it's easy to see how someone could feel that way, just take a few steps . . ."

Tristan didn't react.

Baker said, "Guilt can make a person feel that way."

Tristan retorted, "Or just plain life going to shit." He dropped his head, pressed his cheeks with his palms.

Baker said, "Son, you're obviously a smart guy so I won't insult your intelligence by spinning a lot of theories. But the fact is: confession can be good for the soul."

"I know," said Tristan. "That's why I told you."

"Told us what?"

"I was thinking of doing it. The river. Did Mom send you? All the way from Kentucky?"

"Send us for what?"

"To stop me."

Baker rubbed his bare head. "You're thinking we picked you up for attempted suicide."

"Mom said if I ever did it again, she'd have me arrested."

"Again," said Lamar.

"I tried twice before," said Tristan. "Not the river, pills. Her Prozac. I'm not sure it was really serious . . . the first time. It was probably one of those . . . a cry for help, to use a cliché."

"Your mama's pills."

"She had her purse open. I needed some cash and she's cool with me just taking whatever money I needed. She left the pills in a vial on top of her wallet. I was just hungry for sleep, you know?"

"When was this, son?"

"You keep calling me 'son.' " The boy smiled. "Nashville PD's babysitting me. Amazing what money can buy."

"You think we're doing this for your mama?" said Lamar.

Tristan smirked and now they could see the spoiled rich kid in him. "Everyone knows the eleventh commandment."

"What's that?"

"Money talks, bullshit walks."

"Tristan," said Baker, "let me give you some education: we are not here to babysit you or to prevent you from doing whatever you want to do to yourself. Though we think that would be pretty stupid—jumping into those muddy waters. We have not talked to your mama since we interviewed her yesterday at your house and she led us to believe you were in Rhode Island."

Tristan stared at him. "Then, what?"

"You are being questioned regarding the murder of Jack Jeffries."

Tristan gaped. Sat up straight. "You think—oh, man, that's ridiculous; that is so psychotic *ridiculous*."

"Why's that?"

"I loved Jack."

"Your new dad."

"My always dad, we were . . . ," said Tristan. He shook his head. Clean blond hair billowed, fell back into place.

"You were what?"

"Reuniting. I mean, he felt it and I was starting to feel it—the bond. But we both knew it takes time. That's why he came to Nashville."

"To bond."

"To meet me."

"First time?" said Lamar.

Nod.

"You get together?"

"Not yet."

"So when'd you give him your song—'Music City Breakdown'?"

"I mailed it to him. Five Oh Two Beverly Crest Ridge, Beverly Hills 90210."

"How long ago?"

"A month. I mailed him a bunch of lyrics."

"Before that, did you exchange letters?"

"We e-mailed. We've been doing it for six months; you can check my computer, I've saved everything between us."

"Why'd you send him 'Breakdown' using snail mail?"

"I wanted him to have something . . . something he could touch. It was part of a whole notebook I sent him, all my lyrics. Jack liked four of them, the rest he said were too shapeless—that was the way he put it. But those four had potential to be songs if they 'grew up.' He said he'd help me grow them up. He said we should concentrate on 'Breakdown' because even though it needed work, it was the best. Then, if it . . . I was thinking about moving to LA, maybe getting into a creative writing program at UCLA or something."

"You and Jack making plans."

Long silence. Then Tristan shook his head. "Jack didn't know about that. We were concentrating on 'Breakdown.' "

"To grow it up."

"We were supposed to do it before the concert—he was playing a concert at the Songbird. If it came together, he was going to sing it and then call me up on stage and introduce me as the writer. And maybe more."

"His son."

Slow, tortured nod. "Now she ruined it."

"Who?" said Baker.

Silence.

"No theories, son?"

"No offense," said the boy, "but that makes me feel worse, not better, sir. Hearing you call me 'son.' "

"Apologies," said Baker. "Who ruined things for you?"

No answer.

Baker said, "She as in . . ."

"Mom."

"You think she killed Jack?"

"I don't see her actually stabbing someone, too messy."

"What, then?"

"She'd hire someone. Maybe some Lexington bad dude; she's got all sorts of people working on the farm. I hate that place."

"Don't like horses?"

"Don't like horseshit and all the racism that's part of the whole scene."

"Some Lexington bad dude," said Baker. "What reason would your mama have to kill Jack?"

"To prevent me from entering his world. That's what she called it— *his* world, like it was some Hades thing, some nether-hell of deep, dark iniquity. All those years, she's been bragging about knowing Jack, how she used to hang with all those rock stars."

"Not in front of Lloyd, though."

"Sometimes, if she was drinking."

"Did it bother him?"

"He'd smile and go back to his paper."

"Easygoing sort," said Lamar.

"That," said Tristan, "and he had all his girlfriends."

His smile was weary. "It was what you might call a free environment, sir. Until I wanted to invent *my* own brand of freedom. Mom wasn't pleased."

"The music scene," said Lamar.

"She calls it the lowest of the low."

Lamar quelled another urge to look at Baker. "You really think she'd murder a man to stop him from being a bad influence on you?"

"She went to warn him off," said Tristan.

"When?"

"The night he flew into Nashville. At least, that's what she told me she was going to do. Drove straight to where I was supposed to meet him. Told me to forget about going there, you stay away unless you want an ugly scene you'll never forget."

"Go where?"

"The place Jack was gonna be. Someplace on First, where there's no other clubs."

"The T House."

"Yes, sir."

"You were supposed to meet up with Jack there."

"Yes, sir. He called me that night, said he was going there, I should bring the extra verses I was working on—for 'Breakdown'—and he was going to check them out. Then I was going to drive him back to the hotel and we were going to pull an all-nighter so the song would be in shape to sing at the concert."

"But Mom warned you off and you didn't go."

"I called Jack and asked what to do about it. He told me to be cool, he'd calm her down, and we would meet up."

"How'd you feel about all that?"

"Angry as hell, but Jack promised me we'd get together with enough time before the concert."

"The concert was important."

"He was going to bring me up on stage."

"Where'd you go instead of to the T House?"

"Nowhere," said the boy. "I stayed home and worked on 'Breakdown.' I fell asleep, maybe at three, four, I don't know, it was at my desk. Then I got up and worked some more. Check my computer logs, when I write something, I record the time."

"Why?"

"To preserve it. Preserve everything about the process. You can have my computer, if you want to prove it. It's on the backseat of my car."

"You seem real anxious for us to get hold of your computer."

"Anything about me is going to be on my hard drive."

Lamar said, "We find your computer was used at a certain time, doesn't tell us who used it."

The boy scowled. "Well, it was me—ask Amelia, our maid. I was in all night and never left."

"How'd you end up at the river?"

"I went there after I found out what happened." Tristan's eyelids swelled as if allergic to remembering. "It was like a big hand entered here and ripped me." Knuckling his solar plexus.

"What time?"

"Seven, nine, in the afternoon, I don't know. I just drove like I was in a dream."

"Where?"

"Up and down the highway, all over."

"Which highway?"

"The I-Forty."

"Anyone see you?"

"No, it was just trees—I drove to the old prison, down west, where they film movies? There were these—with the white-striped blue pants? I guess they're minimum-security prisoners, they're always walking around, cleaning up."

"Sounds like you go there a lot."

"It's quiet," said Tristan. "Helps me think. I was there that morning. Parked on top of the hill and looked down at all those dirty gray walls and one of them saw me. He had a rake, was raking leaves. He saw me and waved, I waved back. I sat there a little more, drove back to the city, parked near the river, sat in an empty building and . . . that's what I was doing when the cops found me."

"Thinking about killing yourself."

"I probably wouldn't do it."

"Probably?"

"It would be selfish, right? Like her."

"Your mama."

"She hated Jack," said the boy. "Told me so, when she was screaming no way I was going to meet him, she'd make a scene."

"Why'd she hate him?"

"For leaving her in the first place, then for coming back when she didn't want him to."

"She was married to Lloyd when she conceived you."

"But things weren't going so well," said the boy. "Least that's what she told me. She was bored and thinking of leaving Lloyd. My mom used to be Jack's main groupie, she made like it was more, but that's what it sounded like to me. Then he dumped her and they didn't see each other for a long time. Then, she was visiting a friend in LA, looked him up. They hooked up for a couple of days. After she found out she was pregnant, she called him about it but he didn't answer. So she went back to Lloyd and forgot about Jack."

"And now he was coming back," said Baker. "And being a bad influence on you. You really think she'd have killed him over that?"

"You don't know her, sir. She sets her mind to something, she's not going to be convinced otherwise. She's got all sorts of people working the farm. Lots of trash." Some animation had spread across Tristan's face. "You don't believe me because she's rich and cultured."

"Well," said Baker, "if we had some evidence."

"If she didn't do it, who did?"

Baker sat back, placed his hands behind his head. "As a matter of fact, son, we've been thinking about you."

The boy shot to his feet. Big boy, all those muscles. His jaw was tight and his hands were clenched. "I *told* you! That's fucking *insane*! Meeting Jack was the coolest thing in my *life,* I was going to go to *LA!*"

"Your plan, not his."

"He would've been into it!"

The detectives remained in their seats. Tristan glared down at them. Lamar said, "Sit back down, son."

"Stop *calling* me that!"

Lamar rose to his full height. Tristan was unused to looking up at anyone. He flinched.

"Please sit down, Tristan."

The boy obeyed. "I'm really a suspect?"

"You're what we call a person of interest."

"That's crazy. Fucking crazy. Why would I kill someone I loved?"

Baker said, "Maybe he changed his mind about singing your song."

"He didn't," said Tristan. "But even if he did, that's no reason to kill someone."

"People get killed for all sorts of reasons."

"Not by sane people—anyway, it never happened, he loved my songs. Read my e-mails, everything's positive, everything's cool—my laptop's in the back of my car, it's out of power but you can recharge it. My passwords DDPOET. Short for Dead Poet."

"We'll do that," said Baker. "But no matter what your e-mail says, it doesn't mean that Jack didn't change his mind and decide not to sing your song."

Lamar said, "People change their mind all the time. And Jack was real moody."

"He wasn't moody with me," said Tristan. "I was *important* to him. Not like the others."

"What others?"

"All those loser trailer trash women claiming they had his kids, sending him pictures of their loser kids. And stuff—songs, CDs he never listened to. I was the *only* one he was sure of. Because he liked my songs and because he remembered the exact day it happened."

"The day you were conceived?" Baker asked.

"He told you about it?" Lamar questioned.

"It's in one of the e-mails—if you ever get around to reading the computer. He even forwarded an e-mail she wrote him five years ago, when he was thinking of coming out to see me. She told him that she didn't want to risk losing Lloyd and that I would never accept him because I was close to Lloyd. That unless he wanted to destroy her and me and everything she'd built with Lloyd, he needed to stay away. And he agreed. For *my* sake. It's all in there. And he saved it for years."

Lamar said, "Mom didn't want to risk losing Lloyd."

The kid smirked again. "Didn't want to risk what Lloyd gave her. Eleventh commandment."

"Jack had money, too," said Baker.

"Not as much as Lloyd. Money has always been her first and only love."

"You have strong feelings about your mama."

"I love her," said Tristan, "but I know what she is. You need to talk to her. I'll give you her number in Kentucky. I know she's there, even though she didn't tell me she was headed there."

"How would you know?"

"She always goes to the horses when she's disgusted with me. Horses don't talk back and if you put the time into them, you can eventually break 'em."

They retrieved an IBM ThinkPad from the backseat of the VW, booted it up, spent an hour with Tristan's old mail and sent mail. A tech ran a basic scan of the boy's Internet history.

"Weird," said the tech.

"What is?"

"Just music stuff—downloads, articles, tons of it. No porn at all. This must be the first teenage boy in the history of the cyber-age who doesn't use his laptop as a stroke-book."

Lamar snickered. "We know what you do at night, Wally."

"It keeps me busy and I don't have to brush my teeth beforehand."

The mail between Jack Jeffries and Tristan backed up the boy's story. There was at least a half year of correspondence transitioning from initial reserve on both their parts, to amiability to warmth to professions of father–son love.

Nothing smarmy or sexual, the letters could've been how-to-communicate instructional tools from Dr. Phil, or one of those other preachers with doctorates.

Jack Jeffries praised some of his son's lyrics, but he never gushed. Criticism of weaker songs was tactful but frank, and Tristan reacted to every received comment with lamblike gratitude.

No indication Jack had ever changed his mind about "Music City Breakdown."

They spent another hour phoning the new hi-tech penitentiary and finding out the names of the trustees who tended the old prison grounds. Two of the inmates remembered seeing the green VW atop the hill just before water break, and one recalled waving to a distant figure standing near the car.

None of which provided an airtight alibi; the murder had taken place before that, when Tristan Poulson claimed to be working on his song and sleeping and surfing the Internet. No doubt Amelia, the maid, would back him up.

Even without backup, the detectives were starting to doubt Tristan as a prime suspect. The boy had plenty of time to develop a real alibi, but hadn't bothered. There had been an openness to Tristan's manner, despite all he'd gone through. If either man had been able to admit it, they would have called it touching.

And as far as the detective could tell, the boy hadn't lied.

As opposed to his mother.

Baker and Lamar agreed that Tristan's theory about her was intriguing.

Repeated calls to Al Sus Jahara Arabian Farms were met by a recorded message so brief it bordered on unfriendly.

Lamar Googled the place. It had a thousand acres of rolling hills and big trees and gorgeous horses. Champion bloodlines, big antebellum mansion, paddocks, stables, stud service, cryogenic semen storage, the works. A place that hoo-hah, one would think there'd be a person at the other end, not voice mail.

Unless someone was in hiding.

By day's end, and after reviewing the situation with Fondebernardi and Jones, they decided Cathy Poulson had grown to the status of "serious suspect," but they had no easy way to get evidence on her.

Before they went about digging around in Belle Meade social circles, they decided to recontact an eyewitness—of sorts. Someone who'd seen Cathy and Jack, shortly before Jack's throat got cut.

14

The Happy Night Motel looked no better than it had in its bordello days. Gray texture-coat stucco had flaked, leaving chicken-wire lesions. The green wood trim was bilious. A couple of big rigs were parked in the cracked asphalt motor court. One filthy pickup and a primer-patched Celica made up the rest of the vehicular mix.

The night clerk was an old, crushed-faced guy named Gary Beame—flyaway white hair, grease-stained shirt, ill-fitting dentures, rheumy eyes that jumped all over the place. Maybe a barely reformed homeless guy the owners had hired on the cheap.

He made the detectives right away, rasped through cigarette smoke. "Evening, Officers. We don't hire out to whores. Mr. Bikram's a clean businessman."

It sounded like a rehearsed little speech.

"Congratulations," said Baker. "Which room is Greta Barline's?"

Beame's face darkened. He yanked out his cigarette, scattering ash on the *Star* magazine spread atop the counter. "That little—I knew she was gonna get Mr. Bikram in trouble." Scratching the corner of his collapsed mouth, he peered at something, flicked it away. "All that dirty whorin' and then she stiffs Mr. Bikram for a week's worth."

Lamar said, "She was hooking out of here?"

"Not like you're thinking," said Beame. "Not waltzing out to the street in them halters and hotpants."

"Like the good old days."

"I wouldn't know about that," Beame lied.

"So what, she'd just be here and they'd show up?"

"Who?"

"Johns."

"I never saw no one sneak in," said Beame, warming to his false-hood sonata. "Not on any regular schedule, anyway. I'm all alone here, cain't be bothering to watch all the comings and goings."

"Then how do you know she was hooking?"

Beame puffed manically, working his jaws while constructing his answer. "Only way I found out was we had a family staying in the room next door, tourists from Missouri or someplace. Mother calls me up complaining about three different guys in one night. The noise was coming through the wall. Bad enough they had to hear it, but they had kids."

"What'd you do about it?" said Lamar.

"What could I do?" said Beame. "My responsibility's up here. What I done is phone Mr. Bikram. They tell me he's back home visiting. That's Calcutta, India. Mrs. Bikram says when he comes back in three days he'll deal with it. Next time I see Barline coming in, I try talkin' to her. The little whore has the nerve to ignore me. When Mr. Bikram comes home, I tell him what happens and he marches straight over there. But she's gone with all her stuff. Then we found out she passed a bogus money order. The little whore still owes a week. You find her, you tell me. Or you can call Mr. Bikram direct. Here's his card."

"Your housekeeping staff never informed you about the prostitution?"

"What staff?" said Beame. "We got a couple Mexicans come during the day. They don't even speak no English."

They asked to see Greta Barline's room.

Beame said, "Sorry, can't do. I gotta a couple of people in there."

"More respectable tourists?" said Baker.

No answer.

"Maybe one-hour tourists?" said Lamar.

"Hey," said Beame. "They pay, I don't ask. They might even be married. You find that little whore, you call Mr. Bikram."

"Any idea where we *can* find her?"

Beame finally gave some serious thought to a question. "Well, mebbe one thing. I saw her go off with a guy once. This wasn't no trucker. Suit and tie, drove a Lexus. Silver. It had a white coat hanging in the back. Like a doctor."

———

Out in the motel parking lot, they thumbed through their notes for the name of the dentist who owned The T House.

"Here we go," said Lamar. " 'Dr. McAfee. Lives in Brentwood.' "

Baker said, "If she was telling the truth about that."

"About anything. Hooks, passes bad paper, real sweet kid." Lamar looked up. "Maybe there's something to the churchgoing lifestyle."

"At the very least, you know where the kids are on Wednesday and Sunday." Baker rubbed his head. "Let's talk to the good doctor and find out what other games Gret likes to play."

Motor Vehicle records placed Dr. Donald J. McAfee's house six blocks away from the Drs. Carlsons' white contempo.

"Must be a medico thing," said Baker, as they headed there.

The house was a shingle-topped ranch with an oddly sloping roofline that suggested pagoda. A little stone fountain in front and a patch of mondo grass said someone loved the whole Asian thing.

Two vehicles were registered to McAfee, a silver Lexus sedan and a black Lexus Rx. Neither was in sight but a ten-year-old red Mustang sat in the driveway. It was dented and sagging, rust on the bumpers, a cracked rear side window.

Texas plates.

Lamar said, "So much for Gret not having any car. Why lie to make yourself poorer than you are?"

"Tugging at our heartstrings," said Baker.

"For what reason?"

"The little gal thinks she can sing. Maybe she's into acting, too."

Not much light over the red door. They knocked.

A gonglike chime sounded and Greta Barline's voiced trilled, "One second."

When the door swung open, she was standing there with her blond hair all long and combed out, wearing a tiny little lace apron, spike heels and nothing else. Flour whisk in one hand, round-tipped frosting knife in the other.

Few people look better naked than clothed. This girl was the exception. Every visible inch of her was smooth and golden and nubile and voluptuous and all sorts of other good adjectives. She'd come to the door licking her lips and grinning. But that died fast.

Baker said, "Sorry to interrupt the production, Gret."

The girl's eyes widened and then, darn if her little pink nipples didn't get hard and all puckery around the rosellas or whatever you called them.

Lamar said, "Dressed for business?"

He'd never admit it but he'd been distracted by those nipples when she went after him with the frosting knife.

They subdued her, but it took surprising effort. Even cuffed and face-down on a red silk Asian print sofa, she kept up the kicking and screaming—lot of nonsense about rape.

The interior of the house looked like someone had raided every tourist trap in Bangkok. Lamar found Greta Barline's clothing in the master bedroom—a wide, shag-carpeted space dominated by a huge plaster Buddha spray-painted gold. In a teak dresser, one drawer was reserved for bikinis, thongs, and crotch-less panties. A section of the walk-in closet held negligees, wife-beaters and T-shirts and three pairs of size-4 Diesel jeans. Tons of makeup and other female products in the bathroom. She'd made a real mess of the place, leaving wet towels on the floor, along with crumpled-up *National Enquirer*s.

Living here, on and off, when she wasn't bedding johns and belting out karaoke.

Lamar selected the most modest clothes he could find—a yellow tee, along with a pair of jeans—and brought them back to the living room. Maybe calling for a female officer would've been the smart thing but they didn't want to wait around with this foulmouthed naked girl screaming rape.

The detectives managed to wrestle her into the duds, but it made them sweat.

Then Lamar remembered: no underwear. Like she'd care.

They sat her up, and had just gotten her something to drink, when a big, florid middle-aged guy wearing a Domino Pizza delivery uniform showed up. The duds were a size too small and downright stupid-looking on a paunchy, gray-haired idiot with steel-rimmed eyeglasses.

Trembling hands clutched a pizza box.

"Dr. McAfee?"

The dentist's eyes got wild, as if he were contemplating escape.

Baker said, "Bad idea, sit over there." He took the box and in-spected it, finding a packet of ribbed condoms, an aerosol can of whipped cream and some creepy-looking big old plastic beads on a string.

"Talk about nutrition," said Lamar.

The dentist clutched his chest and when that didn't work, flashed a nice set of white teeth and looked over at Greta. "Don't know her, just met her, Officers. She insisted on coming over. It was just going to be some old-fashioned fun in the privacy of my own domicile."

"Fuck you!" screamed the girl. "You said I was the best!"

McAfee's look was ripe with pity.

Greta Barline squinted. "I'll kill you, you bastard. I'll cut you like I cut him."

McAfee blanched. "Guess I'd better be more careful who I allow to pick me up."

Baker and Lamar hauled the girl out of there. When they reached the door, McAfee was still standing there in his ludicrous delivery duds.

"May I change?"

Baker said, "You better."

15

"He deserved it."

Same interview room, same chairs, a different kid.

Lamar said, "He deserved it because . . ."

"He wouldn't stand up," said Gret Barline.

"For what?"

"His responsibilities."

"To who?"

"All that sperm he shot around, like it was drain water." The cuffs had been removed from the girl's slender wrists. The heavy theatrical makeup she'd worn for her role-play with the dentist glowed salmon-orange in the bright light.

"A fertile guy," said Baker.

He and Lamar were proceeding cautiously. The girl had made what could be construed as a spontaneous confession during her tirade against McAfee: *if* one construed "him" to mean Jack. But who knew what a judge would make of that? They hadn't Mirandized Greta Barline out of fear that she would lawyer up.

And because they had no grounds, just the certainty that came from years of dealing with the messes that people made of their God-given lives.

Baker sensed the girl was a sociopath. But he wasn't totally without sympathy. In the end human beings were frail beings.

Now she said, "Fertile turtle," and laughed at her own wit. Her brown eyes were hot and a little scary, maybe to the point of craziness.

When they traced her NCIC records, they found out she was twenty-eight, not the twenty, twenty-one they'd assumed.

Pushing thirty and old beyond even those years.

Ten-year history of bad checks, trespassing, soliciting, forgery, petty larceny. She'd served maybe a total of half a year, all of it in county lockups. There were muscles in those smooth little arms. A butterfly tattoo in the small of her back. Lamar remembered how much effort it had taken for both of them to restrain her. When they booked her, she came in at a hundred and eight, fully clothed.

He said, "So what was he supposed to stand up for?"

"Not what, freak-a-leak, *who*!" she said. "He was supposed to stand up for me—his flesh and blood."

"You know for a fact that you're kin?"

"My mama told me and she don't lie about things like that."

"When did she tell you?"

"As long as I can remember. I never had a live-in dad, just foster assholes and assholes who'd come in and out to see Mama." Another laugh. "Plenty of in-and-out. Mama was always talking about him: Jack this, Jack that." Wicked smile. "Jack had a nice little beanstalk on him."

"How'd she meet him?"

"He and Denny and Mark did a concert in San Antone."

Talking about the other two members of the trio like they were favorite uncles.

"And?" said Baker.

"And she had a friend who was working security and he got her a backstage pass and she got to meet all of them. They all liked her, but Jack liked her the most. She used to be real sexy before she put on a hundred extra pounds."

Pantomiming a watermelon paunch and sticking her tongue out in disgust.

"So Jack and your mama started hanging out," said Lamar.

"They fucked all night is what they did," said Gret. "And the result is *moi*." She pointed to her chest.

Nipples poking through the yellow tee, darn, he should've thought of a bra. Lamar said, "You've known your whole life."

"I followed his career when I'd see a computer, like in an Internet café, I'd Google him. There wasn't much happening in the last . . . ten years, but I still did it. Trying to figure out if I should try."

"Try what?"

"Try to meet him. Maybe he'd see me and . . ." Nervous laugh. "People meet me, they like me."

"I can see that."

She batted her lashes. Arched her back.

Lamar said, "So you finally decided to . . ."

"I moved to Nashville about six months ago. For my singing career, you know. So it seemed like fate when I found out he was coming here."

"Were you living in the Happy Night right from the beginning?"

"A couple other places before that. Happy Night was the best of 'em."

"Then you got yourself a job at The T House."

"Yeah."

"How'd that happen?"

Gret drank from the Starbucks they'd brought her and rattled off the chronology. The horn-dog dentist had been one of many who'd showed up at the motel. Since he was richer, she extended herself to him and his little stage productions. Being long-divorced with no one else in the house, McAfee decided to move the show to Brentwood for occasional fantasy games. When the tourist family complained, she figured it was time to relocate permanently.

"When did you find out he owned a club?"

"Soon after," she said. "I saw the bill for the karaoke machine, he told me what it was for. I said that's bogus cheap shit, you should get a band. He said no way, I'm losing money as is."

"Then you started working at the T."

"It was the perfect match," she said. "I got my stage and he got me. I need to *sing*."

"Creative drive," said Lamar.

The term puzzled the girl but she smiled and nodded.

He said, "So when did you intend to meet up with Mr. Jeffries?"

"*Mister* Jeffries," she said, shaking her hair and taking a long time to fluff the yellow strands. "He don't deserve the title. He's a dog, just like Mama said."

"Why'd she say that?"

"He left her knocked up and never returned her letters."

"Why didn't she file a paternity suit?"

"She tried, got a stupid San Antone lawyer. He wrote a letter and got a call from a big-time *Beverly Hills* lawyer who told her the choice was take some cash now and shut your face forever, or go to court and go broke because they had the money to drag it out for years. She took the money."

"Your mama told you all this," said Baker.

"All the time," said Gret. "All the all the *all* the time. It was like her favorite bedtime story."

"When you were a kid?"

"Even after. What I'm saying is she told it so many times it put *her* to sleep." Laughing. "She snores like a pig."

"What happened to the money?" Lamar asked.

"Well, let's see. Hmm—oh, yeah, she drank away half of it. The leftover . . . uh, let's see. Oh, yeah, she smoked *that* away. I figure there had to be more where that came from. I'm *owed*."

"So how'd you know where to find Jack Jeffries?"

"A week before he was supposed to come, I called the hotel and said I had a flower delivery for when he arrived. They told me when to deliver."

"How'd you know which hotel?"

"I tried them and the Loews Vanderbilt. Where else is he gonna stay?"

Baker said, "Did you try to see him personally?"

Gret grinned. "I didn't just try, I saw him."

"How?"

"Went there. Got all dressed up pretty and waited in the lobby. I had an iced tea . . . paid ten bucks out of my own pocket to drink and sit there and watch rich folk. Finally, he came out. Then he remembered something and started walking back to the elevators. I rode up with him. Pushed a button on the same floor and pretended to be staying there. We had a nice conversation."

"About what?"

"First," she said, "I sweet-talked him . . . things like 'I recognized you right away, you look just like you do on the CDs.' Which is bogus bullshit, *he* put on like a hundred pounds and he's *old*. But he liked hearing those lies, everyone has their own favorite lies. That's when I told him I was going to the Songbird concert . . . singing backup for Johnny Blackthorn. He said, No kidding, Johnny's an old bud, and we started talking music. I know all about music, it's my life."

"All this is in the hall?" Lamar asked.

"At his door. I knew I could have gotten inside, but I didn't want to. He'd try to fuck me and that would be gross."

"Gross because he's your father."

"That for sure. But also, *he* was gross." She stuck her tongue out.

"So how'd you get him over to The T House?"

"I told him I'd be singing and also helping out with the serving 'cause my daddy owned the place. I told him he should stop by, hear some good music if he wasn't too tired. Then I told him I was thinking about giving up music because the lifestyle was tough. I told him I got into Vanderbilt dental school, maybe I'd do that."

"Why dental school?"

"'Cause it sounded educated. Jack was impressed, and said that sounded cool. Then he said, 'But if you really love to sing, don't give up your dream.' "

"You were getting him on your side," said Baker.

"I wanted him to hear me sing 'cause I'm worth listening to," Gret said. "But I knew I had to be casual. That's the way you got to do it with them."

"Them being . . ."

"Men. They're like fish. You cast the line, wiggle the bait a little, move it around real casual. I figured he'd show up. And he did."

"What time?"

"Toward the end of my last set. A quarter to."

"Quarter to midnight."

"Yeah."

She'd told them around eleven fifteen, eleven thirty the first time. Lying for the sake of it.

"What happened then?"

"I greeted him like a long-lost friend and sat him right in front. I even gave him free tea and yellow-raisin scones. Then I sang. Did a KT Oslin and a Rosanne Cash. Finished with 'Piece of My Heart'— the Janis way, not what Faith Hill did to it. He was listening. Then . . ." Her blue eyes clouded over. "He just up and left. I gave the bastard free tea and he didn't even have the courtesy to say good-bye."

Just like he did to Mama, Lamar thought. "So you went to the door and saw . . ."

"The rich bitch with the red Mercedes. My car's red, too, it's my favorite color. I could never get it to shine like that . . ." Tossing her hair. "They talked like they knew each other, didn't look so friendly. Then she drove away and he started walking."

Reaching for her coffee, she sipped. "Um, this is good and creamy! Thank you, sirs!"

Baker said, "Then what?"

"Pardon?"

"What happened next?"

"Nothing."

"Gret," said Lamar, "we found that knife in your purse. It matches perfectly to the wound on Jack's neck. We also got your fingerprints on his clothes and his neck."

Blatant lies. They were days from processing all the evidence.

Silence.

Baker said, "I reckon you carry that knife because johns can get rough, right?"

"Right."

"We can understand that," Lamar added. "A girl needs to take care of herself."

"Right."

"So why don't you tell us exactly what happened between you and Jack Jeffries?"

"Hmm," she said, finishing her coffee. "Can I have another creamy latte? They're so expensive. I can't afford to buy more than one a week."

They got her the coffee and a croissant. She finished both and asked to go to the bathroom.

"Sure," said Lamar, "but first I've got to bring a senior CSI technologist in to scrape under your fingernails."

"Why?" said Gret.

"To match it to Jack's skin."

"I washed my hands," she said.

"When?"

"Right after I . . ." Looking at the ceiling and toying with her hair and letting one hand wander to her right breast.

Lamar said, "You need to finish the story, Gret. We need to hear the whole thing."

"*I* need to use the little girls' room."

Fondebernardi came in, pretended to be a crime scene tech and did the scrape. Greta Barline was accompanied by a female officer to the restroom and returned looking refreshed.

"That was good," she said, focusing on Lamar.

Baker said, "Please finish the story."

"It's not much of a story."

"Do us a favor and tell it anyway."

She shrugged. "I saw him walking and I went after him . . . to ask him why he left without saying good-bye. Asshole gave me a funny look and kept going . . . ignoring me. He was all pissed off . . . probably because of that woman. Ain't my fault, but he took it out on me, you know? A whole different Jack from the Jack in the elevator. I kept walking with him. It was real dark, but I could see the hostility in his . . . manner. The way he had his arms folded in front of him, looking straight ahead. Like I didn't exist. That made *me* super pissed off."

"Because he wouldn't talk."

"Because he was being *rude*. Being rich doesn't give you any right to be rude. Uh-uh, no sirree, Mr. Jeffries. The world don't work like that."

Her second delusion. The first was thinking she could sing.

Baker said, "It sure isn't fair."

She looked at Lamar. He said, "Downright rude."

"I mean who is he thinking he is? A big fat ugly gross disgusting person who used to be famous but now no one gives a *shit* about him? Who's *he* to go all silent and pissed and leave without saying good-bye? Still, I minded my manners. I said, 'What's wrong? Did the tea taste bad?' "

Lamar said, "He was being rude but you held on to your dignity."

"Exactly! Dignity's what it's all about. Everyone deserves a little dignity, right?"

"Darn right," Baker said. "So then what happened?"

"He just kept ignoring me and I just kept walking alongside him. We keep walking and walking and walking and then he stops again and makes a sharp turn . . . like that's gonna confuse me." She let out a laugh. "Except now he has no idea where he's going and he ends up in this empty lot. I stick right with him. He turns around, not looking where he's going, and his foot hits a wall. He starts cussing and swearing and then . . . and then, he starts screaming at *me*. That I should stop *stalking* him, can you believe that?"

The detectives shook their heads.

She touched her hair, licked a finger and ran it over her eyelids. "He sounded crazy, I was scared. I tell you, Detectives, that old boy was on drugs or something."

"Did you try to leave?"

"Too scared." Gret made her eyes go wide. "It's all dark and he's going crazy on me. He starts calling me horrible names—a lyin' no-talent little bitch, if you must know."

She sniffed, grimaced, and rubbed her eyes, trying to dredge up some tears. The floor had been dried since Tristan Poulson's sob-fest. It stayed that way.

"It was horrible," she said. "No one ever, ever, *ever* talked to me like that. That's what I said to him—trying to stop him from being so *rude*. Then I looked him straight up in the eye and said 'Shut your mouth for a second and hear the truth. I'm your *daughter* and you know what, I don't even *care* about that, it means *nothing* to me! And you know what else? I'm lucky you weren't never in my life, you don't deserve to ever be in my life, you sorry-ass, has-been *motherfucker*!' "

The room fell silent.

"You told him off good," Lamar said.

"Wait, wait, it gets better. Then he gets this wild look, this really wild crazy look gets in his eyes, and he says, 'You're lying, it's just another lie, you been a lying little bitch since the moment I laid eyes on you.' And *I* say, 'I'm the daughter of Ernestine Barline. You knew her as Kiki. Remember that night you fucked her all night? The result is *me*.' "

She stopped. Panting, sucking in breath.

Finally, the tears came . . . a constricted trickle that ended with a gasp.

Lamar said, "What did Jack say to that?"

"His voice got real quiet and he gave me this look. Not the wild-eyed one, but a different one. Scarier. Cold, real, real cold. Like I was nothing . . . but . . . dirt. He smiled, but not a nice smile, an ugly smile. Then he said, 'I don't remember *her* and I don't give a shit about *you*. And even if I did fuck her, no way you were the result. Know how I know?' "

She gasped, covered her eyes. Lamar thought of patting her shoulder, but hesitated. Baker reached over and did it for the both of them.

"I didn't answer him," she said. "But he told me, anyway." She shivered.

Neither detective spoke.

Gret's hand dropped from her face. For a second, she looked young, untouched, vulnerable. Then the brown eyes sparked with fury.

"The bastard touched me here." Gret fingered the bottom of her chin. "Chucked it, you know? Like I was some baby, some stupid little baby thing." Another shiver. If she was faking her emotion, she was Oscar-quality. "Then he said, 'I know you didn't come from me because you got no *talent*. You sing like shit and I'd rather listen to nails on a chalkboard than to hear you screech like a crow. I knew Janis and she's the lucky one, being dead so she didn't have to be subjected to that sorry-ass, ultra-fucked-up abortion you did of her classic. Girl, your voice should never be used except for talking, and not much of that, either.' "

She took awhile to catch her breath. Stared at both detectives as if she'd seen the afterlife and it wasn't pretty.

"Oh, man, that's cold," said Lamar.

Baker said, "God, what a bastard." Sounding as if he meant it.

Greta Barline said, "He's saying those things . . . those horrible things . . . cutting me . . . cutting my singing . . . cutting my life . . . I can't even speak, it's like I'm *bleeding* inside."

She gnashed her teeth, clawed her hands.

"*Then* he starts pushing at me, *pushing*—like to get away. Honestly, I don't know what happened. He was so big and I'm so little and he's pushing at me, pushing at me. I was so scared. I don't know how the knife got into my hand, I promise. All I remember is him holding his neck and looking at me and making this gurgly noise. Then, he fell down and made this thud noise. And then he gurgled some more."

A strange, distant smile skittered across her lips. "I'm just standing there and I'm thinking about that gurgly noise and I say out loud, 'You don't sound so good, yourself, Jack Jeffries.' After that, he got quiet."

The room felt as if all the air had been sucked out of it.

Lamar waited for Baker to speak, but El Bee had a funny look on his face, kind of glassy-eyed.

Lamar said, "Thanks for telling us, Gret. Now I'm gonna have to read you your rights."

"Just like on TV," she said. Then she perked up. "So what do you think, it's self-defense, right?"

16

Lamar got home at four thirty AM. Sue was sleeping but she woke up, brewed some decaf and sat with him while he ate cold pasta, a couple of hastily fried breakfast sausages, and five pieces of toast.

The usual case-closed munchies.

"Another one bites the dust," she said. "Congrats, honey."

After he told her the details, Sue said, "The girl's obviously disturbed but you can see her point."

"About what? She cut the poor man's throat for insulting her singing."

"If what she said is true, he was brutal, honey, just dumped on her dreams. Of course, it doesn't justify what she did. But still, to be rejected like that." She touched his face. "Maybe I'm being a bleeding heart, but I guess I understand her a little."

"If it's even true," said Lamar. "She lies about everything." But he knew he was denying the obvious. For all Greta Barline's lies, he was certain she'd spoken the truth about that final encounter.

Jack Jeffries had paid for it. Now Greta Barline was going to ante up.

They'd closed the case, a high-profile whodunit, they'd get their names in the paper. Maybe even be there at the press conference.

He should've felt more satisfaction.

Sue said, "How'd Baker react?"

"To what?"

"The way it ended."

"He seemed okay." Lamar immediately regretted the lie. He was always honest with Sue, no reason to change that, now. "Actually, he didn't react at all, hon. Once she signed the confession and he made sure the tape had recorded he just left. Fondie called Jones and Jones called in to congratulate us and Baker wasn't there to hear it."

"Maybe he's got a point, Lamar."

"About what?"

"The business, all those dreams, a thousand people come to town, nine hundred ninety-nine get stepped on and shattered and the one who gets a chance doesn't last long either."

Lamar didn't answer. Thinking about his own arrival in Nashville, fifteen years ago, from New Haven. Good solid bass player, he had the moves, extra-long nimble fingers able to span eight, nine frets. A darn good ear, too. After a couple of listens to something, he could often play it back note-perfect.

He couldn't invent, but still, an ear like that counted for something. Everyone back home telling him he was great.

In Nashville, he was good. Maybe even real good.

Meaning not even close to good enough.

He felt cool hands on the back of his neck. Sue had gotten up and was massaging him. She wore that old Med Center 10K commemorative T-shirt and nothing else. Her smell . . . her firmness and her softness, pushing against him.

He said, "Let's hit the hay. Thanks for the grub, Nurse Van Gundy."

"Anything for you, Favorite Patient."

"Let's hear it for Marvin Gaye."

She laughed, for the thousandth time, at the in-joke. Time for Sexual Healing. Lamar wondered if he should find some phrases that weren't music-connected.

Sue didn't seem to mind. She took him by the hand and laughed again.

By the time they reached the bedroom, they were kissing deeply.

17

Baker went home to an empty silent house, popped a beer, and sat in the kitchen with his feet propped up on the Formica dinette table.

Fifty-year-old table, everything in this place was older than he was; since inheriting the house, he'd bought virtually nothing.

Hanging on to all the discount-outlet crap his parents had bought when they moved in.

Danny and Dixie.

When he thought of them that way, they were strangers.

When he used their real names, it was different.

Danville Southerby and Dorothea Baker had met when he was sixteen and she was fourteen, singing in the choir of the First Baptist Church of Newport, Tennessee.

The town, nestled on the edge of the Great Smoky Mountains, was rich in music and folk art and memory, poor in everything else. Danny's father barely broke even farming tobacco and Dixie's daddy didn't do much better with corn.

Singing hymns threw the teenagers together. Blinding love soon followed and within two months, Dixie was pregnant. The child, a small, squalling, pink-faced boy they named Baker, was born three weeks premature, one half year after a hastily arranged church wedding. Dixie bled a lot and the doctor told her she'd never conceive again. She cried, as much from relief as regret.

Like a lot of people in the church, the teens were highly musical. Danny had a clear tenor voice, played piano and organ and guitar without ever taking a lesson. Dixie was on a whole other level, a mandolin prodigy with an astounding vibrato and, some said, technique better than Bill Monroe's. Top of that, her soprano, always nice, smoothed out and stretched following the delivery of her baby. Maybe singing to the cranky little red-faced tot helped, or it could've been one of those strange hormonal twists. Either way, listening to her was a privilege.

The young couple lived on the corn farm with her family, doing scut work and sinking low emotionally. In their spare time, when someone else would take the baby, they sat and played and sang—softly, so as not to share the precious thing they had with anyone else. It was the only private time they had. In those moments, each of them wondered if life wasn't slipping away, but they never shared the thought with each other.

One night, after Dixie's daddy scolded Danny for indolence, he got up in the middle of the night, woke Dixie and told her to get dressed. She watched him pack a bag, carry it out of the house, then return for his guitar and her mandolin.

"What—"

He shushed her with a finger. She got dressed, followed him out to the old Dodge his daddy had given him last year but which he never got to drive, being stuck on the corn farm, working like a mutt.

They pushed the car away from the house so as not to wake anyone. When he got far enough, he started up and hit the road.

Dixie said, "What about the baby?"

Danny said, "They all love him. Maybe even better than we do."

For the next two years, all their families got were postcards. Gaudy souvenir cards from tourists spots all over the South—places Danny and Dixie never visited because instead of seeing the sights, they were doing the roadhouse circuit, playing one-nighters. Mostly the new stuff called Rockabilly, but also bluegrass standards, and gospel hymns when the audience was open to that, which was almost never.

Making petty cash but it was more than Dixie's dad had paid them for working the cornfields, which was nothing because they were supposed to be content with room and board. Top of that, they were doing what they loved and getting paid for it. Meeting people, all kinds of people, having all kinds of eye-opening experiences that no way would've happened back in Newport.

Christmas, they sent store-bought toys to Baker, along with sweet notes in Dixie's hand. The baby became a quiet, determined toddler, unlikely to give up whatever he was working at, unless forced to.

When he was three, his parents showed up at the corn farm, wearing fancy clothes and driving a five-year-old Ford van full of instruments and music and costume changes and talking about meeting Carl Perkins and Ralph Stanley, all those other famous people in "our world." Talking about colored singers doing that rhythm and blues, sometimes you could be safe in those colored clubs and it was worth listening.

Dixie's father scowling at that. Spooning his soup and saying, "I won't hold it against you, running off like that, and leaving your problem with us." Meaning the little boy, sitting right there. Talking about him like he didn't understand. "Be up tomorrow at five to atone. We got a whole edge of the north field to do by hand."

Danny fingered his leather string tie with the piece of quartz up near the collar, then smiled and stood and laid down a fat wad of bills on the table.

"What's that?" said his father-in-law.

"Payment."

"For what?"

"Babysitting, back rent, whatever." Winking at his wife.

She hesitated, avoided her family's eyes. Then quaking so hard she thought she'd fall apart, she scooped up Baker and followed her husband out to the van.

As the Ford drove off, Dixie's mother said, "Figures. They never took their gear out the back."

Baker Southerby grew up on the roadhouse circuit, learning to read and write and do arithmetic from his mother. He picked things up quickly, making her job easy. She hugged and kissed him a lot and he seemed to like that. No one ever talked about the time that she and Danny had gone and left him.

She told him to call her Dixie because everyone did and, "Sweetie, you and me both know I'm your mama."

Years later, Baker figured it out. She'd been all of seventeen, wanted to see herself as that pretty girl with the lightning fingers up on stage, not some housewife.

When he was five, he asked to play her Gibson F-5 mandolin.

"Honey, that's a real precious thing."

"I'll be careful."

Dixie hesitated. Baker stared at her, with those serious eyes.

She ran her hand over his blond crew cut. He kept staring.

"All right, then, but I'm sitting right next to you. Want me to show you some chords?"

Grave nod.

An hour after he started, he was playing C, G and F. By the end of the day, he was coaxing forth a respectable version of "Blackberry Blossom." Not at full speed, but his tone was clear, his right hand nice and smooth.

"Dan, come listen to this." Listening to him, watching how careful he was, Dixie was comfortable letting him play the mandolin without her hovering.

Danny came in from the porch of the motel, where he'd been smoking and strumming and writing songs.

"What?"

"Just listen—go ahead, sweetie-pie little man."

Baker played.

"Huh . . . ," Danny said. Then: "I got an idea."

They bought him his own mandolin. Nothing high-priced, a forties A-50 they picked up in a Savannah pawnshop, but it had decent tone. By age six, Baker had a trunk full of stage-duds and a thirties F-4 almost as shiny as Dixie's F-5 and he was a full-time headliner. The new act was officially The Southerby Family Band: Danny, Dixie and Little Baker the Amazing Smoky Mountain Kid.

Mostly there wasn't room for all that on any marquee so it was just The Southerbys.

Baker's chord repertoire ran all the way down the fretboard, encompassed the majors, minors, sevenths, sixths, ninths, elevenths, and thirteenths, along with diminished, augmented, and a whole bunch of interesting extensions he came upon himself that could be called jazz, even though the closest they got to jazz was a few Texas swing songs that always ended up sounding bluegrassy.

By the time he was nine, he played cleaner and faster than his mother and to her credit, she reacted with nothing but pride.

Homeschooling—though that concept hadn't been invented—continued and Baker was smart enough to get a year ahead of his age group. At least according to the intelligence test Dixie had clipped out of *Parents* magazine.

Baker grew up on fast food, tobacco smoke and applause. Nothing seemed to alter his quiet personality. When he was twelve, a smooth-talking man who'd heard them play at a honky-tonk outside of Natchez told Danny he'd give all three of them a recording contract, make them the new Carter Family.

They went into the studio, laid down five old standards, never heard back from the guy, tried calling a few times, then gave up and went back on the road.

When Baker was twelve, he announced that he wanted to go to a real school.

Danny said, "Just like that? You give it all up?"

Baker didn't answer.

"Wish you'd talk more, son. Kind of hard to know what's going on behind those eyes."

"I just told you."

"Giving it all up."

Silence.

Dixie said, "That's what he wants, maybe it's not such a bad idea."

Danny looked over her. "Yeah, I been feeling that's coming."

"What has?"

"Itching to settle down."

"Could've done it years ago," said Dixie. "I was waiting."

"For what?"

She shrugged. "Something."

They moved to Nashville, because it was in Tennessee and, theoretically, not a big deal to visit their families. The real reason was: Music City.

Danny was still a young man, though sometimes he felt like he'd lived three lifetimes. The mirror told him he looked sharp, and his pipes were good; guys a lot less talented than he were making it big-time, why not give it a shot?

He used some of the cash he'd saved from years on the road and bought a little frame house in The Nations. Nice white neighborhood, full of hardworking people. Dixie wanted to play house that was fine; he'd be over on Sixteenth Street.

Baker went to junior high and met other kids. He stayed quiet but managed to make a few friends and, except for math where he needed some catch-up, classes were pretty easy.

Dixie stayed home and played her mandolin and sang "Just for the sake of it, Baker, which is music at the purest, right?"

Sometimes she asked Baker to jam with her. Mostly, he did.

Danny was out most of the time, trying to scare up a career on Music Row. He got a few gigs playing rhythm guitar at the Ryman when regulars were sick, did some club dates, paid his own money to cut demos that never went anywhere.

When the money ran low, he took a job teaching choir at a Baptist church.

After a year and a half of that, over dinner he announced it was time to hit the road again.

Baker said, "Not me."

Danny said, "I didn't mean you." Glancing at his wife. She screwed up her mouth. "I put on weight, nothing's gonna fit."

"That's why God invented tailors," said her husband. "Or do it yourself, you used to know how to sew."

"I still do," she said, defensively.

"There you go. We're leaving on Monday."

Today was Thursday.

Dixie said, "Leaving for where?"

"Atlanta. I got us a gig opening for the Culpeppers at a new blue-grass club. Nothing fancy, all they want is S.O.S."

Family talk for the Same Old Shit.

Meaning the standards. Danny, seeing himself as a modern man, had come to despise them.

"Just like that," said Dixie. "You made all the plans."

"Don't I always? You might want to get some new strings for your plink-box. I overheard you yesterday. The G and D are dead."

"What about Baker?"

"He can take care of himself, right, son?"

"He's not even fourteen."

"How old were you when you had him?"

Talking about him as if he wasn't there.

Baker wiped his mouth, carried his plate to the sink, and began washing it.

"So?" said Danny.

Dixie sighed. "I'll try to sew it myself."

From then on, they were gone more than they were home. Doing a month on the road, returning for a week or ten days, during which Dixie doted on Baker with obvious guilt and Danny sat by himself and smoked and wrote songs no one else would ever hear.

The summer of Baker's fifteenth birthday, Danny announced they were sending him to Bible camp in Memphis for six weeks. "Time to get some faith and spirituality, son."

By sheer coincidence, Danny and Dixie had been booked for a six-week gig exactly during that period. Aboard a cruise boat leaving from Biloxi.

"Hard to get phone contact from there," said Dixie. "This way we know you'll be safe."

During the last week of camp, Baker ate something off and came down with horrible food poisoning. Three days later, the bug was gone but he'd lost seven pounds and was listless. The camp doctor had left early on a family emergency and the Reverend Hartshorne, the camp director, didn't want to risk any legal liability; just last summer some rich girl's family had sued because she'd gotten a bladder infection that developed into sepsis. Luckily that kid had survived, probably her fault in the first place, she had a reputation for fooling with the boys but tell that to those fancy-pants lawyers . . .

Hartshorne found Baker in his bunk room and drew him outside. "Call your parents, son, so they can pick you up. Then start packing."

"Can't," said a wan, weak Baker. "They're on a ship, no phone contact."

"When were they figuring on picking you up?"

"I'm taking the bus."

"All the way to Nashville?"

"I'm okay."

Lord, thought Hartshorne. These new families.

"Well, son, can't have you being here, all sick. Got a key to your house?"

"Sure."

"I don't mind Nashville. I'll drive you in."

They started out in Hartshorne's white Sedan Deville at three PM, made a single stop for lunch, and pulled into Nashville at nine fifteen.

Lights out in the little frame house.

"You okay going in by yourself?"

Baker was eager to get away from Hartshorne's Bible speeches and the odors the reverend gave off: bubble gum and body odor and for some reason, an overlay of Wheatena cereal.

"Sure."

"Okay, then. Walk with the Lord, son."

"Yessir."

Baker got his duffel and his pillow from the back and fished out his door key. The Cadillac was gone before he reached the door.

He walked into the empty house.

Heard something.

Not empty—a burglar?

Laying his duffel and pillow on the floor, he tiptoed into the kitchen, snuck all the way back to the laundry room where Danny kept his pistol.

Ancient Colt, Danny called it protection for the road though the only time he'd had to use it was when some Klan-type guys loitering near their motel in Pulaski made remarks about seeing them going into a nigger juke-joint.

One flash of the Colt and the idiots dispersed.

Remembering that now—recalling the power that came from a couple pounds of honed steel—Baker hefted the pistol and advanced toward the noise in the back.

His parents' bedroom. Some kind of commotion behind the closed door.

No, not completely closed; the thin paneled slab was cracked an inch.

Baker nudged it with his finger, got a couple more inches of view space and aimed the pistol through the opening.

Dim light. One lamp on a nightstand, his mother's nightstand giving off a pinkish light.

Because of some silky material that had been tossed over the shade.

His mother on the bed, naked, astride his father.

No, not his father, his father was off to the side on a chair and another woman, blond and skinny, was astride him.

The man under his mother, heavier in the legs than his father. Hairier, too.

Two couples, panting, heaving, bucking.

His gun arm froze.

He forced himself to lower it.

Backed away.

Took his duffel and left his pillow and walked out of the house. Made his way to a bus stop and rode downtown and got himself a room at a motel on Fourth.

Found the marine recruitment office the next morning, lied about his age, and enlisted. Two days later, he was on a bus to Camp Lejeune in North Carolina.

It took another week for a panicky Dixie Southerby to locate him.

The marines told him to come back in two years and sent him home.

Dixie said, "What'd you do that for?"

Baker said, "I got restless. Can I go to military school?"

"You don't want to live at home?"

"I'm big enough to go away."

Danny said, "That's a mature decision, son. It's time for your mother and me to hit the road, anyway."

Military academies turned out to be too expensive but Fall River Bible School and Seminary in Arlington, Virginia was flexible about tuition for "students with spiritual leanings."

Baker settled in, met some nice people, and was starting to think he might even fit in somewhere. A month into the first semester, Mrs. Calloway, the head counselor, called him into her office, with tears in her eyes.

When he got here, she hugged him. Not customary for Mrs. Calloway. Not much touching went on at Fall River, period.

"Oh, you poor boy, you poor lamb."

Baker said, "What?"

It took a long time for her to tell him and when she did, she looked scared, as if she'd be punished for doing it.

The van had been hit head-on, by a drunk on I-40.

Danny and Dixie returning to Nashville from a gig in Columbia. Grand opening of a car dealership, two-hundred-dollar fee, not bad when you figured it was only a one-hour drive.

All those years on the road without a mishap. Fifteen minutes out of town, the van was turned into scrap.

Both of them dead on impact, their stage clothes strewn all over the interstate.

Danny's guitar had sustained irreparable damage, sliding around the rear of the van, its soundboard crushed, its neck severed and splintered.

Dixie's mandolin, its hard-shell case covered by a newer Mark Leaf space-age plastic supplementary case and swathed in three packing blankets, the way she always wrapped it, came out unharmed.

Baker went and retrieved the instrument from the closet, same way he'd done so many times before.

Stared at it, touched the taut strings, the ebony bridge, the mother-of-pearl tuners with their gold-plated gears.

Not too many F-5s were gold-plated or triple-bound. This one was and everyone who'd seen it opined that even though it was dated 1924, not '23, it was from the same batch as Bill Monroe's. Monroe's had gotten damaged years ago; the story that circulated was some jealous husband had caught the bluegrass king in bed with his wife and taken out his anger on the instrument.

Stupid, thought Baker. It was people who deserved punishment, not things.

Staring at the F-5 and realizing what he'd just told himself.

Maybe he should smash this thing. What did music bring other than sin and misery?

That poor girl.

That rich boy, was he any better off?

Maybe he'd call that shrink, Delaware, ask if he had any ideas about helping Tristan.

Nah, the guy was long gone back to LA, by now. And what the hell was it his business if the boy had emotional issues, that mother of his . . .

He'd done his job.

So why was it gnawing at him?

Like the girl, like the boy, like everyone else in this goddamn world, they were just people. With their talents and their weaknesses and their heartbreaks and their egos.

People. If there was a God, he had one hell of a sense of humor.

Or maybe there was wisdom behind it.

People, able to change. Able to better themselves, even though so many failed.

The people he and Lamar met day after day . . .

Maybe there was more . . .

Hands—must've been his, but it felt like they were someone else's—lifted the mandolin out of its case. The back all shiny, those silky, sculptural contours where some Michigan craftsman had carved and tapped and carved some more under the watchful eye of the chief acoustical engineer, a genius named Lloyd Loar.

Loar had signed the instrument on March 21, 1924. Anything with his name on it was worth a bundle to collectors.

Baker's fingers grazed the strings. EADG. Perfect tune, after all these years.

He knew because he had perfect pitch.

His left hand formed a G chord. He told his right hand not to move but it did.

A resonant, sweet sound rang out, bounced against cold walls devoid of art or family mementos, ricocheted against discount-outlet furniture and linoleum floors. Ended its flight and burrowed into Baker's skull.

His head hurt.

His hands moved some more and that helped a bit.

An hour later, he was still at it.

ABOUT THE AUTHORS

JONATHAN KELLERMAN has brought his expertise as a clinical psychologist to numerous *New York Times* bestselling tales of suspense, including the Alex Delaware novels. His most recent novel, *Gone,* was a #1 *New York Times* bestseller. He has won the Goldwyn, Edgar, and Anthony Awards, and has been nominated for a Shamus Award.

FAYE KELLERMAN is the *New Tork Times* bestselling author of the Peter Decker/Rina Lazarus novels, as well as the historical thrillers *The Quality of Mercy* and *Straight Into Darkness* and the short story anthology *The Garden of Eden*. She has won the Macavity Award and has been nominated for a Shamus Award.

ABOUT THE TYPE

This book was set in Sabon, a typeface designed by the well-known German typographer Jan Tschichold (1902–74). Sabon's design is based upon the original letter forms of Claude Garamond and was created specifically to be used for three sources: foundry type for hand composition, Linotype, and Monotype. Tschichold named his typeface for the famous Frankfurt typefounder Jacques Sabon, who died in 1580.